...born and bred New Yorker, **Nicki Night** delights in ...ting hometown heroes and heroines with an edge. As ...vid reader and champion of love, Nicki chose to pen ...ance novels because she believes that love should be ...hlighted in this world, and she delights in writing ...temporary romances with unforgettable characters ... just enough drama to make readers clutch a pearl here ... there. Nicki has a penchant for adventure and is ...rently working on penning her next romantic escapade.

...ndrea Laurence is an award-winning contemporary author who has been a lover of books and writing stories since she learned to read. A dedicated West Coast girl ...nsplanted into the Deep South, she's constantly trying ...develop a taste for sweet tea and grits while caring for ...r boyfriend and an old bulldog. You can contact ...ndrea at her website: andrealaurence.com

Also by Nicki Night

Blackwells of New York

Intimate Negotiations
Her Chance at Love
His Love Lesson
Riding into Love

Also by Andrea Laurence

What Lies Beneath
More Than He Expected
His Lover's Little Secret
The CEO's Unexpected Child
Little Secrets: Secretly Pregnant
Rags to Riches Baby
One Unforgettable Weekend
The Boyfriend Arrangement
From Mistake to Millions
From Riches to Redemption
From Seduction to Secrets

ONE MORE SECOND CHANCE

NICKI NIGHT

PROMISES FROM A PLAYBOY

ANDREA LAURENCE

MILLS & BOON

First Published in Great Britain 2021
by Mills & Boon, an imprint of HarperCollins*Publishers* Ltd
1 London Bridge Street, London, SE1 9GF

www.harpercollins.co.uk

HarperCollins*Publishers*
1st Floor, Watermarque Building,
Ringsend Road, Dublin 4, Ireland

ISBN: 978-0-263-28299-3

0721

ONE MORE SECOND CHANCE

NICKI NIGHT

One

"Don't become bridezilla, Savannah!" Phoenix Jones closed her eyes, took a deep, soothing breath. She massaged her temples with her fingertips. "It's all going to work out just fine, sis. Don't get worked up." Phoenix spoke in a calming tone. "In less than forty-eight hours we will be on a plane to one of the most beautiful places on this globe. Let that sink in." Her sister was like their mother, Nadine. Dramatic. Phoenix was more like their dad, not easily rattled.

"But she knew what day we were leaving. I told her several times." Savannah's voice was laced with frustration. Her pitch grew higher and higher. "What if it's not ready by tomorrow night?" Her voice cracked. "What am I supposed to do about a veil at this point? I'm going to end up getting married without one! It should have been done a week ago."

Phoenix realized her sister was on the verge of tears. "Honey," she said softly, "it will be ready. I'll call her myself and reiterate how important this is for you. And if it's not ready, we'll pick some of the most exotic flowers that Fiji has to offer and make a beautiful crown to place on that pretty little head of yours. You may be working yourself up for nothing. Let's wait and see what happens. Okay?"

"Ugh!" Savannah huffed. "There's still so much to do. I don't see how I'm going to get it all done."

"You're a perfectionist. No matter what happens, your wedding will still be perfect because that's just how you operate. It will be fine. I promise you. We've got a lot to do, so don't let this stress you out too much," Phoenix said.

"I'll try." Savannah sounded defeated.

"I'll come by after work to help with anything you need. Cool?"

"Thanks." Her tone was flat.

"Girl! You're about to get married to the man of your dreams on the island of your dreams at the wedding of your dreams. I'm going to need you to sound a little happier."

Phoenix could hear Savannah sigh through the phone. She wanted her sister to feel better. Planning a wedding wasn't easy. Even though Phoenix's wedding never happened, she knew firsthand how stressful they were to plan.

"You're right. I'll try to calm down. See you tonight?" Savannah asked.

"What time do you want me there?"

"Seven good?"

"See you at seven, sis. And try not to drive your husband-to-be crazy before I get there."

"I can't make any promises. Love ya!" Savannah let out a small laugh and Phoenix returned the sentiment. After ending the call, Phoenix sat back and smiled for the first time since she arrived at work that morning.

Phoenix's day started with tension. Actually, the tension began the evening before when Brent, the guy whom she'd been seeing, started questioning her about a conversation she'd had with her male coworker and friend. He wanted to know why her coworker had called her after business hours. That was normal for their team. They were close and often spoke outside work. If they got great ideas, they'd call to run them by each other. Brent's jealous nature was coming to the surface along with a few other red flags, and Phoenix didn't like what she'd been witnessing. She ended their dinner by telling him it was best for them to go their separate ways.

Her cell phone rang and she picked it up. Phoenix's boss, Indra Lee, asked her to come join the team members in the conference room. Phoenix could tell by her boss's tone that she didn't have good news to share. Needing a few minutes to brace herself for whatever was about to come, Phoenix swung her office chair around to face the windowed wall. She never tired of the view down Sixth Avenue. The rhythm of New York City pulsed. She took in the picturesque landscape with neat rows of traffic-filled streets framed by magnificent tall buildings. Usually, this view soothed her mind, but at the moment the pressures of life dulled the joy she got from gazing at the skyline.

Grabbing her cell phone, pad and a pen, Phoenix headed to the conference room as instructed. The two women were the only females in Aida, a small, male-dominated technology firm that created technological platforms using AI—artificial intelligence—to help improve systems for small and midsize companies. As one of Aida's founding partners, Indra recruited Phoenix and helped her develop into a leading tech professional. In the few years that Phoenix had been with the company, they'd grown exponentially and shared their good fortune with their staff. Phoenix loved what she did and got paid extremely well for the work she put in. What more could she ask for?

As Phoenix made her way to the glass conference room in the center of their sleekly designed office, she hoped that whatever they had to meet about wouldn't add extra work to her plate. She was leaving for vacation in two days and already had too much to close out before her departure. When she entered the conference room, the look on Indra's face didn't give Phoenix hope. Indra's smile seemed forced, apologetic almost. Technology moved so fast that it made the industry volatile. Phoenix hoped she wasn't losing her job.

Phoenix sat and waited. Over the next several moments their team of twelve employees made their way into the conference room, engaging in small talk. It was obvious that the others weren't sure why they were there, either. Indra sat at one end of the conference table and her partner, Dean Ochoa, sat at the other end. The two sighed simultaneously before Dean nodded. Indra took that as her cue to begin speaking. The simple sound of her voice called everything to order. The staff members who were standing took seats. The room settled into a quiet hush. Indra started by thanking everyone for coming. Phoenix found that odd. The next words that came from her mouth shocked everyone in the room, except Dean.

"I know." Indra looked around at the surprised expressions in the room. She pressed her lips together after dropping a verbal bomb. Some team members looked stunned, others sad and a few faces were completely blank. "This is big news, though bittersweet."

Bitter. Yes. For Phoenix, there was nothing sweet about what Indra had just said. She didn't know how to feel. Had her boss just told them that their company had been sold and was moving clear across the country to Silicon Valley? What did that mean for Phoenix?

Dean began to speak as if he'd heard the question in Phoenix's mind. "This will be a big ask, but we want to offer all of you the opportunity to stay with the company." Dean paused.

Indra picked up where he'd left off. It was like a well-choreographed dance. "That would mean you'd have to agree to move to California with us. Unfortunately, they want all of our employees in California so there won't be any opportunities to work remotely from here."

"Yes." Dean jumped back in, shaking his head. "Much of this work is tech focused and can be done right from our computers, but our team has proven to work better and smarter when we're physically together. That's what makes us so strong."

"We're prepared to offer generous relocation packages," Indra added, taking back the verbal baton. She looked around and tilted her head sympathetically. "I know this is a bit of a shocker. But I promise you it's really, really good news. Jabber has made us an offer we would be foolish to refuse. This is a huge opportunity. We do understand how you might feel, but we would be delighted to keep our entire team intact."

Phoenix's head filled with questions but she found it difficult to speak. Jabber, a technology giant, had been gobbling up smaller tech firms for the past few years. However, they didn't just buy any company—only companies they knew would earn them billions. The fact that they considered buying Aida was a testament to how successful they'd become. Their offers were often too generous to leave on the negotiation table.

Phoenix didn't want to leave New York. Her entire family was here. She'd visited the Bay Area, but never entertained the thought of living there. What if she did move? She'd miss her family terribly. Her dad was scheduled for hip surgery after the wedding. Phoenix was sure she'd have to pitch in and help her parents out while he healed. If she stayed? She'd have to find a new job. She raised her hand. Questions continued to fill her head.

"Phoenix." Indra called her gently, like a teacher giving her young student the floor to speak.

Despite the softness, Phoenix felt somewhat betrayed. How could Indra have kept something this huge from her? "How much time do we have to make our decision?" Phoenix heard herself ask. It was like an out-of-body experience. She felt blindsided and hadn't shaken the feeling yet.

Indra seemed to have squirmed a bit. She possibly knew how Phoenix felt.

"Six weeks." Dean interjected.

A collective gasp blew through the room. Murmurs ensued.

Dean held a hand up, quieting the room. "In six weeks these offices will shut down and we will officially move into our new offices just outside the Bay Area. We'd greatly appreciate your decision within the next two weeks so that we will know what our hiring needs are. We'd also like for all of you to stay on for the full six weeks and will compensate your dedication."

The room went silent again as everyone digested what Dean had said. After a few moments Indra broke the silence. "For those of you who decide not to join us, we hate to see you go. You are family." She paused and inhaled slowly. Indra blinked rapidly as if she was fighting back tears. "We're prepared to give you a generous severance package. Our hope is that it will fill any salary gaps while you seek out other employment opportunities."

"Well, that's very nice of you, Indra and Dean," Delano, one of the software engineers, said. "I don't need six weeks. I can tell you right now that I will not be able to relocate. Our daughter is just a few months old and my in-laws are caring for her while my wife and I work. In fact, my wife just started a new job. My siblings and I take turns caring for our aging parents. I hate to pass this up but the timing is just not right for me."

Indra pressed her lips together and tilted her head. Delano was sitting next to her. She placed a supportive hand on his shoulder. "We understand."

"We'd love for you to stay on for the full six weeks. It's okay if you need time here and there for interviews. Are you willing to do that?"

Delano shrugged. "I'm happy to."

"Thank you," Dean said.

A few others explained why they would or wouldn't be able to make the move. Some were excited and started side chats about apartment shopping and Bay Area hot spots. Phoenix remained quiet, taking it all in. There was too much to consider to make a decision like this so quickly. She didn't have children but she did have a pretty robust life and a close-knit family. Recently, her father started having a few health issues. Phoenix and her sister had been helping their mother with their dad's doctors' appointments. Perhaps with fewer family issues and more time to prepare, she could have been more excited about moving across the country. She hadn't thought about leaving New York and wasn't sure she wanted to.

After a few more questions from the staff, the meeting was called to a close. Phoenix went to her office, shut the door and quietly sat facing Sixth Avenue. Then she lifted her head and stared at the ceiling. She got lost in thoughts around the offer that Indra and Dean had made. A light tap at her door caught her attention. Indra pushed the door open slightly and stuck her head through the small opening.

"Can I come in?" Indra asked.

Phoenix looked at her with a sideways glance and twisted lips. After a sharp exhale she said, "Come on in."

Normally, she wouldn't speak to her boss that way, but Indra had become her friend. She flashed Phoenix an apologetic look.

"How come you didn't tell me?" Phoenix chided.

"I'm sorry, Phoenix," Indra said. "Legally, I couldn't utter a word to anyone. I didn't even tell Rich," she said, referring to her husband. "He found out when the ink dried on the deal the other day."

"You know you can trust me." Phoenix was hurt.

"Of course, but any missteps could have blown the entire deal," Indra said. "I hated to drop this bomb on you just before your vacation but we wanted to make the announcement when everyone was in the office, and today was our first chance to do it. Besides, they didn't give us much time to make the transition. They want us in their headquarters ASAP. I had to push to get the six weeks."

"Silicon Valley?" Phoenix rolled her eyes. "That place is overrun by twelve-year-old gamer geeks."

Indra laughed. "You're so silly." She sat on the corner

of Phoenix's desk. Her smile faded and her face turned serious. "You coming?"

Phoenix grunted and let her head roll back. "That's a big decision."

"I know. But what's holding you here? Try it and if you don't like it, come back home."

"It's not that easy," Phoenix said.

"I don't want to lose you. To be honest, moving is the only part of the deal I tried to fight. Rich won't be joining me until the end of the school year. I'm going ahead to get things settled. He and Cody will come in a few months. We didn't want to disrupt Cody's school year. I guess I'll fly back and forth as much as possible until my family gets there."

"Are you excited, Indra?" Her question came across more solemn than she intended.

Indra put her hand on her heart. "Extremely. This is the deal of a lifetime."

Phoenix held her hands in the air. "That's what matters most. Congratulations."

Indra slid off the desk, walked around to Phoenix and put a hand on her shoulder. "Why don't you take tomorrow off? Start your vacation early and give yourself time to absorb all of this. Think about joining us in California and let me know what you decide."

"Thanks, but I have too much work to do before my vacation. I promise I'll give this serious consideration."

"That's all I ask," Indra said.

Phoenix watched Indra leave her office. She knew that whether she went or stayed behind that she and Indra would likely stay in touch, yet she couldn't help but feel like she just lost one of her closest friends.

"What else could happen?" Phoenix asked aloud and regretted the moment the words left her lips.

Two

Carter Blackwell wished he could snap his fingers and magically appear at the airport. This vacation couldn't have come at a better time. The volatile stock market had made a few of his high-net-worth clients extremely anxious. He'd been trying to alleviate their anxiety on calls day and night. A major business opportunity recently gained steam and he needed to make some major decisions to move forward soon. And he was in his cousin Jaxon's wedding. Carter, Jaxon, his brothers Lincoln and Ethan and a few friends had recently returned from a long weekend of partying in Las Vegas. That was more than a week ago and Carter still hadn't caught up on his rest. Now he had to deal with the pressure of closing a number of loose ends before leaving for vacation in less than two days.

With work, his business venture, family and a robust social life all operating at a high, Carter was weary and desperately needed to unplug. He was more than ready for the beauty and serenity of Fiji.

Carter looked at his watch and took a deep breath. The afternoon seemed to have passed without his realizing it. In another thirty-six hours he would be on the airplane, leaving all of these worries behind him for ten days. That made him smile.

Carter had meant to leave work a bit early to get a jump on packing. He hadn't even pulled his suitcase out yet. He contemplated turning off his work cell phone but decided against it. There were still a few major stops he had to make before heading home.

The moment his foot hit the stoop of his brownstone near downtown Brooklyn, his cell phone rang.

"Hey," Carter said through a smile as he greeted the woman he'd been dating for the past few months. This was one call he didn't mind taking. Her company, among other things, could help ease his mind.

"Um," Sinai Killington sighed. "We need to talk."

Carter's smile faded. *What now?* "Something wrong?" he asked.

"Have you made it home yet?" Sinai asked, not directly answering his question.

"Just getting here," he said as he turned the key and pushed the door open. "You're still coming tonight, right?"

Carter heard her clear her throat. "Yes. I'll be there in about twenty minutes."

"Okay." Silence ensued. After a few beats Carter asked. "Everything all right?"

"We will talk when I get there."

"Okay," he repeated. "See you soon."

Sinai ended the call without saying goodbye. Carter looked at the display wondering what happened.

Brushing off the abrupt end to their call, Carter placed his keys onto the hook in the kitchen. Standing still, he took a deep breath, and then rubbed his tight shoulders and sore neck. He worked out regularly, but this wasn't soreness from the gym. Carter understood this tightness to be the tension that had been building from a long, grueling workweek. He hoped that whatever Sinai wanted to talk about wasn't going to be too heavy. He already had so much on him.

Sinai's visits usually helped him relax. She was sleeping over the next two nights so they could get up and catch their early flight to Fiji. They weren't exclusive but they really enjoyed each other's company. Carter felt like if he really wanted to get serious in a relationship, Sinai would definitely be a top contender. She was smart, beautiful, ambitious and great in bed. She didn't take life too seriously and was always ready for a good time.

All of Carter's friends were getting married. Out of his brothers, he was the only one who wasn't in a committed relationship. Even Ethan had snagged a beautiful wife and now they had a baby on the way.

He looked around his home. It was perfectly suitable for a family, but Carter wanted to raise his children on Long Island where he'd grown up. He'd always imagined a large home buzzing with warmth and activity even though he wasn't ready for all of that now. Not yet.

More than not being ready, Carter didn't believe he had come across the *right* woman yet. He'd dated his share of beautiful women, but he was looking for much more than beauty. Sinai had a lot going for her, but… What exactly was he looking for? Carter wasn't sure. Phoenix was the one whom he'd let go. Was he looking for another version of her? Carter shook his head as if to get rid of that thought. That bridge had burned and was pretty much unsalvageable.

The doorbell rang, bringing Carter out of his thoughts. He realized he hadn't made it beyond the kitchen since he arrived at home. He thought about all the packing he needed to do as he headed to the door to let Sinai in.

"Hey," Carter said after he opened the door. He leaned forward to kiss her pink glossed lips.

"Hey." Her response was flat. She puckered but didn't kiss him the way she usually did.

Carter stepped aside to let her in. He admired her pretty face and curvaceous figure as she walked into his brownstone. His brow furrowed when he noticed she wasn't carrying a suitcase.

"You need me to grab your bags from the car?" he asked.

Sinai stopped walking and slowly turned around. "I'm not going, Carter."

Carter reared his head back. "What? Why?"

Sinai dropped her hands to her sides. "Carter…" She paused, trying to find the right words. "It's time for us to go our separate ways."

Carter closed the door pensively. "What's this about?"

Sinai chuckled. "I know you've been super busy lately, but you couldn't have been so busy that you didn't see this coming." She stepped closer to him, rose on her toes and kissed him.

Carter kissed her back but was still confused. He stepped back and studied her brown eyes. "I don't understand."

"It's been a few months now and we have not progressed as a couple at all. I feel like I'm just a friend and you have no intentions on making me a true girlfriend. The other night made that painfully clear."

The other night? Carter wasn't sure what she was referring to. He scrunched his face. "The other night?" he asked aloud.

"Dinner the other night…" Sinai tilted her head. "You don't remember," she said matter-of-factly and shook her head.

Carter tried to think of what had happened.

"While we were at the table, my friend London asked about what's next for us. Your response was, 'We're just having fun.' It's been almost six months, Carter." Sinai's hand flopped against her thigh. "I want more than to just have a little fun. You've invited me to join you in Fiji but I've never met a single family member of yours. It feels awkward to meet them for the first time at your cousin's wedding and you have no desire to commit to me in any way. I don't want to experience Fiji like this."

Carter opened his mouth to say something.

Before he could speak, she smiled softly and held up her hand. "Let me finish, please. This isn't easy for me." Sinai paused a moment before speaking again. "You avoid any conversation that touches on a future when it comes to us.

I've ignored these signs for a while but now I understand you don't want more. You're content. This…" Sinai waved her hand as if presenting the space around them. "This is fine with you." Sinai paused again. "But it's not okay with me." She placed a hand across her heart. "I want more, Carter. I deserve more."

Carter opened his mouth. Realizing he had no rebuttal, he closed it.

"It's okay, Carter. Really."

She was right. She was like a friend with benefits all this time. He liked her but didn't see being with her for the long haul. His inviting her to Fiji was about having more fun. It wasn't about taking anything to the next level.

"No hard feelings, Carter. I'm a big girl. I get it and I'm okay. At least now I am. At one point I hoped things would change but I have to do what makes me happy."

"I'm sorry." Carter quietly acknowledged the reality they were standing in.

"I'm sorry, too. It would have been nice." Sinai touched his face. "Going with you to Fiji wouldn't make sense for me if nothing is going to change. I hope you understand."

Carter looked at the ceiling and then back at her. "Is there someone else?"

Sinai tilted her head and grinned. "No. There's no one else."

"Oh," Carter said. He wasn't sure what else to say. This was unexpected.

"I really enjoyed our time together," Sinai said.

"Me, too." Carter touched her face. He stared at her for a moment. "So this is really goodbye?" Carter tried to absorb what was happening.

Sinai took the hand that Carter gently placed on her face and planted a soft kiss in his palm. "Yes." She closed her eyes and sighed. "This is goodbye." She smiled again. She blinked and a lone tear rolled down her cheek.

Carter's chest tightened. He felt bad but he didn't want to mislead her. He wiped her tear with his thumb. "You deserve the best."

"Thank you. I agree." She giggled. More tears fell. "You're a good dude, Carter. Maybe one day you'll come to believe in love."

Carter let her words bounce off him. There was too much happening in his head for him to think clearly. The one thing he knew was that it was time to let Sinai go. It was only fair.

"Goodbye, Sinai."

Sinai puckered her lips. Carter lowered himself to meet her. Their kiss was brief and sealed the fate of their relationship.

Sinai grinned, patted his chest and said, "Enjoy Fiji." With that she left, leaving Carter to absorb the moment and her absence.

Carter watched Sinai leave. He stood unmoving, stunned by what had just transpired. Sinai's words played over and over in his mind. *Maybe one day you'll come to believe in love.* She was the third woman in the past year who'd mentioned his apparent lack of belief in love. Admittedly, he was more interested in his career. That came first. He looked around his beautiful home. Suddenly, it felt empty. Carter brushed off the coolness that had settled over him.

There was too much to do. He had to pack. He faced major business decisions. Work was demanding. A relationship would just have to wait.

Three

The entire bridal party traveled together except Ethan and Zoe Blackwell. Zoe was expecting a baby and wasn't feeling well before the flight so they opted to change their departure so she could see her doctor before leaving.

As a gift to the bridal party, Savannah and Jaxon invited them to arrive a few days early to party and bond prior to the wedding. It was a token of their appreciation for agreeing to travel halfway across the globe on just a few months of notice.

Phoenix strolled through the hotel lobby and out the back to the area where the villas stretched out over the water. The grounds were lush and vibrant, with beautiful tropical plants lining the walkways. The colors were more vivid than the images the resort boasted on their website. She entered her villa and reveled in the breathtaking views of the ocean right outside her room.

The flight from New York to Fiji was more than fifteen hours. Then their group boarded a seaplane for another forty-five-minute flight to the private island where they would stay for the next ten days. Phoenix helped Savannah with last-minute preparations the night before leaving so she hardly slept. She was especially happy to see that her sister's veil had arrived in time. When Phoenix got back to her house, she packed and repacked several times to make sure she had everything she needed. Despite how exhausted she was, she didn't sleep well during the flights. Maybe it was the excitement of everything that kept her from getting rest.

Phoenix's body hit the plush mattress in her villa like a large piece of lead. She needed a nap if she was going to be able to get through the welcome party later that evening. She looked forward to all the festivities despite feeling a bit uncomfortable about having to be around her ex-fiancé, Carter. She was over him, but it still felt awkward knowing they would be in such close proximity for so many days. She managed a small smile and had actually said hello to him when she saw him at the airport. That was the extent of their communication. Their families lived in the same neighborhood and socialized in the same circles since they were children, but since the breakup, they had managed to keep their distance from one another.

Phoenix felt like she was sinking into a cloud of plushness on the king-size bed. She looked at her cell phone. The welcome party would start in a few hours. She rolled over onto her back and studied the leaf-like blades whirring on the ceiling fan, aware of how heavy her eyelids were becoming. Thoughts of how much fun and relaxation she was looking forward to having in Fiji carried her to sleep.

Banging on the door woke Phoenix with a start. At first, she thought the knocking was in her head. She didn't realize she'd fallen asleep until this moment. She stretched and then sprung from the bed. "Coming!" she yelled through her yawn. Savannah was calling her name.

"Geesh!" Phoenix said when she opened the door. She walked back through the spacious villa toward the balcony with Savannah in tow. "What's going on?"

"You weren't answering. I knocked hard because I figured you had fallen asleep. We have a little issue," Savannah said.

Phoenix whirled around. "What happened?" She was ready to protect her younger sister.

Savannah stopped in her tracks and flinched at how fast Phoenix spun around. "Let's go sit on the balcony and I'll explain everything."

Phoenix narrowed her eyes at Savannah. "Okay," she sang. "You're making me nervous."

Savannah huffed but said nothing more until they reached the balcony. The ladies sat. A slight breeze greeted them. Savannah closed her eyes and lifted her face to the sun. She remained like that for a few moments. Phoenix followed suit.

Savannah exhaled and started to speak. "It doesn't look like Ethan and Zoe are going to make it."

"Oh no! Is she okay?"

"The doctor sent her to the hospital. She'll be there a few days under observation. When she goes home, she'll be on strict bed rest."

"Oh!" Phoenix's hand spread across her chest. "Poor thing. I hope she's going to be okay. She seemed so excited about this baby when I met her at the engagement party."

"Yeah. Ethan said she's pretty scared, but he's by her side and his mom is staying back so his dad will be coming by himself."

"Wow. This is so unfortunate. How's Jax taking the news?"

"He'll be okay. He hates that Ethan and Zoe will miss everything but he just wants her and the baby to be okay. It would be heartbreaking if they lost that baby."

"Of course. How about you? Are you okay?" Phoenix asked Savannah.

"I'm fine. Just hoping for the best for them. I'm going to try to speak to her again tomorrow."

Several moments passed in silence.

"Phoenix."

The way Savannah said her name made Phoenix raise a brow. "Yes, Savannah?"

Savannah grunted but said nothing.

"Spit it out!" Phoenix admonished.

Savannah closed her eyes and the words rushed from

her mouth. "Jax wants Carter to replace Ethan as his best man."

Phoenix's entire body stiffened. She tried her best not to show any emotion. This was her sister's wedding and she refused to do or say anything to ruin it. But something about having to walk down the aisle arm in arm with the man who had walked away from her the night before their wedding didn't sit well.

"Phoenix?"

She couldn't say the words running through her mind so she kept her mouth clamped shut.

"Fifi?" Savannah softly called her by her nickname. This time she leaned forward and looked into Phoenix's face.

"Yes, Savannah?"

"Say something. Please."

"I told you when you announced your engagement to Jax not to worry about me. This is your wedding. You and Jax have to be happy. I will be fine. I meant it then and I mean it now."

Savannah threw her arms around Phoenix's neck. "Oh! Thank you, Fifi! I was so worried. I love you, sis! I didn't want you to feel uncomfortable. Jax went over to talk to Carter. We wanted to make sure you two were okay with everything." Savannah's words spilled from her lips so fast she had to catch her breath when she finished.

Phoenix returned her sister's tight hug.

"Thank you for understanding." Savannah continued. "I may not be a big fan of Carter, but he and Ethan are not just Jax's cousins, they're the best of friends." She sighed. "I was so worried. I'll let Jax know. I told him you were over Carter anyway." Savannah stood. "Let me get back. The welcome reception is about to start and I still have to get dressed. See you there, okay?"

Savannah rambled when she was nervous. Phoenix stood

with her sister and placed a hand on her shoulder. "Don't be nervous. Everything will be fine. See you at the reception."

Savannah took a deep breath. "Okay." She went to leave and paused. Turning back toward Phoenix, she asked, "Are you sure you're okay?"

"I'm fine." Phoenix placed her hand or Savannah's back gently.

"Say the word, sis, and I'll tell Jaxon it won't work out."

Phoenix waved away Savannah's concern. "It's all good. I get it."

Savannah hugged her sister tightly. Then, she left. Phoenix closed the door and leaned her back against it. She didn't know how to feel but she couldn't let on that she was not happy about this new arrangement. Walking down the aisle with Carter at anybody's wedding would require strength that Phoenix wasn't sure she could manage.

What else could go wrong? Phoenix slapped her hand across her mouth. She thought it but refused to say it. Every time she uttered those words the universe found a way to show her.

Four

Carter paced back and forth in his overwater bungalow. He couldn't believe his fate. Carter knew he'd have to be around his ex-fiancée, Phoenix, and he'd prepared for that. The two hadn't spoken much at all since that fateful night before their wedding. It wasn't for lack of trying on his part. Once he told her that he couldn't marry her she didn't want to hear anything else he had to say. In fact, he never got the chance to explain why he needed to call off the wedding. That was five years ago.

Despite living in close proximity and occasionally seeing each other at functions, it was years before Phoenix would even acknowledge his presence. Eventually, she'd utter a contrite greeting here or there but it was nothing he could count on. He'd wanted to explain the whole story to her on several occasions but it was too late for that now. The pain had been buried. He'd been hurt, too. Calling the wedding off was the hardest decision of his life but he was left with no choice.

He stopped pacing long enough to look at his cousin Jaxon, who was sitting on the sofa in the living room of the bungalow. Carter shook his head at Jaxon. "Does Phoenix know?"

Jaxon inhaled, held his breath a moment and then exhaled with a grunt. "Savannah is telling her now."

"I don't want to make anyone uncomfortable." Carter shook his head adamantly.

Jaxon stood up from his chair and shrugged. "Neither do I, but without Ethan there's no one else I'd pick for my best man besides you."

"Yeah." Carter parked his hands on his hips and groaned.

"Who wouldn't expect that?" Jax said.

"Ugh!" Carter laid his hand across his forehead. "You know she hates me, right?" he asked, referring to Phoenix.

Jaxon waved him off. "She doesn't hate you, man."

Carter stopped pacing and looked at Jaxon sideways.

"Okay, maybe she does hate you just a little but that was a long time ago."

"Not long enough," Carter said.

"Five years, dude! You both moved on since then—dated other people. You just have to walk down the aisle with her after the ceremony. What is that? For two quick minutes you'll have to be close to one another. You can survive that, right?"

"And what about all of this other stuff you and Savannah planned for this week? This…this team building…stuff. Clearly, we have to spend a lot more time around each other than a walk down the aisle after the ceremony."

Jaxon sank into his shoulders. "Savannah just wanted everyone to bond before the wedding. We wanted you all to have a good time."

Carter just stared at him.

Jaxon walked closer to him. "Come on, man. Tell me this isn't going to be fun. Four-wheeling? Zip-lining? Kayaking? Yacht parties?"

Carter lived for these activities. "Of course they'll be fun," he admitted.

"All kidding aside, Carter, you have to be my best man. Without Ethan, it has to be you. I need you, man," Jax repeated.

Carter threw his hand up. "You know I'll do anything for you. It's just that this…this is…ugh! This won't be fun. You and Savannah will have to somehow be the buffer. I don't know how Phoenix is going to respond to this."

"Look. Phoenix is a smart, reasonable woman. I'm sure she'll understand."

Carter wasn't so sure. Yes, Phoenix was intelligent. Brilliant, even. But she was also scorned by Carter. She'd proven time and time again that she wanted nothing to do with him.

"Think about this." Jaxon interrupted Carter's thoughts. "Maybe, if you two dare to become cordial enough, you could finally have the chance to tell her why you called off the wedding in the first place."

Carter stopped pacing abruptly and huffed. "That would probably ruin this entire trip."

"Think about the fact that you could finally be able to close that chapter."

Carter glanced at Jaxon and looked away, waving him off. "That chapter has been closed."

"Yes. You're over it. I get that, but you know what I mean. After all this time she still doesn't know. You, Uncle Bill, Aunt Lydia, Ethan, Lincoln and I are the only ones who know the whole story. I never uttered a word to Savannah. She just thought you were a jerk with cold feet that wasn't ready to give up your bachelor ways. Maybe if you told Phoenix, she wouldn't hate you so much."

Carter plopped on the couch and let his arms fall heavily to his sides. "Do you have any idea how many times I tried to talk to her? She never wanted to hear it. She can't see any reason for me to call off the wedding on such short notice. She wouldn't even give me the chance to explain that night."

"I get it. She was hurt. She…" Jaxon searched for the right words.

"Felt rejected." Carter filled in the blank for him.

"And embarrassed," Jaxon added.

"I know." Carter felt bad all over again.

"Look. All I'm saying is that if things don't go crazy, maybe you guys can be cordial enough to perhaps have a normal conversation. This may be your opportunity to let her know the truth even if it happens after the wedding is over. She deserves to know."

"Maybe." Carter wouldn't cosign Jaxon's idea just yet. He knew it would take work to get Phoenix to hear him out, and ten days in Fiji might not cut it. Why bother at this point anyway? Weren't both of them over it?

"It's hard enough to deal with the fact Ethan is going to miss my wedding and I pray that Zoe is okay. We never imagined moments like this without each other. The most important thing is making sure their baby comes out healthy and strong. You with me?" Jaxon held out his hand.

Carter stood, took Jaxon's hand and pulled him in for a hug. "I'm with you, Jax. Let's hope this goes over well with Phoenix."

"Let's hope. Either way, we will get through this together," Jaxon said. He threw his hands out to the sides. "Dude! We're in Fiji! I'm about to get married!"

A huge smile spread across Carter's face. "Sounds like it's time to celebrate!" Carter walked over to the bar inside his villa. "Let the celebration begin." He poured two glasses of scotch and handed one to Jaxon.

They held their glasses up and clinked them together. Carter began to say something.

"Uh uh uh! Save it for the toast. Until then, let's just have fun."

The two men lifted their glasses again and threw the amber liquid down their throats.

"Ah! Nice," Carter said.

"Yeah," Jaxon said, putting down his glass. "We need to get ready for the welcome reception. Let me get back to my villa before my wife-to-be sends out a search party."

Jaxon headed for the door and paused. He turned back toward Carter and chuckled. "Maybe this is fate."

"What are you talking about, Jax?"

"Sinai decided not to come. Ethan can't come. And now

you and Phoenix will walk down the aisle together. There might be something to this."

"Man!" Carter picked up one of the pillows on the sofa and tossed it at Jaxon.

He ducked, avoiding the hit, and hurried toward the door. "Just a thought." Jaxon chuckled. "See you at the reception." He let himself out and Carter could hear him laughing beyond the closed door.

Carter couldn't get mad. If the shoe was on the other foot, he would have teased Jaxon just the same. That was how they were with each other. Carter poured himself another drink and sat on his balcony overlooking the pristine water surrounding his villa. This time he sipped the whiskey slowly, wondering what these next few days could bring.

Carter hadn't had a serious relationship since Phoenix. Although he thought he was doing the right thing back then, he'd hurt Phoenix badly. But what could he do about that now? That was the past. He had his whole life ahead of him and several other large fish to fry. He just needed to get through the rest of the festivities and this vacation. He needed to enjoy himself. He deserved this break.

Big decisions awaited his return to the States. Carter looked forward to his time in Fiji being somewhat of a reprieve before starting new chapters in his life. Chapters that he was excited about, despite making other people unhappy, namely his father. While he was away, perhaps he could find the right words to let his father know that his days at Blackwell Wealth Management were numbered. Bill's dream for his sons taking over the company was dissipating. Carter had other plans and he'd sacrificed enough of his time to appease his dad. It was time for him to strike out on his own. Losing that promotion to Ethan was a turning point for Carter. Bill had given each of them the chance to prove themselves when they opened their branches. Ethan's branches out-performed Carter's and Dillon's giving Ethan the upper hand. Now his brother was his boss. It was time to make *his* dreams come true, not his father's.

Carter walked back inside and put his glass in the small sink on the wet bar. He didn't have time to ponder the past. He had an entire future ahead of him despite the challenges it held. Right now he was in Fiji on a well-deserved vacation, ready to have fun and celebrate his cousin and his beautiful fiancée. Carter wasn't about to sit around mulling over what could have been. He did what he had to do. As for what was next, when he got back home he would do what was necessary. Right now it was time to party!

Five

Phoenix dressed for the welcome reception that was taking place under a cabana on the beach. Her strapless, flowing maxi dress was perfect for the seaside festivities. Phoenix closed the tube of nude lip gloss and stared at her reflection in the bathroom mirror. She took a deep breath, sighed and rolled her eyes toward the ceiling. “It’s for Savannah,” she said to herself.

Savannah’s wedding was the important thing here, not her own feelings about Carter. How bad could it be? A walk that wouldn’t last more than a few minutes couldn’t be so terrible.

Phoenix groaned. She wished it could have been anyone else. She and Carter were supposed to walk down the aisle together as husband and wife five years ago. That never happened because he called it off the night before the wedding. She never anticipated fate would bring her to a moment like this. She was over the situation and wasn’t interested in ever getting close and personal with Carter ever again. This trip would be the first time in years that they would have to spend time around each other in close proximity for more than a few minutes.

“This is for Savannah,” she repeated as she stuffed her gloss, mascara and eyeliner back into her makeup bag. “I’m going to have a good time.”

Phoenix put the bag inside her suitcase, straightened her back and headed out her villa door. As she made her way through the tropical surroundings and smiling natives, she decided not to let the circumstances bother her. She moved on from Carter a long time ago. One stroll down the aisle for her sister’s wedding wouldn’t change a thing.

Other than tight cordial greetings at events by mutual friends, she and Carter never talked. All she had to do was to continue being cordial. Carter was just another ex.

By the time Phoenix reached the area on the beach where the reception was being held, she was smiling. It could have been the ocean breeze caressing her skin, the beautiful scenery or the fact that she was finally starting to settle into her vacation. Regardless of what it was, Phoenix was happy to feel free of all worries. The next ten days were going to be amazing, fun and peaceful. That was just what she needed.

A handsome Fijian gentleman handed her a colorful drink as she approached the cabana designated for the reception. She smiled and waved at Lincoln and Ivy, Carter's siblings, and continued through the space. The bridal party was small and made up of mostly family. It was originally eight members but now that Zoe and Ethan had to stay behind, there were six of them left that included Carter, Lincoln and Jaxon's buddy Angel. Carter's sister, Ivy, was among the women along with her and Maya, Savannah's good friend. Angel and Maya were the only members of the bridal party that weren't family.

Because a few changes were made, and Carter was now the best man, he was partnered with Phoenix in the wedding since she was the maid of honor. Lincoln was walking with Maya, and Angel was paired with Ivy.

Phoenix hugged and kissed Maya when she stepped under the cabana. Maya and Savannah were college roommates and had become inseparable in the past few years. You would have thought they were friends since childhood. She greeted the others, chatting briefly as she sipped her drink and enjoyed the ocean breeze. Carter and Lincoln hadn't arrived. She continued mingling.

Phoenix would be around everyone for most of the trip and didn't mind, but she also longed for a few quiet moments. She spotted a cozy-looking chair near a corner of the cabana and excused herself from the small crowd. That would give her some quiet time until her sister and Jaxon arrived. They weren't the quiet types.

Phoenix thought about their engagement as she sat. It certainly wasn't a long one. They'd known each other since grade school and weren't interested in a long engagement. The day after Jaxon proposed they scheduled a date a few months out and began planning for their destination wedding. Savannah dreamed about marrying in exotic locations since she was a teenager.

Phoenix ran her hand across the white leather covering the comfortable chair and wondered how they managed to keep them so clean. Phoenix looked around and took in the all-white decor, curtains, seating and flowers, and smiled. The space looked pure, fresh and blissful.

Phoenix took a sip of her drink, closed her eyes and lifted her chin. She could smell the sea and taste the salt on her lips. She felt like all of her worries could roll away with the waves. She listened to the melodic Fijian music playing in the background. With her eyes still closed, she swayed to the rhythm.

"I see that you're enjoying the vibe."

At the sound of that voice, Phoenix felt a bit of her peace slip away. She opened her eyes to find Carter standing over her. Her heart quickened. Not because she was annoyed by him disturbing her moment, but because Carter looked unreasonably handsome. More handsome than the last time she saw him. She figured it was the beauty of Fiji filtering everything around her.

"Hello, Carter," Phoenix said and nodded before sitting up straighter. Taking a sip, she looked at him over the rim of her drink. "It's nice to see you." That was all she had to say. Phoenix hadn't thought about actually having a conversation with him.

"May I?" Carter gestured toward the chair adjacent to her.

"Sure." Phoenix sat back, getting comfortable again.

For several moments they sat in silence. Phoenix wondered how long Carter would stay seated next to her. She closed her eyes again and tried to get back into the music. Her heart rate had returned to normal and the initial tension she felt from Carter's presence was waning. Perhaps this wouldn't be as grueling as she'd anticipated.

After a while Carter finally spoke. "It's beautiful here."

"Yes. It is." Phoenix hadn't opened her eyes.

After another long pause Carter began again. Phoenix gave him her attention. "I just wanted to say hello and..." Carter paused. That made Phoenix open her eyes. Carter blinked in that thoughtful way that Phoenix remembered him doing whenever he was choosing his words carefully. "Having to walk down the aisle with me is probably the last thing you want to do. I just wanted to let you know that I understand if it makes you uncomfortable. I'm doing my cousin a favor and other than that, I'll stay out of your way."

"Same." Phoenix flashed a quick, cordial smile. "You don't need to do this, Carter. I'm sure you had the same conversation with Jaxon that I had with my sister. It's about them, not us."

"I'm glad we're on the same page," Carter said.

"Me, too," Phoenix agreed.

Silence expanded between them again and so did a sense of awkwardness. She thought about asking for another drink. Hers was getting low. Maybe Carter would say something else. They were no longer used to sharing companionable silence. Instead, Phoenix felt the strain of his presence. She thought about coming up with small talk but she sat in the thickness of the silence instead.

"By the way, you look amazing," Carter said.

Phoenix didn't know why his compliment made her smile. But what ex didn't want to hear that they still had it?

"Thanks."

"Hey, everybody!" Savannah burst onto the scene, holding Jaxon's hand. Relieved by her arrival, Phoenix took note of how happy her sister looked and how lovingly Jaxon looked at her. "Are you all ready to get this party started?" Savannah's cheerful voice carried throughout the cabana. She and Jaxon took the drinks the Fijian gentleman handed to them.

"Yeah!" Several members of the wedding party raised their glasses and shouted.

Savannah and Jaxon's arrival succeeded in breaking through the tension surrounding Carter and her.

"Let's start with a toast to beautiful Fiji." Savannah raised her glass. "And I want to toast to each of you for accepting our invitation to come a few days early."

"Yes," Jaxon interjected. "We're a long way from home and Savannah and I wanted to take this time with you to show you our appreciation. So the next few days will be filled with a bit of fun and adventure on us."

"So we can thank you." Savannah picked up where Jaxon left off. "Thank you for agreeing to be a part of our special day, for being here and for being amazing family and friends."

"Cheers!" Jaxon said.

Everyone who had glasses raised them and repeated, "Cheers."

After a sip, Savannah continued. "As you know, Ethan and Zoe won't be able to join us this week. We spoke to them and Zoe is stable but won't be able to leave the hospital for several days. We wish them well."

A few people groaned. Ethan's and Zoe's presence would definitely be missed.

"Since they couldn't join us, I want to thank my cousin

Carter for stepping up and taking on the role of my best man." Jaxon raised his glass toward Carter. "Love you, man."

Phoenix noticed Ivy look from Carter to her, and then lock eyes with Lincoln. This was news to them too.

"Love you back, dude! Anything for my little cousin."

"We all know you're older, Carter!" Jaxon teased. "We'll be sure to remind you of that when it counts the most." A few chuckles erupted from the crowd.

"We've put together a schedule so you'll know what to expect."

Savannah and Jaxon talked for a few more moments to let everyone know what they'd planned over the next few days. Phoenix was well aware of the plan since she worked with them to schedule some of the excursions. She looked forward to having a good time but suddenly wondered about the activities that required partners. For some of the excursions, she and Savannah had paired the members of the wedding party based on who they were walking with. This meant that she would be paired with Carter. They would definitely be too close for comfort. She was fine with being around Carter as long as they kept a cordial distance. Phoenix quickly realized that walking down the aisle with Carter wasn't the only time she'd have to engage with him.

Lost in her thoughts, Phoenix missed the last few moments of Savannah and Jaxon's announcement. "Now, let's party!" Phoenix heard Jaxon yell.

Phoenix looked to the side and noticed Carter watching her. Savannah nodded at the woman assigned to assist her with the wedding party. The lady disappeared for a moment and then reggae music blared from speakers settled in the sand. The party officially started. Everyone danced with drinks in their hands, surrounding the soon-to-be newlyweds, cheering and shouting their names. All seemed to be lost in the excitement of the moment except Phoenix.

Phoenix looked at the happy couple in the center of the bridal party as they danced. Jaxon and Savannah's love for one another oozed into the atmosphere. Unbridled joy danced in their eyes as they gazed at each other and moved to the reggae beat. Phoenix attempted another discreet glance at Carter but he was no longer watching her. Yet, like her, he didn't seem caught up in the fun like the others. Or perhaps, like her, he needed something else to look at besides the blissful couple. Watching them love so open and intimately made Phoenix realize how far she was from that in her life.

Six

Carter pulled out his phone and sent a quick text to Ethan to check on Zoe's status. He acted instinctively, not thinking about the time difference at first. The day was new in Fiji, but with the seventeen-hour time difference it was almost midnight back in New York. Ethan was a night owl. Carter was pretty sure he was still awake. And he was. Ethan texted him back almost immediately, letting him know there was basically no change in Zoe's status. She was still in the hospital but in good spirits and he was right by her side. Their mom had left the hospital a few hours before.

Carter knocked on the door to Lincoln's villa, which was right next door to his, and turned his face toward the rising sun as he waited for him to come out.

"Ready to go," Lincoln said as he stepped outside.

"You look tired," Carter said.

"I was up late so I could talk to Brit and the kids. They can't wait to get here. I see you and Phoenix are playing nice so far."

"Yeah. No reason not to."

"I know, but I imagine it must still be a little awkward."

"It is," Carter admitted.

"Wait!" Lincoln stopped walking. "What happened to Sinai? I just noticed that she wasn't here. I thought she was coming with you."

Carter released a sigh that ended in a chuckle. "Yeah. We're not dating anymore."

Lincoln reared his head back. "Since when?"

"The night before I left. She said I wasn't ready for a commitment, and coming here with me wouldn't have helped our situation."

"Ha!" Lincoln snickered.

"What's so funny?" Carter asked but already knew the answer. No one knew him better than his brothers. Before Lincoln could answer, Carter had already started laughing with him.

"Didn't the last one say that?"

"Is it that obvious?"

"Don't worry. When the right one comes along you won't have to question that."

Jaxon walked into the hotel lobby where he met up with Carter and Lincoln. "What's up? You guys ready?" Jaxon rubbed his hands together as if he was plotting.

"We're ready," Carter said and looked at Lincoln for confirmation.

"Let's do this," Jaxon said and looked around. "I see the women haven't made it here yet, but our chariot awaits." He pointed to the shuttle bus idling in front of the hotel. "I'll let the driver know we need a few more minutes."

Just as Jaxon stepped out of the hotel doors, Carter noticed Phoenix and Savannah making their way toward them. Phoenix was gorgeous. She always had been a flawless beauty—at least to him. He tried not to be obvious but couldn't turn away until he'd taken all of her in. Her hair was pulled back into a ponytail, revealing every beautiful detail of her face. Carter remembered the way he used to trace the outline of her dimples and place his finger in their deep crevices. It always made Phoenix smile harder. He remembered being the one who kept a smile on her face. The simple denim halter and shorts with gold sandals that Phoenix wore gave her a youthful appeal. Carter tore his gaze away, assured that she had not noticed him watching. He remembered so much about her in that moment. There were plenty of other beautiful women out there, possibly less stubborn than Phoenix.

"Good morning!" Carter gave the ladies a cheerful greeting.

"Good morning," Phoenix said in return and nodded at both Carter and Lincoln.

"Hey, guys!" Savannah said. "Where's Jax?"

"He just went out to talk to the shuttle driver."

"Thanks! See you outside." Savannah headed toward the exit.

Carter looked beyond Phoenix and saw his sister, Ivy, walking with Maya. It looked like most of them were there. He was sure that Angel wasn't far behind. He waved at the approaching ladies and headed out to let Jaxon know.

The crew boarded the bus. Carter expected to get some sleep during their hour-long ride but Jaxon and Savannah had other plans. They played trivia, asking questions to see how much their family and friends knew about their relationship. As tired as Carter was, he enjoyed himself.

"Okay, next question," Phoenix said, giggling.

"This isn't fair!" Maya said, folding her arms and pouting playfully. "You guys have known them all your life. You have all the answers."

"She's right," Jaxon said. "Let Angel and Maya try to get this one before any of you chime in," he instructed.

"That's not fair," Carter said.

"You just want all the damn prizes," Carter's sister, Ivy, said.

"What? I'm competitive." Carter shrugged.

Laughter filled the shuttle.

"Here's the question. Where did Jaxon and I meet?"

Maya jumped up. "I know this one. Grade school, right?"

"Yep. Which one."

"Pr…" Carter started.

"Unh uh uh!" Savannah put her finger up, stopping Carter from answering. "You can't answer! We all went to the same school, silly. Of course you know. Give Maya a chance. Geesh. I should have picked more creative questions." Savannah laughed.

"Wasn't it something, something prep school?"

"Close enough!" Jaxon laughed. "You get a point for that one."

"See, Carter, I know some of this stuff." Maya gave Carter a look that appeared more flirtatious than friendly.

Carter thought he noticed a vibe coming from her at the reception the night before, but brushed it off. He figured she had to know that he dated her best friend's sister. *Dated* was putting it lightly. Weren't there some girl codes that she was possibly violating? He glanced over at Phoenix. She didn't seem to pay attention. That was fine, too, since there was absolutely nothing going on between the two of them, and based on their history, the chances of anything ever happening between Phoenix and him were extremely slim. Maya was a beautiful woman, but dating her was out of the question. It was too close to home.

That thought made Carter wonder about the possibility of becoming more than cordial with Phoenix, and immediately shook that thought away.

They moved on to another game. This once pit the men against the women. Soon after, they arrived at the destination.

"Okay, guys! We're here. Oh my goodness. This is going to be so much fun. I really hope you all enjoy this. I know you will, Carter. You and Phoenix love adventure."

Carter looked at Phoenix. She gave a quick smile and turned her head.

The tour guide boarded the shuttle and gave everyone instructions. The woman spoke perfect English despite her Fijian accent. The more she spoke, the more Carter became excited. This was his kind of excursion, one that would take away all the tension he'd been holding in his body for the past several weeks. He was ready to let go and live.

The group grabbed their knapsacks and got off the bus. They browsed a gift shop on their way to the area where they were to be matched up with horses. The beautiful animals were their rides up the mountain.

Carter chose a stunning jet-black stallion and wasn't surprised when he saw that Phoenix chose a gray-and-white one that looked like the one she rode back home as a teen. She'd named him Sparkle because of its flecks of gray coloring. It took nearly a half hour to get to their destination. The well-trained horses followed one another in a straight line with the tour guide in front and another employee for the tour company trailing the group from behind. Carter assumed that they wanted to ensure there were no stragglers.

Carter actually closed his eyes a time or two during their ride up the mountain. He breathed deeply, taking in the clean, fresh air. He looked out over the mountain terrain, which seemed like lush, natural artwork. Carter watched the leaves move with the breeze. He had all but forgotten about every worry he'd left behind. By the time they reached the area where they were to dismount the horses, he'd also forgotten about keeping his distance from Phoenix. Carter was caught up in a blissful peace.

"That was nice."

Carter looked up, a bit surprised that Phoenix had actually said something directly to him. He hesitated a moment to make sure before responding. "Yes. It was."

"I needed that," she said.

"Me, too."

"How are you guys doing?" the tour guide said.

"Great. Wonderful. Fantastic." These were some of the responses.

"Some of those paths were a bit narrow, don't you think?" Maya said. "I'm glad that ride is finally over. Wait! How are we getting back down the mountain? Do we have to get on those horses again? I'd rather walk." Maya shook her head.

Savannah laughed. "Come on, girl." She took Maya by the hand. Worry about that part when we get there."

"Savannah!" Maya groaned. "That was scary. My horse walked way too close to the edge of the cliff. I closed my eyes and started praying. I mean, I know God hasn't heard from me in a while, but I promised if he got me through that trail, I'd reach out to him a whole lot more."

Savannah held her stomach and doubled over laughing. The rest of them laughed, too.

"Maya! You're nuts," Savannah said. "Come on, more adventure awaits!"

Maya moaned and followed Savannah.

Carter chuckled the whole time. Maya was beautiful, but her personality was over-the-top. Even if he hadn't dated Phoenix in the past, he would have to pass on dating her. She wasn't his type.

"On the way back down, maybe I could ride on the back of Carter's horse. He seemed to have a good handle on his stallion."

Carter raised a brow. Maya's comment was bold and her tone seductive. He wasn't expecting that. From the look on everyone's faces, neither were they. Maya flashed a flirtatious smile. Ivy, Lincoln, Jaxon and Angel all looked at Carter at the same time. Ivy barked out a laugh. Lincoln raised a brow. Angel snickered. Jaxon shook his head. Phoenix gave no reaction at all.

"Girl, come on." Savannah yanked Maya's arm. "You'll be fine."

"We have a short hike to our next activity," the tour guide chimed in, bringing everyone's attention back to the excursion.

Moments later they arrived at a platform and were fitted for gear to zip-line. The guide explained that there would be sixteen zip lines and the highest point was 16,400 feet in the air.

"Sixteen thousand! Oh, Lord! Where's my horse?" Maya shouted. "I can't do that."

"Yes, you can," Savannah said.

"You can go alone or partner up if that makes you feel more comfortable," the guide said in an attempt to calm Maya.

"Carter, will you partner with me?"

"I'll go with you," Savannah said quickly before Carter could respond.

Carter was caught off guard again. As a ladies' man, he always had a quick comeback for a pretty woman. Maya was coming for him hard and fast. But this was different. He didn't feel comfortable flirting like that in front of Phoenix.

"Don't you want to go with Jaxon?" Maya asked Savannah.

"We always go by ourselves," Jaxon interjected.

"If it makes you feel safer, I'll go with you." Carter felt obligated to say something. Savannah and Jaxon were trying their best to clean things up.

"That's okay, Carter. I'll go with her. She'll scream your ears off," Savannah said.

"Okay." Carter shrugged.

Glancing toward Phoenix, Carter wondered again if Maya knew anything about their history. Phoenix still seemed unfazed. Maya and Savannah's friendship blossomed after their breakup so there was a chance that she wasn't aware of Phoenix's and his relationship.

"Okay, guys. Here we go," the guide said in a melodic accent.

Lincoln clapped his hands together. One of his frequent gestures. "I'm ready for an adventure."

"Yeah!" Jaxon pumped his fist in the air.

"Ha!" Carter chimed in with a laugh.

The crew hooked Maya and Savannah up first and sent them soaring across the zip line. Maya screamed the entire way, leaving the rest of them on the platform chuckling.

"Saved by Savannah, huh?" Lincoln said, looking at Carter.

"She's coming for you hard, brother," Ivy said and then looked at Phoenix. "She must not know."

"It's not a problem, Ivy." Phoenix waved away any concern she appeared to express. "Maya wasn't around back then and the past is the past."

Carter chuckled and shook his head but something about Phoenix's cavalier attitude made him feel a certain way. What way? He wasn't quite sure but he felt something.

For the next hour they zip-lined at jaw-dropping speeds over treetops. From their vantage point, they took in breathtaking landscapes and views of the ocean. Then they explored caves with exotic ecosystems like nothing Carter had ever seen.

The last part of the tour included a therapeutic dip in the mud pool. Savannah grabbed a gob of mud and tossed it onto Jaxon's chest. Jaxon picked her up and sat down in the mud, covering Savannah up to her neck. Pure joy spilled from her lips as she laughed.

"What are you laughing at?" Savannah said to Phoenix after standing back up. She grabbed another handful of mud and tossed it at Phoenix.

Phoenix let out a sound akin to a hoot and slung some mud right back at Savannah. Savannah ducked and the mud hit Carter square in his face.

"Oh my goodness! I'm so sorry." Phoenix's hand flew to her mouth. Ivy howled, pointing at Carter.

"Who are *you* laughing at?" Carter slung mud in Ivy's direction and also hit Lincoln.

Before long, mud was being slung everywhere. Everyone was covered. They eventually exited the pool and lay in the sun to let the mud dry before a refreshing cleansing in the hot springs. After an authentic Fijian meal they headed back to the shuttle completely spent.

Maya switched her seat. This time she sat next to Carter. He had no trouble sleeping on the way back. At one point he woke to find Maya resting her head on his shoulder, and Phoenix looking his way. They locked eyes for a quick moment before she snickered, shook her head and turned away.

The sun was preparing to set when they were approaching the resort. Carter watched it for a while before nudging Maya awake. He looked around and noticed how quiet the shuttle bus was. They all had fallen asleep. He lifted Maya's head from his arm. He smiled out of kindness. He knew he would have to find a polite way to let her know he wasn't interested. The situation with Sinai was still fresh and something about flirting with Phoenix around didn't settle right.

Maya moaned and stretched. "You're going back to your room?" she asked Carter.

As forthright as Maya was being, Carter wondered if he'd heard her correctly.

"Pardon me?" Carter looked directly at her to make sure he heard her this time.

Maya twisted a finger in her hair and tilted her head. "Are you—" she touched his chest with her index finger "—going back to your room right now? Would you like company?"

Carter smiled. "Thanks, but I don't think that would be a good idea."

"Why? You scared?" Maya pouted.

"Not at all. But thanks. I'm definitely flattered."

Maya twisted her lips. "Well, you know where my villa is in case you change your mind."

Carter simply lifted his brows and smiled. He hung back while everyone exited the bus. He specifically waited for Maya to leave.

"See you guys later," Ivy said. "I need a shower." One of the first to leave, Ivy waved at the rest of the crew and disappeared through the lobby.

"Lincoln, give me a second," he said to his brother, who was waiting to walk back to his villa with him.

"Phoenix..." Carter jogged to catch up with her.

Phoenix turned toward Carter. A slight smile played on the edges of her lips.

"Listen. I...there's nothing going on with Maya and me."

"Why are you telling me this, Carter?"

"I just felt you needed to know."

"There's also nothing going on between you and me. What you do with other women is none of my business."

"There's no need to get snippy, Phoenix."

"I'm not snippy!" she huffed. "You don't owe me any explanation. That's all I'm saying."

"I didn't say I did. I'm just trying to make this less... uncomfortable."

"Fine!"

Carter blew out a frustrated breath. "Maybe you could try being a little nicer."

"Nicer, Carter? Really? All I have to do is get through the next few days. This is about my sister and Jax, remember? Not you!" Phoenix's raised voice caught the attention of Lincoln, who was standing several feet away, and a few other guests.

Carter looked around and lowered his voice. "I didn't say it was about me. I was only trying to be up front."

"Thanks." Phoenix's voice was close to a whisper as she looked around. "It's not necessary."

"You know what…fine. Forget I said anything." Carter turned in frustration.

Carter walked toward Lincoln. "Let's go." His frustration wouldn't let him engage in any small talk as they walked back toward their villas.

Seven

The next morning, Phoenix almost missed the soft knock on her door. She looked out before letting Savannah in. Her sister was in a white swimsuit and matching cover-up. In fact, almost every outfit that Savannah wore was white. Between the white attire and the tiara brandishing the word *Bride* in sparkling crystals, there would be no mistaking who was the bride among them.

Phoenix plopped on the couch with one leg folded under her, sipping a cup of instant coffee. Savannah came and sat beside her.

"You okay, Fifi?"

Phoenix stopped midsip and looked at Savannah. "Sure. Of course. Why?"

"Maya's behavior yesterday, especially last night."

Phoenix rolled her eyes. "Why is everyone so worried about Carter and me? She could have him if she wants."

Savannah twisted her lips unbelievingly. "First of all, who is everyone?"

Phoenix tilted her head. "Why are you looking at me like that?" She closed her eyes for a few seconds before answering Savannah's question. "You and Carter seem to be so worried about how I feel about Maya. It's no big deal."

"You can talk that crap with anyone else but me. I know."

"That was in—"

Savannah held up her hand. "Yes. It was in the past. I know. But whether you still hold a torch for him or not, no one wants to see their ex frolicking with another woman so close to the fold."

"I do not—"

"Yes! Again. I know you no longer have feelings for

Carter," Savannah said mockingly and then tossed Phoenix a sideways glance, but then her expression softened.

"What?" Phoenix groaned and then shrugged.

"I'm sorry." Savannah touched her sister's leg. "I knew you wouldn't love having to partner with him for the ceremony and we couldn't avoid having him here because he's so close to Jaxon, but I didn't realize how much this would affect you."

"What's that supposed to mean? I'm fine." Phoenix put her coffee cup down on the end table.

"Tell that to someone who will believe it. This is me, Fifi. No one knows you better. You haven't been yourself since we've been here. You've been trying so hard to seem unaffected by his presence that you're not even having real fun. I can see that you're just going through the motions. It makes me feel horrible."

Phoenix stood and walked toward the view of the water. "Trust me. I'm fine."

Savannah walked up behind her. "I saw the way you looked when Maya was coming on to Carter yesterday."

"Savannah!" Phoenix spun around and faced her sister. She didn't mean to call her sister's name so harshly, but Savannah was hitting close to home and she wanted this conversation to end.

Phoenix had to admit to herself that she still felt the sting of his betrayal, and even after five years she still didn't have a solid answer as to why he walked away from her the night before their wedding. She didn't want to care about it, but she couldn't seem to help herself.

"Savannah," Phoenix called her name gentler this time. "Please don't worry about me. This trip is all about you. Yes. It's awkward for me, but I'll get over it. I haven't been around him like this since before our break up. It just takes some getting used to. I don't care if Maya wants Carter. Who am I to stand in the way of that?"

Savannah stood firmly in her spot and folded her arms across her chest. "There's more to this. I know there is."

Phoenix looked away. "You're going to be late. We have another day full of adventure that starts in less than an hour."

Savannah dropped her arms. "We're not done with this conversation." She started toward the door. "I told Maya that you guys dated in the past but that was all I said."

That made Phoenix laugh. She walked behind her sister to let her out.

Savannah stopped in the frame of the door and turned back toward Phoenix. "Try to have some real fun today, please."

"I've been having a great time."

Savannah cut her eyes to the ceiling. She went to her sister and hugged her. "Don't be late," she called out as she left.

Phoenix closed the door and rested against the back of it. She thought she'd done a better job of hiding her angst. She had to let go. Whether she got the answers she felt like she needed or not, nothing would change. She and Carter were done. The pit of her stomach knotted. She wanted to be done, but truthfully, there were too many loose ends dangling for that to actually be possible. When everything had happened, she was in too much pain to hear what he had to say. What could he possibly tell her that would make things better? He turned her entire world around the night before the biggest day of her life. She kept everything in after that and tried to convince everyone she was fine. Maybe being around him now was bringing old anger to the surface. She wasn't interested in having Carter back, but maybe she was ready for answers. However, getting answers from Carter would require that she gave a few of her own and she definitely wasn't ready for that. What good would it do now? She decided to leave it alone.

Phoenix got dressed so she could meet everyone downstairs. Admittedly, she felt a little silly about her behavior the night before. It was actually considerate of Carter to reassure her about his intentions with Maya. The truth was Maya's flirtation *did* bother her. She just wasn't willing to admit that to anyone but she certainly felt that twinge of jealousy. She caught Carter's glances but refused to acknowledge them, wanting to appear unfazed. Despite her feelings, she vowed to have more fun for the rest of the trip. Why should she miss out?

When Phoenix reached the lobby, she tapped Carter's shoulder and asked if she could talk with him for a moment.

"What's up, Phoenix?" She could hear Carter's frustration with her in his response.

He had certainly put more effort into making this easier to deal with. She hadn't matched that effort until now. She promised to try.

"I wanted to apologize for last night. I shouldn't have snapped at you like that. Truce?" She held out her hand.

Carter looked at her outstretched hand for a moment before shaking it. "Truce. I'll continue to stay out of your way."

"No need. As two reasonable adults, I think we could manage despite the little bit of history between us. I'm sure you want to enjoy this trip as much as I do."

"Yeah." Carter chuckled. "A little bit of history."

"Just a little." She pinched two fingers together, jokingly. She saw Maya coming their way. "I know who'd like to make a little bit of history with you," Phoenix said, teasing him about Maya's flirting and then discreetly nodded in her direction.

Maya was cheerfully saying hello to everyone so Carter didn't have to turn around to know who Phoenix was referencing. "No, thank you!"

"Ha! Not your type, huh?" Phoenix said sarcastically

but couldn't hold in her laughter too long. She of all people knew Carter's type. Both of them chuckled.

Phoenix felt lighter.

"Our next excursion awaits!" Jaxon yelled, capturing their attention. He waved one arm and grabbed Savannah by the hand to lead her to the shuttle.

"Hey, Phoenix." Maya hung back as the rest of the party headed outside. "Can I chat with you one moment, please?"

"Uh. Sure." Phoenix stopped walking and waited for Maya to catch up.

"Savannah said you and Carter used to date?"

"Yeah. Something like that," Phoenix said.

"All this time and I never knew that. I guess it's because I never really see you around when I'm with Savannah."

"I suppose," Phoenix said.

"That was before Savannah and I became really close, right?" Maya smiled. "He's really good-looking."

"Mmm-hmm." Phoenix nodded in agreement.

"Knowing that you two have history, I was just wondering how you felt about…you know…me flirting with him. I'm really harmless."

A barrage of words flashed through Phoenix's mind. "It's no big deal," and "as long as he's on the market," were the only ones she allowed to pass her lips.

Maya seemed to glow after Phoenix's comment. "Is he? I don't see that he's here with anyone."

Phoenix looked toward the ceiling and thought a moment. "Actually, I don't know."

"Okay. Thanks!" Maya practically skipped away.

Phoenix inhaled slowly and held it for a moment. She was having to work harder to stifle that twinge of jealousy the kept rising up.

Everyone boarded the shuttle, and two hours later they were riding quads across a dirt trail.

"Partner up! It's time for our relay race," Savannah said.

"Girls against boys!" Phoenix yelled.

"What? No! It wouldn't be fair. The girls would lose," Maya said.

"What girls!" Ivy and Phoenix said at the same time. They looked at each other, giggled and slapped high five.

"Me. This girl." She pointed at herself with both thumbs. "Didn't you see me lagging behind everyone?"

"Don't worry. The first round will be men versus women," Savannah said.

"We'll do a relay from here to that big rock over there," Jaxon said. "And then we'll pair up with our or original partners."

"And your partner is the person you're walking in with for the ceremony. So Phoenix, you're with Carter. Lincoln, you're with Maya, and Angel, you're with Ivy. And me..." Savannah looked at Jaxon and wiggled her shoulders. "I'm with my sweetie." She snuggled up against Jaxon.

"I wanted to be on Carter's team," Maya said but must have felt Savannah's eyes on her. "I'm sorry," she said immediately.

Phoenix and Carter looked at each other and shared knowing smiles.

Jaxon jumped on his quad next to Savannah's. "Babe. Should we apologize to them now for leaving them in the dust?"

Savannah threw her head back, laughed and then high-fived Jaxon. "Maybe we should."

"Don't waste your time. We got this. Right, Carter?" Phoenix said.

"No question," Carter answered confidently.

Phoenix and Carter weren't new to four-wheeling. It was one of their favorite things to do when they were together.

Maya caused the girls to lose the men-versus-women round. Unlike the other ladies, Maya wasn't very good at adventures like this. She complained at how dirty her sneakers were getting and how she'd have to toss them when they got back to the resort. They switched to partners. Each round became more competitive with Savannah and Jaxon winning the first, Angel and Ivy winning the second, and Phoenix and Carter winning the last two, which gave them bragging rights. Lincoln and Maya came in last each time. Maya's whining gave them much to laugh about.

Phoenix forgot how much fun Carter could be to hang out with. Together they talked trash about their double win. She looked over at Carter laughing and suddenly noticed how his ripped abs and athletic build pressed against his tank top. Being covered in splattered dirt gave him a sexy, rugged appeal. Something warmed her belly and she turned away, chiding herself for being turned on by Carter's confident stance, muscular arms and taut chest. She never could deny his good looks. And his laugh. Sound spilled from his lips like a baritone melody. She swallowed hard.

"Should we do one more time?"

"No!" Lincoln and Maya yelled.

"Yes!" everyone else said.

Savannah giggled. "Majority rules."

"We're ready to win again. Right, Carter?" Phoenix held her hands up in victory.

"Yes we are," Carter said.

"We were just getting warmed up," Ivy said and Lincoln cosigned with a nod.

Maya said nothing. Phoenix was pretty sure she knew she was the reason they'd lost.

The last race was the closest of them all. Savannah and Phoenix were neck and neck. One would gain a small lead and that would soon be devoured by the other. As they neared the finish line, Phoenix maneuvered around Savannah to get the win. Her ATV hit the side of a rock, causing it to flip on its side, tossing her from the quad. She flew through the air and landed with a thud, hurting her knee. She yelled in pain.

"Phoenix!" Savannah screamed, jumped off her quad and ran to her sister.

Everyone else got off their ATVs and raced to Phoenix rolling on the ground, hugging her knee. She groaned. Carter was the first person at her side.

"Phoenix! What hurts besides your knee? Where does it hurt?" Carter leaned over her.

"M…my…my knee." It took all of the breath in Phoenix's body to speak through the pain. Other parts hurt but her knee was by far the most painful.

"On my goodness, Phoenix," Savannah cried.

Phoenix looked up at all of them around her. Their eyes were filled with worry. Taking turns, they kept asking how she felt or if anything else hurt. Her aching knee took her breath away. She couldn't speak. Carter scooped her off the ground and carried her like a baby.

"We need to get her some help." Despite the weight of Phoenix, Carter moved swiftly. He positioned her on his ATV and jumped on. "Hold on tight."

Phoenix wrapped her arms around Carter's waist and leaned into his back, groaning from the pain. The rest of them jumped back on their quads and followed Carter as he cautiously maneuvered back toward the rental reception area.

"Just hold on." Carter was breathless, too. Phoenix could hear the concern in his voice. "I got you."

Phoenix moaned. It was the only response she could muster. Tears rolled down her face, wetting Carter's T-shirt. She nestled her face in the center of his back and allowed herself to cry.

"It's going to be okay," he assured her all the way back.

From the second that Carter lifted Phoenix into his arms, she knew innately that Carter would take care of her. The past didn't matter right now. Neither did Maya. What she felt in that moment almost shocked her as much as her accident did. Phoenix felt safe in Carter's arms. Like an old, familiar place, she felt like she belonged there.

Eight

Carter and the others paced outside the room as the doctor on-site examined Phoenix's knee. No one spoke. Fortunately, they didn't have to leave the facility for her to be seen. Carter thought they'd have to find a hospital but having someone on staff made sense. Surely, there were accidents all the time.

Savannah was with her. Carter wanted to be inside, as well. His heart felt like it dropped into his stomach when he saw her fly off the ATV. He couldn't get to her side fast enough. The way she hit the ground scared him. Hearing her yelp gave him a small bit of relief. Nothing mattered more in that moment than making sure she was okay.

Now, as they waited, he pondered his response. He didn't think; he reacted instinctually. Phoenix was in danger and he hurried to her side to help. Surely, if it had been his sister, Ivy, who had gotten hurt, or even Maya, he would have responded the same way. Of course he would have helped; yet, Carter couldn't deny that there was something about seeing Phoenix hurt that compelled him to be the first by her side. Maybe it was guilt.

Savannah came out of the room. Everyone looked toward her at the same time. Carter was next to her instantly.

"What did they say? Did she break anything? She's going to be all right?" The questions rushed from his mouth.

Jaxon put his arm around Savannah.

"She's going to be okay. It was a bad fall, but nothing is broken. She's got some swelling, bruising and pain of course. She's going to have to stay off her feet. They were giving her crutches but she refused them. The doctor insisted so she said she'd take one."

"That's Phoenix for you," Carter said. As pretty and dainty as she appeared to be, Phoenix was tough.

There was a collective sigh. "I'm glad she doesn't have any broken bones," Ivy said.

"He's giving her something for the pain now and said the shuttle could stop by the pharmacy on the way back so she can get some regular pain medicine. He didn't believe she needed anything that required a prescription. He's wrapping her up now and then we can go."

"Do you think she'll be up for game night later?" Maya asked.

"I don't know. The pills he gave her can make her drowsy. She may need the rest." Savannah laid her head on Jaxon's chest. "I can't believe this."

Jaxon wrapped his arm around Savannah and rubbed her back. Carter watched as he comforted her. The love they had for each other was undeniable. He wondered if he was even capable of sharing love like that with someone. Then his thoughts careened toward the unpleasant. This accident could have been much worse. Life was fragile and could be cut short at any moment.

The door opened and Phoenix wobbled out with a crutch on one side and the doctor supporting her on the other. Carter ran to the doctor's side and helped Phoenix along.

"Why all the somber faces?" Phoenix said, snickering. "Y'all are not getting rid of me that easily."

Relief was evident in everyone's sighs and expressions. Leave it up to Phoenix to act like this was no big deal.

"You scared the daylights out of me!" Savannah admonished, carefully hugging her sister. "Good try but you're still going to be in this wedding." She wagged her finger at Phoenix, pretending to be annoyed.

"Ah, man!" Phoenix steadied herself on the crutch and snapped her fingers. "Seriously. What's it going to take to get out of this thing?"

"It's a good thing your dress is long and will cover up that swollen knee. I don't want to hear anything about you not wanting to take pictures because your knee looks fat." The women laughed hysterically at Savannah's joke. She shook her head as if she was really frustrated. "Wait until I tell Mom how you tried to get out of my wedding."

The sisters' bantering put everyone else at ease. Moments later they had all climbed into the shuttle and were headed back to the resort. Phoenix sat in a row by herself with her injured leg across the seat next to her. Carter sat nearby to keep an eye on her. Before long she was fast asleep. Both the four-wheeling and the emotional toll had drained them all. One by one, they each fell asleep except Carter. He was wound up in his feelings and couldn't rest. Instead, he examined life as it was.

Carter thought about everything that awaited him at home, including the big decisions. Again, he thought about Sinai and her comment about him.

Then it hit him. Carter knew what his problem was when it came to a serious relationship. He couldn't control it. As an alpha male born with leadership in his DNA, Carter didn't like things he wasn't able to control. Maybe that was behind his need to leave the family business. His entire career has been under his father's thumb. And once he gave his heart to a woman, he was no longer in control of that, either.

Nine

Phoenix rested her head against a cushion and sank lower into the large spa tub. She added a few drops of the essential oils she'd traveled with. Lavender and eucalyptus was her favorite combination and just what she needed after the day she'd had. Phoenix had returned to her room both dirty and battered. Her entire body ached from her accident. Something else had been shaken that day. Her will.

Phoenix thought back to how Carter had run to her side, how he carried her and how she cried into his back. She remembered how safe she felt in his arms. It felt right. She didn't like feeling so at home in Carter's arms.

Phoenix had planned to let go and have fun but she didn't count on enjoying Carter's company so much. It had been a long time since she'd been this adventurous. She and Carter used to do those kinds of things all the time. None of the other men she'd dated since then thirsted for adrenaline rushes the way she and Carter had. They always had fun together.

Phoenix grunted. She wanted to stop thinking about Carter but he wouldn't leave her mind. She didn't want to be mad at him forever. Yet, she also wasn't looking to be his friend. There was too much pain between them for a friendship to work.

Phoenix took her time rubbing the scented scrub into her skin. Her knee throbbed, but not as bad as it did before she took painkillers. Again, Carter popped up in her thoughts. It was awkward being friendly with him. It wasn't like friendship was foreign to them. They grew up in the same community and considered themselves to be good friends even while they dated. But that changed when he came to her the night before their wedding and told her he couldn't marry her. What kind of friend did that? She was so distraught she wouldn't hear anything he said after those horrific words. No explanation seemed sensible. She screamed at him. Told him to get out of her house. She never wanted to see him again. He said he wanted her to keep the engagement ring. She took it off and threw it at him.

That following day was supposed to be the happiest day of her life. They had plans to share that joy with over three hundred guests at one of the Hamptons' most beautiful venues. Excited, her mother, Nadine, arranged for press, which Phoenix tried to talk her out of. The cancellation became the big story. The humiliation was publicized. She relived the pain of being jilted every time she had to explain to someone new that the wedding was off. Phoenix's parents were furious, especially her mother, and the relationship between the families was strained for the next few years. She distanced herself from Ivy, also. Though they knew each other growing up, they'd grown much closer as Phoenix was planning her wedding. Once it was called off, she distanced herself from Carter's siblings, as well. Phoenix sucked her teeth, bringing herself back to the present.

She got into the tub to relax, not to get assaulted by her past.

"Dammit, Carter!"

She was supposed to stay mad at him. It was better when she kept her distance. Feelings of anger were easier to manage than what she was feeling now. Phoenix couldn't articulate what she felt but she didn't like how unsettling it was. She was trying to be nice, trying to reclaim the joy of being on vacation. She didn't expect to remember what she used to love about Carter, or notice how gorgeous he looked, or enjoy his company as they did things together that they once cherished. That wasn't supposed to happen. This was the Carter she remembered and loved. This Carter was grounded. Mature. Different. Phoenix hated that she liked what she saw.

When they'd returned to the resort, Carter insisted on carrying her to the room. Then stuck around and helped her get settled. The way he anticipated her needs gave Phoenix pause, leaving her heart and mind in a state of flux. Carter took charge and made sure she was taken care of. That was something else she used to love about him. He didn't seem to think about it. It happened just like when they were together, intuitively. Finally, she told him to leave. No, she insisted that he leave.

Phoenix washed the body scrub from her skin. She couldn't sit in the room all evening battling thoughts of Carter. She was going to get dressed and meet the rest of the party at Savannah and Jaxon's villa for game night even if she had to hop all the way there.

Phoenix carefully emerged from the tub, delicately wrapped her knee and dressed as comfortably as she could. She chose a maxi dress. Grabbing her one crutch, she cautiously hobbled to Jaxon and Savannah's honeymoon villa.

Everyone was already there. Carter jumped up and met her at the door. She refused his help.

"I got it." Carter stepped aside and raised both hands in the air. Again, Phoenix didn't mean to come off so snippy. She kept doing that with him. "Thanks," she said in a softer tone as she hobbled toward a free spot on the couch. "I need to do this by myself."

"Fifi, you should be resting," Savannah said.

"I did get some rest and I took a long, hot bath." She averted her eyes from Carter. "I just wanted to get out for a bit. What are we playing?"

Ivy told Phoenix what games were played and explained what they were about to play when she came in. It was some game where they had teams and categories and each player only had seconds to come up with the answers.

"I love that game. I'm in," Phoenix said. She felt better now that she was with everyone. It didn't matter that Carter was there. Being alone with her thoughts was more troubling.

This was one game where the girls excelled, beating the guys in every round.

"How do they keep winning?" Jaxon said.

"We're smarter," Phoenix smirked, sharing high fives with the rest of the women.

Getting lost in the fun, Phoenix was able to keep her mind off Carter. Still, every now and then, when Carter would say something, she'd glance over at him and the memories would rush back. She couldn't help it. Most times she'd find that he was already staring at her.

Phoenix stayed long enough for her knee to start aching again. It was time for another painkiller and she hadn't brought any with her.

"Okay, guys. This was fun. I'm glad I came but I need to head back now. My knee is starting to ache."

"I'll walk you back," Carter said and stood.

"No!" Phoenix said fast and loud. "I mean. I'll be fine. I got over here by myself. I'll take my time."

Carter let his hands fall to his sides. "Okay, superwoman."

Phoenix narrowed her eyes at Carter. Calling her superwoman dredged up a few more memories. He used to always say that when she refused someone's help.

"I've got it." Phoenix was going to show that she didn't need assistance. She steadied one hand on the seat of the chair she was in and held the crutch with the other. She went to stand. Her knee wobbled, sending her crashing back into the chair.

Carter came to her and held out his hand. "Come on, superwoman."

Phoenix rolled her eyes at him, but took his hand. Savannah snickered. Carter wrapped his arm around Phoenix's torso to support her as she stood. She hissed from the pain once she put weight on her leg. With Carter on one side and the crutch on the other, she made her way to the door.

Everyone bid her a good-night as she and Carter left.

The walk from Savannah's villa to hers seemed to take forever. They had to stop several times to give her a moment to rest. Awkward silence filled the space between Phoenix and Carter again. Besides the pain in her knee, Phoenix's body was sore, which caused her to walk even slower.

When Phoenix and Carter finally reached her villa, he held her as she lifted her digital bracelet to the keypad on the door. They heard the locks click. Carter pushed the door open, making way for Phoenix to take her time stepping inside. Carter hovered over her as she hobbled to the sofa and sat down.

"You don't want to go to the bedroom?"

"I'm fine here." Phoenix could have used his help getting to the bedroom, but she just wanted him to leave. His presence challenged her will again. The more time she spent around him, the less angry she was and the more she was reminded of the Carter she once loved.

"Where are your painkillers?" he asked.

"By the bed."

Carter went into the bedroom and returned with the pill bottle. He went to the mini refrigerator and grabbed a water bottle.

"Thanks!" Phoenix took the pills and washed them down with a gulp of water. When the liquid hit her stomach she was reminded of how hungry she was. She decided to order room service once Carter was gone. Meanwhile, Carter got the remote for the television and put it within Phoenix's reach.

"Need anything else?" he asked.

"Nope, I think I'm good. Thanks, Carter." Phoenix

smiled. This was her attempt to dismiss him. "You can go now. I'll be fine." A second after she finished her statement her stomach growled. The sound seemed amplified in the quiet room. She looked at Carter. Carter looked at her. Another beat passed before both laughed.

"When is the last time you ate?"

Phoenix stopped laughing long enough to think about it. She twisted her lips at the thought. Consumed by the aches and pains, Phoenix forgot about eating. Her last meal was just before they rode the ATVs. "It's been a while."

Carter picked up the menu. "What do you want?"

"I can order my own room service, Carter. I'm fine."

"I know. But how will you get it when they arrive with the food?"

"I'll walk to the door and open it."

"The same way you walked to your room? It took you ten minutes to get down the hall."

"Ugh! Okay. Fine." Phoenix held her hand out and Carter gave her the menu.

She flipped through and picked a few items.

"Hungry, are we?" Carter teased. Phoenix tossed one of the pillows on the sofa at him.

"Ha!" Carter swatted the pillow with a karate chop. Carter took Phoenix's order and called it in. Picking up the remote, he turned the television on and sat on the couch with Phoenix, leaving ample space between them. They sat quietly watching Carter flip channels. "How are you feeling now, besides hungry?" Carter asked, breaking the silence.

"I've been better. I'll be great when this medicine kicks in."

"Remember when we decided to go get in-line skates out of the blue?" Carter pulled a distant memory out of the past.

Phoenix had just taken a sip of water and had to cover her mouth to keep from spitting it out after Carter's questions. "Oh my goodness! You tumbled down that hill so fast I couldn't keep up."

"I was in pain for days! What made us decide to go in-line skating that day?"

"You did! I think you challenged me or something like that." Phoenix tried to remember.

"Oh yeah. I was going to prove to you that I still had it," Carter recalled. Phoenix chuckled and shook her head. "I was wrong, but it was fun."

"You and your silly challenges. You're so competitive."

"And they were always fun, weren't they?"

Phoenix rolled her eyes. "I'll give you that."

Phoenix and Carter reminisced until her food arrived. Carter went to the door, tipped the gentleman delivering the food and laid everything out before Phoenix.

"Thanks," Phoenix said quietly. "I appreciate this." She truly did. As much as she wanted to send Carter away, his sticking around helped.

"You're welcome," Carter replied. They locked eyes. Both looked away instantly. "Um," Carter said as the mood turned awkward. "Need anything else?"

"No. I don't think so. I'm fine. Thanks for everything." She looked around, trying to avoid looking directly at Carter.

"Okay."

Neither of them moved. Carter didn't head for the door. Phoenix didn't reach for her food. Instead, she fiddled with her fingers. Carter stuffed his hands in the pockets of his linen shorts. Time slowed. Phoenix liked having him there. She didn't want him to leave but didn't dare say that. It seemed that Carter wasn't ready to leave, either. Maybe it was the painkillers kicking in.

"I guess I'll head out now," Carter said. "Let me know if you need anything."

"Yeah," Phoenix said and then the last thing she ever expected happened.

Carter bent over and kissed her forehead. "Feel better. I'll check on you in the morning." With that, he quickly walked out, leaving Phoenix spinning in her emotions.

Phoenix wanted to tell him that checking on her in the morning wasn't necessary, but she could only think about the kiss. The kiss wasn't romantic. It was caring. Normal. Familiar. It felt like something they did all the time without thinking. She watched Carter leave, clamping her mouth shut. She could feel herself getting ready to tell him to stay. She couldn't do that, especially after the kiss, even though it wasn't romantic. Still, it was a kiss. Carter had kissed her. She hadn't felt the touch of his lips in over five years. She felt another stir in her emotions, like a slow unraveling.

Ten

Carter thought about the kiss all night long. It was still on his mind when he woke in the morning. Before he knew it, he'd bent over and his lips were on Phoenix's forehead. He was surprised that Phoenix hadn't objected or pushed him away. He wasn't sure why he'd done it. Yet, it felt natural.

Carter made it his business to try and work cordially with Phoenix, even though she had been snippy. He understood. He hadn't wanted to partner with her in this wedding any more than she wanted to walk with him. How ironic was it that he was supposed to walk with her down the aisle and they had never made it down the aisle of their own wedding? When Jaxon first asked, he felt like karma was playing a cruel joke on him.

This vacation was supposed to take his mind off his issues, not add to them. Yes, they were two mature adults but so much had transpired in their past, Carter wasn't sure how this would turn out. He anticipated that Phoenix wouldn't be happy about the matchup. What he didn't anticipate was remembering how much fun it was to hang out with her. He didn't expect to notice her beauty or enjoy the sound of her laughter. He didn't expect to feel the need to run to her aid when she had the accident. Something shifted in him when he saw Phoenix's body fly off that ATV. The fall scared Carter and he didn't want to see her hurt. He had once loved the woman. Somehow, he felt like he was supposed to be there for her.

Jaxon and Savannah had another full day of activities planned for the bridal party. Phoenix would have to sit this one out. There was no way she'd be able to endure water sports. She could get the rest she needed and join them for the yacht party later that evening.

Their parents and the rest of the guests were due to arrive throughout the day. Phoenix would need her rest to be able to participate in the wedding the next day.

Carter decided to stop by her villa before heading to the lobby to meet the others. Savannah was coming out of Phoenix's door when Carter got there.

"What's wrong, Savannah?" Carter asked.

She huffed. "Phoenix. I feel bad."

"Something happened?"

"No. Phoenix is in no condition to join us today. I told her I was going to stay and help her get around today. She insisted that I join the rest of the party as planned and practically told me to get out so I could go have fun, but I'm going to stay back and help her out anyway. You should see her hobbling around that villa. Jaxon can handle the group without me."

"Savannah. You're the guest of honor. You have to go."

"I can't. I need to be there for my sister."

"I'll stay back. I can help her if she needs anything. She can call me."

"No, Carter. I couldn't ask you to do that."

"I helped her out last night. I can help her today. Besides, I could use a day to just chill. There's plenty to do here at the resort. I'll see you at the yacht party tonight."

"Really? You'd do that for me? For Phoenix?"

"Believe me it's not a big deal. I'll be close by in case she needs someone. Go have fun."

"Are you sure, Carter?"

"Absolutely sure. Enjoy yourself. You've got a big day tomorrow."

Savannah wrapped her arms around Carter and hugged him tightly. "Thanks, Carter."

"No problem."

Savannah went to walk away and turned back. "Between you and me. I was really happy to see you and Phoenix getting along yesterday."

Carter smiled. "Me, too."

"Thanks again, Carter."

"You're welcome."

Savannah headed in the direction of the lobby. Carter turned and knocked on Phoenix's door.

"Savannah!" Phoenix yelled from the other side of the door. "I told you I don't need a babysitter."

"It's not Savannah," Carter said.

"One sec," Phoenix said.

Carter waited several moments, imagining Phoenix limping toward the door. Finally, the door creaked open slowly. Carter stepped in as Phoenix headed toward the couch and plopped down.

"How are you feeling?"

"Blah."

"No jet-skiing today?" Carter teased.

"I could go if I wanted."

"Yeah, right. Superwoman is at it again." Carter sat on the couch next to her. Phoenix laughed. "I'm resting up so I can carry out my maid of honor duties tomorrow."

"Good."

Phoenix looked at her cell phone and turned her attention to Carter. "Shouldn't you be in the lobby with the rest of the group? The shuttle bus is scheduled to leave in a few minutes."

"I'm not going."

"Carter!"

Carter held his hand up. "I volunteered to stay back so your sister could go."

"No! You don't have to miss the action because of me. I'm a big girl and can handle myself." Phoenix struggled to stand. "Go on with the rest of them."

"My decision has been made. I'm sticking around. If you need anything I'll be right here."

"In my room?"

"If you want me to. After yesterday I could use a day to chill."

"No. Carter. I don't need you to do this."

"You don't have a choice. I'm sticking around."

"Ugh!" Phoenix's grunt was loud. It filled the open space.

Carter stood and walked to the sliding door and opened it. The sound of the waves crashing against the shore filled the room. He took a deep breath, taking in the salted air. Carter closed his eyes.

"This is good for both of us. I've been on the go since my plane touched down. Now I can actually sit back and enjoy the view." Carter turned back toward Phoenix. "Have you had breakfast?"

"No. I was just about to head to the dining room."

"Feel like walking? I can get it for you or we can order room service and you can enjoy breakfast right on your patio."

Phoenix took a moment to respond. "I'd rather get out of this room for a bit."

"Say no more." Carter picked up the phone in the villa and called for a golf cart to come take them to breakfast. "Your chariot will arrive in several minutes," he said, holding out a hand as a servant would with their queen.

At first, Phoenix narrowed her eyes at him. "I don't know who's worse, you or Savannah! Help me up so I can get my things."

Carter helped her to her feet and watched as she slowly walked to the bedroom. Carter continued watching as Phoenix stuffed a towel and a book in a straw beach bag. She slid a pair of shades over her eyes. As she walked back toward the living room, he noticed she had on a swimsuit with a long cover-up that flowed in the slight breeze behind her. Carter took a breath. Phoenix looked both sexy and regal. The hotel attendant tooted the horn outside her villa. Carter held the door open so she could take her time getting through it.

Breakfast was outside overlooking a different part of the ocean. Initially, both Carter and Phoenix remained silent. Soon after, they engaged in small talk about how delicious their meal was. Like the day before, they were laughing and talking as if there wasn't a heartbreaking history between them. Carter was intrigued at how easily they slipped into comfortable banter. He thought about his conversation with Jaxon. Now that he and Phoenix were speaking, he wanted to let her know how sorry he was about what happened between them. He wanted her to know that his intent wasn't to hurt her. He was just trying to do the right thing. He may not have this opportunity again and decided to have that conversation today. Carter needed to get it off his chest but the timing had to be right. *Would the timing for that subject ever be right?* Carter thought.

"So what were you planning on doing today?" Carter asked, sipping orange juice.

"Lie on the beach. Enjoy some cocktails. Read. Bathe in the sun. It's a welcome respite after being so busy with all these excursions."

"Okay. After breakfast I'll walk you over to the beach and leave you alone to enjoy your book. If you need anything just call or text me. I won't be far so I can check on you."

"What are you going to do?" Phoenix said, placing her fork down. She pushed her plate back and rubbed her stomach.

"Not sure yet. I'll see what they have going on around here."

"Well..." Phoenix stopped talking abruptly.

"Well, what?"

"You're welcome to join me on the beach for a drink."

Carter nodded. "I think I will."

They finished breakfast and found a spot on the beach to lounge. Carter ran back to the room and changed into swimming trunks. It was as relaxing as he had expected. Phoenix read while Carter swam a few laps and took a ride on a rented Jet Ski. He didn't venture far into the water and kept his eye on Phoenix. By early afternoon they'd shared several cocktails, taking off any remaining edge as they lounged in the tropical sun.

Phoenix lifted her empty cup and the waitress taking their orders nodded. She would soon arrive with a fresh drink for her and Carter. "This is just what I needed," Phoenix said. "And this—" she held up her cocktail "—is why I skipped the painkillers this morning." She lifted her face toward the sun. "I wish I could stay here all month. There's so much waiting for me back home."

Carter groaned. "You, too?"

"Yes. Work, home, everything."

"That and more. My partner and I are starting a new venture. We're waiting on a few pieces of the puzzle to fall into place before we can launch."

"That's great news, Carter. Sounds exciting. Congratulations."

"It is. Thanks."

Phoenix sat up and looked at him. "You don't sound excited. What's up?"

"I am. I'm not looking forward to telling my father about leaving the company."

"He doesn't know yet? Yikes!" Phoenix sat back.

"His dream was for his sons to take over the business. He won't be happy. There are a few other big decisions awaiting my return. Oh, and the girl I was dating broke up with me the night before I left to come here. She basically said I was allergic to commitment. She's the second or third one this year."

"Ha!" Phoenix covered her mouth to keep her drink from spraying all over her and Carter. "Sorry. I shouldn't have laughed at that. I know a little something about your commitment allergies."

"Really, Phoenix?" The way she laughed made Carter laugh, too.

"That was cynical but funny!" Both chuckled this time. "To be honest, I probably shouldn't laugh at you. Your life sounds a lot like mine. Two days before I left, my boss told me my company was moving to the Bay Area and remote work won't be an option. How do they expect us to uproot our entire lives and make a decision to follow them across the country in a matter of weeks?"

"Whoa! Are you going?" Carter asked, suddenly alarmed by the fact that she might be moving. He had to tell her now or he'd never get the chance.

Phoenix slowly shook her head. "I really don't know. My dad needs surgery and my mom is going to need us to help with his recovery. I want to be here for them but the opportunity to move comes with a lot of perks. I don't want to leave New York but I hate to miss out on a great opportunity. I need to give my boss my answer within thirty days. It's just so sudden."

"Wow." Carter sipped his drink.

"Oh. And the guy I was seeing isn't so happy with me, either, so that's pretty much over." Phoenix chuckled. "I guess I have some commitment allergies of my own."

"Who would have thought!" Carter chuckled, feeling a bit relieved by her admission.

"Phoenix." Carter's tone was serious, devoid of the teasing lightness from moments before.

"Yes, Carter?"

This was his chance. He searched his mind for the right words. "I had a baby on the way."

Phoenix scrunched her face. "What?"

"That's why I called the wedding off."

"No! We're not doing this." Phoenix sat up and swiped her arm across her body as if cutting Carter's words off. She reached for her beach bag.

Carter swung his leg over the side of his lounge chair and faced her. "Please." He gently grabbed her wrists, stopping her from tossing more stuff into the bag.

"No!" Phoenix twisted her arms from his grasp. "That was the past."

"Please! You should know. Before we got back together and decided to get married, I was dating Taylor." The words came in a rush. Carter knew he only had minutes to get this out. "The week of our wedding, she came to me—pregnant. She was sure it was my baby. I was sure it was mine. The timing made sense."

"I don't want to hear this." Phoenix shook her head.

"You deserve to know. I didn't love Taylor, but I wanted to do the right thing and be there for my child. It was the hardest decision I ever had to make in my life. I did what I thought was best for everyone involved."

"Well, where's this baby now, Carter? Huh? Ugh!"

"It turned out not to be mine. It was months later when I found out. I'm sorry." Carter watched Phoenix shake her head. "I'm sorry," he said again. "I've wanted to say that to you for years. I never meant to hurt you." Phoenix blinked rapidly. Carter felt like he was breaking her heart all over again. He didn't mean to. He just wanted to finally tell her the truth and get past it. The damage had already been done.

Phoenix's mouth fell open. "I need to go." She ambled her way to her feet, tossed her bag across one shoulder and steadied her crutch under the other. Carter stood to assist her. She held out her hand to stop him. “No. I don’t want your help.”

Holding both hands in the air, Carter stepped back and let her go. He watched her as she carefully disappeared into the lobby. Carter wanted to walk her to the room, but knew she needed a moment. He would check on her later, if she allowed.

Carter hadn’t expected the conversation to go well, but knew he had to tell her. After carrying that information around for years, he felt lighter now. He meant it when he told Phoenix that she deserved to know. He needed her to know.

Eleven

Phoenix avoided Carter for the rest of the day. Instead of sitting on the beach, she lounged on her balcony, taking in a more private view of the water. The rest of their family and friends were due to arrive at the resort by the evening, but Phoenix decided to remain low-key to deal with her emotions. She listened to music, ordered lunch and read her book, but none of that would take her mind off what Carter had revealed.

"Dammit!" Phoenix grunted as the thoughts took over her mind once again. She put her book down on the small table next to her lounge chair. She'd been reading for at least twenty minutes and had no idea what she'd just read. Her mind was on Carter. Why did he have to tell her all this now? Pregnant. It was a pregnancy that ended their engagement. How interesting. This was too much for Phoenix to bear.

Phoenix remembered Taylor. She was the one constant during her and Carter's on-again, off-again relationship back in college. It was as if she waited for them to break up. Days later Phoenix would see Taylor hanging off Carter's arm somewhere on the campus. Carter's dating Taylor wasn't the problem. It was the pregnancy.

Tears fell from Phoenix's eyes. She swatted them away. Carter's admission had torn open old wounds. Why did he have to bring that up? She was growing comfortable with the idea of walking down the aisle at her sister's wedding with Carter. The tension had melted away and Phoenix had actually started to enjoy Carter's company. Now she wasn't so sure.

Phoenix poured a glass of the wine she'd ordered and

sat back to take in the evening sun. The beauty of the sky with its spectacle of lights should have brought her joy. It didn't. Phoenix huffed.

At least Phoenix now had the answer she'd avoided for so long. Her heart had broken into pieces the night he called the wedding off. And now it was breaking all over again. Back then she didn't want to hear what he had to say because no explanation would have made a difference. After he'd said he couldn't marry her the night before the ceremony, there was nothing else she needed to hear from him. Scenes from that night flashed before her. She'd gone from shocked to angry. Phoenix had pushed him. She screamed, cursed and told him to get out of her sight. She shouted that she hated him and that she never wanted to see him again. A few times after that she wondered what would make Carter do that to her and always arrived at the same conclusion. It didn't matter why he did it. What mattered was *that* he did it.

The days following were the worst days of her life. They were supposed to honeymoon in Belize. She went alone but hardly left her room at the resort. The solitude was what she'd needed. Savannah, her mother and friends tried to talk her out of going. When they couldn't, they decided to go with her. She insisted on going by herself. In Belize she hadn't had to answer anyone's questions about why the wedding had been called off. She couldn't tell that story one more time.

So many painful memories flooded her thoughts. New emotions battled with old ones. After the breakup she was angry and then numb. Now she was confused. This news changed so much and now her heart ached all over again. She tried not to be angry with herself.

It made sense that Carter hadn't wanted to embarrass her. That was what she would have expected Carter to do. He was a stand-up man even when he was running around college trying to be the most eligible bachelor of the campus during their breakups. It wasn't hard. Carter had always been gorgeous with his smooth brown skin, dreamy eyes and athletic build. All the Blackwell boys were charmers. Girls would dote all over them and be jealous of any other girl who seemed to hold their attention for a few weeks at a time.

A barrage of what-ifs came to mind. What if they had talked things out that fateful night? What if she had known about the pregnancy then? What if Phoenix had told him her secret? Things would have been different. They might have been married. Maybe not.

"Ugh!" Phoenix shook her head as a fresh batch of tears fell. She had to stop her mind from going back. None of those what-ifs mattered now. She'd made her decision then. It was too late now.

Phoenix had spent the better part of her afternoon reeling about the news Carter had dropped on her. Now evening was approaching and the yacht party would start soon. She needed to get herself together. There would be no excuse for her missing it. But this news was heavy on her heart and mind.

Phoenix took one last sip of wine and headed to the shower. Setting her phone to her favorite pop music playlist, she washed the leftover sand from her body, oiled her skin and put on another sundress. This time it was soft pink. She brushed her tresses, stuck her feet into comfortable flat sandals and considered herself ready. Phoenix checked her reflection before leaving her room. She didn't want to look like she'd been crying.

Phoenix dabbed on some makeup to freshen her appearance. She wished she had eye drops to reduce a bit of the redness. Looking at herself in the mirror, she smiled. It was practice for when she got together with the rest of the bridal party. The smile was to push back the pain. To make her appear happy. To hide the emotions bubbling to the surface. To keep her from falling apart. Phoenix blinked back a new threat of tears. She looked into the mirror again, staring directly into her eyes. She smiled once more, then took a deep breath.

When Phoenix stepped out of her villa, she saw Carter coming her way. A rush of air swirled in her lungs. She took three quick breaths. The last quivered as she released it. She'd prepared for being in front of everyone. She hadn't prepared for seeing Carter's face. Phoenix bit on the inside of her lip and then forced herself to smile. That smile covered a multitude of emotions.

"Hey," Carter said when he approached.

"Hey," Phoenix said back.

"I just wanted to make sure you got to the boat okay."

"Thanks." Phoenix leaned on her crutch and started walking. "It's actually better now. There's not as much pain." Her tone was tight and her words short. Phoenix thought about how ironically the pain seemed to move from one place to another, from her knee to her heart. "I'll be fine. You can go ahead."

"I'll just give you some space, superwoman."

Why did he have to say that? When he said it before today, it was funny to her. It brought back cute memories. Now it was like pouring verbal salt into her open wound. She hated feeling so vulnerable.

"Fine."

True to his word, Carter walked several feet behind her. Lincoln caught up with them by the time they reached the area where they were to dock.

"Hey, y'all! Up here!" Savannah was waving from the top deck.

Savannah looked so pretty in her white halter dress and her hair flowing in the breeze. Jaxon stood beside her as handsome as could be with one arm around Savannah's waist. They looked perfect together. Phoenix smiled for real this time. Her sister was so happy. She would use Savannah's joy to get her through the night. It was contagious.

By the time Phoenix approached the stairs, Carter was behind her, making sure she made it up without incident. Once she got onto the deck, everyone cheered.

Savannah hugged her. "You made it!" When Savannah pulled back she stared into Phoenix's eyes. "You okay?"

Phoenix grinned and shook her head. "I'm fine."

"You sure?" Savannah asked. Phoenix avoided Savannah's penetrating stare. After another moment Savannah asked, "Any pain?"

"Actually, I feel much better. I think I really needed the rest."

"Great! You don't have to move around much. Just try your best to have a good time, okay?"

"I will."

Jaxon and the others came over and checked on Phoenix, as well.

"Thanks everyone, but this party is about my sister and her dapper hubby-to-be here. I'm good. Where's the food?"

"That's my sister." Savannah laughed.

Phoenix stole a glance in Carter's direction. He was looking right at her. She wondered what he was thinking. Did he know she'd been crying? At that moment they went back to cautiously avoiding each other like they had when they first arrived in Fiji. Phoenix needed to get through the party and the wedding so she could return to her life and forget all about Carter and the what-ifs of the past five years.

Twelve

Carter wasn't sure how to take Phoenix's distant behavior at the yacht party. She didn't speak and barely looked his way. He hadn't expected her to take the news with a hearty smile, but didn't expect her to be this upset. He thought she was over it. The timing was right. They were finally speaking. No one else was around and once they got back to the US, there was no telling if he'd ever get another chance to tell her.

Carter's mind drifted to the past. His decision to walk away from their engagement wasn't easy. He'd tried to figure out better ways to handle the situation. He knew it would hurt her. That was the last thing he wanted to do. Taylor, the woman who claimed to be carrying his child, was fun to be with and always made herself available to Carter. But he didn't share the same history with her as he had with Phoenix. He met Taylor while they were in college. She was also from New York and stayed on campus at the same university as Carter and Phoenix. They'd dated off and on in college and occasionally during grad school. Their relationship hadn't been as serious as the one he'd shared with Phoenix.

Carter had had a crush on Phoenix since middle school. They finally started dating in high school. He knew then that one day she'd be his wife. But first, he needed to get his wanton lust for girls out of his system. He and Taylor ended their fling just before Carter and Phoenix reunited. They got back together in the spring before finishing graduate school, decided to marry and scheduled their wedding for that same summer. Then Taylor showed up pregnant. She was several months by then with a noticeable bulge.

Carter wrestled with his emotions for months after the cancellation. He found it hard to eat and lost weight. He buried his pain and focused on Taylor, doing everything he needed to do to be there for her and their baby. Carter didn't love Taylor, but still put in the effort to make a relationship work. His father said it was the right thing to do. He figured he might grow to love Taylor. Most of all, he wanted to be there for his child. Blackwells weren't deadbeat dads.

Carter had accompanied Taylor to doctors' appointments, made midnight runs for ice cream, rubbed her aching feet at night and shopped for baby furniture. Pride filled his chest when the doctor announced they would be having a boy. Despite moving forward with Taylor, they maintained a low profile around his family. His mother, who always had a sixth sense about things, never took to Taylor. Carter figured his family was used to Phoenix and would soon adjust, especially once the baby came.

At his mother's insistence, Carter requested a DNA test shortly after the baby's arrival. He had found out the baby wasn't his. He was furious and let Taylor know exactly how he felt without mincing words. Carter was also torn. He had gotten used to life without Phoenix and settled into the idea of having a son with Taylor. He loved the child before he was born and was instantly smitten with his big brown eyes the moment he entered the world. He bonded with that baby boy and was crushed a month later when he learned he wasn't the father. He was crushed again after learning that he didn't have to wait until the baby was born to confirm that it wasn't his. The woman who'd administered his DNA test told him he could have found out as early as nine weeks into Taylor's pregnancy. Carter wouldn't have had to call off his wedding. He had to live with the decisions he'd made.

"What's on your mind, bro?" Lincoln's voice pulled Carter from his bitter memories. He handed Carter a drink.

Carter sighed. "Too much," he said as he took the drink from Lincoln and sipped.

"This is the life," Lincoln said, leaning on the railing as he and Carter faced the setting sun.

"It is! Cheers." Carter lifted his glass to Lincoln for a toast.

"Wanna talk about it?" Lincoln asked.

"Not now."

"Okay. Phoenix seems to be doing better. That was scary," Lincoln said, referring to Phoenix's incident. He shook his head. "I'm glad it wasn't worse."

"Yeah. She's a tough one. Always has been," Carter reminisced.

"Come on. Join the party. You've been over here looking like your dog died long enough," Lincoln said and laughed at the common phrase his family used to describe when someone seemed down.

"Ha! Whatever, bro. You're right, though. I just have a lot on my mind. I need to get back to the party."

The two of them walked over to where the rest were dancing, chatting and nibbling on hors d'oeuvres. Carter checked his demeanor on the way.

"Welcome to the party, cousin-in-law," Savannah announced. "Glad you decided to join us."

"Yeah, Carter. What's up? You act like your dog died," Ivy teased.

That got Carter laughing again. "Lincoln just used that on me."

"Ha! That's a Blackwell for you," Ivy said.

He glanced at Phoenix and averted his eyes before she or anyone else could catch him looking. "Just a lot on my mind. And that water is mesmerizing. Did I miss anything good?"

"Just Jaxon's silly jokes. I see why he's marrying Savannah. She actually laughs at them," Ivy said.

"That's my baby!" Jaxon said, squeezing Savannah in his arms. It was evident that the cocktails he'd been consuming were working on him.

"We might need to turn the party up a notch." Carter walked away to ask one of the attendants if they could turn the music up and play one of his favorite songs.

The popular melody sailed through the deck and everyone jumped to their feet to dance, except Phoenix. She danced from her chair, raising her crutch in the air to the rhythm of the party tune. The rest of their time on the water was filled with good music, dancing and the group reminiscing about their favorite songs. By the time the boat docked, most of them were in high spirits from the drinks and the fun they had. Carter had almost forgotten about his worries until he saw Phoenix struggling to get down the stairs. It seemed that everyone expected that he'd be the one to help her along.

Phoenix didn't object this time. Yet, she still hadn't spoken to him. Quietly, he proceeded to walk her to her villa. The awkwardness that initially settled between them was back. Only this time it was accompanied by a thick tension. The walk seemed longer. Both cleared their throats several times.

"Listen." Carter broke the silence when they reached her door. "I didn't mean to upset you."

"Don't worry about it." Phoenix cut him off, held her wrist up to the door and turned the knob.

"I thought the timing was right. We were getting along and…"

"It's evident you still have an issue with timing," Phoenix snapped.

Her comment stung. Carter took a deep breath and exhaled slowly. He tried not to lose his patience with her. "Fine," his tone was even. He took a step back, adding space between them.

"I'm sorry. I shouldn't have said that." Phoenix carefully stepped over the threshold and turned back toward Carter.

"I'm sorry, too," he said. "Hopefully, we can move on. It was nice being friendly. Maybe one day we could go back to that."

Phoenix looked away. When she looked back at Carter there was something unreadable in her eyes. Had she been more affected by his news than he realized? Their eyes locked. Carter felt himself moving closer to her.

"We just need to get through the wedding tomorrow and the next few days and we can go back to living our normal lives. You won't have to see me and I won't have to see you."

"You're right," he said outwardly. Inside, he didn't like the idea of never seeing her again. The past few days awakened something in him. Even the tense moments reminded him of what they once shared.

Carter kept his eyes on hers. She held his gaze. Old feelings returned, stirring his emotions. Perhaps those feelings never left and remained dormant in his soul. His heart quickened. Desire flooded him and he wondered what Phoenix would do if he kissed her. She still hadn't looked away. Was she waiting for him to leave? Did she want to kiss him as much as he wanted to kiss her? Maybe she was having some of the same crazy thoughts. Maybe old feelings were coming to the surface for her, too.

Carter stepped closer to Phoenix. She didn't move. Carter noticed the rise and fall of her chest become more intense. He stepped closer. She stayed put. He watched her throat shift as she swallowed. He smelled the sweet scent of perfume. He wondered if he could taste the salt on her skin.

Carter wasn't sure what he was feeling, but he felt something. It was more than lust, despite the horrible timing. He missed Phoenix. The thought of her absence burned in him. In this moment he realized every woman since her was an attempted replacement. That was why none of those relationships worked. But Phoenix would never have him. Would she?

Random thoughts flashed in his mind. What if Taylor was never pregnant? What if he had known the baby wasn't his before calling off the wedding? Did he still want Phoenix? In this moment he did.

Carter closed the space between them so tightly he could feel her breath. He brushed her cheek with the back of his fingers and whispered, "I'm sorry."

Phoenix closed her eyes and a tear fell.

Something quickened in Carter's chest. Her tears weakened him. Why was she crying? He wanted to take care of whatever caused her to cry. He wiped her tear, leaned forward and kissed the wetness that it left behind. Phoenix stiffened slightly. He kissed her cheek once more. Carter wanted to kiss her again and again. She didn't move but hadn't objected. Carter wanted to be with her. The feeling overwhelmed him. He kissed her again. This time closer to her lips.

He gently placed his hands behind her head and pulled her to him. "I'm sorry," he whispered again, brushed his lips against her nose and rested his forehead against hers. He felt the heaviness of her pain in her breath. He longed to be her salve. Carter couldn't seem to pull himself away. He felt compelled. He craved Phoenix, wishing he could erase the past and rewrite it.

"I wish it never happened." His desire for her consumed him with heat. He pulled away to gather himself. He looked into her eyes. More tears fell. He hated seeing her cry.

Carter kissed the new tears. He felt Phoenix's body relax. She sniffled. He wished he never caused her pain. He kept kissing her, finding his way to her lips. Phoenix opened her mouth, hesitantly at first. Then she received him fully, passionately, hungrily. She invited him in. Carter's eyes closed, elated by her acceptance. Phoenix kissed him back with an urgency that matched his. When their lips parted, both were breathless.

"I'm sorry." This time Carter apologized for taking liberties even though she hadn't objected. Inside he was a happy man. The kiss was a breakthrough. He couldn't believe his thoughts. He wanted Phoenix but didn't realize how much until that moment. But was that even possible?

"Stop apologizing," she whispered, out of breath.

This time she reached for him. Carter happily obliged, kissing her passionately. The welcome feel of her soft lips almost sent him over the edge. Together they hobbled in the door enough to be able to close it. Carter felt his erection stiffen and pulled away. Phoenix looked down. He knew she felt it, too.

Carter didn't want to push Phoenix too far. If the door to her heart was opening, he needed to enter with care. Phoenix's heart wasn't something to play with. Neither was his. They had been through too much.

"I'd better go."

Phoenix gnawed on her kiss-swollen bottom lip. "Yeah. Maybe you should go." Her voice was low.

Carter wanted to pull her in for another kiss, pick her up and carry her to the bed. He restrained himself, willing his desire to be curtailed. "Good night, Phoenix."

"Good night, Carter." Her words came out in a whisper.

Carter backed out, keeping his gaze locked on Phoenix. When he cleared the doorjamb, she closed it slowly.

Thirteen

Phoenix woke in the morning to a bright sun shining down on her in the bed. She was in a haze, wondering if her memory served her right; if she really had kissed Carter the night before.

After closing the door on Carter last night, Phoenix leaned against it. She'd stayed there listening until she finally heard Carter walk away. She'd been glad when he did. It had taken everything for her not to open that door back up and invite him into her bedroom.

Carter had just kissed away her tears. And she'd let him. She was convinced that she was over Carter. Being around him these past few days had softened her resolve. Now she wasn't sure about that at all. His kiss soothed her soul and lit a fire inside her. It felt right and it shouldn't have. She yearned for more. What was she to do now?

Phoenix's tears surprised her. She never meant to cry in front of him but couldn't help herself. She'd believed him when he said he was sorry. His apology made all the feelings and memories from earlier that day come rushing back. The what-ifs returned, too. So many things could have been different had she calmed down enough to let him explain that night.

Phoenix huffed. She had to stop thinking about Carter. She was scheduled to meet her family for breakfast. The rest of the guests arrived between yesterday evening and this morning. There was so much to do to get ready for the wedding. A wedding where she would have to walk down the aisle arm in arm with Carter Blackwell. A part of her couldn't wait to see him while another part of her dreaded being in his presence because of how he made her feel.

Phoenix put her crutch aside and walked cautiously to the bathroom. Her body didn't ache as much as it had before. She'd gotten much better at walking without the crutch as long as she wasn't too tired.

Phoenix focused on getting dressed but her thoughts kept going back to Carter. "Ugh!" Those kisses were going to increase the level of awkwardness during the wedding.

What would it be like when she saw Carter? How would she feel?

Phoenix called to see if her parents and Savannah were ready. At breakfast their mom, Nadine, fussed over Savannah. She couldn't contain her excitement about her daughter's wedding. Their dad, Christopher, sat back and smiled broadly.

"I have something to tell you, Mom," Savannah said.

"What is it, sweetie?" Nadine said, reaching for her flute of mimosa.

Savannah cast Phoenix a quick glance before blurting out, "Savannah is walking with Carter in the wedding."

Their dad, Chris, sat straight up and sighed. Nadine paused with her glass midway to her mouth. "What did you just say?"

Savannah rushed to explain. "Ethan couldn't make it. Zoe is in the hospital and you know how close Jaxon is to his cousins…" Savannah continued speaking but Nadine's eyes were on Phoenix.

"Phoenix," Nadine said, calmly putting her glass down.

Savannah stopped talking. It seemed like everything stopped moving when Nadine said Phoenix's name.

"Yes, Mom?" Phoenix thought about her and Carter's kiss and felt like she was about to be scolded. Nadine had been especially upset after the wedding was called off. In fact, she stopped speaking to Carter's parents for a while until she got over it.

"How do you feel about that?" Nadine asked.

"I'm fine with it. Carter doesn't bother me. It's not like I didn't know he would be in the wedding. Jaxon is like his best friend." Phoenix shrugged off Nadine's concern.

"You sure?" Nadine eyed her skeptically.

Phoenix tried not to squirm. "Yes, Mom." She smiled. "I'm fine."

"If you say so." Nadine picked up her glass and finally sipped her mimosa.

"Are you sure, baby girl?" Christopher asked again.

"Yes, Daddy. I'm sure." Phoenix smiled, hoping it would convince him. She could never tell them about the thoughts she had about Carter. They would think she had lost her mind. They didn't know what she knew.

Christopher and Nadine looked at each other and then back at the girls.

After breakfast everyone met in one of the hotel's conference rooms to greet the rest of their family and friends. Phoenix, Savannah, Maya and Ivy went for a spa visit to get their hair and nails freshly done for the wedding. Phoenix's villa was the designated bridal party's headquarters. After the spa the girls met there with their dresses and accessories as they got dressed and helped Savannah prepare for her big day. Savannah flopped on the couch and gushed about how excited she was to become Mrs. Blackwell.

"If it were okay with Phoenix, I might try to become a Blackwell, too. That Carter is a catch."

"Maya!" Savannah chided.

"Well, Phoenix acts like she couldn't care less about Carter but I've seen the way he looks at her. I caught you tossing a few looks his way, too, Phoenix."

"I wouldn't get into that if I were you," Ivy said. "There's more history there than you know."

"Well, he already shut me down gently." Maya scrunched her face. "He's such a gentleman. I doubt he'll stay single long."

"That's enough, Maya," Savannah said sternly.

"I'm just kidding, Savannah," Maya said.

Phoenix smirked. Maya's comments hadn't fazed her one bit. She of all people knew what it was like to pass on a man like Carter.

"Be careful what you wish for, Maya." Phoenix laughed.

"Yep." Ivy laughed with her. The two slapped a high five. They had made amends years ago, and this trip made Phoenix even more comfortable with Ivy. "You don't know my brother," Ivy added and clucked her teeth. "Come on, ladies. Let's get Savannah ready to marry her sweetheart!"

"'Meet me at the altar…'" Phoenix sang an old-school R & B song. The girls joined in. "'In your white dress!'"

Savannah picked up her garter belt and swung it around in the air as they sang.

"We need to play that!" Maya said and pulled out her phone. After a few swipes the song flowed from her phone.

Maya's playlist continued as they dressed. When they were done, Phoenix, Maya and Ivy looked at Savannah in awe as if they'd collectively created a masterpiece.

"Savannah! You look…" Phoenix covered her mouth. She paused to think of the right word. "Beautiful!" Tears filled her eyes.

"Absolutely stunning," Ivy said, shaking her head.

"Girl. I didn't think it was possible for you to look more gorgeous!" Maya said.

Savannah stood and spun around. She glowed in her elegant strapless gown with its sweetheart neckline. The lace dress outlined her curves and flared at the bottom with a small train in the back. Ringlets of curls cascaded down one side of her head and her makeup was flawless. Tears welled up in Savannah's eyes.

"No! No!" the girls yelled in unison and then scrambled to find tissues.

"You cannot mess up that makeup job!" Maya said.

"Suck it up!" Phoenix said. That made Savannah laugh.

Ivy wiped her tears. "It's time." She smiled at Savannah.

There was a knock on the door and Nadine stuck her head in. She gasped.

"My goodness, honey. You look gorgeous." Nadine held one hand to her heart and blinked away tears. "Oh!" she said after a moment. "I almost forgot. The photographer is here."

"Yes. Tell her to come on in." Savannah waved her hand, welcoming the petite woman.

The photographer took pictures of Savannah and staged a few shots of the girls helping her get ready. It was time for the wedding. Ivy, Maya and Nadine surrounded Savannah as they led her to the stunning beachfront area where the ceremony would take place. Phoenix went ahead to make sure everyone else was ready. Jaxon stood under a white trellis adorned with flowers. Carter stood beside him, looking more handsome than Phoenix could stand. The setting sun and mesmerizing sea were the perfect backdrop.

Phoenix gave the nod and the music started playing. Savannah and Jaxon had chosen the song "You Are" by Charlie Wilson. Nadine made her way down the aisle and was seated. Following her were Jaxon's parents, Benjamin and Sabrina Blackwell. The bridesmaids linked with their groomsmen partners and slowly made their way down the aisle with Phoenix bringing up the rear. The music changed. The attendees stood. Chris linked his arm with Savannah's and patted her hand as he fought back tears. Everything about the moment was breathtaking.

Phoenix watched her sister, whose eyes were on her husband-to-be. Jaxon looked as if he would be the next to shed tears. He held it together. The love in the air and beauty of the moment softened Phoenix's heart. She made the mistake of looking at Carter. His eyes were already trained on her, his gaze—penetrating. It weakened her. Phoenix's breath caught. Carter wouldn't take his eyes off her. She couldn't help but wonder what it would have been like if it was their wedding. Suddenly, her heart felt heavy. She fought to keep it together.

Fortunately, the ceremony was delightfully quick. It was time for the bridal party to walk back down the aisle. Air swirled inside Phoenix's chest as Carter linked her arm in his. His touch triggered a whirlwind of emotions. It also sparked warmth deep on the inside. She longed for his kisses. Phoenix steadied herself and actually counted her steps to focus on walking without falling. She was sure her injured knee would buckle. Jaxon and Savannah eventually stopped to greet their guests. That was when Phoenix realized she'd been holding her breath. She exhaled. A few more steps and she could let go of Carter. She survived. Now she just had to get through the wedding pictures and the reception.

Phoenix had fun at the reception. Their intimate group of family and a few friends got along well despite their past differences. Everyone seemed to be over the situation between her and Carter except the two of them. Phoenix sat at the dais and watched everyone else dance. She wished she could join in but after a full day she was tired and her leg was starting to ache. She'd left her crutch in the room and needed her strength to get back without it.

Phoenix watched Carter and the rest of the bridal party on the dance floor. She was no longer upset with Carter for telling her about why he'd called off the wedding and the pregnancy. Carter was right; she deserved to know. She'd secretly wondered long enough. They were now on their way to true closure. When they got back to the States, she wouldn't have to deal with it anymore. She had to admit it was comforting to know there was a real reason behind what Carter had done. She'd battled with rejection since then and was just coming to understand that it played a role in why she ran from commitment in other relationships. Maybe that would change now, though there were still loose ends.

"How are you doing?" Carter's deep voice soothed her. She looked up at him standing by her side. His effect on her was startling.

"I'm fine. It's been a long day," she said.

"You must miss being able to dance. I know how much you like it. Wanna try?" Carter held his hand out.

Her heart fluttered. Why did she feel like a girl being asked to the prom? This was Carter, for goodness' sake. Still she hesitated, thinking of what her parents would think of her dancing in Carter's arms.

"I don't think I could manage that right now." She wished she could. She wanted to have Carter close to her again.

Carter took the seat next to her. "Are you okay about last night? I didn't mean to be too forward."

"We're good, Carter."

"Okay." He sat with her for a long while.

Neither of them said much. It was a companionable silence. Phoenix felt comfortable the way she used to with him.

Once the reception was over, the girls went back to Phoenix's room to gather their stuff. She couldn't take her mind off Carter, the way he looked, how gently he handled her as they walked, and the way he sat with her while everyone else danced. He'd catered to her every whim so effortlessly. The kiss still lingered on her lips, and desire lingered in her loins. Seeing him today only amplified her renewed longing for him.

She recalled the vision of him standing at the altar beside Jaxon. Carter looked especially handsome against the beautiful backdrop of the sea. Phoenix had discreetly taken him in from his Italian shoes to his gorgeous face. The tan suit, chosen to reflect the sand, fit his taut body ridiculously well. Instead of blazers they wore vests, white shirts and ties the hue of the water. His smooth skin glowed under the brilliant colors of the setting sun. Clean-shaven and good-looking, his eyes sparkled when he looked at Phoenix. His tall stature gave him a godlike presence. She released a sharp breath.

What if she just showed up at his door tonight? What about her mother? She saw the way she looked at Carter at the wedding. Nadine was still upset at how Carter had hurt her. Phoenix could tell. Nadine didn't mess around with her girls. Despite that, Phoenix wanted Carter. She wanted him even more now. Something had been stirred in her. She wanted to feel him even if it was just one more time. Maybe it was the ceremony that was making her this way. There was something romantic about the air in Fiji. She didn't understand why the urge was so strong but she couldn't ignore it.

Phoenix thought about drawing a bath. Just as she was about to head to the bathroom, she heard a knock. She hoped it was Carter. Phoenix opened the door. Carter was leaning against the frame with a bottle of champagne in one hand and two flutes in the other. He looked sexy as hell with his hanging tie and untucked shirt.

"Tired?" he asked, his voice setting her core ablaze.

A sly smile spread across her face. She stepped aside and waved him in. Carter stepped in slowly and paused just beyond the door. Phoenix pushed it closed.

"I just wanted to check on you." Carter's voice was seductive.

"With champagne?" She chuckled. "I'm doing just fine."

The two stood before each other, with minimal space between them. Little fires ignited along the edges of Phoenix's skin. Moments passed and they said nothing yet stared into each other's eyes. It was like Carter was waiting for her to make the first move. He seemed to want her approval.

Phoenix rose on her toes and kissed his lips. She closed her eyes. It felt like falling into clouds. Still holding the champagne and glasses, Carter wrapped his arms around her and held on as if his life depended on his holding her. Phoenix melted into his arms. It was exactly where she wanted to be and felt better than she imagined.

The kiss ended slowly.

Phoenix said, “How about that dance?”

Carter smiled. He put the bottle and glasses down. Pulled up a playlist on his phone and lifted Phoenix into his arms. “I wouldn’t want you to hurt yourself.” Carter danced with her in his arms.

When the song finished, he gently placed Phoenix on her feet. She took him by the hand and led him to the bedroom. Once again Carter lifted her up and delicately laid her on the bed.

“I miss being with you. This trip made me realize that,” he whispered.

Phoenix placed her hands behind his neck and pulled him to her. Carter kissed her lips and made a trail of kisses down her neck and across her bare shoulders. He helped her out of her dress.

“Are you okay with this?” he asked as she lay naked before him.

Phoenix put her finger on his lips, quieting him. “What happens in Fiji, stays in Fiji.” Phoenix unbuttoned his shirt, ran a finger down his taut chest and then reached for his belt. Carter dropped his head back. She released the erection straining against his zipper. That was his answer. Carter kicked off his pants and continued tracing her body with steamy kisses. Phoenix hissed and her back arched at his touch.

Carter went to say something else to her and Phoenix put her finger up to his lips. She shook her head. Carter seemed to understand. She didn’t want this to be complicated. She wanted him and he wanted her. In that moment that was all that mattered.

Carter slid Phoenix farther up on the bed and buried his head between her legs. He nibbled at her pearl until she flailed against the bed and grabbed handfuls of linen. Phoenix covered her mouth with a pillow and screamed into it. Her body shuddered hard and she moaned, writhing on the bed until the orgasm finally released her. Carter kissed her with her own juices. Carefully, she rolled over and took his long, hard erection into her mouth. She wanted to give him the same pleasure he'd just given her.

Carter hissed as she took him in with long strokes, pulling out when he couldn't seem to take any more. Then he hovered over her and entered her warm canal. Phoenix's breath caught. He filled her up and she snatched the sheets so hard they snapped from the corners of the bed. The sense of delight was euphoric. Phoenix met him stroke for stroke until a guttural groan rumbled through him and out of his mouth. He held Phoenix tight and drove himself deep inside her. She clenched him with her walls until his muscles convulsed. Carter squeezed his eyes shut and refused to stop stroking until Phoenix was sated. Suddenly, she began to grunt, one short grunt after the other until they strung together in one long howl. The climax claimed her ability to control her own body, causing rigid spasms to roll through. Carter entered her faster until both howled together and collapsed, spent from giving their all. Carter wrapped his arms around her. She held him back.

"Are you okay?" he asked.

"I'm better than okay. I can't believe we did this," Phoenix said.

"I'm glad we did," Carter said and traced the line of her nose. "The question is where do we go from here?"

Phoenix wasn't ready to answer that. Instead, she massaged him back to attention for round two.

Fourteen

For the past few nights, Carter had gone to bed just before dawn. He'd spent the past three nights with Phoenix. After sunbathing, hanging with their family and more activities, Phoenix would end up in his room or he would end up in hers. They would always return to their own rooms just before dawn to keep from being detected. They didn't have any discussions about what they were doing. Instead, they laughed, joked and reminisced like old times. They had always communicated well, stretching conversations all the way from literature and politics to their favorite childhood cartoons. They reclaimed that comfortable, familiar place that used to exist between them.

They enjoyed being discreetly reconnected. Carter didn't intend to push anything. He couldn't reasonably expect anything to continue between them beyond their trip. He had his hands full with life anyway. Phoenix might move across the country. Phoenix no longer hated him. That was what mattered. He'd carried the guilt of causing her so much pain for far too long. Now he could finally let that go.

Carter wasn't sure how well they were covering up their secret. He supposed his brother Lincoln may have suspected something but now that his wife and kids were in Fiji they kept him occupied.

Carter had gotten into the habit of calling Ethan and Zoe to check in on them each morning. It was nighttime for them. He was always glad to hear that Zoe was in good spirits, despite being on strict bed rest. Carter grabbed his phone so he could talk with Ethan as he took a stroll on the beach to catch the sunrise.

After the call Carter continued walking along the shore.

His nights with Phoenix were amazing. This would be their last one together. Carter knew it would be special. There was no telling when he would see her again once they made it back home. Despite that, he would always cherish this time with her.

Carter chuckled when he remembered her words. *What happens in Fiji, stays in Fiji.* This would always be their little secret. Carter could imagine how they would exchange knowing glances on the few occasions they would end up in the same place.

Carter continued walking for a while and eventually came across a secluded area along the shoreline. Large rocks created a small alcove. He decided to bring Phoenix there later. Her leg was much better now and she could handle the walk. Carter headed back and joined his family for breakfast in the main dining room.

"Uncle Carter!" Lincoln's son and daughter sang as they ran up to him. Carter picked them up and swung them around in the air one by one. He kissed his sister and sister-in-law on the cheek and greeted his father and brother with a handshake. He missed his mother's presence, but Lydia refused to leave Ethan and Zoe behind alone. She wanted to make sure her grandbaby made it here.

After several days of nonstop activities, Carter and his family decided that their last day in Fiji would be a relaxing one. They spent most of the day poolside enjoying drinks, eating, talking and lying in the sun. Carter was anxious for the day to end so he could spend his last night with Phoenix. He had seen her and her family during breakfast and a few other times during the day. It seemed that they had the same idea of sticking around the resort and chilling out. When Savannah, Jaxon and Phoenix did stop by and chat with them during lunch, he and Phoenix hardly exchanged glances or words. They kept their interactions friendly and general.

At nightfall Carter sat at the bar with Ivy, Maya, Angel and Phoenix, listening to music and watching people with really bad voices sing karaoke. One by one each left, leaving him and his sister behind. Ivy finally left, insisting she needed to pack to get ready for their flight the next day.

Carter headed straight for Phoenix's room, told her to grab some towels and led her along the shore by the hand.

"Can you believe us?" Phoenix giggled, leaning against his shoulder. "Savannah would die if she knew what we've been doing."

Carter faced her and brushed his finger across her chin. "And what exactly have we been doing, Ms. Jones?"

"Ha!" Phoenix threw her head back and laughed. "You really need me to spell it out for you, Mr. Blackwell?"

"No!" Carter laughed. "Not at all." He took her hand and continued walking. "Let me know if you get tired of walking."

"I will."

During their silent moments Carter tuned in to the sound of the water rolling up on the shore. He watched the moonlight ripple in the waves on the surface of the water. The blackness of the horizon was eerily fascinating. Finally, they came to the area Carter had found earlier. Just as he'd hoped, there was enough light to keep the area from being too dark.

"Give me the towels," he told Phoenix.

She pulled them from her beach bag. Carter spread them over the sand and the two of them sat side by side, facing the sea.

Phoenix leaned her head against his shoulder. "I enjoyed my time with you."

"I'm just glad you don't hate me anymore."

"What?" She swatted him playfully. "I never hated you—exactly. I mean, I wouldn't call it hate. I was hurt."

"I know. I hated that I hurt you."

Phoenix looked serious and turned away.

"Did I say something?" Carter wondered what it could have been.

"Oh. No. I'm… I was just thinking about something."

"Care to share."

"Uh…no. It's nothing. So…what's the first thing you're going to do when you get back home?"

"A better question is what won't I do. That list is shorter," Carter chuckled. "There's so much on my plate."

"Preach! I'll have a few weeks to decide about moving to the Bay Area or finding another job. I'm just concerned about my dad. I spoke with my mom and sister about it. My mother insisted I not worry and make the best decision for me. She's actually looking forward to coming to visit if I move. All she and Savannah want to do is shop."

"I've got some major paperwork and hard conversations waiting on me back home. It almost makes me want to stay at least another week."

"Yeah." Silence settled between them. Phoenix drew shapes in the sand. "As much as I love it here, I'm ready to go home. I need to sleep in my own bed."

"There's nothing like your own space," Carter said.

"Yeah." Phoenix paused and looked out over the sea. "Everything goes back to normal."

Carter knew she was referring to this thing between them. For a moment he wondered, what if they continued seeing one another? Then he dismissed the idea almost as soon as he thought it.

"This is our last night."

Phoenix turned to him. She gently touched his chin. "Yeah. Who would have thought?"

Carter leaned toward her and covered her mouth with his. Between kisses he told her how much he was going to miss her.

Carter's hands roamed her body as he kissed her, gently squeezing her supple breasts and pulling her closer to him. Phoenix climbed over and straddled him. His erection pushed against his shorts and nestled right between her legs. Her presence summoned him to attention.

Without breaking their kiss, Carter unsnapped her bra, lifted her dress and pushed her panties aside. He fingered her jewel, making it moist and ready to receive him. Phoenix unzipped his shorts, pulled out his erection and stroked it to a level of rigidness that Carter deemed potentially dangerous. He needed to be inside her. He came prepared this time. Carter reached in his pocket, removed the foil pack and then sheathed himself. Phoenix moaned as he entered her.

Carter gently guided her hips up and down. "Are you okay?" he asked, checking in.

"Yes." Her response was breathless. Phoenix licked her lips and groaned.

Up and down, she rode the full length of his shaft, creating a sweet rhythm. He met her stroke for stroke. Carter wanted to look her right in the eyes, but hers were closed, and her head was back. Their tempo quickened. Phoenix opened her eyes. Their gazes locked. The intensity increased. They bounced against each other harder, peering into one another's eyes. Carter loved when she stared at him boldly while they made love. Phoenix held her arms around his neck tight.

She cushioned him with the walls of her canal. Carter almost howled. He wanted her to keep looking directly into his eyes. He wanted this feeling to last forever. A wave of pleasure washed over him, threatening to send him over the edge. It was too soon. Carter needed more of Phoenix. He lifted her off him, flipped her over onto her knees and entered her from behind.

"Yes!" Phoenix chanted over and over again. "Oh, Carter!" she moaned.

"Ph… Ph… Phoenix." Carter was so overtaken by pleasure, he could barely get her name out.

His impending climax threatened to send him to euphoric destinations. He removed himself again, turned Phoenix onto her back and nibbled her pearl between his lips. He licked and teased her until her body shuddered uncontrollably. Once her peak had ravaged her completely she lay in a ball, moaning, trying to catch her breath. Carter wouldn't give her rest. He wanted to please her until she couldn't be pleased anymore. He kissed her swollen lips. Took her nipples into his mouth. Licked hot trails of kisses down her torso and entered her again.

Phoenix grunted, raked her fingers down his chest. She grabbed handfuls of sand, arching her back and bucking. Carter's long, steady strokes turned urgent and wild. Soon, he grunted each time he drove himself inside her. His body tensed. His back arched. His eyes rolled back. His pace quickened. Sweet, melodic screams escaped her mouth. Guttural moans rumbled through his chest and out through his lips. His long, deep strokes turned into quick, erratic thrusts until he pushed himself inside one last time and exploded.

Carter's muscles spasmed, forcing him to buck and hold, buck and hold. He couldn't control his muscles. They tightened with a fierce grip that wouldn't let him go. At the same time Phoenix wrapped her arms around his neck and her legs around his back and pushed against him hard. Then her body bucked and spasmed, too. Her groans rode her release until she finally lay spent, and Carter collapsed on top of her. They lay there together until their heartbeats and breathing returned to a normal pace.

Then they lay on their backs, looking into the clear midnight sky, pointing out the stars to each other.

"You make me not want to leave," Phoenix said.

"We could stay one more day. Then we wouldn't have to sneak around," Carter laughed.

"I wish."

After a while Carter asked. "Ready to head back?"

"You coming to my room or am I coming to yours?" Phoenix asked.

"Whatever your pretty little mind desires."

Carter picked up the towels and shook them out. They walked back hand in hand until they got closer to the villas where their families stayed. Carter thought he saw Lincoln walking up to his room but looked the other way.

They came to Carter's room first and dipped inside to avoid the risk of possibly being seen by anyone else. Inside they showered together, washing the sand from one another's bodies. They made love in the shower and again once they hit the bed. Carter couldn't get enough of Phoenix. The feel of her drove him to the edge of a pleasurable madness. When he reached a peak with her, it took forever for the deeply sensual sensation to loosen its grip. Making love to her was more indulgent than he ever remembered.

"I can't stay all night this time. I need to pack."

"Okay. I'll walk you over."

"No. I can manage. Besides, I don't want anyone to see us."

Carter felt a shift in her demeanor. Maybe it was because this was goodbye.

"I need one more kiss." They kissed and then Carter held her for some time.

He felt himself dozing off when he heard her calling his name softly. "Carter?" It sounded like a question and the tone had completely changed. Carter was alarmed.

"What's up?" He lifted and leaned on his elbow.

"I have to tell you something."

Carter sat completely up in the bed. Phoenix swung her legs over the edge of the mattress. She sat pensively for a moment before standing. She paced a bit and then stopped. Carter noticed how she wrung her hands.

He jumped up and went to hold her. Phoenix held her hand up, stopping him.

"What is it, Phoenix?" Carter wondered if she was having second thoughts about the past few nights. Maybe she wanted to continue seeing him. Carter wondered if that would work. He had to be ready for Phoenix. She wouldn't give him her heart twice for him to break it.

Phoenix continued pacing.

"Phoenix!" She flinched. The volume of his tone startled her. "I'm sorry. What is it that you want to say?"

Phoenix stopped pacing and closed her eyes. She inhaled long and deep. When her eyes popped open, her mouth did, too. "I was pregnant, too."

Carter was confused. "Pregnant. What? When?"

Phoenix huffed. "Carter." She spoke slowly. "I was pregnant. I was going to surprise you and tell you on our wedding night."

"Wh—! No. No. No. No. No!" Both Carter's hands waved in the air. "Phoenix, what are you saying?"

"It's time you knew. I was carrying your baby when you called off the wedding. That's why I was so angry and didn't want to hear what you had to say."

Carter felt like time had slowed down. Confused, he sat on the edge of the bed and held his head in his hands. "What are you saying? Wh…what happened to the baby? Phoenix. Wh…where's the baby?" Carter had trouble getting his words out. He couldn't breathe.

Phoenix took a while to answer. When Carter looked up to see why she hadn't spoken, he saw the tears in Phoenix's eyes.

"I…lost it." Phoenix's hands crossed her stomach as if it ached. She caught her breath. "It happened when I got back from Belize. The doctor said it could have been from the stress. I wasn't eating… I… I couldn't eat. I… I…"

Carter grabbed Phoenix and held her in his arms. She sobbed.

"I lost the baby, Carter," she repeated.

Carter didn't know what to say. His anger only subsided due to his looming sense of guilt.

"Why didn't you tell me?" he asked, still holding her.

Phoenix pulled herself out of his embrace. "You left me! The day before our wedding. You left. I let you go, because I was angry. You hurt me. You hurt me bad. I was an emotional wreck. I wanted you out of my sight. I was going to tell you when I got back from Belize. I needed to go and clear my mind. I didn't expect to lose our baby. By then you were gone. You were with Taylor. People saw you so I didn't say anything. I thought you left me for her. I didn't know she was pregnant until you told me the other day. I never knew we were both carrying your child!"

That stung. "Taylor wasn't carrying my child. You were. You were my fiancée. You were going to be my wife and you didn't tell me."

"And you walked out on me!" Phoenix shouted, stabbing the air with her index finger.

"I would have never left if I knew you were carrying my child. I could have worked something else out. Ugh! I was just trying to do the right thing." Carter stood and paced circles at the end of the bed.

The weight of all Carter had lost crushed him, making it difficult to breathe. The words scrambled in his mind and wouldn't make sense coming through his lips.

Phoenix dried her tears. Picked up her beach bag to leave. He followed her to the door not sure of what to say. She paused once she opened the door. "You had to know." The pain in her voice was evident. She softly closed the door behind her.

What was Carter to do with this information? They had messed up and it was a cost they could never recover. Carter went back to the bedroom, lay back on the bed and stared at the ceiling.

Fifteen

Phoenix was happy to be home, but after a bad case of jet lag and the string of sleepless nights she had spent in Carter's arms before she left, she wished she could sleep twenty-four more hours but she had to go back to work. She lifted her hand and smiled at the doorman in her luxury condo in downtown Brooklyn. The older gentleman returned her customary greeting with a nod.

Phoenix hit the sidewalk and maneuvered through the throngs of people heading to work during the morning rush hour. She loved the vibe of her new neighborhood. It was alive and breathing with its own pulse. Within a few short blocks, she had access to coffeehouses, galleries, boutiques, fitness studios, poetry lounges and restaurants boasting cuisine representing every culture across the globe. Moving to Brooklyn from Long Island had shortened her commute to work significantly. Her office was a short train ride to a renovated brownstone on the other side of downtown. She even loved the noise of the city, chatter, cars, dogs barking, horns, music flowing from car windows or through the doors of coffee shops. It all synced together to create its own rhythm—a musical backdrop. It was so different from the neighborhood she grew up in on Long Island's Gold Coast, with large homes on sprawling grounds and eerily quiet, tree-lined streets.

Brent offered to pick her up at the airport when she returned but she refused, preferring a drama-free ride with the car service she'd ordered. He also reached out to her as she was stepping into work. She responded with a text, can't right now. She thought she made it clear to him that she wanted to break up before she left for Fiji. Their situation had passed its expiration date way before she ended it that night. Yet, he called and texted her several times about her not reaching out to him while she was away.

Brent texted again to say that he needed to talk to her, and asked if he could stop by after work. Phoenix wished she were back in Fiji with Carter. However, she was sure Carter wasn't too happy with her, either. She hadn't spoken to him since she left his room several nights ago after telling him about the baby. Whenever she thought back to that moment and seeing the look on Carter's face, her stomach tightened. Phoenix thought she had buried those memories and the pain that came with them. Carter reopened those wounds when he confessed his true reason for calling off the wedding. It was hard to relive that moment, but harder to reveal to Carter the secret she held for all those years. She couldn't decide whose revelation was worse, and hated to think that had she just listened to him that night or had told him about the baby, things may have been very different. She didn't know whether to direct her anger at him or herself. She had absolutely no idea what to do with the guilt she'd been feeling.

Not even her parents knew about her pregnancy. Phoenix couldn't tell them before telling Carter but then she never got to tell Carter. Savannah knew about the miscarriage. She was the one Phoenix called when she woke up to gut-wrenching cramps and blood-covered sheets. She'd sworn Savannah to secrecy back then.

Phoenix looked at the time on her cell phone. She managed to reach her office without running into anyone. She had arrived early but expected Indra and Dean to be around. Getting settled, she put on some music, turned it down low and started up her laptop. Coming back to work after being away for two weeks was wonderful, but the four hundred emails in her inbox made her wish she has checked in a few times while she was out.

A knock on her office door pulled her attention away from the emails. Indra stuck her head in and then stepped all the way into the room. "Hey! How was the trip?"

"It was—" Phoenix thought about all that had transpired, from the announcement that Carter was going to be the best man to her accident, reconnecting with Carter and things she'd learned "—part amazing, part interesting."

"You look tanned and refreshed."

"Thanks. I still haven't recovered from jet lag. If I start sleepwalking don't trip me."

"Ha!" Indra laughed. "I wanted to drop in and say hello. Dean and I have to fly out to the Bay Area for meetings. I'll be back midweek. I know you're just getting back but do you think you'll have an answer for me?" Indra tilted her head. "We'd really love for you to join us."

Phoenix felt like a belt was tightening around her chest. "I'm working on it."

"Good. Call me if you need me. We'll do a video call with the team with updates after all of our meetings. See you when we get back."

"Safe travels," Phoenix said and smiled. As soon as Indra left and shut the door, the smile fell off Phoenix's face.

Phoenix had two weeks left to make one of the biggest decisions of her life. She'd visited California a dozen times and loved it but had no interest in living there. If she didn't go, she needed to find a new job. The idea of injecting herself into the job market search was another headache she didn't look forward to.

Just then, her phone rang. It was her mother, letting her know that their father's surgery date was pushed up. She remembered how carefully he walked in Fiji. Her mother wanted everyone to make sure they were available the evening of the surgery to see their father. Phoenix made the adjustment on her calendar and her phone rang again. Phoenix cocked her head to the side and shook it.

"Hello, Brent." If she didn't answer he would keep calling.

"You didn't answer my text. I really need to talk to you tonight. Can I come by?"

She flicked her gaze upward. "Meet me at Mona's at seven."

"Thanks. See you there..." Brent paused. "I miss you."

"I have to go, Brent. See you later." Phoenix ended the call.

Brent's words didn't make her miss him. They made her think of Carter. She missed his presence. She wondered how he was dealing with the news about the baby since they'd never spoken after that. She'd been wondering since she boarded her flight back home. Carter was hurt and so was she. Phoenix wondered if the weight of their decisions to hold on to this information for so long weighed as heavily on him. She was tired of considering all the possible scenarios in her head. If they had talked, perhaps they would have been married now.

Phoenix stood and rounded her desk. She picked up her phone and dialed Savannah's number. She was the only person on whom Phoenix could have possibly unloaded all of the thoughts she'd been carrying.

"Hey, Fifi. What's up? Aren't you at work?"

Phoenix was having second thoughts about bringing up the conversation. "Yeah. Brent keeps calling me. He wants to meet." She couldn't bring herself to start the conversation about Carter. She needed more time to navigate through her feelings. Phoenix wasn't even sure where to start.

"I bet he wants you back. What are you going to do?"

"Ugh!" Phoenix rubbed her brow. "I told him I'd meet him at Mona's tonight. I don't want him coming to the house."

"Noted. If I hear of a disturbance at Mona's I'll know it's you. Hopefully, you won't have to hit him with some of the Brazilian jujitsu you've been learning." Savannah cackled loudly.

That brought a smile to Phoenix's face. "Hopefully not." There was another knock at Phoenix's door. She held the phone away from her face. "Just a moment," she said and then turned her attention back to her sister. "I gotta go. I'll let you know what happened." Phoenix walked over and opened the door. Both Dean and Indra were standing on the other side. They looked as if they were up to something. "Hey," Phoenix said. "How can I help you?"

Dean stepped in first and then Indra. They were silent until they closed the door behind them.

"We know you're still thinking about your decision, but we wanted to share something with you," Dean said and glanced at Indra.

Indra jumped in. "We really want you to stay with the team. So..."

"If you decide to join us, we'd like you to run our research and development department. It will require more responsibility and of course a salary increase," Dean said.

"We hope this will help with your decision." Indra handed Phoenix a folder. "Please consider this offer while we're away."

Taken aback, it took a moment for Phoenix to take the folder from Indra. "Thanks. I'll definitely look through this carefully."

"That's all we ask," Indra said. She took Phoenix's hand in hers. "Thanks."

"You're welcome," Phoenix said. She groaned when they left. Indra and Dean were doing everything they could to convince her to go. Maybe she should give it a chance for a few months and see how it worked out. But would she be happy in California?

Phoenix spent most of her day catching up on emails. She left in time to go home to change into more casual clothing before meeting Brent at Mona's. She chose the coffeehouse instead of a restaurant because she wanted this meeting with Brent to be as brief as possible.

As she expected, he arrived before she had. Brent waved her over to the small table by the window. It was the place she loved to sit when they went there together.

"Hey." Brent stood. He leaned forward to kiss Phoenix on the cheek.

"Hey." Phoenix returned his greeting.

Brent stood for another awkward moment with his hands stuffed in his pockets.

Phoenix sat down and Brent followed suit.

"How was your trip?"

"It was good. The wedding was nice." Carter flashed across Phoenix's mind again. He would forever be the dominant memory for her when it came to Fiji.

"Great!"

A barista came over and placed two mugs in front of them.

"I ordered you a chai latte," Brent said.

"Thanks!" Phoenix wrapped her hands around the mug. She always loved feeling the warmth of a hot drink. She took a sip. "What did you want to talk about, Brent?"

"I know I upset you before you left and you said you wanted to cut things off. I apologize for getting a little… crazy over things at times. I figured if we both had a little time to think things over, then maybe we could start fresh and give it one more try."

"Brent."

"Let me finish. I don't know why I get so crazy when I think of another man even having a conversation with you. It's just that you're a beautiful woman and I know what it's like to have someone I love taken from me."

Phoenix blinked rapidly. "Brent?"

"Yes. I said *love*. I love you, Phoenix, and I don't want to lose you. I want to give us another try."

Phoenix squeezed her eyes shut and rubbed her forehead. In her mind she saw a sea of red flags. Brent was a nice guy and very good-looking but his negative traits outweighed his good ones—the jealousy, the quick temper, comparing her to his previous relationships. He'd managed to hide these traits when they first started dating, but then the real Brent showed up. Phoenix knew none of that would change. If she said yes, she'd go back to feeling suffocated. Carter popped into her mind. She remembered how easily they got along, how they could talk for hours, how he knew her so well and how he anticipated her needs. Carter wasn't jealous. He exuded confidence. Then she wondered why she compared Brent to Carter. He had nothing to do with their relationship.

"You don't have to answer me now. I didn't want to do this by text."

"There's no need to prolong this. I'm sorry, but this is over, Brent."

He slammed his hand against the small bistro table, causing the cups to wobble. Phoenix flinched and then narrowed her eyes at him. Coffee and chai tea latte spilled over the rims. Patrons sharply turned their way. "Dammit, Phoenix. You didn't even think about it."

Brent seemed completely oblivious to the scene he caused. Phoenix's jaw clenched.

Phoenix tilted her head back and gazed upward. Then she looked at Brent for a moment. She thought about explaining how his actions were part of her reason for leaving but then realized that explaining wouldn't change the way she felt. She wanted a man that treated her like Carter had in Fiji.

"Brent. There's nothing more for me to think about

here." Phoenix stood. "Thank you for the chai. Goodbye." She calmly walked out. With all that she had on her plate, there was no room for Brent's antics. She didn't bother telling him she might not be around in another month anyway.

Phoenix walked back to her apartment. Her encounter with Brent only made her miss Carter's presence more. She wished he could sneak to her apartment and spend the night with her like he had in Fiji. But she wasn't sure that Carter would want to talk to her anyway.

Their baby would have been almost five years old. If only she had dealt with Carter differently when he came to her that night…

Sixteen

Carter thought he saw Phoenix walk into the coffeehouse next to the bodega where he got his bacon, egg and cheese breakfast sandwich from each morning. He picked up his pace, jogging to the entrance, only to realize it wasn't her. That was the third time in the week since he'd been back from Fiji that he thought he saw Phoenix in his Brooklyn neighborhood. From what he knew, Phoenix lived on Long Island. Carter was convinced that his mind was playing games with him.

He attributed these "sightings" to the trauma of knowing that he actually had a child by the woman he loved but that baby didn't make it. He walked out on Phoenix to be with a woman who lied to him about carrying his baby. It was ironic and unfair. He was angry that Phoenix withheld that information from him. The pain of losing that child that he hadn't known about felt surreal. His anger subsided when the guilt took over. Had he not canceled their wedding, maybe she wouldn't have suffered from so much stress and lost their baby. What could he do now besides torment himself with possibilities that he couldn't do anything about?

Carter had more immediate concerns. One of his investors was threatening to pull out of the deal for his new business venture with his partner and friend, Harris Cooper. He needed to figure out a way to save the deal. The money was one thing, but this investor came with connections that were critical to get their technology business off the ground. His father had just gotten on him about not being focused with work and he still hadn't told

Bill about leaving. If they were able to convince this investor to stay, they would be able to get things rolling in weeks. Harris and he already had office space picked out in downtown Brooklyn.

Carter was back to the horrible sleeping patterns that he'd had before vacation. He hadn't gotten the rest he anticipated on vacation, either, especially once he and Phoenix started hooking up. Now that he was home, the workload from Blackwell Wealth Management, along with his business ventures, left him with little time to sleep.

The time with Phoenix brought so many feelings to the surface. He wished she were coming to his room tonight to soothe all the stress of work. Yet, they agreed that their time together would be over after Fiji. Too many issues were stirred with both of their admissions and after that last night, he had no idea where they stood. Despite it all, he missed her. He was angry with her. He cared about her. He was sorry for what he'd done all over again.

Carter looked at his watch. If the cook didn't hurry with his sandwich, he would end up running late. They had meetings at Blackwell Headquarters today. All the regional managers would be there except Ethan. He was still spending every day by Zoe's side at the hospital, hoping she'd be released soon and praying they wouldn't lose their baby.

Carter's phone rang. It was Harris. "What's up?"

"Roberts is out!"

"What?" Carter said loud enough for the other people in the store to look at him. He lowered his voice. "Dammit! What went wrong? Let me call him."

"I'm not sure if it will do any good," Harris said.

"I need to at least try."

"Call me back if you get him."

Carter ended the call and dialed Jacob Roberts. Roberts didn't answer. "Ugh!" Carter tried again. This time he left a message, asking for Jacob to call him back. Carter finally got his food, made his way out of the crammed bodega and headed for his train.

Carter made it to the Blackwell offices just in time. Like his father, Bill, he was a stickler for time, considering tardiness a form of disrespect. This morning's meeting was a quarterly one where they reviewed the state of the business and strategized on how they could remain on track to meet and exceed their goals in the next quarter. It required brainpower that Carter wasn't sure he could manage. He was tired, had too much on his mind and was now facing a major issue with regards to this new business. If they didn't find another investor willing to offer as much as Roberts with some of the same connections there was a chance that his business wasn't going anywhere.

His brain hurt from trying to think of how they could fill the gaping hole Roberts's departure would leave in their financial plan. This tech company wasn't a cheap start-up. They needed to invest in the best technology experts to attract the kind of business that would get them the right returns. It came at a high cost. The market research confirmed that there was a gap they could fill effectively and scale up quickly.

Carter headed into his office at the headquarters, closed the door behind him and called Harris back.

"I called a few times. He's not answering. It's early so I'll try again when we get a break," Carter told Harris.

"In the meantime, let's reach out to our other prospects," Harris said.

Carter decided to try Roberts one more time before heading to the conference room.

"Roberts!" Carter was surprised he answered.

"Blackwell?"

"We need to talk," Carter said.

"I'm not sure it will matter, Carter."

"I'm about to run into a meeting now, but I have an idea. It's a bit of a renegotiation."

Carter could hear Roberts sigh. "I'll hear you out, Carter. Noon. How's that?"

Carter pumped his fist. "Perfect. Will this number work?"

"Yep. I'll only have about an hour. I'm flying out to Seattle this afternoon so after that you won't be able to get me."

"I think once you hear what I have to say you'll be ready to jump back on board."

"We will see."

"Talk to you later," Carter said and ended the call. He wasn't willing to let Roberts go so easily. Carter was used to getting what he wanted most of the time.

Getting the meeting gave him one less thing to worry about. Now he could focus on what was ahead of him at Blackwell.

Carter gathered his laptop and a few files but before he could make it to the door, his father, Bill, rushed into his office. "Carter, it's Zoe!"

Carter's stomach tightened like a rock. "What happened, Pop?" His father's fair skin looked pale. Small beads of sweat lined his forehead. This didn't look good.

"Ethan called. He was distraught. I could hardly understand what he was saying. We need to get to the hospital now. Your mom, Lincoln and Ivy will meet us there. I already arranged for a car."

Carter became aware of every beat of his own heart. It thumped with fear. He said a discreet prayer as he stuffed his laptop into a bag. He could only imagine what Ethan and Zoe were going through right now. He couldn't bear his brother and wife losing their baby.

Seventeen

Phoenix opened the folder from her bosses again and spread the contents across her desk. The offer was incredible. She loved her work. She was used to money. It was the perks that were most convincing. They offered Phoenix a huge promotion, a company vehicle, compensation for relocation services, stock options in Jabber and more. They even gave her extra time to make her decision, which would allow her to join them in California several weeks later. That took some of the pressure off. Until this point, none of the other jobs she'd applied for had called her back. She didn't want to move, but the more they sweetened the deal, the more she considered it. Maybe she could try it out for a few months and see if she'd like it. Her main concern was her father's health.

Phoenix was glad that her dad's surgery was pushed up but then they found that he had formed blood clots, which brought on a new set of concerns. Her mother tried to remain calm but Phoenix could tell from the bags around her eyes that she hadn't had any sleep. Today she was going to the hospital after work to stay with him for the evening so her mom could go home and rest.

Her parents were getting older. Savannah had a new husband. Phoenix expected to be the one to fill in for her mother when needed. She couldn't do that from California. She'd just purchased her brownstone in Brooklyn months ago and absolutely loved her new neighborhood. Silicon Valley was nothing like Brooklyn. As much as she loved traveling, she never had a desire to live outside New York. Maybe it was time she did something different, unexpected. Had Savannah been given this offer she probably would have packed up her house already. She was spontaneous and sometimes flighty. Phoenix was practical and calculated.

Phoenix left work early so she could avoid traffic on her drive from Brooklyn to Long Island. Her dad was resting when she arrived. She didn't want to wake him so she tuned in to an audiobook until he woke up.

"Sweetie," Chris's voice was groggy.

"Hey, Daddy."

Phoenix leaned over and gave him a kiss on his forehead. She pulled her chair closer and sat next to his bed. "How are you feeling?"

"I've had better days," Chris said.

"Feel like talking? You can mostly listen while I talk."

"Sure. What's on your mind?" Chris cleared his throat.

Phoenix updated him about work and explained her trepidation about moving.

"You don't worry about me and your mother. We will be fine. What else do you think is holding you back?"

"I love home. I love my new place. I'll have a few coworkers but I don't know anyone else there. West Coast living is so different."

"You're comfortable," Chris said matter-of-factly.

"Yeah. I am," Phoenix said proudly.

"And you know comfort can be the enemy of progress?"

"Oh! Yeah." She sat back in her chair.

"You just don't want to become stagnant. Then you stop growing altogether."

"I know, Dad. But does progress have to mean moving across the entire country?"

"Not at all. The options are endless. Heck! Start your own business."

"Hmm." Phoenix thought for a moment. She'd considered starting her own business in the past but not seriously. "Thanks, Dad." Phoenix's phone vibrated. Savannah's name lit up the screen.

"Hey. I'm here with Dad."

"Hey, Daddy," Savannah yelled into the phone.

There was no need to transfer the message. Though the phone wasn't on speaker, Chris heard Savannah, chuckled and said hello back.

"Have you spoken to Carter?" Savannah asked.

"Me? No. Why?"

"Jaxon just told me that Zoe went in for an emergency C-section. Ethan is completely distraught. They have to take the baby."

"Oh no! When did this happen? Why?"

"Earlier today. I'm not sure what caused it. They didn't say. I'm hoping everything turns out okay." Savannah's sigh was clear through the phone. "Jax is trying to find out more. I just wanted to let you know. Jax and I are going to go by the hospital later."

"Okay. Keep me posted."

"I will. Talk to you later. Tell Daddy I said bye," Savannah said and ended the call.

Phoenix stayed with her father a while longer before excusing herself to call Carter. She checked the family lounge. No one was there so she stepped in. Phoenix held her phone in her hand, staring at Carter's name for a while before she dialed his number. This was the first time she would hear his voice since their last night together in Fiji.

"Hello," Carter answered. His voice was listless.

"Hey. Carter. Um, I heard about Zoe. Is she okay?"

Carter cleared his throat. "We hope so. She's in surgery now. I'm here with Ethan. He's worried."

Phoenix's hand slowly went to her heart. "I pray everything will be okay."

"Me, too." Carter sounded tired.

"You sound exhausted," Phoenix said.

"Yeah."

Neither spoke for a few moments.

"I'm so sorry about all of this. Please tell them I'm thinking of them." Phoenix was generally concerned. "Would you mind keeping me posted?"

"I will." Carter paused. "Thanks."

There was a long pause. "Carter?"

"Yes?"

"Let me know if there's anything I can do for you."

"There is," Carter said.

"Oh. Okay. What is it?" Phoenix asked.

"Let me come see you tonight."

Eighteen

Carter sat in the car outside the address that Phoenix had given him on the phone. He contemplated whether or not he should go in. It was past ten at night. He had asked her if he could come by without thinking about it. She'd said yes. That surprised Carter. Messy issues resided between them but despite that, he needed her. Carter needed to feel the way he felt during those nights they'd spent together in Fiji. He knew then that it was temporary. Tonight would be temporary, too.

Carter's day couldn't have gone worse. After his father told him about Ethan and Zoe, he completely forgot to call Roberts at noon. He hoped he hadn't completely botched his chances of getting him back on board as an investor. Never had Carter had so much weighing on his mind at once. Going home to an empty house was the last thing he wanted to do.

Carter left the hospital after Zoe was out of surgery and back in her room. She still had a long road to recovery and so did the baby. Born prematurely, their little girl was sent to the neonatal intensive care unit where she was likely to spend the next few months. When Carter had left the hospital, Ethan had fallen asleep in a chair next to Zoe's bed. They were still holding hands. Carter couldn't remember the last time he'd seen his brother cry. He could never say he understood what Ethan was going through, but the situation made him think of his own past with kids. It hurt him to walk away from the son that Taylor had told him was his. He had already bonded with the little boy. And it hurt even more when he found out about Phoenix's losing the baby and having to deal with that loss on her own.

Carter looked at his watch. It was almost half past ten. If he was going in to see Phoenix, he needed to get out of the car now. After a few more moments he pushed the car door open and headed to the lobby of her building. The slate gray and glass building looked like a work of contemporary art nestled between older structures. He told the doorman where he was headed and he guided him to her apartment.

Carter lifted his hand to knock and paused. After a deep breath he tapped lightly. Moments later Phoenix opened the door. One look in her eyes and he felt some of his burdens lighten. She was beautiful even with her hair piled on top of her head in a messy bun. He'd never seen a pair of lounge pants and a tank top look sexier. The fluffy slippers made him smile. She stepped aside and welcomed him in.

"Hi," she said.

"Hi," he said back. Carter looked around. The decor was simple, elegant, feminine and cozy. Pale gray walls were adorned with interesting colorful art. The artwork set the stage for the colorful accents that popped against the muted backdrop. A basket sat in the corner with plush throws rolled inside. One large knitted throw lay across the back of the couch.

Carter stood in the living room, several feet from the door. He still wasn't sure he'd made the right move by coming over. His mouth operated without his brain.

"Are you okay, Carter?"

He shook his head. Phoenix went to him. At first, she looked directly into Carter's eyes. She embraced him. Carter held her back. He didn't want to let go. He belonged in her arms. She looked at him once again. Time slowed. Carter gazed back at her. There was that pull again. He needed to feel her lips. Leaning forward, his lips connected with hers. Heat surged through him as well as something more primal. He needed Phoenix even if it was just for the night. Not just her body. He needed the comfort she gave him.

Carter released his passion in their kiss. He held her by the waist. Phoenix's arms were around his neck. Carter pressed his body against hers. Phoenix showed no signs of resistance. She pressed back against him. Another heat surge.

"I need you," he whispered without pulling his mouth away from hers.

Phoenix nodded, giving Carter the green light.

Carter lifted Phoenix. She wrapped her legs around his waist. Carter felt his way through her apartment and into her bedroom. He found it with ease as if he'd been there before. Gently, he laid her across the well-made bed. They tore at one another's clothes until they were naked. Carter admired her body, running a finger from the crook of her neck to her navel. He planted teasing pecks on her mouth and down her torso. They were quick and moist.

Phoenix's skin was on fire. That drove Carter's desire higher. Phoenix pulled protection from her side drawer and held it up. Carter lifted his chin. Phoenix unwrapped it and slid it onto his erection. She massaged it before lying back and letting him enter her wet canal. Carter went as far as she could take him, driving himself inside her with long, deep strokes. The intense pleasure threatened to send him over an immediate edge.

Phoenix's nails dug deep into his back. The pain brought Carter pleasure. His strokes were slow and deliberate. He watched Phoenix's face. Her eyes were closed and her mouth agape. Her expression, euphoric. Carter wanted nothing more than to please her. When she bit her bottom lip, an involuntary spasm started in his groin and spread through his lower body. Making love to her was indulgent. He wanted to stay inside her but couldn't take much more.

Carter pulled out and kissed her body from head to toe

before returning, zoning in on her pearl. He buried his face between her legs and lapped at Phoenix until her legs trembled. Covering her mouth with a pillow, she released her bliss in a series of groans until her body stopped convulsing.

Just as she came down, Carter entered her again, driving her back to euphoria. This time he held her in his arms as he drove himself deep within her walls. Phoenix held him back, squeezing him tighter as she neared another climax. This time they rode the pleasure wave together, bucking and convulsing as their twin orgasms rolled through them like violent waves. Neither released their hold until their bodies stopped quaking and their breathing returned to normal.

Carter lay facing Phoenix, staring into her eyes. For a long time he basked in their afterglow, still feeling remnants of pleasure in smaller, less frequent waves.

Phoenix touched his face. "Are you okay?"

Her question jolted him. He came to Phoenix for comfort but didn't plan for them to end up in bed. Carter embraced the relief that being in her presence offered.

"I don't want you to think I just came for this."

Phoenix rolled her eyes upward. "I know. We can say that it just happened."

Carter kissed her lips again. "Thank you for letting it happen." He chuckled.

"I guess we need to talk," Phoenix said. She got up and went to the bathroom.

Carter stayed on the bed, folding his hands behind his head. He thought about his day. He was glad he came. He thought about the talk they needed to have and felt some trepidation.

Phoenix returned to the room with a robe on and two glasses of wine. She placed the one for him on the dresser while Carter took his turn to freshen up.

When Carter came out of the bathroom, Phoenix was on her balcony. Carter slipped into his slacks and put on his shirt, leaving it unbuttoned, and then joined her outside with his glass.

At first, they just sat, taking in the starry night. A slight breeze rolled through. Carter sat back and exhaled.

"Thanks again for letting me come by."

"How's Zoe and Ethan?" Phoenix asked.

"She's resting. The baby is in the NICU. Only two pounds. She'll have to stay in the hospital for a while."

"Wow! Thank God she made it. I can't imagine..." Phoenix stopped speaking abruptly.

Carter knew why she stopped. Her situation wasn't the same, but he was sure it was just as stressful.

"About that," Carter said.

Phoenix swung her legs over the lounge chair she sat in and faced him. "I should have told you," she said. He remained quiet. "I realize that now. Back then, I was just angry, and distraught and scared."

Carter sat up and faced Phoenix. "You shouldn't have gone through that by yourself. That wasn't fair to you or me. My guilt won't let me be angry with you."

"Guilt?"

"I caused that stress that led you to your miscarriage. You lost our baby because of me." A lump lodged in Carter's throat. He swallowed hard and blinked harder. "Who else knows?"

"Just Savannah." Phoenix lay back again and stared at the sky.

"I left for a baby that wasn't mine and lost the one that was mine."

"I let you go without knowing you had a baby on the way."

Carter lay back now, too. Both kept their gazes toward the sky. Several beats passed before Carter sighed. "We screwed up, Phoenix."

"We did."

Nineteen

"You snuck out early," Phoenix said when she answered her cell phone. The morning sun poured through the window as she lay in the bed.

"I have early meetings and didn't want to wake you," Carter said.

"I'm exhausted." She yawned.

"I know. That's why I'm calling—to make sure you got up in time."

"Thanks," Phoenix said. "But I'm a big girl. I can handle a few late nights." Her smile radiated from deep inside.

"Okay, superwoman. See you later?"

"Why not?" Phoenix ended the call. She loved teasing Carter.

They were at it again. This was the third morning Carter woke up at Phoenix's house. Again, it was their secret.

Phoenix couldn't believe she was actually having a rendezvous with her ex-fiancé. It would have to remain her salacious secret. Her mother would burst a blood vessel if she knew that she had been sleeping around with Carter. But the two of them fit together seamlessly. Phoenix had never felt so secure and complete with another man. Too bad it was temporary.

Happy thoughts followed Phoenix to the shower and work. She arrived early to take a phone interview. She wanted to get it over with before anyone else came into the office. It had been a while since she'd been on the job market. Phoenix was nervous about the interview but felt like she'd aced it. If they called her back, the next meeting would be in person.

Phoenix was glad that she was finally getting callbacks.

The number of applications she'd submitted was too numerous to keep up with. She usually kept spreadsheets for things like this. Instead, she kept track of the job boards she used. Most were geared specifically to the technology industry. Phoenix also created a wish list of local tech companies to which she applied. A remote position would have been great also.

Indra knocked and stepped into her office.

"Morning!" she said.

"Morning!" Phoenix returned her greeting.

Indra sat on the edge of her desk. "We're making arrangements to fly the team out together the week after next. I was hoping we would know whether or not you were joining us."

Phoenix sat back. "I'll have an answer for you soon."

"Good. How's your dad?"

"Still struggling. He's still in the hospital. Another clot formed."

"Oh no! Sorry to hear that." Indra shook her head. "I know you have a lot going on. I don't mean to pressure you, but we need to know soon. We're hoping the extra time we gave to you to make the decision helps. If you can't join us when the team goes together, we're happy to fly you out later. But we can't wait too long."

"I understand. Just a little more time."

Indra cocked her head sideways. "I understand."

When Indra left, she thought about Carter. She hadn't mentioned anything about leaving since they'd been back from Fiji. A ball of angst formed in her stomach. She and Carter hadn't defined what they were doing. However, every moment they spent together slowly mended the damage they'd done in their past. She enjoyed his company. Being with him came with ease. She never intended to desire his company so much, among other things. Leaving would mean that this thing they had between them would have to be over. Phoenix wasn't sure she wanted that.

They had plans for dinner later. She decided to bring it up then. Thinking of him made her want to end her workday early. She giggled, thinking about the things they'd done to each other the night before. He'd fed her strawberries, kissing her between bites. The more they were together the more adventurous they became in bed and the more fun they had. Anticipating their date put a smile on her face that lasted the rest of the day.

Phoenix headed home to change before meeting up with Carter. The restaurant they chose was downtown, not far from either of their houses.

Phoenix's phone rang as she was getting into the shower. The display read Brent's name. She sent the call to voice mail. Brent had called two more times by the time she left her house. Instead of moving her car and worrying about finding parking on busy downtown streets, Phoenix took an Uber. Brent called again while she was in the car. She hesitated but answered.

"Yes, Brent?"

"Phoenix!" He sounded as if he'd been running.

"Everything okay?"

"Yes. I've been thinking. I want to apologize for my behavior. Let me come by so we can talk."

Phoenix drew in a sharp breath and released it in a rush. "That's not a good idea, Brent." She only answered the phone because he called back-to-back. There could have been an emergency.

"Phoenix…"

"I'm sorry, Brent. I truly wish you the best. I have to go. Good night." Phoenix ended the call and rubbed the back of her neck. How had she missed so many red flags with him? He was nothing like Carter. Brent called back but she refused to answer.

The car pulled up in front of the swanky restaurant. Phoenix exited and sauntered inside. She couldn't wait to see Carter. He greeted her with a kiss once she stepped in. They checked in and Carter placed his hand on the small of her back as the host led them to their reserved table. Carter pulled out her seat. Phoenix loved a man who treated a woman like a lady. That was another problem with Brent. He missed the mark on small things.

"You look amazing."

Phoenix had put special effort into her preparation. The black lace cocktail dress hugged her in all the right places. She'd even added false lashes, which made her feel sexy when she batted her eyes. Savannah would be proud. All this for Carter. Phoenix giggled.

"Thanks! You look quite handsome yourself." She wanted to say *delicious* but figured she'd save that for later. "So is this a date, Mr. Blackwell?"

"Phoenix."

She thought she heard her name. But it wasn't Carter who had called it.

"Phoenix!"

This time she knew she heard her name. Both Carter and she looked around. Brent was heading in her direction fast. Phoenix scrunched her face in frustration, then closed her eyes a brief moment to collect herself.

"Who is this, Phoenix? Is he why you won't talk to me?"

"Brent!" She spat his name. Carter stood. "Carter, no!" Phoenix was on her feet now. Every neck in the restaurant snapped in their direction. The host stepped toward their table. "How did you know I was here?"

Brent didn't answer. "Who are you?" Brent directed his question to Carter.

Carter's chest lifted. He took a step toward Brent. Phoenix maneuvered between the two men. Carter held her by the waist. Brent's eyes followed Carter's hand.

Brent turned to Phoenix. "Is this why you won't talk to me?"

"Brent. I told you it was over. You need to accept that."

"You heard the lady," Carter said calmly. "I'd advise you to leave now."

Brent shook his head. He took a step toward Phoenix. Carter gently moved her aside and stepped to Brent. "It's time for you to go." Carter was firm.

Brent didn't move. He looked from Carter to Phoenix. She hoped they wouldn't have to cause more of a scene than they already had.

"It's over, Brent. It's been over. You need to leave. Now!" Her nostrils flared. Heat flushed through her body.

Brent stood firm for another moment. All three held their stances; none of them backed down. The host was now at their table. Brent huffed. Shook his head at Phoenix and walked away. She hoped she was seeing the last of him.

Once Brent was gone, Phoenix sat with her head in her trembling hands. She was furious.

"Want to get out of here?" Carter asked softly.

"Yes."

Carter placed money on the table. When Phoenix stood, he took her by the hand and led her outside. In silence they walked to Carter's car, got in and drove for a while. Phoenix didn't know where they were going and didn't bother asking. Carter pulled up by Canarsie Pier. He got out, rounded the car, opened Phoenix's door and held out his hand. She placed her hand in his. Carter led her to the railing where they could overlook the water.

"I come here when I need a moment of peace."

Phoenix smiled. "Thank you."

"No need." They remained silent for a while longer. Phoenix started to feel better.

"Where'd you find that guy?" Carter said.

Surprised, Phoenix looked at him and found him laughing. She laughed, too.

Carter put his arms around her. She leaned onto his shoulder. Together they watched the moonlight ripple in the waves. There she was again. Safe in Carter's arms.

Before long they were swapping stories about their day. Carter updated her on Ethan, Zoe and the baby, and Phoenix updated him on her father's condition.

"So how long is your list of crazy exes?"

"Ha!" Phoenix swatted him playfully.

"I just need to know what I'm in for now that we're dating."

"Who said we're dating?" She narrowed her eyes at him and chuckled. Carter shrugged. They laughed but the comment tugged at Phoenix's heart. She couldn't seriously date Carter. Besides the fact that she may be leaving in a few weeks, her family would never accept him.

"Well, whatever it is that we're doing, I like it," Carter said. He kissed her. "I even brought strawberries."

"Your house or mine," Phoenix teased, knowing he was being naughty.

"Let's go." He took her hand, kissed it and walked her back to the car.

The attention he gave her made Phoenix giddy. They reached Carter's brownstone in record time. The door was barely closed before they started kissing. Peeling each other's clothes off, they left a trail from the entrance to the kitchen. Naked, they stood before his subzero refrigerator and pulled out a carton of strawberries. Carter washed the fruit and then laid Phoenix on her back across the large island. She flinched from the coolness of the countertop.

"I guess it's time for dessert." His voice was deep with desire. He took one of the strawberries, bit it and fed the rest to Phoenix. It wasn't long before he swept her naked body off the counter and carried her to his bed.

By the time they were done feasting on one another, their stomachs growled. Phoenix's stomach out-growled Carter's. Embarrassed, she covered her mouth with one hand and her belly with the other. Then she threw her head back and barked out a laugh.

Deciding to order in, they picked a comedy to watch and ate in bed. With her head against his muscular arm, she remembered what she meant to tell him. She watched him watch TV. Taking in his features as if she wanted to remember them precisely.

"Carter."

"What's up?" His eyes were on the television.

"I might be leaving soon."

Twenty

"Thanks, everyone, for your work tonight. This was good," Carter said to his colleagues at the Brooklyn branch office.

This was the last of several afternoon meetings his team had hosted in the past few days to quell their customers' growing anxiety about the volatile stock market. Carter hoped that would ease the angst of the few clients who called him every time a stock dipped in price. His wealthiest clients were used to the ups and downs. It was his newer and younger clients who required more hand-holding.

The staff left, but Carter went back to his office to send a few more emails. He rounded his large mahogany desk, trying to think of ways to connect with Roberts and secure his investment in the company. He still hadn't had the chance to meet with him since that day he missed their appointment. The longer it took, the more worried Carter became about being able to convince Roberts to stick with him and Harris. The investment needed to launch; this company was massive. Having the right people involved was just as important as having the money they needed. He wanted to get this deal with Roberts solidified so he could deal with his father. Carter sat in his high-back executive chair and released a sigh. Bill wasn't going to be happy but he at least wanted to show his father that he had a solid plan.

It had always been hard to appease Bill. His brother Ethan worked so hard at gaining their dad's approval. For Carter, those efforts were too exhausting. It wasn't that he didn't think his father loved them. Bill seemed to believe that he needed to be extra hard on his boys. This was his way of preparing them for the world. The pressure to meet

Bill's standards was often overwhelming. He had a vision for Blackwell Wealth Management that included all of his sons. Lincoln had already gone his own way and now Bill looked to Ethan and Carter to carry the mantle. What was he going to say when another son told him that Blackwell wasn't part of his future plans? Carter braced himself for his father's disappointment. Bill wasn't going to stop him from being his own man. He dreamed of building his own empire. That was something his father should be proud of. He couldn't stay under Bill's shadow forever.

Carter sat back in his chair, thinking of the best way to pin Roberts down. Instead of trying to catch him during the day, he thought of another way. Carter picked up his phone.

"Coop!" He called Harris by the name they called him in college.

"You heard from Roberts?"

"He hasn't gotten back to me yet. I've been trying to schedule meetings during business hours. Why don't we just meet him for dinner? We can do Louie's," Carter suggested. Louie's was a posh steak house and popular spot in downtown Manhattan for major deals.

"Let me know what night works for you two and I'll make it happen on my end."

"You got it. I'll call you as soon as I hear back from him. Hopefully, it will be soon."

"Hope so!"

"All right. Check you later, bro." Carter ended the call.

With his business venture hanging in the balance and the most recent news bomb that Phoenix had dropped on him, Carter didn't have the capacity for much more stress.

Phoenix had a way with timing when it came to delivering news. Carter never expected that his one visit would turn into the two of them continuing to see one another on a consistent basis. After dealing with the past, he could now see a future for them. Hearing that she may be leaving the state made him realize how much he wanted a future with Phoenix. Would that consist of dating? An exclusive relationship? Carter wasn't seeing anyone besides her, nor was he interested. But now she may be moving across the country. Carter didn't want a long-distance relationship. He wanted Phoenix here with him. He hoped those other jobs she mentioned called. Then she wouldn't have to leave. It became clear to Carter that he wanted a second chance.

Carter called Phoenix to find out her plans for the evening. He told her to be ready for him around eight. The summer was approaching its end and the nights descended with a welcome breeze. Carter took that into consideration as he prepared for later. He made a few calls, pulled a few strings and his ideas were set in motion. That motivated him to shut down his laptop and leave the empty office.

Being in the Brooklyn office made it easy for him to get home quickly. Carter moved about efficiently. He showered and called the car service his company contracted for certain occasions. Instead of driving around New York City and searching for parking, he wanted to use that time to focus on Phoenix.

Carter moved like he was on a mission. Once his mind was made up, he didn't waste time. Within a half hour, Carter was well dressed in a black custom suit and white shirt. The car arrived right on time. The driver easily navigated the several turns it took to get from his brownstone to Phoenix's building. He still found it odd that she lived so close to him. Those sightings weren't his imagination. He was sure he'd seen Phoenix at local neighborhood businesses.

Carter stepped out of the car, tugged his jacket in place and headed to Phoenix's apartment. She opened after the second knock.

"Wow!" she said when she saw him. She finished placing an earring in her ear and looked down at her dress. "I need to change."

"You look beautiful." Carter laughed. "But go ahead if you must."

Phoenix went into the room and returned with a stunning black dress that draped off her shoulder. Carter, nearly speechless, could only stare in response. He shook his head. "And now you look stunning."

Phoenix winked. "That dress wasn't cutting it. So where are we going again?" Phoenix picked up her purse from the couch.

"I never said where we were going. However, you should probably bring a shawl."

"Oh. Okay." Phoenix went back into the room to grab a shawl. "So this is some sort of surprise."

"Maybe. As long as none of your ex-boyfriends show up."

"I doubt we have to worry about that."

Carter held out his elbow. Phoenix maneuvered hers around his.

The evening sky displayed a stunning show of orange, pink and yellow blends. It would be dark by the time they reached their destination in Manhattan. They filled each other in on their day during the ride.

Phoenix looked out the window when the car stopped. The driver opened the door and reached for her hand, helping her out of the car. Carter rounded the vehicle from the back, took Phoenix's hand in his and stepped into a contemporary structure squeezed between two traditional-looking buildings. They took the elevator to the penthouse floor and were greeted by a tall, well-structured gentleman in a tux.

"Mr. Blackwell! It's good to see you." The man gave a slight bow.

"Hey, Jeff. How are you this evening?"

"Well, sir." He turned his attention to Phoenix and nodded. "And you look stunning tonight, ma'am."

"Thank you." Phoenix smiled. She looked at Carter, pressed her lips together and lifted her brows. "Impressive," she teased.

Carter winked.

The gentleman led them onto the rooftop dining area with only a few couples seated sparsely to provide privacy. Their reserved table was the best in the house. It was a corner setting that offered an unhindered view overlooking Gramercy Park. He pulled out Phoenix's seat and then Carter's.

"Someone will be with you shortly to take your drink orders."

"Thanks, Jeff," Carter said.

"Well, this is special. What's the occasion?" Phoenix said once the host walked away.

"Another try at a real date."

Phoenix blushed. "Thanks."

"My boy, Carter!" Renowned Chef Chase Williamson declared as he reached their table. He flipped a towel across his shoulder.

"Chase!" Carter stood and hugged his friend and owner of the exclusive establishment.

"And this must be Ms. Phoenix." Chase took her hand and kissed the back of it.

Phoenix chuckled. "Hello. Just Phoenix is fine. I believe I've seen you on TV a time or two." She shook his hand.

"Tonight I prepared my special just for the two of you." Chase rubbed his hands together. "Coconut curry salmon over wild rice for you." He nodded in Carter's direction. Carter's mouth watered. "And for the lady, braised lobster over risotto topped with a creamy garlic and butter sauce and roasted Brussels sprouts on the side."

"I'm impressed." Phoenix smiled. "Thank you, Chase."

"Would you still like to start with the clams oreganata and grilled prawns?"

Carter glanced at Phoenix. She took that as her cue to answer on their behalf and nodded.

"Wonderful," Chase said cheerfully. "Bon appétit!"

"You're gaining points here, Carter. What's up?"

He smiled with Phoenix but his face quickly turned serious as he prepared his words.

"I want us to be together again."

Phoenix's water didn't make it to her mouth. She put the glass down. "Carter. Really?" Her brows furrowed.

"I know we've been through a lot. I take ownership of everything I brought to the table. I'm sorry. I want your forgiveness. I never meant to hurt you. I never thought we'd speak again." He took her hand across the table. "Being with you these past few weeks made me realize why I never committed to another woman. They were not you."

"Carter." Her voice was a whisper.

"I know now that I never stopped wanting you. But wanting you has stopped me from being with anyone else."

"Wow." Phoenix took that drink of water. She cleared her throat. "I may be leaving in a few weeks."

"Maybe you won't have to leave. You could start your own business."

"What about our families? My parents won't respond to this well."

"They will get over it," Carter said firmly. "It's what we want that matters. You know what I want. What do you want?"

"I… I don't know. I never thought we'd be here, either. I'm sorry for not telling you about the baby. But you hurt me so bad I couldn't think straight."

"And if you let me, I will make that up to you." Carter gazed directly into Phoenix's eyes.

Phoenix cast her eyes toward the ground.

"I know." Carter stood and rounded the table. He took her hand and led her to stand. With his index finger, Carter delicately lifted Phoenix's chin. "Give me this second chance." He kissed her lips. "Let me show you how much I care about you." He kissed her again. Phoenix lifted her chin and kissed him back. Carter licked his lips. She tasted sweet.

"And the move?" she asked.

"We will deal with that when and if it happens," Carter said. Now he had to find a way to get her to stay.

Twenty-One

"Phoenix!" Nadine's rasping breaths rushed through the phone. "Oh, my Lord. Phoenix!"

Phoenix snapped straight up in the bed. "Mom! What happened?" Her heart pounded in her chest. Carter sat up beside her. Concern was etched into his expression.

"Your father! Oh my goodness. Phoenix, he fell. We were going to the bathroom and he fell. He won't respond to me, Fi."

"Mom!" she shrieked. Phoenix threw the covers back, jumped out of bed and scampered around in search of her panties and leggings. Carter followed her lead, picking up his jeans from the floor. "Call the ambulance. I'm on my way. I'll call you when I'm on the road to find out where they're taking him." Phoenix heard her mother sniffle. "I'm coming, Ma! Daddy's going to be all right." Phoenix wanted to believe that. Tears spilled down her cheeks. "I'm coming." She tried to keep the fact that she was crying out of her voice.

"Please hurry, Fifi."

"I will, Ma." Phoenix pulled a college hoodie over her head, maneuvering with one hand at a time as she held the phone. "Wait! Did you call Savannah?"

"No. You're the first number I called."

"Hold on." Phoenix put her mother on hold and dialed Savannah. A quick glance at the clock and Phoenix realized it was after two in the morning. It took two attempts to get her sister on the phone.

"Hello." Savannah's voice was groggy. She cleared her throat.

"Savannah! It's Daddy."

"What! What's going on?" Savannah's voice was full now and laced with panic.

"Hold on." Phoenix merged the call and filled Savannah in on what little she knew. Savannah announced that she was on her way. "Savannah, let me know where they take him," Phoenix said, referring to the ambulance. "See you as soon as possible." As soon as she ended the call her tears started to flow. She prayed her dad would be okay.

Savannah lived on Long Island with their parents. Phoenix knew she would get there much sooner than her coming from Brooklyn. By the time she brushed her wild tresses up into a haphazard ponytail and left the bathroom, Carter was fully dressed, waiting on her.

"Where do we have to go?"

"We?"

"Yes. We. Don't argue with me. You're in no condition to drive. Now take off your shirt and put it on the right way before we leave."

Phoenix looked down and realized her sweatshirt was inside out. She chuckled through her tears but then burst into a full-on cry. She couldn't break down while she was on the phone with her mother. Carter wrapped his arms around her and held her trembling body. After several moments Phoenix pulled back and wiped her tears with the sleeve of her shirt.

Carter lifted the shirt over her head, righted it and put it back on, working with Phoenix as if she were a child, still needing help getting dressed.

"I'll drive." Carter kissed her forehead and led her by the hand.

Phoenix didn't protest. She could barely see through her tears. There was no way she could safely drive from Brooklyn to Long Island alone. She'd just tell Carter to stay in the car when they got to the hospital. She wasn't ready to explain to her family why she was with Carter Blackwell at nearly three in the morning.

Phoenix called her mother back when they got in the car. Nadine was inside the ambulance with her dad. She could hear the commands and commotion of the EMTs. Nadine whimpered as she tried to encourage her father.

"Hold on, honey. We're almost there." She told Phoenix which hospital to meet them at.

Next, Phoenix called Savannah. She and Jaxon were en route behind the ambulance. At that moment Phoenix felt like Brooklyn was too far away. It would be at least another twenty-five minutes before she got to them.

She ended the call, sat back in the passenger seat of Carter's SUV and let the tears roll down her cheeks. Carter took her hand in his, navigating the car as fast as he could with the other. Any other time she would have urged him to slow down. She needed to get to her family.

Finally, they arrived. Phoenix jumped out of the car and scurried through the entrance to the emergency room. She moved so fast she wasn't sure if she'd closed the door. She looked back. It was closed.

Phoenix's heart pounded in her chest. Her mouth dried. She begged God not to let anything happen to her father. Inside she inquired at the registration desk about her father. "Yes. Jones. Christopher. Yes."

The woman had soothing, sympathetic eyes. She directed Phoenix through a set of double doors manned by a burly security guard. He held the door for her. Phoenix scurried through the corridors, passed beds with patients lying asleep until she reached the number she was given.

"Ma!" she said when she thought she'd heard Nadine's voice.

"Phoenix!" Nadine poked her head outside the curtain. Her family was there but her father was not.

Nadine fell into her arms. Savannah wrapped her arms

around Phoenix and Nadine. The three of them stayed that way for a while. Jaxon stood behind Savannah, rubbing her back.

When they released her, Phoenix said, "Where's Dad?"

"They're running tests," Nadine said.

Air swirled in Phoenix's chest like a rushing wind. She needed her father to pull through. She looked at her mother and held back tears. Nadine's weary eyes looked as if they hadn't seen sleep in days. Her usually flawless skin looked pale and dull.

"What did the doctors say?" Phoenix asked.

"It may be congestive heart failure. We'll know more when they're done running tests," Nadine said.

This could take all night. Phoenix felt her knees wobble. Savannah dropped her head into Jaxon's chest and cried.

"Okay." That was all Phoenix could say. She held Nadine's hand. She was at a loss for words. Again, she prayed for God to spare her father.

Jaxon left to find another chair. Phoenix sat when he returned. A moment later Phoenix heard her name. It was Carter. She froze. In that short amount of time, she'd forgotten he was with her and she hadn't told him to stay in the car. Now he was in the hospital at three in the morning. How would she explain that?

"That sounds like Carter," Jaxon said with his brows furrowed.

Nadine's face scrunched. "Why in the world would Carter be here?"

Phoenix said nothing. Nor did she move.

"Phoenix?" Carter's voice filtered through the curtains again. He was looking for her.

Jaxon stood and stepped outside the curtain. "Hey, man. What are you doing here?"

"I drove Phoenix."

"Oh...okay," Jaxon said.

Nadine looked confused, but then narrowed her eyes. Realization spread across Savannah's face. She raised her brow. Jaxon stepped back inside the curtain with Carter in tow. There was nothing to explain now. Carter's presence at almost three in the morning was explanation enough. She'd deal with her family later.

"Good evening, Ms. Jones." Carter nodded respectfully.

"Good evening, Carter," Nadine said but her eyes were on Phoenix's. "Thanks for bringing her to the hospital." She finally looked his way. Her tone was weary yet dry.

Nadine gave a tight nod in return and looked at Phoenix. She was certain that she was going to hear more from her mother later. He hugged Savannah and stood near Phoenix. Nadine watched all of their interactions.

The doctor stepped up and relieved her from the tension she was steeping in. He was a sturdy man with large shoulders, soothing blue eyes and a salt-and-pepper beard. He introduced himself as Phoenix tried to slow her heart rate with deep, cleansing breaths. The updates on her father's condition seemed bleak. They listened intently, crowding around the doctor as he spoke. Their father needed emergency surgery to open clogged arteries. It would take hours. He encouraged the family to go home, get some rest and return later.

"I'm not going anywhere," Nadine said. She was firm but polite. "You ladies go and I'll call you when he's out." She turned to the doctor. "Doctor, where can I wait?" Phoenix's heart broke for her mother. She wasn't going to leave her father's side.

"There's a family lounge. I can have someone show you there," Dr. Blake said.

"We're staying, too," Phoenix said, looking at her sister. Savannah nodded in agreement. Jaxon and Carter shared a knowing glance. They were staying, as well.

"So be it. I'll have someone show you there right away," Dr. Blake said. "She'll be here shortly."

Moments later a petite brown woman led them to the family lounge where they could wait for her father to get out of surgery.

In the hours that they waited, few words passed between them. They took turns napping on the uncomfortable chairs until the sun rose. Nadine paced, her arm folded across the other. Red lines wiggled through the whites of her eyes. Phoenix didn't think she'd gotten any sleep at all. Her mother went to the vending machine.

"Ms. Jones," Carter said. Phoenix's head snapped in their direction. "Jaxon and I will get you something to eat."

"I'm not actually hungry, Carter." Nadine's tone was friendly. She seemed grateful. "I just need something to drink."

Carter stepped up to the machine and paid for five bottles of water and handed them out. Then he went to where Jaxon sat with Savannah's head resting in his lap. Phoenix stayed by her mother's side.

Moments later Jaxon and Carter announced that they were going out to get everyone something to eat. Taking orders they hurried off, leaving Phoenix, Savannah and their mom alone for the first time.

Nadine looked at Phoenix but she couldn't read her mother's expression. Phoenix stirred under her mother's gaze. "No need to talk about this now. Let's focus on your father."

Phoenix exhaled. Savannah's smile was sly. Phoenix was sure their mother didn't see it. Sometime after that Nadine went off to the ladies' room.

"What's up with that?" Savannah whispered when Nadine was completely out of earshot.

"What do you think?" Phoenix whispered back.

"I knew it." Savannah chuckled. "I'm kind of glad."

Phoenix shifted in her seat. "Why?"

"I just am. Did you tell him about the baby?"

Phoenix huffed. She gnawed on her lip a moment before saying, "Yes."

Savannah took Phoenix's hand in hers. "How did you feel?"

"Like a boulder has finally rolled off my shoulders." Phoenix looked down at Savannah's hand covering hers. "He called off the wedding because his ex, Taylor, was pregnant and she told him it was his baby. They dated just before we got back together and decided to get married. He found out after the baby was born that it wasn't his. He said he was only trying to do the right thing and be there for the baby. He said he didn't want to embarrass me with an illegitimate child months after we got married."

Savannah had covered her mouth with her other hand. "Oh my goodness! You plan on telling Ma?"

"For what? Carter and I are just…you know…enjoying ourselves. It's nothing permanent."

Savannah eyed her skeptically.

Phoenix thought about her job. Her father. Carter. She swallowed hard. It was too much to carry. She didn't want to talk anymore. But she did admit to herself that she was grateful for Carter's presence. Luckily, Nadine was on her way back toward them. Savannah's glance told Phoenix that she wasn't done with this conversation. The girls sat on either side of their mother and rested their heads on her shoulders.

Twenty-Two

"Roberts." Carter nodded and shook his hand. "Looking dapper as always." Carter noted his black designer suit, black shirt and fancy silk pocket square. Roberts's appearance was always polished with the slight essence of a well-dressed used car salesman.

"Evening, Blackwell."

"Cooper will be with us soon." The men had a thing about calling each other by their last names.

Carter nodded at the hostess in the posh steak house and she led them to their table.

The dim lighting and dark wood decor gave the decor a masculine feel. Empires were created over the dinner tables at Louie's Steak House. Carter planned to do just that, put the final piece in place to start his new technology empire. Carter and Harris agreed on the name Weller, combining the ends of their last names.

Snapping the napkin, Carter placed it in his lap. "How's the family?" He started with small talk. Cooper arrived soon after.

"Pardon my tardiness, gentlemen," Cooper said as he sat.

The waiter quickly took their orders and they continued engaging in small talk until their dinner was served.

"Why the hesitancy, Roberts? Your feedback is important to me." Carter got right to the point.

"No investment from Blackwell. Your family is deeply entrenched in finance on the East Coast, real estate development in the Midwest and media on the West Coast. I found it odd that there was no backing from them."

"I see." Carter kept his cool. "Did you discuss this with my father?"

"Not directly. I realized he didn't know about it and that concerned me even more," Roberts said.

"I see." Carter leaned aside as the waiter placed their drink orders on the table. "I can assure you that Blackwell backing is in place." *Even if it wasn't coming directly from the head of Blackwell Wealth Management, Bill Blackwell.* "You could have asked me directly."

"At the same time, I'd been tapped for three other ventures and truthfully, the others were moving a bit faster. I had to make a decision to go with one of the others that were further along than yours. I doubt that any venture associated with Blackwell wouldn't be successful. But when the top Blackwell seemed oblivious to the opportunity, I questioned if it made sense to move forward. Speaking directly with you wouldn't have changed that."

"And your decision to meet with us today?" Harris asked.

"To let you know face-to-face."

"I can respect that." Carter glanced over at Cooper. He wanted to know how much Roberts had told his dad. Bill hadn't given any indication that he'd known about his and Cooper's goals. "And my reason for wanting to meet with you today is for you to reconsider. I'd like to make you another offer for your investment."

Roberts lifted his chin as he slowly chewed the piece of filet mignon he'd just placed into his mouth. He nodded. That was Carter's cue to continue.

"I won't deny that having you among our pool of investors is impressionable. I know you're a staunch businessman. I also know that your investment in the other company won't hinder your ability to invest in Weller. We value not only your investment, but also your strategic mind and the strength of your network. And I know that we'll have better access to both with your investment. So this is a strategic ask and we're willing to sweeten the deal when it comes to your return. Also, Blackwell's support is guaranteed. I can send you numbers later if you're willing to hear more."

Carter placed a piece of steak into his mouth and waited for Roberts to respond. He buttered him up in preparation for the ask. His father had always taught him when to stop talking during deals. This was one of those moments. If Roberts was interested in hearing what else Carter had to say, he was sure his offer would urge Roberts to seal a deal with them.

Quiet filled the table except for the scraping of knives and forks and nearby chatter. The silence lasted long enough to begin to feel uncomfortable. Carter refused to speak.

"I'm listening," Roberts finally said.

Cooper flashed a quick smile.

"We're ready to up your stake in the company, fifteen percent, and would like for you to sit on the board. We're willing to pay a bit more for the added influence." Roberts smiled, confirming that Carter had stroked his ego. That was what he wanted. The promise of 15 percent guaranteed that Roberts would be the largest investor besides Carter and Cooper. "We need to know tonight."

Carter added that additional squeeze. He knew Roberts had the resources to meet the offer. He liked being schmoozed. He and Cooper had already agreed that their ceiling would be 15 percent with only one investor. They also had a feeling Roberts would be the one they'd ended up offering it to. Carter placed a tender piece of steak into his mouth and savored it.

Roberts put his fork down, wiped his hands on his napkin and shook his head. "You're strategic. Blackwell taught you well." He reached his hand over the table. Carter wiped his hand and shook Roberts's. Roberts did the same with Cooper. "We've got us a deal."

Carter felt like pumping his fist. Instead, he smiled. "I look forward to doing business with you." He raised his hand and got the waiter's attention. "Your best Cab, please." He turned to Roberts. "That is your favorite, right?"

"And you have a good memory," Roberts said and chuckled.

Carter's smug smile spread into laughter. The men enjoyed the rest of their meal. Their conversation turned to other subjects. They broached sports, travel, golf and the latest political scandals. Then Carter remembered something.

"Your other venture involves AI, correct?" Carter asked.

"Yes. Some great new technology, but I can't reveal anything about it," Roberts said, sitting back and sipping on his third glass of Cabernet.

"I have a friend in AI. She may be looking for a change and she's absolutely brilliant."

"They're in the process of building their team now. Have her give me a call."

Carter raised his glass. "Will do!"

Harris and Carter went over the changes to Roberts's deal on the phone once they were back in their cars. Carter felt like he could walk on clouds. This deal was back on and he was excited. The only thing he didn't look forward to was telling his father. He had to tread carefully now that Roberts revealed that he'd attempted to have a conversation with Bill. It concerned him that his father may have an idea about his venture without him being the one who told him.

He couldn't wait to get to Phoenix's house and fill her in. She'd be tired after spending another evening at her father's bedside. After spending that first full day with them during his surgery, Phoenix insisted he didn't have to come back. He knew why. Surely, Ms. Jones had thoroughly questioned his presence. Carter would never forget the shocked look on her and Savannah's faces when he walked into that emergency room. He caught Savannah's smirk. Jaxon looked surprised, too. Carter hadn't shared the fact that he was seeing Phoenix with him or his brothers. Until then, Phoenix was his secret. However, Carter wasn't interested in keeping her a secret anymore. These past few weeks confirmed for him that his heart still beat for her. She hadn't quite confirmed it, but he knew Phoenix felt the same way. But just like with his father, her parents wouldn't be elated about their reunion. He understood Phoenix's hesitancy but was convinced they could get over that.

Nadine had to know that if Carter was around at two o'clock in the morning to drive Phoenix from Brooklyn to Long Island, it wasn't because Phoenix couldn't call an Uber. It had to be obvious to all of them that night that there was much more going on between Phoenix and him. That night also confirmed that she'd been keeping him a secret from her family the same way he had been keeping her a secret from his.

Carter was getting everything he wanted. The last thing he needed to work out was finding a way for Phoenix to stay. She would be more likely to stay in New York because of her father or a career opportunity and not just for him. He understood that.

Carter had been hoping that one of the positions she'd applied for would call her with an impressive offer. That hadn't happened yet. Hopefully, Roberts could deliver on that.

Carter pulled up to Phoenix's building and jogged inside. His excitement wouldn't allow him to walk. Positive energy surged through him. Phoenix opened the door. The heaviness of her mood was a sharp contrast to his elation.

"Hey." She leaned forward to kiss him. It had become customary between them. Both her greeting and her kiss were lackluster.

"Hey." Carter snaked his arms around her waist and kissed her again. "Dad okay?"

"He's out of ICU but not out of the woods. My poor mother won't leave his side. She's hardly eating."

"I'm sorry."

Phoenix breathed deep and exhaled with a groan and slipped from Carter's embrace.

"I have good news."

"I'd love to hear it." She plopped on the couch and pointed the remote at the television. The light from the TV flickered throughout the room. She put it on mute. "What happened?"

"Roberts is back in. The deal is still on."

"That's wonderful!" Phoenix managed to muster a bit of excitement for her response. "Have you told your father?"

"This week. I wanted to make sure things were ready to move before bringing it up. Have you heard anything back from the other companies?"

Phoenix pressed her lips together and then huffed. "Nothing since that last callback for a chief technology officer. They said they wanted to conduct an interview but I haven't heard anything back."

Phoenix folded her legs under herself on the couch and leaned on her hand. She looked like she was ready to lose hope.

"What's Indra saying about your move?"

"I bought some time when I told them about my dad. If nothing else comes through, I'll be leaving the middle of next month. They're already working on my accommodations. I'm just hoping my dad is better by then."

Carter sat facing her on the couch. "Just stay."

Phoenix touched his face. "Carter. I can't. I really love my job. California isn't my first choice, but it can't be that bad."

"I get it," Carter said. And he did. Just like him, Phoenix's decisions had to be on her own terms. At that moment he decided not to tell her about the opportunity with the company Roberts was investing in. Instead, he'd find out who was doing their recruitment and he'd make sure they had an eye on Phoenix.

"You seem exhausted. I'll come back by tomorrow after you get in from visiting your father." Carter kissed her lips and stood.

Phoenix caught him by the arm. "No! Don't leave." Her voice was a mix of fatigue and seduction.

Carter smiled deep on the inside. He lifted her into his arms. She loved when he did that. Carter carried her to the bedroom and laid her down. He removed his shirt and pants, climbed into bed and held her. She held him back until they fell asleep together.

Twenty-Three

"Hey, Mom!" Phoenix whispered as she eased out of bed, trying not to wake Carter.

"You're just getting up? No wonder you didn't answer my calls this morning. I was trying to get you to come and have breakfast with me. I want to talk to you."

Phoenix looked at the clock as she tiptoed out of the room. "We could do lunch. What would you like to talk about?" She grabbed a bottled water from the refrigerator and sat on a stool near the breakfast nook.

"Why are you whispering? Is Carter there? Phoenix." Nadine said her name like she pitied her. "What are you doing with him?"

"Mom."

"Don't *Mom* me! You don't remember how much pain, and money and embarrassment he caused you?"

"Yes, Mom. I do."

"What would our family say—our friends, if they saw you taking up time with him after all he had done? How would that make us look?"

"Us?" Phoenix scrunched her face.

"Yes. Us. You didn't go through all that embarrassment by yourself. That was one of the most humiliating events of my entire life!" Nadine was yelling.

"I don't want to talk about this." Phoenix threw her hand up.

"What happened to that other guy you were dating? What's his name, Bob?"

"Brent and he was worse than Carter could ever be."

"Oh, please. Phoenix. I don't get it."

"I know, Mom. And that's okay."

"Okay!" Nadine screeched. "You're not serious about being with him, are you? I would never accept him."

She saw Carter walk from her bedroom to the bathroom. If Nadine knew that they spent almost every night together at her house or his, she'd have a fit.

"I'm sorry, Ma. I have to go." She paused a moment. "I love you." Phoenix ended the call with her mother still yelling her name.

Phoenix expected this. This was why she kept this thing between her and Carter to herself. She even tried to keep Carter at a distance in her heart. It didn't work. She was falling for Carter all over again. Phoenix wanted to be with him more every day. Carter was everything all the men she dated after him were not. She never realized how much she'd missed him. But being with him would create friction between her and her mother. Possibly her entire family. How could she choose between the man she was falling in love with and her own family?

Carter came from the bathroom and sat on the stool next to her. "Feeling better?"

"A little."

"Got plans for the day?"

"A few errands. Going to see my dad. I need to start packing and my mom just asked me to lunch."

"Oh! The packing."

"Don't start, Carter."

He held his hands up in surrender. "I'm not saying anything. I'm heading to Long Island, too. The family is getting together for brunch and then we're going over to see the baby at the hospital."

"How are they?"

"Much better. Zoe's been home for a couple of days now and doing well. The baby is still in the hospital but getting stronger every day. She's a feisty one. The doctors said she'll be able to come home in a few weeks."

"Oh, that's such great news!"

"Shower?" Carter asked.

"Sure." Phoenix slid off the stool and let Carter lead her. "Wait! Carry me."

Carter chuckled and swept her off her feet.

She loved having him around and wanted to get as much time with him as possible until she left. Phoenix wasn't sure what it would be like when she left, but she knew she was going to miss him terribly. It would be like having her heartbroken all over again. She didn't voice how she felt, but was sure he already knew.

As they hit the bathroom door, Phoenix heard her doorbell. Sliding out of Carter's arms, she wondered who it could have been. The series of knocks answered her question. No one rang and knocked like that besides Savannah. That was their signal.

"It's Savannah!" She ushered Carter into the bathroom. "Enjoy the shower."

"All right." Carter kissed her, gathered his belongings and headed to the shower.

The ringing and banging continued. "Okay. Okay. I'm coming."

Phoenix opened the door and Savannah dashed in like a rushing wind.

"What took you so long?" Savannah's energy was always on ten. She craned her ear toward the running water. "Oh! You were just about to take a shower? Good. I came to take you to lunch so we can talk."

Phoenix rolled her eyes. "Like Mom wanted to talk this morning."

"She called, huh? She's been on a rampage since Carter showed up at the hospital, asking me all kinds of questions and getting mad when I told her I didn't know the answers. She told me I was trying to cover for you."

"Ugh! Well, she let me know exactly how she felt a little while ago."

"Save it for lunch. Go get in the shower."

"Um." Phoenix averted her eyes.

"Um. What?"

Phoenix tilted her head in the direction of the bathroom.

"Oh!" Savannah said. "He's here. Is that why Mom freaked out? Hey, Carter!" she yelled. "I'll be out on the balcony." Instead, Savannah walked in the opposite direction toward the kitchen. "After I make me a cup of coffee." She opened the refrigerator. "You got French vanilla creamer? Never mind, I'll find it."

Phoenix headed for the bathroom, shaking her head. "In the refrigerator door."

"Enjoy!" Savannah said and snickered.

Phoenix and Carter dressed quickly. He stopped to say hello to Savannah on his way out.

"Hey, Carter." Savannah's slick smile made Phoenix shake her head. Carter laughed.

"Hi, Savannah. How's the newlywed life treating you?"

"I love it. How's the reunited life going for you?"

"Savannah." Phoenix cocked her head to the side.

She snickered again. "I'm just teasing. I don't think it's bad. Things are usually better the second time around. At the end of the day, you have to do what makes you happy even if it makes others unhappy."

Carter and Phoenix looked at each other.

"See you later?" Phoenix dismissed Carter.

"Yeah. Call me when you get back to Brooklyn." They kissed.

Savannah cleared her throat. "I'm still here but don't mind me. Ha!"

Carter waved at Savannah before walking out. "Later, cousin."

"You're a mess," Phoenix said.

"And you were never fooling anyone. I knew you still held a torch for that man. You were just angry. Heck! I was angry, too. He made a jilted bride out of my sister, but I also knew that you never stopped loving him."

"That's not true." The words rushed past Phoenix's lips.

Savannah's expression turned serious. "I've always been able to see what you couldn't, sis. And what you refused to see. Despite your past you're letting him into a place you haven't allowed a man into for five years." Savannah tapped the center of Phoenix's chest.

Phoenix didn't respond. She couldn't. Savannah was right. That was why Phoenix needed to go ahead and take the job in California. If she stayed, she'd be in Carter's arms every night and she couldn't have Carter and her family. Her mother made that clear.

Twenty-Four

Carter took a few days off to handle business for Weller. Their agreement with Roberts had been signed and the money transferred. Harris took the lead on hiring and Carter worked on getting their offices set up. They were still a few weeks away from an official launch but Carter's window of opportunity to speak with his father was closing. He wanted to give Blackwell at least a month's notice.

On his first day back in the office, the executive team was meeting at the headquarters for monthly management meetings. Carter decided to have the conversation with his father after the meeting was over.

He called Roberts while he waited for the meeting to start.

"Morning. I was checking in about the opportunity with that AI company we spoke about," Carter said.

"Oh yes. You were going to send me your friend's information."

"Yes. However, I'd rather orchestrate an introduction. I don't want her to know that I'm trying to help her."

"I see," Roberts said. "How about I introduce the two of you by email and you can take it from there."

"That sounds like a plan. Thanks!"

"Not a problem."

When Roberts sent the email, Carter planned to share Phoenix's credentials with him and if they wanted to reach out to her, they could. He was sure that once they saw her résumé, they'd want her on their team. He'd let her know that he'd had a small hand in getting her the opportunity if something came of it. His goal was to help Phoenix secure a position in New York so she wouldn't have to leave.

Carter believed he and Phoenix could make it as a couple. Though he kept their situation to himself, he wasn't concerned about what their families had to say. All that mattered was that he was falling in love with Phoenix again. He wanted to spend his life making up for every mistake he'd made with her. He was confident Phoenix cared for him as much as he cared for her but if she moved across the country that would hinder their chances of building a life together.

One by one the rest of the Blackwell management team strolled in, chatting, drinking coffee and eating the pastries the office manager had set up for them in the conference room. Ethan walked in and everyone applauded. It was his first management meeting after his return back to work. He'd been out since Zoe's hospitalization.

"Thanks, guys." He put his head down, lifted it back up and smiled.

Dillon, the regional director for the Westchester branches hugged him. "Congrats, man! We've been rooting for you and Zoe."

"I appreciate it."

"Tell Zoe we miss her," one of the branch managers said.

"Good morning." Bill stepped in with his booming voice and commanding presence. Despite his stature, he still exuded warmth.

"Good morning, Bill!" several people said.

Ethan and Carter greeted their dad.

"Good to see you back, son," Bill said to Ethan.

"It feels good to be back, old man," Ethan said.

Bill chuckled.

"Hey, Dad. You busy after the meeting? I want to talk to you about something," Carter said.

"I always have time for you, son."

"Thanks, old man," Carter said.

Bill cleared his throat, quieting the room. "It's great to see you all. I'll start by saying how glad I am to see my son Ethan return. We've missed both you and Zoe here and continue to wish you the best. We must acknowledge and applaud Bella for her amazing work, stepping in for Zoe at the branch. Blackwell continues to grow. Please grab something to eat or drink and take your seats. We've got a full agenda today and I'd like to get started right away."

The team did as Bill instructed. They got right down to business reporting on the numbers at each branch, company objectives and breaking them down by region and branch.

"Despite market fluctuations, we've been able to calm our clients' fears and still grow our customer base across the entire region. Our information sessions were instrumental in allowing us to stay connected to our clients and led to a significant number of referrals," Carter reported.

Each region gave their reports and before Carter knew it, they were approaching lunchtime. He thought about the conversation he was about to have with his father and rubbed the back of his neck. Once all the reports had been presented, the team applauded, celebrating another successful month in spite of trying economic times.

"Before we close out, I want to make a special announcement." Everyone turned their attention toward Bill. "As some of you may know, I will be sixty years young very soon." He laughed. "And as I approach that milestone, I'm considering my next phase in life. I've made it known that it's been my dream to hand my company over to my sons Ethan and Carter. They have certainly proven themselves capable and I look forward to beginning the process of passing the mantle to these fine gentlemen."

A few began applauding until the entire room clapped and cheered for Ethan and Carter.

"I also want the rest of our team to know we've got our eyes on you, too," Bill continued. "I'm confident that some of you, like Bella, have what it takes to step into bigger roles. We're ready to provide opportunities for professional development and mentorship to help prepare all of you for your next step whether it be with Blackwell or not. I want all of you to be successful."

Everyone in the room seemed to be excited about Bill's announcement except Carter. Without warning, his father had just announced handing over the reins of the company to him and Ethan on the same day Carter planned to hand in his resignation.

The meeting came to a close. Saying their goodbyes, everyone began to clear out. As VP, Ethan now had his offices officially at the headquarters.

"What's my niece up to?" Carter asked Ethan.

"Getting stronger every day. She's developed some set of lungs. I'll be honest. That crying is music to my ears. The doctor said yesterday that we might be able to bring her home sooner."

"What did you expect? She's a Blackwell."

"Ha!" Ethan nodded. "You're right."

"Hey." Bill walked up to them. "You men ready to run Blackwell?"

"As long as we don't have to share offices," Ethan teased.

The brothers looked at each other and laughed. "It was hard enough sharing a room with you as a kid," Carter added.

"Ha!" Bill threw his head back and let out a hardy laugh. He put a hand on each of their shoulders. "You have no idea how proud I am of you young men. I dreamed of the day I would get to hand over the company. The legacy begins." Bill beamed. "Oh. Carter. You wanted to talk to me, right?"

Carter felt his smile fade. "Uh. It was nothing big. I need to get back. I planned to stop by the Queens office today." Carter looked at his watch. "Catch you later, Ethan." The brothers hugged. "I'll see you this weekend, Dad."

Carter would tell his father. It just wasn't going to be today while Bill's chest was puffed with pride.

Twenty-Five

"Taking these?" Savannah held up a pair of black stiletto booties. "You may have a hot date with a cute technology geek!"

Phoenix laughed. "Silly! We're not your everyday geeks." Phoenix tilted her head. "Well, maybe. Throw them in the box."

"I certainly hope you find a nice man. I'm happy you're getting away from that Blackwell boy," Nadine said.

"Mom. Please don't start."

Nadine huffed and waved away Phoenix's reprimand.

"Ugh!" Savannah picked up a box and carried it from the bedroom to the living room and placed it in the designated corner with the others. "When are the movers coming?"

"Friday."

Nadine stopped placing the clothes from the pile on the bed into the suitcase in front of her and sat still. After a moment she said, "What day do you leave again?"

"Next Monday," Phoenix said.

"Oh!" Nadine placed her hand on her heart. "I'm going to miss you so much."

Phoenix went to her mother and hugged her. "I'm going to miss you, too, Mom. Thanks for coming to help me pack."

"Your dad is going to miss you, too. You girls never strayed too far from us," Nadine said in a quiet voice. Her eyes filled with tears. She took a breath, shook her head and breathed deep.

"Yeah." Phoenix sat next to Nadine and laid her head on her shoulder. "I know." Nadine patted Phoenix's hand. They remained quiet for several moments. "I'm so glad he's finally home. I didn't want to leave while he was still in the hospital."

"You know he tried to come and help today." Nadine tsked and shook her head.

"That's Dad," Phoenix said. Both chuckled.

"Hey! You two back here getting emotional while I do all the work?" Savannah parked her hands on her hips.

Phoenix cut her eyes toward the ceiling. Savannah raced to where they sat on the bed and wrapped her arms around both of them and yelled, "Group hug!" making all three of them laugh.

"Let's call it a day. I'm hungry," Phoenix said.

"Me, too!" Nadine said. "Let's order something. I need to get back to Chris. I don't like to leave him alone for too long."

"I'll grab the menus." Savannah hopped to the kitchen.

Nadine chose sushi and the girls followed suit. They continued chatting over their meals on the balcony before Savannah and Nadine headed home.

After saying goodbye, Phoenix grabbed a bottle of wine and a glass, and headed back to the balcony. It was a beautiful night. Stars sparkled brightly against a velvety black sky. A slight breeze caressed her skin. The sounds of Brooklyn mumbled in the distance, cars, horns, the whistle of the air. They all blended into a soft symphony. She was on a high enough floor so the city's natural soundtrack wouldn't be a huge distraction.

Phoenix hadn't been alone on a Saturday night in weeks. If she wasn't at Carter's house, then he was at hers. But not tonight. Carter was with his family. She wondered what it would have been like to hang at his family's house with him like they used to. Would they even welcome her?

Until Savannah's wedding, she'd been cool and distant with the Blackwells. She knew for sure that her parents wouldn't welcome him with warmth and open arms. She'd known people whose boyfriends or girlfriends didn't get along with their family. It was a burden that she didn't want to carry. Despite that, she enjoyed being in Carter's presence and wished things between him and her parents could be different.

She thought back to their time together in Fiji. For a few days, they had been the old Carter and Phoenix, adventurous and fun. There was nothing they wouldn't try together. He got her. No other man after Carter ever did.

Nadine was right. What would it look like if they actually got back together? Phoenix was never one to care much for what people had to say. That was more Nadine and Savannah, but surely there would be lots of buzz. She could just imagine walking into events or showing up for holidays on Carter's arm. Phoenix chuckled out loud. She could see it now, wide eyes and open mouths on shocked faces. Then the whispers would start. Those bold enough would come directly to them and ask silly, obvious questions. "Are you two together?"

Who mattered? Them or her? If Carter was what her heart wanted, why should she care what others had to say? Phoenix groaned. That idea was easier said than lived. Moving allowed her to leave it all behind. Silicon Valley would give her a fresh start. She'd come back for holidays, long weekends and vacations. Maybe she could come back sometime and just let Carter know that she was in town. They could spend the weekend holed up in her apartment without interruption. Phoenix laughed aloud. That didn't make any sense. Who would she be hiding from? Who was she lying to?

Herself.

Phoenix closed her eyes. She breathed deep and groaned. Who was she fooling? She'd fallen in love with Carter Blackwell all over again. But what could she do about it? In less than ten days, she would be on a plane to her new life in California. Even if she stayed, life with Carter would be too complicated to enjoy openly. She hated that she cared so much. Nadine had made herself clear. She was close with her mother and would hate to ruin their relationship. But Phoenix was a grown woman and had never let Nadine dictate her life. Why would she do so now?

Phoenix stood and walked to the corner of her balcony. She could hear the neighbor's music. Her favorite, R & B from the nineties. She'd grown up with her parents telling her that it was among the best music. Love songs today weren't the same as the ones her parents listened to. She felt the love and the pain in the music from the seventies, eighties and nineties. It penetrated their souls then. Hers, too.

Phoenix leaned against the railing, swaying to the rhythm. The song changed; she kept listening. She heard the words "If you think you're lonely now, wait until tonight." Phoenix held up her glass and laughed. She was lonely. As long as she'd been living alone, she never felt lonely, until tonight. Carter's absence left a void.

Her cell phone rang. She wanted it to be Carter. She hadn't called him because she didn't want to bother him when he was with his family. Phoenix walked back to the wicker table next to the chair she'd been sitting in and picked up her phone. It was Carter. Her grin could not be contained.

"Hey, you."

"What are you doing?" Carter asked. The sultry sound of his voice made her yearn for his presence. She was going to miss him so much when she left.

"Relaxing on my balcony."

"I wish I were there with you."

"How's your dad's birthday shindig going?" Phoenix asked. She could hear the celebration in the background.

"Oh. It's great! He's having the best time. My mother and sister really outdid themselves. The venue is on the water.

The view is amazing, the food was delicious and he's surrounded by his family and friends. What more could he ask for?"

"That's great!" She forced a smile. Mr. Blackwell's party sounded wonderful. The idea of being surrounded by family and friends made her sad. Besides coworkers, she'd have no one in California.

"I guess you'll be getting home pretty late."

"Yeah." There was a pause. "Did you do more packing?"

"Yes. My mom and Savannah came and helped me today."

"That's cool.

"I wish you didn't have to go."

"Carter!" she sang, admonishing him.

"I know. I'm not supposed to keep saying that but it's true. I'm going to need to spend as much time as I can with you before you get on that plane. I told you I could come and help you get settled," Carter said.

"And I told you that I'd be fine." Phoenix needed a clean break. The lingering would only torture her. Trying to get through this one night was bad enough. Phoenix wasn't going to tease herself with pop-up visits. The secrecy had already been more than she could stand. She wanted all or nothing with Carter. And she had no choice but to choose nothing.

"Let's make sure this last week together is memorable," Carter said.

"I'd like that," Phoenix said and blushed.

"I guess I should get back to the party," Carter said.

"Yeah. Enjoy." Under different circumstances, she would have told him to tell his siblings she'd said hi.

"See you tomorrow?" Carter said.

"Yes."

"Okay. Good night," he said. Yet, no one ended the call.

Phoenix lay back on the lounge chair with the phone to

her ear. After a while she said, "Call me on your way home if you want to talk."

"I will," Carter said. Still no one hung up. They listened to one another breathe. Finally, Carter said, "I love you."

Phoenix squeezed her eyes shut, opened them and ended the call.

Twenty-Six

Carter thought about how much he'd enjoyed being immersed in family for his father's birthday weekend as he drove through his parents' neighborhood. It was a far cry from the dense streets of Brooklyn and his brownstone that was beautiful and historical, but narrow and tight. He drove through two-laned streets with sprawling homes set far back from the hilly road, with lush trees that gave natural privacy. This was the last of the planned festivities for his father's milestone birthday.

As much as he enjoyed spending so much time with his family, he couldn't wait to get back to Phoenix. Carter missed her presence. He thought about asking her to come with him but he knew she wouldn't. Waking up alone felt odd. He thought about her all through the day, every day. With only a week left, he remained hopeful that something would come through for her and she wouldn't have to leave. The thought of her packing troubled him.

The words he'd said to her last night on the phone played in his head over and over again. He'd felt it but never voiced it. Yet, he'd parted his lips and the words "I love you" escaped his heart easily and naturally. He hadn't given it any thought and only realized what he had said after he'd said it.

Carter didn't want to push Phoenix. They'd been through enough. If Phoenix wished to stay, or love him, he wanted her to come to those conclusions on her own. His call to Roberts was to help her find opportunities she'd already been seeking. If it worked out, then great. If it didn't, he'd have to deal with her absence. Maybe he'd find love again though he knew it would never be like it was with Phoenix. It was as if their past hardships made their bond even better this time.

Carter maneuvered up the private drive and around to the side of his parents' massive home. Several cars were already in the driveway. Unlike the black-tie event of the night before, today's brunch was casual and held at their home with a color scheme of silver and Bill's favorite, green.

Carter needed to tell his father about Weller before he left their home tonight. The office wasn't the right place and over the phone would be unacceptable. Carter would wait until all the guests, which were mostly family, had gone for the evening. He could tell both his mother and father together.

Entering through the garage door, Carter greeted his mother first.

"Hey, sweetie," Lydia said.

"Hey, Mom." He pulled her into a bear hug and lifted her off her feet.

"Put me down, boy," she said, smiling. She popped him in the arm. "Your dad is outside with Eloise and his brothers."

All of Bill's brothers and his only sister flew to celebrate with him. Originating from South Carolina, the Blackwell clan was bred in New York and spread across the country. They had empires in different industries, such as media, real estate development, finance and hospitality. The family was massive and when they got together, the gatherings were massive. Some of them were heading back later that evening. So Carter decided to wait until the majority of them left. In the meantime, he'd enjoy the company of his many cousins.

Carter greeted his father, who was on the upper deck enjoying cigars with his brothers, Tommy, Ben and Melvin. Eloise, his stylish only sister, was on the lower deck with the ladies. Aunt Eloise was a grand Southern belle even though she was raised in Queens until she left for college in Atlanta where she met her husband.

"Hey, Carter." He greeted his uncles one by one with hugs and fist bumps. They teased him about being a bachelor.

"Are you still allergic to commitment?" his uncle Tommy asked. The rest snickered.

"Come back to LA with me," Uncle Ben teased. "There's plenty of beautiful women to choose from there. You see Tyson finally settled down with Kendall. She sings like a beautiful bird. You know she's got another movie coming out."

"I saw that. I'll be the first one at the theater. In fact, where's Kendall and Tyson? I want tickets to the premiere!"

The men laughed. Carter moved on to greet his other family members. Several areas of the house both inside and out were filled with groups of cousins from both his mother's and father's sides.

Carter caught up with his brothers and a few of his male cousins in the guesthouse. The female cousins hung out with the wives and girlfriends. For the next few hours they ate heartily, talked trash and told embarrassing stories from their childhood. Several times Carter wondered what it would have been like had he and Phoenix married. They would have been among the married cousins swapping stories about the kids and married life. Phoenix would have been there with him.

"Carter!" Lincoln said his name.

"What's up?" he answered.

"Dude! I called you three times. What's on your mind?"

"Ah! Work." Carter said the first thing he could think of. Between the conversation he had to have with his father and thoughts of Phoenix constantly creeping up, Carter couldn't help zoning out. "Thinking about some stuff I have coming up this week."

"No thinking about work!" one of his cousins said. "Not today."

"You're right." They pulled Carter back into the conversation.

As family members began to say their goodbyes, Carter went through the motions but his mind was on "the talk." He sat at the island and rubbed his hands across the smooth marble countertop and then down the legs of his pants. Finding something to do with his hands had become a challenge. Bill walked in through the double doors leading from the backyard. Carter stood.

"Heading home now, son?" Bill asked.

"Yeah. Can I have a word with you for a moment before I go?"

"Sure." Bill's brow furrowed. "Is everything all right?"

"Yeah. Let's talk in your study."

Bill headed in that direction. Carter followed and closed the door behind them.

"Do I need a drink?"

"Well..."

"What is it, Carter?"

Carter took a breath. "I'm leaving Blackwell."

His father's expression fell. A combination of anger and disappointment flashed across his hooded eyes.

"Carter!"

"I realize you're getting ready to retire. I appreciate all that you've taught me, but I want to build my own empire."

Bill's jaw squared; the muscles in his face seemed more rigid. He sat back in his executive chair, hard. With his hand on his chin, he wore a pensive gaze. He didn't look in Carter's direction. He didn't speak.

Carter became uncomfortable in the thickening silence.

"I built this company for you. For my children. To leave a legacy. I want to leave it in the hands of my heirs."

"I'm sorry, Dad. I want the same thing, but my own."

"So your kids can disappoint you and toss everything you built back in your face? First Lincoln. Now you! Ethan will have to carry this company on his own shoulders!" Bill stood and groaned. His comment stung Carter. He knew he would be upset, but that cut. "When do you plan on leaving?"

"Thirty days."

"What are you going to do?"

"Harris and I have been working on a venture. We finally have all of our investors in place. The name is Weller, a technology firm."

"Those are expensive and risky investments."

"You've taught us to never run from risk."

Bill narrowed his eyes at Carter.

"Dad. I need to do this. If it doesn't work, hopefully, you'll welcome me back. But I have to give it a try. My heart, money and all of my resources are in this thing."

"Why are you just telling me?"

"Because I knew how you'd react."

Bill sat back. He rubbed his chin for a long time. Emboldened, Carter stood firmly in the tension that threatened to suck the oxygen from the room. He couldn't wait any longer. It wouldn't be fair to him or his father.

"I'll need you to figure out your replacement. We will announce your resignation tomorrow." Bill stood and walked out of the room.

Carter ran his hand across his forehead. The hard part was over. He'd had the conversation with his father. He got his business. Now he needed to get his woman.

Twenty-Seven

The first email in Phoenix's inbox was from a recruiter. They wanted to speak with her about a position at a new company that was launching in New York. She tried not to get too excited. After closing her office door, she returned to her chair and dialed the number in the signature line. Normally she would have just responded by email, but she was anxious so she took a chance by calling.

"Leah Dresner." The woman's voice was full of life for a Monday morning.

"Hello, Ms. Dresner. This is Phoenix Jones, calling regarding your email about an opportunity with a technology company launching in New York."

"Yes! Ms. Jones. I'm so glad you called. We came across your information. Your credentials seem impressive. I wanted to speak with you regarding a position our client is seeking to fill. I can give you some insight now and you can let me know if you're interested in having me set up an interview."

"Sure. I'd love to hear about it."

Phoenix listened to Leah describe the company and the opportunity. The more she spoke, the more Phoenix became excited. This start-up must have had an incredible amount of financial backing. And they seemed to know quite a bit about her accomplishments. The offer was more impressive than what her current boss wanted to give her. The idea of being on the ground floor of such an amazing opportunity in tech enticed her even more.

"Does that sound like something you'd be interested in?"

"Absolutely!"

"Wonderful. Would you be available to come in for an interview next week, Wednesday?"

Leah had just put a pin in her excitement bubble. "Unfortunately, I will be leaving town on Monday. Is it possible to get an earlier interview?"

"I'm not sure, but I'll check. Is this a good number to call you back on?"

"Yes. It's my cell."

"Okay. Great. I'll see what we can do and get back to you ASAP!"

"Thanks. I look forward to speaking to you."

Phoenix ended the call and squealed. Hopefully, this one would work out. She pulled up the website the recruiter had given her to find out more about the company. She also found a few articles touting their launch. They were brand-new but backed by some major players. Projections about how they would fare were very favorable. Phoenix sat back and thought for a moment. She hadn't applied for a position with them. How had this recruiter found her? She assumed it was through one of the job boards.

The first call she made was to Carter.

"Good morning, beautiful. I missed you last night."

"I missed you, too. I have good news. Well, it's still too early to tell but I'm excited about it." Phoenix told Carter about the job.

"That's great! So if this comes through, you won't have to leave."

"If! And that's a big *if.* I may not be able to get an interview before I leave."

"How about I come take you out to lunch to celebrate?"

"I've got meetings all day. I'm going to be glued to this desk. How about dinner?"

"I'll take it. Good luck. I'll keep my fingers crossed for you."

"Great!"

That call put Phoenix in a great mood. She opened her door again. There were only a few people left at the office. Those who were not moving and one who was leaving next week like she was. Indra and Dean had been in California for the past two weeks.

Phoenix headed back to her desk and prepared for back-to-back meetings. She sailed through the day on her excitement. Her mood changed when she realized it was after two in the afternoon and she hadn't heard back from Leah Dresner. She thought about calling her back, and changed her mind. Phoenix handled some work before her next meeting. As she was about to leave her office and meet her coworkers in the conference room, her phone rang. It was Leah.

"Phoenix Jones."

"Ms. Jones. Leah Dresner. How are you?"

"I'm well. And you?"

"I'm well, thanks. We were able to get an interview moved up but the window is tight. Would you be available to meet tomorrow morning?"

"I would have to move some stuff around but I could definitely make it happen."

"Great! How's nine thirty?"

"Perfect. Where?"

Leah gave her the address. The office was right in downtown Brooklyn, not far from Phoenix's current job. They finalized the details. When the call was over, Phoenix jumped up and danced around her desk. She hoped this worked out. The closer she got to her move date, the more she realized she wasn't interested in leaving New York. The only relief it would have provided was leaving Carter behind so she wouldn't have to deal with how complicated life had become. She wanted him but didn't like the burden that came with being with him because of her family. If she stayed, she'd have to deal with that somehow.

Phoenix remembered Carter's words the other night when she was on the phone. He'd said he loved her. She already knew that. She knew Carter. She also knew that she loved him, too. If it didn't come up she didn't have to face it. But Carter brought it up and made her acknowledge her own feelings.

Phoenix shook away those thoughts. She didn't want to deal with that now. If this job didn't come through, she was back to her original plan of leaving. Whether she left or stayed, it wouldn't make life easier. Leaving Carter behind would be an adjustment. If she stayed, finding a way to love Carter and keep her bond with her family would also be a challenge.

At five on the dot, Phoenix shut down her computer. She was anxious to get to the next morning but had to get through the night first. She looked forward to seeing Carter after not laying eyes on him all weekend. That was the longest she went without being with him in weeks. Saying good-night to her coworkers, Phoenix bounced out of the building.

Carter was leaning against his car outside her building. The smile that graced her lips radiated from the inside.

"What are you doing here?"

"Ready to start celebrating?"

Phoenix sauntered to him. "Sure."

Carter kissed her passionately right there on the busy city street. "I missed you." He stepped aside and opened the passenger door for her before rounding the front of the car and getting in on the driver's side.

"Where are we going?" she asked.

Carter wouldn't answer. Instead, he laced his fingers in hers as he maneuvered the car into traffic.

Phoenix sat back and enjoyed the ride. Carter filled her in on his busy weekend with the family. She knew their destination was in Manhattan when he crossed the Brooklyn

Bridge. Keeping her distracted with conversation, Carter asked her about the call she had with Leah Dresner in the afternoon. She gave him the details about the interview in the morning.

"So I can't keep you up too late tonight?" He winked.

"No. You can't." Phoenix grinned.

Carter rode through busy Manhattan streets, dodging wild-driven yellow cabs as he made his way to Midtown. He pulled into a parking garage on the west side of Sixth Avenue. Carter pulled a duffel bag from the trunk, tossed the keys to the valet, got his ticket and led Phoenix through the garage.

"What's in the bag?" she asked, her curiosity getting the best of her.

"It's for where we're going."

"I figured that. You don't plan on telling me anything, do you?"

"Nope!"

They walked two city blocks to Bryant Park. It looked like hundreds of people were out on the lawn, sitting on blankets. Near the Sixth Avenue side was a massive movie screen.

"Oh, Carter! I've always wanted to do this." She kissed his cheek, not missing a step.

"It's the last one of the season."

They walked around the great lawn in search of the perfect spot. As large as the screen was, any spot would have been fine.

"How about right there?" Phoenix pointed to a spot right near the center.

"This works."

Carter opened the bag and spread the blanket over the grass. Next, he pulled out two glasses, a corkscrew, a prepackaged charcuterie and a bottle of wine. The two of them sat down. They still had time before the movie started.

Carter poured two glasses of wine, handed one to Phoenix, lifted his glass and said, "Cheers."

Phoenix clinked her glass against his.

They sipped and Carter looked deep into her eyes. Phoenix felt as if he were trying to see into her soul.

"You heard me the other night," Carter said matter-of-factly.

"I did," Phoenix admitted.

"I need to know how you feel."

"Honestly. I love you, too, Carter. I never thought I'd say those words ever again."

"They're music to my ears."

"Things are complicated. I'm moving. I've never wanted a long-distance relationship."

"Not if you get this job."

"We both know that's not guaranteed. And what if I do get the job? I'll admit, I want to be with you, but..." Phoenix sighed. "My family. I have yet to hear the end of it after you came to the hospital with me that night. I don't want to feel like I have to choose between you and my own family."

"I'll speak to your family. I owe them that."

"Carter." Phoenix loved him more for saying that but didn't think it would do any good. "I don't know."

"So what, we just keep going on like this? Keeping each other a secret. I want you. All of you. I want to go to family functions with you. Hang out with friends. I want what we had before but better."

"Is that even possible?"

"We won't know if we don't try. The question is, are you willing to try?"

Phoenix looked to the sky. She wanted to try. She wanted to do more than try. Phoenix wanted the same things he wanted. It seemed perfect but reality didn't work that way. "I do, Carter. But—"

"Then let me do my part to fix it."

Phoenix pulled him to her and kissed his lips. She didn't care that they were sitting among hundreds of people in a public New York City park. Carter had done it again. He still had the ability to make her feel like everything would be all right.

Twenty-Eight

Carter paced back and forth in his office at the headquarters as he waited for Phoenix's call. His future with her resided in this job opportunity. When he left that morning, he wished her luck on her interview.

Bill knocked on his open door, catching his attention. "Everything okay, son?"

"Uh. Yeah."

"You're pacing. Is it the business deal?"

"Actually, no."

"Something you want to talk about?"

"You know what? Yes."

Carter closed his office door, gestured for his father to sit and parked himself in his chair. Carter told Bill all about Phoenix.

"The only thing that matters, son, is how you feel for each other. Everyone else will have to get over it. If your heart is leading you back to her, then follow it."

"Thanks, Dad."

"As a man, I agree you need to go to Christopher and Nadine and speak with them. You do owe that to them. Want me to come?"

"No. I'll be fine by myself, but thanks, Dad."

"Anytime." Bill went to stand.

"Dad. Did you come in here for something?"

"Yes." Bill sat back down. "I've been thinking since our talk Sunday. While I'm still disappointed, I'm proud of you. A man has to do what a man has to do. There's nothing like having your own. I wish you the best in your new company and I support you. If you need anything let me know. If it doesn't work out, the door here at Blackwell will always be open for you. Something tells me you won't need to come back. You're a hard worker. You know how to get results. I'm sure you'll do well."

Carter exhaled long and loud. "Thanks, old man. This really means a lot to me."

Bill stood. "Keep me posted on the situation with Phoenix. If you need me, let me know. Most important, take good care of her heart."

"I will."

When Bill left, Carter looked at his watch. Only twenty minutes had passed. Phoenix was still in her interview. Carter needed to get busy, or thinking about Phoenix and this interview would drive him batty.

Carter grabbed his laptop and went to Ethan's office to discuss his conversation with Bill, update him on Phoenix and share some ideas he had about objectives they were looking to meet in this quarter. He'd confided in Ethan and Lincoln about his goals. They'd supported him from the start.

After being with Ethan for a while, Carter's cell phone rang. It was Phoenix.

"How'd it go?"

"You won't believe this. The interview was amazing. They offered me the job and asked me to give them a few days to put together my package. Also, the other job called me back for a second interview. It looks like I'm staying."

"Yes!" Carter pumped his fist. Ethan raised a brow. He forgot he was in his office. "It's time I speak to your family."

Phoenix got quiet. After a while, she said, "Okay. Okay. I'll set it up."

"Before you do?" Carter paused and cleared his throat. "I have to tell you something."

"Lord! Carter, what is it? I don't like the way you said that. You're scaring me." Phoenix huffed.

"It's not like that but I do need to confess something to you."

"Carter!" he could clearly detect the uneasiness in her voice.

"I want to make sure there are never any secrets between us again." He paused again waiting for her to respond.

"I'm listening," Phoenix said.

"I'm the person who made sure Leah Dresner received your information so that you would be considered for the job."

"What? How?"

"Jacob Roberts, the lead investor for my company is also a major investor in the tech start-up that's hiring you. I told them how brilliant you were and he agreed to look at your credentials. That's all I did. You got yourself the job," Carter said.

Phoenix didn't respond for several moments. Carter waited until he couldn't stand the silence anymore.

"I knew you didn't want to move to California and leave your family. I didn't want you to leave me, either. I'll be honest, I wanted to be helpful but I was also selfish. I may have helped you get the interview, but you're the one who impressed them enough for them to offer you the position so quickly."

Finally Phoenix sighed. Carter was happy to hear some kind of a response even if it wasn't a verbal one.

"I apologize for not saying something before," he continued. "You wouldn't have wanted me to meddle but I don't regret my actions at all. I hope you'll forgive me and I promise that's the last secret I'll ever keep from you."

"Carter…" Phoenix groaned but didn't say anything more.

He wondered what she was going to say. The silence was torture.

"Thank you," she finally said. He could feel her smile through the words.

A broad smile spread across his face. "You're welcome."

"No more secrets!" she commanded.

"Never again," he agreed.

"See you later," Phoenix said.

"I love you, superwoman." Carter's words lingered for a moment.

"I love you right back."

Together, Carter and Phoenix pulled up in front of her parents' home in Great Neck, Long Island. Phoenix fidgeted the entire ride. And now she looked as if the color had drained from her face. Carter insisted that she invite Savannah and Jaxon, as well.

Carter was nervous but determined. He held Phoenix's hand up the walk. She used her key to enter.

"Mom. Dad."

"In here, honey." They were in the family room. Her mother's tone was clipped. The tension had already begun to rise in the atmosphere.

Phoenix rubbed her hands together and hesitated before walking toward the family room.

"Good evening, Mr. and Mrs. Jones."

"Good evening," Chris said, peering over his glasses. His greeting lacked warmth.

"Mmm-hmm." That was Nadine's greeting. She pursed her lips.

Carter went to Mr. Jones and shook his hand.

"Have a seat, son," Chris said.

Nadine's eyes followed him across the room. Phoenix stayed at the door initially, but then went to sit next to Carter on the sofa.

"What do you want to say to us?" Chris asked.

"Sir, I'd like to start with an apology. Phoenix and I

worked things out between us, but I felt it was only right to address this with you directly. I love your daughter. In fact, I've never stopped loving your daughter and I'm not the man I was five years ago. Back then…" Carter told them about Taylor, the baby and why he called off the wedding.

"I can understand that you tried to do what you thought was noble, but there was a better way to handle that. You hurt our daughter, caused us to waste a lot of money and humiliated our family," Chris said.

"I know. I plan to make that up to her."

"M-Mom. Dad."

Nadine peered at Phoenix. "What is it, honey?" Chris said.

"I have something to tell you also."

Nadine's brows furrowed. "Don't tell me you're pregnant!"

"Not now. But I was then."

"What?" Chris and Nadine said at the same time. Nadine scooted to the edge of her seat.

"What are you talking about?"

"I was pregnant. I wanted to surprise Carter on our wedding night, but the wedding never happened. I was so hurt and angry. I wouldn't let him explain why he was calling off the wedding." Both Nadine and Chris's mouths hung open. Each leaned in, taking in every word that fell from Phoenix's mouth. She swallowed. "I should have said something that night but I didn't. I just needed to think. I figured going to Belize by myself would give me a chance to get my thoughts together. But when I got back I had the miscarriage…"

Just then, Savannah and Jaxon walked into the room.

"Did you know about this?" Nadine asked Savannah.

Savannah nodded.

Phoenix continued. "I didn't know what else to do. The doctor said there could have been several reasons for the miscarriage, including stress. I should have said something." Tears fell from Phoenix's eyes. Carter took one hand in his and used his free hand to rub comforting circles on her back. "He thought he was doing the right thing by being a father. I understand that. Unfortunately, that baby turned out not to be his, and I lost our baby. Had I heard him out that night, maybe this could have been avoided. Who knows?"

"Mr. and Mrs. Jones, Phoenix and I have a second chance here and we want to take it. I promise all of you that I will handle her heart with care."

"Phoenix." Chris looked intently at his daughter. "Is this what you want?"

"Yes, Dad. It is." She looked from her father to Carter. At that moment Carter felt all the love he held for her.

"Phoenix, are you sure?"

"I am, Mom."

"Well, you two are going to have to work on your communication skills." Chris chuckled and the weight enveloping the room lifted.

"Chris, what will people think?" Nadine said with a hand on her heart.

"Honey, it doesn't matter what people think. What matters is that they love each other. My concern is her happiness. If he makes her happy, then so be it." Chris looked at Carter. "And that this young man is responsible for our daughter's heart." He pointed at Carter. "Don't you forget that. I'll be watching."

"Never," Carter said. "I will never forget that or the responsibility that comes with that. With your blessing—" Carter pulled a box from his suit jacket "—I want to ask Phoenix again, if she would do me the honor of being my wife."

Phoenix's mouth fell open. She covered it with both hands. "Oh my goodness, Carter!"

"That would be up to my daughter. Right, Phoenix?" Chris said.

"It would," Nadine cosigned.

Phoenix looked at everyone in the room. A slick smile slid across Savannah's face. "You knew about this?" Phoenix asked.

"Of course." Savannah snickered. Phoenix narrowed her eyes at her sister.

Phoenix turned to Carter. "That's why you insisted she come." Phoenix teasingly rolled her eyes at Savannah.

Unfazed, Savannah laughed. "Answer the man."

"Phoenix, will you marry me?"

"Yes! Yes. I will marry you!" Phoenix wrapped her arms around Carter's neck and squeezed him tight. He couldn't wait to get his fiancée home.

* * * * *

PROMISES FROM A PLAYBOY

ANDREA LAURENCE

Prologue

Finn was startled awake by a loud bang and a rumbling that made the plane shudder with turbulence. Normally flying on the corporate jet was smooth sailing, the epitome of luxurious travel, so he instantly knew something was wrong.

His heart was pounding in his chest. He tried to get up out of his seat, but the shaking of the plane knocked him back into the chair. There were five people on board—Finn, the pilot and copilot, a flight attendant and a manufacturing consultant that had joined them at the last minute. The consultant's original flight on a commercial carrier had been canceled and Finn had offered him a ride back to the US from Beijing. As he turned to look at the terrified man in the seat across the aisle from him, he knew the man now regretted taking him up on the offer.

Pushing up and bracing himself on the next seat, Finn fought his way to the front of the plane. He ignored the calls of the buckled-in flight attendant pleading with him to return to his seat.

"What's going on?" he shouted over the chaotic beeping of sensors, the frantic Mayday calls of the pilot and the uncharacteristically loud roar of the engine.

"Mechanical failure," the copilot said as he turned around and looked at Finn with worry lining his brow. "Something has gone wrong with the engine and we're not going to make it to Salt Lake City. We're trying to reroute to Sea-Tac for an emergency landing. You should return to your seat and put on your seat belt, Mr. Steele."

"Screw the seat belt! Put on your parachute," the pilot shouted as he fought to control the steering. "There's one under each seat."

"Parachute?" Finn stumbled and gripped at the door to the cockpit to steady himself. "Are you serious?"

"If we don't make it to Seattle in time, we might have to bail. I'm trying to bring us down to a safer altitude just in case."

Finn swallowed hard. The idea of leaping from the jet into the dark night had never crossed his mind. He was the family wild child, but the risks he took were with women and fast cars. He wasn't the type to jump out of a perfectly good airplane.

The plane jerked hard, sending him stumbling forward. Another shrill alarm sounded from the control panel. Then again, he thought, this was not a perfectly good airplane. He stumbled back to his seat and pulled out the package underneath. The man beside him nervously did the same, slipping the parachute straps over his arms while still securely belted into his leather lounging chair.

Finn put on his own parachute, snapping the clasps over his chest to secure it. His father had insisted that each plane be equipped with parachutes for emergencies. They'd gone over how they worked once when they first bought the planes, but he wasn't sure he'd really listened. He honestly never thought he would need to use it. Who would expect a fancy private jet like this to be anything less than flawlessly maintained?

He groaned and lowered himself into his seat as they rumbled through the air. His father would be incensed if one of the multimillion-dollar corporate jets crashed. And somehow, Finn knew it would be his fault. Everything was always his fault in the end.

Finn was reaching for his seat belt when another loud bang deafened him. The bang coincided with a fireball and the sudden whip of wind through the cabin as the blast created a large hole in the side of the fuselage. Half a heartbeat later, Finn was sucked from his seat and flung into the dark night.

In an instant, there was the sensation of freezing cold with the wind whipping around him. The blackness enveloped him with only pinpoints of light visible in the distance. He couldn't breathe at first. His brain could barely keep up with it all; he was in complete sensory overload.

Finn had no idea how high he was or how far he was from the ground, but he could feel himself start to get light-headed. Gritting his teeth, he pulled the cord and the parachute jerked him to a slower descent. That done, he gave in to the swimming sensation in his head and blacked out.

When he came to, he could see the tops of trees highlighted by the moonlight. He came in hard and fast, blowing through the thin upper branches as he descended into what appeared to be a densely wooded area. Considering they'd been over the Pacific Ocean not long ago, he was ecstatic to find trees underfoot instead of miles of inky black sea.

At least until the sharp twigs and leaves started whipping at him. They cut at his skin like a hundred icy knives. As he descended lower, he tried to cover his face with his arms and he could feel the branches snagging at his clothes.

Then he jerked to a sudden stop.

He looked up and realized the same branches that had attacked him had snagged his parachute. Now he was dangling from his harness, unsure if he was five, ten or thirty feet from the ground. Finn squirmed, hoping he could untangle the parachute enough to get closer to the forest floor, but there was no getting loose.

Finn considered his options for a minute. He needed to get down from this tree, but there were no tree trunks within his grasp. He couldn't just dangle here until morning and hope someone found him. He could be in the middle of nowhere for all he knew, and he was too exposed up here in the treetops without shelter from the wind. He started to shiver in his thin dress shirt and summer suit coat. Beijing had been a lot warmer in September than wherever he was now. Maybe it was the cold, or maybe it was shock of the accident starting to set in. He couldn't be sure. But he knew what he had to do.

With trembling fingers, he fumbled with the harness. The lower buckle unsnapped easily, but he fought with the second. When it finally gave way, he had no time to react before he slipped out. He fell for what felt like minutes, branches slamming into his ribs and whipping at his arms and legs before he took a thick branch across his forehead and everything went black.

One

Willow Bates was enjoying the brisk morning air on her back deck with a large mug of coffee in her hand. The weather was just starting to cool down in the San Juan Islands community that she called home. Somewhere between Victoria, British Columbia, and Seattle, Washington, the smallest of the islands—Shaw Island—was her blessed retreat. Fall was coming. Unfortunately, that also meant that their stormy season was coming.

And judging by the thick black clouds on the horizon, she wouldn't be enjoying the outdoors for a few days. The weatherman said a severe thunderstorm with high winds was heading their way. That meant she'd likely be cut off from the mainland for a day or two, but she didn't mind. She rarely left her island. There was nothing for her in Seattle but painful memories and traffic.

Her shaggy white-and-gray husky mix traipsed over to her and laid his head on her lap. He looked up at her with his big ice-blue eyes. She scratched him behind his pointed ears and sighed. “We need to get your walk in early today, Shadow. It’s going to rain for a few days. I probably need to get out of the house and away from the computer for a while, too.”

Shadow lifted his head and replied to her with the grumbling *woo* sound that was common for his breed.

She did need a break. It had been a long week filled with highs and lows, frustrations and breakthroughs. As a writer, she had a lot of times like this. It was the creative process. But it could give you a headache staring at the computer for hours on end, lost in another world that was completely under your control and yet totally uncooperative at the same time.

If her older sister, Rain, were here, she would’ve nudged Willow at some point and thrust a plate of food in front of her. She’d done that all through college as Willow studied and ignored her basic needs. “Coffee is not a food group,” Rain always said.

Willow thought of that every time she poured another cup instead of fooling with making herself something real to eat. It wasn’t as though she didn’t eat at all. Her rear end would argue otherwise. But she did live entirely on easy-to-prepare foods she could get in bulk at the warehouse store when she bothered to take the ferry to Victoria or Seattle. She kept a stash of protein bars, enough cans of soup and boxes of crackers to survive a nuclear winter, industrial-size jars of peanut butter and jelly, and an assortment of breakfast cereals that would make any six-year-old proud.

Sure, her sister would argue that they’d grown up

as vegans and her diet was seriously lacking in fresh vegetables and fruits. Rain could keep her lecturing for her two-year-old son, Joey, and leave Willow out of it. If cancer hadn't succeeded in killing her, protein bars and coffee surely wouldn't.

She took the last sip of her coffee and set it aside. "You ready to go?" she asked Shadow.

Her dog danced excitedly around the deck and howled at her. He was always ready for a walk.

"Okay, okay. Let me get my jacket."

Willow opened the back door and slipped into the jacket she'd thrown over the kitchen chair. She put her keys, phone and a canister of bear repellent in her coat pockets, then went back outside where Shadow was waiting.

"Are we headed to the beach today?" she asked as they went down the steps of the deck and into the wooded area behind her house.

Shadow's fluffy curled tail disappeared ahead of her into the trees. He liked to roam free but he didn't go too far. He was too protective of Willow to leave her alone for long. She had gotten him as a puppy not long after she'd moved to the island. She'd finished her last cancer treatment in Seattle a year ago and was keen to get as far away from all of that as she could. Rain had worried about her being alone, so Willow silenced her sister's concerns with the blue-eyed ball of fur.

With a new house and a new puppy, Willow had started her new life here. Shadow had been by her side ever since then. He could read her moods and feelings like a book, forcing her to take a break when she needed one. He wasn't a trained therapy dog, but he had become so much more than just a pet to her.

The woods were very active this morning. The birds in the trees squawked loudly, probably anticipating the weather. She pressed through across the spongy forest floor, stepping over fallen trees and following the makeshift trail she and Shadow had worn into the dirt on their way to the beach.

As she reached the tree line, Shadow greeted her with a loud howl. He'd found something on the beach he was excited about. That could be anything from a fish he'd hauled out of the shallows, the perfect throwing stick or something dead and decaying, which was endlessly fascinating to him for some reason.

"What is it, fuzzy butt?" she asked.

He pranced about and then shot off across the beach toward his prize. She squinted her eyes to try and see if she could spy it in the distance. There was definitely something out there. It was bigger than a fish and not moving. Maybe a seal. They didn't get many of them here, but they did show up from time to time. She walked along the shoreline until the shape became clearer and she realized what she was looking at.

It was a body.

Willow ran across the beach until she got close enough to see it was the figure of a man slumped back over a piece of driftwood. He seemed to be in his thirties or so with golden blond hair and a strong jaw—features that clearly highlighted his handsomeness—but he'd obviously had a bad night. He was beaten and battered with dirty and torn clothing, and there was a large knot on his forehead that had dripped blood down the side of his face.

It was like seeing some angel fallen to earth, cast out of the heavens. His golden curls and perfect skin gave him a cherubic appearance like an old Renaissance painting.

But this man was real. And possibly still alive. There was a bit of color in his cheeks and she could see the faint rising and falling of his chest. She knelt down beside him and reached out to touch his throat. His pulse thumped against her fingertips and she sighed in relief. "Sir?" she asked, but he didn't stir.

Not quite willing to pull her hand away, she reached up to cup his cheek and feel the rough stubble of his beard against her palm. She wasn't inclined to caress strangers—especially ones who looked like they'd been beaten and dumped on a beach by some thugs—but she couldn't stop herself.

When was the last time she'd touched a man? Hugging her two-year-old nephew and brother-in-law, Steve, didn't count. Neither did the poking and prodding from the doctors and nurses at the hospital. Honestly, she didn't really know. Too long.

Shadow sniffed at the man's clothing with enthusiasm, eventually licking the man's face and howling loudly with excitement. That did the trick. The man started at the noise, then winced. Willow jerked her hand away as he groaned loudly and brought a hand up to his bleeding head.

"Damn," he muttered under his breath as his eyes fluttered open.

Willow sat back on her heels and sucked in a ragged breath as the man turned and looked at her. Despite the shape he was in, the man was beautiful, and more so now that he was awake. His large dark brown eyes were fringed with thick lashes any woman would kill for. His gaze ran over her for a moment and a smile curled his full lips, revealing a dimple in one cheek. "Well, hello there, beautiful," he said in the slurred speech of a sleepy drunk. He shifted his weight and groaned again in pain.

"Don't move," she said, ignoring the injured man's flattery and reaching out to press him back to where he was lying. He obviously wasn't in good condition if he thought she was beautiful. She wore no makeup and her hair was a mess under the cap she'd tugged on before she left. "You're hurt pretty badly."

"Don't I know it," he replied with a dry chuckle despite the obvious pain. He looked away from Willow and scanned the beach around him with a frown of confusion lining his forehead. He stopped when he found himself face-to-face with the interested, but patiently waiting, Shadow. The dog was sitting beside him panting heavily, with his pink tongue hanging out of the side of his goofy doggy grin.

"I'm on a beach," he said matter-of-factly.

"Yes, you are."

"With a wolf," he added, as he studied the dog and his large, exposed canines warily.

"Technically he's a wolf dog. Mostly husky, though. He won't bother you unless you mess with me."

"Noted," the man murmured and turned back to look at her. "I'd probably bite any man that messed with you, too."

Willow winced and reached out to examine his head wound. It must be worse than it looked for him to talk like that. "Can you tell me how you got out here?"

He shook his head gently. "I wish I knew. I don't even know where *here* is. What beach am I on?"

"You're on Shaw Island," Willow explained. "Off the coast of Washington State."

"Huh," he said thoughtfully. He wrapped his arm over his ribs and pushed himself up from the sand and rocks until he was sitting upright. "I've never hurt so badly in my whole life. My ribs feel like someone has taken a free shot at me with a baseball bat."

"Is that what happened?" Willow asked. Her island wasn't exactly an epicenter of hard crime. With less than three hundred year-round residents, you couldn't get away with much. The last newsworthy occurrence on the island had involved a rebellious teenager and a joyride in the sheriff deputy's car. But nothing violent that she knew of.

"I have no idea."

Willow frowned. She couldn't understand how a guy could be in this kind of shape but have no clue how he'd gotten that way or where he even was. He must've hit his head pretty hard. "What's your name? Maybe I could call someone for you."

The man opened his mouth to answer and then stopped with a puzzled expression on his face. "I don't know that, either," he admitted.

Maybe he had a concussion. What was she supposed to do for that? Ask questions? "Do you know what day it is?"

"Not a clue."

"Do you know what two times two equals?"

"Four," he answered without hesitation and then shook his head. "I don't get it. I know my alphabet and who the president is. How to tie my shoe… I think. But anything about myself or what happened to me seems just out of my reach."

Willow nodded. "I think we need to get you to a doctor."

A large crack of lightning lit up the sky over the water, followed by a deep rumble of thunder. They also needed to hurry before they got caught in the incoming storm. This beach wasn't accessible by road, so their best shot was to go back to her place.

"Do you think you can stand?" she asked. "My house isn't very far away. If we can get back there, I can call someone to come look at you. We don't have a hospital here or I'd take you there instead."

"I'm not sure, but we can try."

Willow put one of the man's arms over her shoulder and helped slowly hoist him to his feet. He continued to lean heavily on her as they made their way down the beach together. Shadow trotted happily beside them with a piece of driftwood in his mouth.

They had to take their time, but they reached her back deck just as the first few drops of water fell on their heads. Willow unlocked the door and brought him inside, forcing Shadow to leave his prize outside before he could come in.

She helped him to the living room and over to her recliner. The chair had been a lifesaver on long nights when chemotherapy or surgery pains kept her awake and uncomfortable. "Let's put you here," she said.

He lowered gently into the old, squeaky recliner and sighed in contentment. "I think this is the most comfortable chair in the whole world."

"How do you know?" Willow asked, curiously. "You don't even know your own name."

"I *know*," he insisted. "I know a good chair when I sit in one."

Willow shook her head and pulled her phone out of her pocket. "I'm going to call the local doctor and see if he can come by."

"Okay," he said. "I'm not going anywhere."

"Let me just check one last thing..."

The only doctor living on Shaw Island—a retiree who went by Doc—pressed his fingers against his rib cage, and it was like daggers exploding in his chest. He jerked away and made an involuntary screech like an injured animal as tears welled in his eyes.

"Yeah, if they aren't broken, they're at least badly bruised." The older man narrowed his gaze at him and nodded. "Two, probably three of your ribs are cracked is my guess without an X-ray to look at."

He groaned and clutched his abused chest with his hand. "I could've told you that without the jabbing."

"Do they need to be wrapped or something?"

He turned his attention to the woman who'd saved him as she spoke up. She'd told him her name was Willow once she returned after calling the doctor. He didn't think she looked like a Willow. She was very thin, waif-like in figure, with short, dirty blond hair and large, dark brown eyes. She was intriguing to look at, with thick eyelashes and faint freckles across her cheeks. She just didn't look like a Willow to him. Then again, he didn't know what he thought someone named Willow should look like.

"No, it's best to just leave them be," Doc explained. "The muscles of the chest are strong enough to hold the bones in place until they heal. They're not at a risk of puncturing his lungs or anything serious. Really, it's a good break to have."

He flinched at the doctor's words. "Are you serious?"

"Well, it won't feel great at first," Doc said with a small chuckle. "No, you're going to feel like you're being stabbed every time you try to move for two or three days. The pain medicine will help, but you'll do good to just lie still. But then, surprisingly, you'll wake up one morning and be mostly okay. Just a little sore. Ribs are funny that way."

"I'm not laughing," he quipped.

"Good," Doc said with a serious expression. "It'll hurt like hell if you do." He turned to Willow. "I thought I might call Ted and see if he had room at his place to take our John Doe in until we can get him transported to the mainland."

As if on cue, a large flash of lightning lit the picture window and the corresponding rumble of thunder shook the walls of the house a moment later.

"He may be stuck here a few days. It's supposed to be a hell of a storm. Early in the season for it, too."

"Don't bother Ted. He has enough going on with Linda sick. I'll keep him here. I have a guest room he can stay in until we can get him to a hospital."

He watched Doc frown at him with concern.

"I don't like the idea of leaving you here alone with a stranger," the doctor said to Willow.

"What's he going to do to me? He can barely lift an arm without crying. I'll be fine. I have Shadow and a shotgun, and if he doesn't have all the sense knocked out of him, he'll stay in bed and behave." Willow turned to look at him. "Are you going to give me any trouble?"

He started to shake his head and winced. Every movement seemed to send a painful shock wave through his whole body. “No, ma’am. I’ll be a saint. A very still, very cautious saint.”

“See?” She turned back to Doc. “It will be fine. I’ve faced more dangerous things in my life than John Doe here.”

“Okay, but I’ll be checking in regularly just in case.” Doc peeled off a prescription from his pad and handed it to Willow. “This is for some pain medication, muscle relaxants and an antibiotic to keep his cuts from getting infected. I put it under your name since he doesn’t have one.”

She looked up from the pad and seemed to eye him warily. “What about his head? He says he doesn’t remember anything.”

Doc walked back over to where he was sitting and eyed the lump on his head. It felt like he had an egg trying to break through his forehead. “He took quite a blow to the head. But aside from the amnesia, he seems coherent. I’m no expert on head injuries like this, but I’m confident that once the swelling goes down, he’ll remember who he is and how he ended up on our little island. In the meantime, though, you’ll need to ice it on and off, and may not want to leave him alone just in case he passes out and falls.”

The wind whistled loudly past Willow’s home, announcing the storm was getting closer. “I’m going to head on out,” Doc announced. “I need to put some plywood over my front windows. You’ve probably got enough time to run to the general store and get these scrips filled before the worst of the storm comes ashore. An hour at the most.”

Willow nodded and walked the doctor out. When she came back into the living room, she eyed him in the chair.

"I'm going to run to the store and get your medications. I won't be gone long. I'm leaving you here with Shadow."

He looked over at the dog. It was deceptively fluffy, hiding big blue eyes and even bigger teeth. It had lain on the hardwood floors and watched him since he arrived. No growling or anything. But the husky watched, and he got the distinct impression that Shadow didn't care for him as much now that he was in his home with his mama.

"Can I go with you?"

She narrowed her eyes at him. "That's probably a bad idea. The road isn't paved on my property and you're going to get jostled around."

"That's okay." He closed his eyes and took a deep breath before forcing himself up out of the chair. "I want to go."

Willow shrugged. "Okay. We'll get some supplies and some clothes for you while Eddie fills these." She held up the prescriptions in her hand before shoving them into a messenger bag and pulling out her keys.

They went outside together where she had a big red pickup truck waiting. It had a step and a handle he used to pull himself up and into the seat. She drove as slowly and carefully as she could on the way to the store, but he felt every divot in the road as they went. He probably should've stayed in the recliner with the wolf dog, but he didn't want to be alone. For some reason, the thought of Willow leaving his sight bothered him. She was his savior, and he was going to stick to her side until he didn't need saving any longer.

To distract himself from the pain, he turned his focus from the road to Willow. He studied the interesting angles and curves of her face as she watched the road…the intricate shell of her ear with the single diamond stud piercing in its lobe… Anything was better than thinking about the pain.

The truck finally met with what seemed like a main, paved highway, to his relief. They'd seemed to be out in the middle of nowhere up until this point. Without the bumps torturing him, he was able to entertain other thoughts—like what a woman like her was doing out here alone. She was young, attractive, self-sufficient, thoughtful…but alone. He was a mystery, but she seemed to be equally confusing.

"You need a name," she said.

"What?" he asked as her words jerked him from his thoughtful trance.

"A name. You don't look much like a John Doe," she said, probably making small talk to distract him during the drive. "But I need to call you something while you're around."

He supposed she was right. He needed a name and John didn't suit him at all. "I guess so. Until I get my memory back, we should pick a name to use. But which one? Most people don't get to choose their names."

Willow made a thoughtful sound as she gripped the steering wheel. "How about… Mark? Allen? Henry? When I was in high school I lived next door to a guy named Jeremy. He was pretty cool."

None of those fit at all. He knew instinctively. But the odds of landing on the right name were slim. They could flip through a baby book, even speak his actual name aloud, and with his head beat to hell, he probably wouldn't know it. "I guess it doesn't really matter. I'll let you pick since I'm in your capable hands. What do you want to call me, darling?"

Her gaze met his for a moment before she turned back to the road with a rosy blush on her cheeks. Apparently men didn't call her "darling" very often. The words had slid from his lips easily, as did the hint of a Southern accent he didn't know he had until that moment.

"Um...since none of those other names seemed to thrill you...what about instead of John, we call you Jack? You look like you could be a Jack."

He didn't hate that. It was simple and easy to remember. "I can live with Jack. Now, all I have to do is remind myself to answer to it."

"Jack it is," she said as she slowed and gingerly turned the truck into a small parking lot. "Now, let's hurry up here so we can get home, give you some pain medicine and get you out of those clothes."

Jack's brow went up suggestively on instinct. "If I wasn't in such rough shape, I'd take you up on that."

Her dark eyes got big as she turned off the truck. "Apparently Jack is a flirt," she said, climbing out.

Jack nodded and took off his own seat belt. He didn't know much about himself, but that seemed to be true enough. At the moment, flirting came easier than breathing. He wished everything else was as simple right now.

Two

Willow left her new patient to wander through the small general store while she headed straight for the pharmacy. There wasn't much trouble he could get into on his own in a place like this. Especially with the store's owner, Mrs. Hudson, watching over everything from her perch at the register.

At the back counter, as always, was Eddie McAlister, Shaw Island's only pharmacist. He was always polite and professional, even helping her with research for her books from time to time when she needed a nontraditional poison to kill off a character or some other medical assistance. As an author, she always wondered if he enjoyed knowing everything about the island residents' private medical matters. Most people, for example, had no idea about Willow's past medical history aside from Doc. It had all happened prior to her moving here. But Eddie knew. He took care of all her hormone replacements. Unless someone handled all their appointments and medical issues off the island or via mail order, Eddie knew.

Small-island life was just like that, she supposed. She'd traded anonymity and privacy for quiet when she moved out here from Seattle.

In her mind, she could easily devise a plot where a small-town pharmacist was murdered to cover up a secret only he was privy to. For a second, she could envision him sprawled out on the floor, papers and pills littering the ground all around him and a knife buried into his chest. *A Prescription for Murder.* Not bad, she thought.

"Afternoon, Willow. Heck of a storm heading this way."

She handed over the prescriptions Doc had written out and shook the disturbing images of Eddie's corpse from her mind. Occupational hazard. "Hey, Eddie. You guys closing up early?"

"Perhaps." He glanced down at the papers curiously and back at her. His weary eyes looked over her with a furrowed brow of concern. "Are you okay?"

"Me? Yes." She realized that the kind of medicine she was requesting wasn't the norm for her. Or for anyone who hadn't been in a car wreck or washed up on a beach. "Those aren't mine. Doc put them in my name, but they're for a John Doe that washed up on the beach. He's pretty banged up but in this weather, we can't get him to the mainland for a few days."

Eddie eyed the prescriptions and then looked out into the general store at the only other person shopping. Willow followed his glance to the tall, blond man who was studying a Snickers bar as though he'd uncovered the holy grail.

"He's had a bump on the head and doesn't know who he is. Doc took a look at him and thinks he may have cracked a few ribs, too. You can put Jack or John Doe on the label if you need to. I know this isn't exactly a normal situation. I'll pay cash for his medicines. I don't know if he has insurance or not."

He looked like he did. Or if he didn't have it, he just paid cash for any medical expenses because he could. Her shipwrecked visitor didn't exactly look like a homeless drifter. The main character of all her books, Amelia Hayes, would note those details about him immediately. Yes, his suit needed to be burned. It was ripped beyond repair, soaked with seawater and crusted with dirt and blood. There were bits of sand and wood stuck to the fabric here and there, likely from his beach nap. But beneath all that, it was a nice suit. When Jack had gingerly slipped out of the suit coat for Doc's examination, she noticed the tag was for Brioni.

A quick Google search on her phone during his exam had uncovered that the custom-tailored Italian suits started at over six grand and went up from there.

Willow was a successful mystery writer. Amelia's Mysteries did well for her. But she estimated her entire wardrobe, shoes included, had cost less than his jacket alone. Her heroine would have a field day trying to determine who this mysterious man really was. *The Case of the Amicable Amnesiac*? Meh. She'd give that some more thought.

Eddie continued to watch Jack as he wandered through the store like he'd never been in one before.

He kept picking up things and studying them before putting them back with a visible wince of pain. "Sure thing," Eddie said at last. "These aren't too expensive without insurance, anyway. It will just take me a few minutes to pull it together."

"Thanks, Eddie. Just give me a shout when it's ready." Willow was eager to return to Jack. She told herself it was because she was worried about him being alone with his head injury. But she also found she just liked being around him. Yes, he was handsome and a bit of a shameless flirt, but she liked his smile and his sense of humor. She wasn't sure what he had been through, exactly, before he showed up in her life, but she wanted to do what she could to help him.

"Washed up on the beach, you say?" Eddie, too, seemed entranced by their unusual visitor. Jack had a commanding presence that demanded it of others, somehow. That or he just stood out like a sore thumb on her boring little island.

"Perhaps. We're not entirely sure. He couldn't have just fallen from the sky."

"Or maybe he did," Eddie said with a conspiratorial wink. "If anyone can figure it out, it's our resident mystery writer. Hey, maybe you can use this in one of your books."

Willow chuckled and turned away from the counter. "You never know," she said as she made her way over to Jack. He was looking at a display of sweatshirts for tourists that said San Juan Islands with a sailboat on the front. There weren't a lot of choices for clothes here, just a few things people might need at the beach or as a souvenir, so he would probably go home with one of those today.

She eyed his broad shoulders and tapered waist. "What size do you think you'll need?"

Jack shrugged. "I don't know."

Willow pulled a sweatshirt from the wall and held it up to him without letting it get defiled by the state of his current clothes. "This looks about right. It's a men's large." She threw the sweatshirt, a T-shirt with a similar imprint, a two-pack of boxer shorts, a pair of jogging shorts and some black sweatpants over her arm. "None of this is very fashionable, but it will have to do for now."

"I'll just be glad to get out of this suit. The wool is starting to get itchy."

"Did you see anything else you wanted? I noticed you looking at the candy earlier."

Jack smiled and shook his head. "I don't need any candy." He bit at his bottom lip for a minute and then laughed. "It's just…and it will sound crazy…but I feel like I've never been in a store like this in my life."

"You mean a little shop like this?"

"No, I mean, like a grocery store. I've walked up and down the aisles looking at dish soap and bags of chips. And while the products themselves seem familiar enough, the surroundings are just completely alien."

"I doubt many people could make it to your age without going into a grocery store. It's probably just the bump on your head. Those memories are locked away with your name and how you got here."

Jack looked at her and nodded, although he seemed unconvinced. "It's bizarre." He reached out for a bottle of soda from the nearby refrigerated case. "I know exactly what this tastes like. I feel like I've had it a hundred times. All these brands are familiar when I see them. I can recall the taste of a Snickers. I know that I prefer them to a Milky Way if given the choice. But other things I should know are just out of my grasp."

"That sounds like it would be very frustrating. Hopefully once the swelling goes down, your memory will return."

"Hopefully."

"You'll also need toiletries," she said and grabbed a nearby shopping basket to carry their purchases. He followed her to the aisle of the shop with soap and other items. "You need it all, so pick out whatever you like."

She watched him look over his choices, selecting a toothbrush and a comb fairly easily. After that, he chose soap, toothpaste and deodorant. "This isn't the right scent, but it will work. How is it I know that I wear Arctic Chill scented deodorant, not Mountain Breeze?"

She shook her head. "Memory is a funny thing. It's why I've never used amnesia in any of my books. It has always seemed an odd thing to me. How can you forget everything, but still remember English? Or how to count? The difference between a cat and a dog? How to walk or even feed yourself? How can you injure yourself in such a way that you can't recall the basic facts of your life and the essence of who you are, but the rest of your knowledge remains? It always seemed like a convenient plot device. Too convenient."

"I assure you this is anything but convenient." Jack grabbed a small bottle of two-in-one shampoo and conditioner. "This should be enough. I'll be happy to get the sand and stink off of me." As he reached to put the bottle in the basket, he winced and clutched his side.

"I think we're done here. Go sit in the truck and I'll be out in a few minutes. Soon we can get some medicine into you and you can finally clean up and get some rest."

Jack seemed hesitant to leave her with all the things he needed.

"Unless you'd rather pay?" she said with a smile. She knew he didn't have a wallet, ID or any money on him.

"Funny girl," he said. "Keep the receipts. Once I get my memory back, I intend to repay you for this fine sweatshirt and all your other kindness."

Willow put the keys in his hand. "We'll run you a tab. Now go get in the truck."

"You want me to what?"

Jack wished he had a camera to capture the look on Willow's face. For a woman who kept a wolf hybrid as a pet and could handle a shotgun, she seemed downright terrified by what he'd just asked her.

"I wouldn't ask you this under normal circumstances, of course, but I need help."

Willow stood frozen like a deer in the headlights. But as the truth of his words became evident, he saw her relax a bit. "I suppose you're right."

"Normally when I ask a woman to help me take off my clothes, I buy her dinner first. Or I'd like to think that I would. But I'm afraid I've misplaced my wallet."

Jack stood with his dress shirt and pants unbuttoned, but at that point, he'd run into a snag. He simply couldn't move the way he needed in order to remove his clothing. The pain pills and muscle relaxants were working their way through his system, along with the tomato soup and grilled cheese she'd fed him for dinner, but he needed to get out of these clothes and take a bath. He couldn't wait for the meds to kick in. So he'd asked for her help. He got the feeling he was used to a warmer response from women than he got from Willow.

"Just stand as still as you can," she said as she came around behind him. "I'll do the moving. You be a mannequin."

"Yes, ma'am."

He could feel her warm breath on the back of his neck as she leaned in to peel the shirt from his shoulders. He bit back a wince of pain as she worked the ruined silk shirt down his arms, then breathed a shallow sigh of relief as she tossed it to the floor.

"The pants should be easier," he said.

"Maybe for you," she muttered and gently tugged the trousers down his narrow hips.

He held as still as he could, grasping his ribs protectively. But through the rustle of the fabric, he thought he heard a soft intake of breath. It wasn't him. He was holding his breath to keep from groaning or drawing in the scent of Willow while she was so close. So it had to be her. He looked over his shoulder and noticed her quick assessment of his rear end before casting her gaze to the floor.

He lifted one leg, then the other, to step out of the pants, leaving him in nothing but a pair of fire-engine red Calvin Klein boxer briefs. He looked at his reflection in the bathroom mirror and had to agree with her assessment of his physique. He did have a nice ass. That was good to know. In fact, he had a nice everything. He was in no condition to preen and flex in front of the mirror, but he really wanted to.

Jack had a hard body. He was tan, lean and muscular with broad shoulders and strong arms. His thighs were solid and his calves were hard as rocks. He looked like he took care of himself. Maybe rock climbed or something. The view was only marred by ugly purple-black bruises and bright red abrasions that spread across his skin. He supposed it was weird to admire himself in the mirror, but as far as he was concerned, he'd never seen himself before. Anything could've been hiding beneath that suit.

The thought led him to look at his face at last, and there, he winced again. Not that he was uglier than he expected—far from it—but he was in rough shape. The ache in his head wasn't nearly as bad as it looked, thankfully. But it certainly seemed like the kind of injury that could wipe the Etch A Sketch of his brain clean. He didn't know what he'd hit his forehead on—maybe a ship railing before or while falling overboard—but he'd gone down hard.

"I think I'm probably pretty hot when I haven't lost a fight with a two-by-four."

Willow sat back on her heels and watched him as he admired his own reflection in the mirror. "Careful, Narcissus, or you'll drown looking at yourself."

She was a sassy one, his savior. He liked that about her. She seemed like the kind who could match his mouth when the situation called for it. "Hey, I didn't know what I looked like until now. We've been too busy worrying about other stuff like broken bones and medicine."

"I'm sorry," she said, climbing to her feet. "I should've told you straight away that you were hot. You needed to know that."

He could tell by her flat tone that she was mocking him. He was okay with that, too. "It certainly contributes to my overall morale. So does knowing I'm one pair of underwear away from soaking in a hot bath."

Jack eyed the huge copper soaking tub that was in the corner of her bathroom. It looked divine. And considering that every inch of his body from the hairs on his head to his toenails ached, it was just what he needed. But when he didn't make a move to take off his boxer briefs, he saw Willow stand up abruptly out of the corner of his eye.

"You don't think you can…?" She hesitated. When he looked at her, her cheeks were nearly as red as his underpants.

He wasn't quite sure what to think of his rescuer. She was old enough to have seen a man naked, practical enough to understand why it had to be done, but she seemed very uncomfortable by the prospect. "I can't really bend over, but I'll try. You seem miserable enough as it is."

She audibly sighed in relief. "I'll run the bath. I have some lavender Epsom salts I'll add to it that will help with the aches and pains."

With her back turned and the sound of rushing water filling the room, Jack was able to wiggle out of his shorts and kick them over with the rest of his clothes. They might be salvageable, unlike the suit. He walked over to the fluffy white towel she'd placed on the counter and wrapped it around his waist. He didn't want her to turn around and get an eyeful of what he had to offer—which was also a pleasant addition to his overall package and completely unscathed by the accident.

His interest was piqued by a lovely scent that filled the warm air of the bathroom. "Did you say that was lavender?"

"Yes," she said without turning around.

"It's very nice."

"I like it." Willow shut off the water and tested it with her hand. "It should be ready. Enjoy your bath." She turned, making a beeline for the door.

"Wait. I can't get in there by myself. And Doc said I shouldn't be left alone."

She stopped short with her hand on the doorknob. He didn't hear her curse aloud, but he was pretty certain she'd said some choice words in her head.

"I'm sorry. Really, I am. I take no pleasure in torturing you like this."

"It's not—" she started to argue and stopped short. "It's fine."

"I'm not asking for a sponge bath or anything. If you can just help me get in and out—do it with your eyes closed if you want—that's all I need. I'll shower after this, I promise. But Doc said a bath tonight would be good."

"I know. I heard him. I just wasn't thinking about what that meant." Willow walked reluctantly over to the bathtub and held out her hands. "Come on, let's get you in here."

She braced him as he lifted one leg, then the other, into the tub. "Don't look, Ethel," he quipped, tugging the towel off and putting it aside.

"There's not going to be a way to do this without it hurting, so I say do it quickly."

She was right. Jack took a deep breath and lowered himself into the tub. A bolt of pain shot through his chest, wrestling a groan from his lips and bringing the shimmer of tears to his eyes. He kept his eyelids tightly shut as he reached the bottom of the tub. Stretching his legs out, he sat back and sighed.

"Here." Willow offered a rolled-up towel to put behind his neck.

He accepted the towel and let himself relax into the water. Getting in hadn't been fun, but the scalding hot water felt amazing. Jack closed his eyes and laid his head back. "Thank you," he said.

"It wasn't so bad," she said.

"Not just for this. Thank you for everything. Food, clothes, shelter, medicine… You've been beyond kind to me, and I'm a stranger. You could've just called the cops or the coast guard and got rid of me." A loud rumble of thunder outside made the bathroom windows rattle as he spoke.

"Anyone would've done this under the circumstances," Willow said as she walked to the other side of the bathroom and pulled out her vanity chair to sit at a safe distance. "You have nowhere to go and if this storm is as bad as they say it might be, the coast guard has other things to worry about. I have the room and the time to do it, so I'm happy to."

"You said you were a writer earlier. What do you write? Would I have heard of you?"

Willow's nose wrinkled delicately as she shook her head. "I doubt it, even if you didn't have amnesia. I'm a cozy mystery writer. I've published about thirty books since the start of my career. I've done pretty well for myself, but I'm no household name by any stretch."

"What is a cozy mystery?" he asked. As much as he

wanted to just close his eyes and drift away on a cloud of Percocet, he knew he needed to stay focused and conscious until he was out of the tub. She didn't need him drowning in her bathroom. So he would ask her questions to stay awake. Besides, it was easy enough to show an interest in Willow. She seemed like the kind of woman who had a variety of layers. He had the urge to peel a few of them back and see what was underneath. If he felt better, he'd start with the cardigan she'd pulled on.

"It's a subgenre of mystery with an amateur detective that solves crimes. Even though there are murders, they're not too gory and we leave out any details that could be a turnoff for our readers. Think of *Murder, She Wrote*, from back in the eighties. Those were classic cozy murder mysteries."

The name of the show was familiar to him. He could remember watching it with someone as a kid, but he didn't know who. It was incredibly frustrating having this head injury. "I always wondered if that old lady wasn't behind the murders somehow. No matter where she went, someone died."

Willow smiled. "You start to wonder after a few dozen people die, right?"

"So you live out on this little island, just you and your dog, and write books about killing people."

She thought about it for a minute and eventually shrugged. "Basically."

He chuckled for a moment, stopping short when the movement hurt his ribs again. "I'm not sure of much, Willow Bates, but I'm pretty sure you're not like other women I've known."

The light in her brown eyes faded. "No," she said,

looking down at the tile floor of her bathroom. "I'm not. I never have been."

Jack's brow furrowed in concern at her response. "I'm not saying that's a bad thing. It's a good thing."

"Is it?" she asked. "Being different hasn't benefited me much over the years. It's actually been pretty lonely."

There was a sadness in Willow's expression as she spoke, and it bothered him. He had plenty of his own troubles at the moment, maybe even more than he knew with his memory failing. But somehow he felt like the best way to repay her kindness was to make her smile. It seemed like an awkward expression on her face when she tried—more like she was baring her teeth to a possible predator. The blank neutrality of her sadness appeared far more comfortable for her, judging by the well-worn frown lines between her eyebrows.

She deserved to smile and really mean it. It lit up her whole face in a way that made her even more striking in appearance. She already had a penetrating gaze, high, prominent cheekbones and full, pouty lips. Her short pixie haircut just accentuated her features and heart-shaped face. A genuine smile would take her from an angst-filled runway model to a radiant cosmetics model in a glossy magazine.

"It is absolutely a good thing to be different," Jack insisted. "Fitting in is boring. There's nothing special about doing and acting like everyone else. I don't think I'd be very interested in a woman that was just a cardboard cutout of what magazines and television shows said she should be."

That brought a real smile, albeit a small one, to her face. "My mother used to say that after she made me, she broke the mold. I would joke that it was because she couldn't handle more than one daughter like me."

"No, not at all," Jack responded with the sincerest expression on his face he could muster. "I'm certain she meant that you're a one-of-a-kind person. And to the right collector, that makes you priceless."

Three

"There," Willow said with a heavy sigh of relief as she tugged down his new shirt. At last, she wasn't alone in the house with the sexiest naked man she'd ever laid eyes on. It was bad enough that he was hard bodied and not particularly shy. But when he started complimenting her, talking about her like she was some rare gift or something, she didn't know what to think. A man had never said anything like that to her. Of course, Jack also had significant head trauma and narcotics in his system. That was more likely to be the cause of his flattery.

It had taken some more careful maneuvering, but Jack was finally bathed and dressed, and now she could suppress whatever wicked thoughts had crossed her mind during his bath and move on with her evening.

Jack looked down at the brand-new San Juan Islands T-shirt and jogging shorts he was attired in and smiled as widely as if he'd just put on a new designer suit. "They fit."

"They're a little big," she noted. He had broad shoulders, but a thinner, runner's physique, which meant he probably spent a lot of time and money getting his clothes perfectly tailored to fit correctly. "But good enough for you to sleep in. Let's go get you settled into the guest room. I hope it will suit you."

"I don't know if it's the medicine or the bath," he said as he followed her down the hallway. "Maybe both…but I feel like I could lie on a bed of nails and still sleep like a baby tonight."

"That's good. I doubt my guest bed is the greatest bed in the world. It didn't make sense to pay a fortune for something that's never used. In fact, no one has ever slept on it before. You're the first actual visitor I've had since I moved to the island."

Willow opened the door to the smallest bedroom, which she'd set aside for the guests she never had. She supposed she did it out of a sense of expectation her mother had instilled in her as a child. She had lived on a commune with her parents, who shared everything they had. When they divorced and her mom moved to Seattle with her and her sister, she was adamant they had a place with room for guests. It was just the way things were done.

So when Willow looked for a house on the islands, she'd chosen one with three bedrooms. One was the master, one was her office and naturally one should be ready for a guest if she ever had one. She'd lived on this island for over a year now and she'd put sheets on the bed for the first time while he was eating his grilled cheese sandwich.

Who was going to visit her? She hadn't been exaggerating when she said she led a pretty lonely life. Her father had vanished. Her mother and grandmother had both passed away. Her sister had her hands full with her husband and a toddler. Her nephew was too young to visit his aunt without his parents in tow. The Bates sisters didn't have any other family left. At least that Willow knew about. She'd lost touch with most of the friends she'd made in school. Those she did speak to were strictly social media acquaintances, not the kind who would visit your home.

Here on Shaw Island, it was just Willow and Shadow, and had been for a while now.

She went ahead of him into the room and pulled back the fluffy down comforter and sheets. The bedroom decor she'd chosen was as cheerful as she could think to buy. The room had white wood furniture and the comforter was yellow with pale pink roses on it. At the store, it had seemed like the perfect little ray of sunshine for a place that usually had gray skies and rain. Of course, it didn't suit her very masculine guest at all, but he didn't seem to mind.

"Considering I slept on a beach last night with a log for a pillow, this will be great, I'm sure."

He slowly limped past her and lowered himself gingerly onto the bed. Jack eased one leg, then the other, under the blankets and lay back against the pillows with a wince and a groan. "It's wonderful," he said. "The most comfortable bed I ever remember having slept in before."

Willow smirked at his cheeky response. For a guy with no memory, he had a pretty good attitude about the whole thing. She couldn't imagine being so laid-back about the whole situation if it were her. Then again, what could he do about it? Especially when he was trapped on this tiny island in a storm?

She watched him settle in and pull up the blankets with a sigh. "I'm going to go get you a glass of water for your night pills," she said.

She disappeared from the room and went into the kitchen. There, she found Shadow sprawled out across the tile floor, keeping cool while he napped. For him, sixty degrees was warm. And with the house thermostat set at seventy, it was downright stifling for his bristly double coat. He lifted his head to watch her as she stepped over him and got a glass to fill at the refrigerator dispenser. Disinterested, he laid his head back down and returned to his nap.

"Don't get too comfortable," she said. "Once I get our guest settled, you've got to go outside to do your business and I've got to get some writing done. With my latest deadline schedule, I can't afford to lose a whole day of work because some shipwrecked amnesiac derailed my afternoon."

One ice-blue eye watched her as he listened, then he grumbled back at her in the way that only huskies would do. She hadn't deliberately chosen a breed that would talk back, but it did help with the loneliness sometimes. Unless he was being sassy, like now.

"I don't want to hear it. Rain or no rain, you're going out. It's only going to get worse later."

Willow stepped back over her dog and returned to the guest room. There, she found her patient was already asleep. He was sprawled out on his back, propped up by a couple pillows and softly snoring. One arm was draped protectively over his ribs and the other was limp at his side.

She put the glass of water on the nightstand beside the bottles of medication he would have to take in a few more hours. She knew she should turn off the light and leave him to get his rest, but she was drawn in by the rhythmic sound of his breathing. She watched him for a moment as she had that morning on the beach. His face was even more beautiful now with the dirt and blood washed away. His thick golden eyelashes rested on his cheeks, which were rosy once again. If it wasn't for the bandage across his forehead, you wouldn't even know he'd probably just lived through one of the worst experiences of his life. In fact, he looked like she could lean down, kiss him, and he would awaken from whatever evil curse a witch had put on him.

With a sigh, Willow turned off the lamp and left the room. She needed to stop listening to those folklore and fairy-tale podcasts. Her visitor was no secret prince under the spell of a wicked queen. He could be a high-end drug dealer who'd gotten thrown overboard when a deal went wrong on some cartel's yacht. Or a partying playboy who'd drunk too much and fell off his own boat. Either way, nice boys didn't wash up on the beach with amnesia. She'd written enough mystery novels to know that much.

Willow forced Shadow outside for a potty break, standing stoically on the back deck in her raincoat and watching the sky. The rain wasn't falling very hard yet, but she knew it was coming. The inky black of the sky was marred with a swirling gray mass of clouds that would periodically light up with a flash of lightning a few miles offshore. The latest weather reports had the worst of it hitting Shaw Island around two in the morning.

While she waited, she walked along the back of the house, closing and latching the shutters to protect all the windows. By the time she was finished, Shadow was back on the deck, his white paws brown with mud.

She cleaned him up, dried him off and then they both returned to her office to settle in for some late-night writing. She sat down at her desk and turned on her laptop. Shadow curled up on his plush dog pillow and covered his face with his bushy tail to block out the light of the computer so he could sleep.

Willow opened up the file for her latest manuscript. She read over the last few pages she'd written to orient herself and prepared to start where she'd left off. But as her fingers met the keys, she found her heart and her head were not in the mood to write. Not tonight. She had too much real life on her mind for a change.

The mystery of Jack Doe was at the forefront of her thoughts, not who had killed the town's librarian with a letter opener during the Halloween festival. The book would have to wait. She sat back in her chair, frustrated, and stared at the screen without really seeing any of the words.

Who was this man who had crash-landed in her life today? He was handsome and rich, if his clothes were any indication. He could be some Seattle corporate guy who'd fallen overboard at some business affair on the company ship. Or the lover of a rich married woman who'd had to jump into the sea when her husband showed up in his helicopter. No matter what, he didn't belong on Shaw Island, so how else could he have appeared on her beach? A man like Jack hadn't simply fallen from the sky.

Or had he? Eddie had made the suggestion and said that she could figure it out even if no one else could.

Willow frowned and slammed shut her laptop. She was wasting brain cells on this. Chances were his memory would come back at any time and his story would be completely sensible and benign without the slightest hint of high-stakes misconduct or television-like drama. And even if he wasn't some criminal or lowlife hiding from the people wanting to kill him—even if he was just a normal guy who'd had a freak accident—what did it matter to Willow?

Really, honestly, would it change anything about her life in the end?

The truth of the words hit her hard. He might not be an average guy, but she certainly wasn't an average woman, either. She was a hermit, a self-sequestered loner, and for good reason. She hid her hollow shell of a body away from the rest of the world, which might look at her and see she was different. It was easier that way. Easier to avoid the looks and questions of well-meaning strangers. Easier than explaining to people why she didn't get married and start a family with a nice boy like her sister. Easier than looking at people's expressions of pity when they learned the truth about her medical history.

Jack was charming. He had a good sense of humor. He had a dimple in one cheek when he smiled that made her kneecaps turn to butter. And if he hadn't basically landed in her lap, she never would've been exposed to a man like him. A walking, talking temptation like Jack simply didn't show up in a place like

Shaw Island, and that made her day-to-day life easier. It made distancing herself and suppressing any kind of emotions or attraction so much simpler.

But now he was here. Lying in the other room. She'd briefly glanced at his naked body when she'd undressed him today and had to turn away as her cheeks flamed with embarrassment and interest. The lure was dangling in front of her, so to speak, making it that much more difficult to be the stoic, chaste loner she'd decided to be.

Even then, there was no point in allowing herself to fantasize that they would ever have more than they had at this exact moment. Jack had a life somewhere. He might not know anything about it, but it was out there. A job, a family, maybe even a girlfriend or a wife. When his memory returned, he would want to go back to all that. And he should. This wasn't where he belonged.

And even if he was interested in her—and she seriously doubted that—it wouldn't last long. Jack was the kind who asked a lot of questions. Tonight, they'd been innocent enough, but eventually he might start wondering about her and why she lived the way she did. It wasn't an easy answer. Or a pleasant one to hear.

When he found out the truth, he would happily return to his old life and she wouldn't blame him. Whatever it was he'd left behind, it had to be more exciting and glamorous than what she had on this little island. His family and friends would be looking for him, and even if he didn't remember who he was, the news of the missing man would reach them eventually.

So Willow had to be careful not to get too attached to Mr. Jack Doe. He wouldn't be around for long.

* * *

Kat Steele paced the kitchen floor, rubbing her very pregnant belly while she walked. Finn was missing. He might even be dead. As complicated as her situation with twins Sawyer and Finn was, losing Finn wouldn't make it any easier. He was her brother-in-law, but he was also the father of her baby. Sawyer would absolutely step up to be the best dad he could be, but she didn't want him to do it because Finn was dead.

She heard her husband, Sawyer, hang up the phone and come into the kitchen. She stopped and looked at him, desperate for some news. "Have they found him?"

"They found the plane," Sawyer said with a somber expression on his face.

She knew this couldn't be easy on him. Possibly losing his brother was bad enough, but Finn was his identical twin. That had to be like losing part of himself, somehow. "And?"

"It crashed in the woods in the middle of nowhere in Washington near the Oregon border. No one else was injured, but they found four bodies in the wreckage."

"How many people were supposed to be on the jet?"

Sawyer didn't meet her gaze for a moment. "Four. Two pilots, a flight attendant and Finn. All four bodies were burned beyond recognition, so they can't positively identify any of them yet."

Kat groaned and lowered herself onto a nearby barstool. "So we won't know for sure until they look at the dental records, right?" She was grasping at hope for the sake of her husband and daughter. But she knew it wasn't likely to end well for them.

"Yes. They're transporting all the bodies back here

once the crash site has been released by the FAA. Then we'll know for certain."

Kat closed her eyes and bit back tears. Finn had been a massive pain in the ass nearly from birth. She'd almost married him, in some mistaken drive to build a proper family. But he had been working hard at becoming a better person lately for his daughter's sake. He didn't deserve to die like this. No one did.

She felt Sawyer's arms wrap around her and she gave in to the embrace. When he held her, it felt like the world couldn't get to her or her daughter. But even Sawyer's strong arms couldn't protect her from this grief. It only added fuel to it, knowing how much he must be hurting, too. How much the whole family must be grieving his loss…

"I want to say something, but I'm not sure how to do it. I can't say it to anyone but you. They'd think I was crazy, but I hope that you'll have an open mind."

Kat sat up and wiped the tears from her cheek. Sawyer was the serious twin, a man of few words, so if he had something to say, she would let him, even if it were crazy. "Tell me."

He glanced over her shoulder at the wall as he tried to figure out the words. "I don't want to upset you or get your hopes up. But I just… I feel like if Finn were dead, I would know it."

"What do you mean?"

Sawyer shook his head. "It's not like I'm saying we had some psychic twin connection or anything like some twins claim. We didn't. We've been opposites from the start. Mirror images of each other. But he doesn't feel dead. I feel like I would know if he were really gone."

Kat frowned. Sawyer had lived a life of privilege, never having to face real loss before. "Losing someone never feels the way you expect it to. When my parents were killed in an accident, it seemed like they were just on a trip and would be home anytime. Even after I identified their bodies, I kept waiting for a call or something from them. When it happens so suddenly, it feels harder to process. At least it was for me."

"I know what you're trying to say. And yes, when they identify him for certain, I'll give up the ghost. But I would be able to feel it if he were dead. I've had a headache since yesterday before the phone call. No medicine will touch it. I think Finn is hurt. Maybe he hit his head. But I believe he's alive."

Kat wasn't quite sure how to be supportive of her husband in the face of his denial. They'd found four bodies. Finn was more than likely amongst them. She hated it for him and his family. She hated it for her daughter, who would never get to meet the funny, carefree man who'd helped to make her. But hating reality didn't change it.

"You don't believe me." Sawyer's face was red with indignation. "I shared something very personal with you and you don't believe me."

Kat sighed. "I don't know, honey. I want to believe you. I want more than anything for Finn to be okay. Maybe he is and you're right." She reached out and stroked his arm. "We will know for sure, soon."

Jack expected to be awoken by the alarm reminding him to take more medication. Instead, he was roused from his sleep by a brilliant bolt of lightning hitting too close to them for comfort. The whole house immediately shook with the thunder, jerking him upright in bed. Thankfully, the rumble smothered his shout of pain as his rib cage protested the sudden and unanticipated movement.

Clutching his ribs, he lowered back against the pillows with a groan. He reached out for the lamp, hoping it would illuminate the clock and prove it was almost time for him to take his medicine. But the click of the knob yielded no results. The room remained dark. The clock face was dark. The house was silent, no hum of the heat or appliances in another room. He realized then that the storm must've knocked the power out.

The creak of the door opening sounded unusually loud in the quiet house. When he looked over, he saw the illuminated face of Willow with a flashlight in her hand. The bright bulb highlighted the interesting angles of her face as her dark eyes searched the room for him. "Are you okay?" she asked.

"Yeah, I just got startled. Hurt like hell, but I'll live."

As if in response, the skies seemed to open up overhead, and the lightning and thunder was joined by the roar of hard rain coming down on the roof and windows. "The power is out," she said. "It will be until tomorrow, at the earliest. We don't exactly have an emergency power crew on standby here. They're all stuck on the mainland in storms like this. I have a generator that will kick in and keep the refrigerator and a few appliances running, but that's about it."

Jack sat up and swung his legs out of the bed as gingerly as he could. "Do we need to do something? Cover the windows?"

"I did all that after you went to sleep. We may want to move into the living room, though. Without the heat running, this place is going to get chilly pretty quickly. You'll be more comfortable by the fireplace."

"Okay." Jack pushed up from the bed and Willow handed him the flashlight.

"If you can take this, I'll get your stuff and bring it out."

He watched her gather his blanket and his medicine and follow him into the hallway and to the living room. The room had vaulted ceilings with heavy wooden beams and a stone fireplace against one wall that went all the way to the top. She put his blanket on the recliner and set his water and pill bottles on the small table beside it.

"Go ahead and get comfortable. I'll get a fire going."

Jack watched with curiosity and a little guilt as Willow moved quickly to light a fire. He noted how carefully she stacked the logs, placing smaller pieces between them along with tiny chunks of what looked almost like sawdust cakes. She was experienced enough that it caught quickly and within a few minutes, the fire was on its way to becoming a large and warm light source for them both.

He turned off the flashlight and placed it on the table beside him. "You must lose power here a lot."

"More than I'd like," she admitted. "But I keep a fire going in here most of the winter anyway. This close to the ocean there's not a lot of snow or ice, but the wind is awful and the cold just goes straight through to your bones."

Jack caught movement out of the corner of his eye and noticed her large dog joining them. He sought out his oversize fluffy pillow by the fireplace and settled onto it. Resting his head on his paws, he watched Jack in a way that made him uneasy. Like the dog didn't trust him with his mama. Jack smothered a smile. His mama could take care of herself. Jack was the one at her mercy.

The rain started coming down harder, filling the room with a loud roar as the wind whipped it into sheets that pummeled the house. Thunder continued to rumble around them with the occasional nearby flash of lightning dancing over the living room skylight that faced the woods. Combined with the hum of the generator that had finally kicked in, Jack was fairly certain he wouldn't be falling asleep again anytime soon.

"Would you like some hot tea or something?" Willow asked. She was standing with the fireplace behind her. The flames had grown enough that the light shone through the fabric of her thin cotton pajama gown. He could easily make out the narrow outline of her hips and the slight cut in of her waist before it widened to her chest. She didn't have a very voluptuous figure, but it was womanly enough and he found himself being tantalized by the unexpected glimpse of it he was being given. The nightgown itself was fairly short, falling midthigh and providing him with a full view of her long, feminine legs and dainty feet with pink toenail polish.

It was a silly detail to notice, but one that made him smile. His savior might seem like a hard wilderness woman on the outside, but there was a soft, unexpectedly feminine side to her that had his full attention, as well.

"Jack?"

His gaze shifted quickly to her face. "Yes?"

"Would you like some herbal tea?"

"Yes, please," he said with a smile he hoped would cover up the fact that he'd been admiring her figure.

"Okay," she said with a curious wrinkling of her brow. "I'll go make it."

Jack leaned back into the recliner with a sigh as she left the room and followed it with a groan as he once again moved too quickly. He welcomed that pain this time, though. The sharp sensation would hopefully dull the arousal that had warmed his bloodstream faster than the fire had. Even with no memory of his past, he now knew for sure that women played a very large and important role in his life.

He was also certain that things with Willow had suddenly become decidedly more interesting.

Four

As comfortable as her recliner was, Jack found himself moving over to the couch, where he could sit beside Willow and share his blanket with her. It wasn't an entirely magnanimous gesture; he wanted to be closer to her, but if he could help her stay warm, all the better. She had pulled a chenille robe on over her nightie when she returned from the kitchen, which disappointed him a bit, but he imagined it wasn't the warmest outfit under the circumstances. She settled in on the other end of the couch and happily tugged her end of the blanket over her bare legs to chase away the chill.

He took a sip of the tea she'd made for him. It had a floral taste with a sweetness he didn't recognize, which wasn't surprising given the situation. "What kind of tea is this?" he asked.

"Chamomile with local honey. It's good for relaxation and sleep, plus it helps with my allergies. I drink it nearly every night. Sometimes I get a little spun up writing and a cup of this helps me turn off my brain and get some rest."

"It's good." He took another sip and looked around the room for what they could discuss next. "So since we're awake with nothing to do, tell me more about you, Willow. I know you're a writer and you live on this island with your dog. What else is there to know about you?"

Her eyes widened for a moment at his question. "There's not much to know. Honestly, I'm not that great talking about myself. I'm better at making things up."

There was plenty to discuss—of that he was certain—but he just had to convince her to open up. "Well, I can't talk about myself. We can't discuss movies or literature. So unless we're going to stare awkwardly at each other all night, how about you start at the beginning."

Willow let a blast of air out of her lungs in resignation. "Okay. Well, I grew up not far from here in a commune on the mainland. My parents were major hippies and vegans before it was really a thing. My dad was one of the farmers that grew food and supplies, and my mother worked taking care of the children in the community. It was a different kind of upbringing. We had electricity, but we didn't have televisions or video games. There was one landline phone everyone shared. We played outside and with the other children. I read every book we had in our little library. My sister and I were basically free to roam because it was a safe place for us. I really loved my life there.

"Then my parents split up," she continued. "My mom decided she didn't want to stay with my father there, so she packed us girls up and we moved to Seattle to live with my maternal grandmother."

"How old were you when you left?"

"I was about eleven, I think. My sister was thirteen."

Jack wasn't sure what his childhood was like, but if he had to guess, it wasn't anything like hers. "I bet that was a shocking transition."

"It was devastating. Public schools, buses, traffic, pollution, fast food, violence, sitcoms…things that were normal to other people were completely alien to us. There were good things, but they were outnumbered by the bad for me. I remember crying and begging Mama to take us back home. She may have even considered it. But then my grandmother got sick and we had to stay and take care of her. We never did go back."

Jack could tell that she didn't like talking about herself, so he was pleased she was indulging him even if he did have to prompt her for details. "Did you opt for college or jump right in to writing?"

"I got an English degree," she said. Willow perked up a bit as though shifting to her writing was far more comfortable a discussion. "I wasn't quite sure what I wanted to do and it seemed like a good way to avoid facing real life for a few more years. I found I really enjoyed my creative writing classes and my professor encouraged me to pursue fiction writing, so I tried my hand at it. It was something I could do while helping out my mom at home when she got sick. By the time she passed away, I had already published a couple mysteries and I was doing well enough to be able to live on my own."

It seemed even discussing her writing wasn't safe. He noticed the sadness in her eyes despite talking of her success. He could tell the cloud of losing her mother hung over it, tainting it. "It sounds like you lost a lot of people in your life at a young age."

Willow nodded. "Cancer is a bitch," she said with a tone of finality that ended that line of discussion.

"When did you decide to move here?" he asked.

"There were a few years where I thought Seattle was where I would stay. I needed to be close to civilization for a while," Willow said with a pained expression pinching her face. "But when I was able to get away, I came here. It reminded me of where I grew up, wild and yet safe at the same time."

"Don't you get lonely out here all by yourself?"

She narrowed her gaze at him. He watched a confusing mix of emotions dance across her face for a moment before she shook her head. "I prefer to be alone. It makes it easier to work without distractions."

"Yeah, I can see that. But don't you want to have a family one day? At least a partner to share your life with? You can't meet someone if you never leave your house."

He watched Willow stiffen slightly before reaching out to set her mug on the table. "No, I don't want any of that. I knew early on that the normal life path wasn't for me. My older sister, Rain, did the husband-and-kid thing. I can always visit her if the urge to cuddle my nephew strikes, but that's a choice I made. There are just certain things about my family that don't need to be passed along to another generation. Motherhood is not in the cards. I don't think love is, either. And I'm okay with that. I have my house, my community. I have Shadow, of course. And dogs are superior to people in so many ways."

She chuckled softly at her observation, but the laughter didn't reach her eyes. There was something sad there instead. The way she looked at him as she spoke told Jack that she was lying to him about how she felt. Perhaps even lying to herself. She didn't want to be alone, not really. She was just…scared…perhaps to be with someone. Perhaps she'd lost too many people in her life to risk having it happen again. Maybe she'd been hurt in a past relationship. He could understand wanting to swear off love if she'd been burned. But not everyone was a bad guy. Not everyone would leave her. Jack, for example, wasn't a bad guy. At least he didn't think so.

It was the way she looked at him then that urged him to lean closer to her. When she didn't pull away, he knew he was reading her right. He reached out to cup her cheek and draw her lips up to his own.

It started off as a soft, hesitant kiss. With no memories of his past, Jack felt like some awkward kid kissing his first girl under the bleachers after school. But it all came back to him pretty quickly. He deepened the kiss, holding her face in his hands, drawing her closer and drinking her in. She tasted like the honey from her tea, and the sweetness caused him to groan against her lips.

Willow reached out and wrapped her warm palm over his knee. Even through the wool blanket, her touch was enough to make his insides turn molten with a familiar need that wore away at his self-control. He wanted to touch her. Explore more of her body and reacquaint himself with the female form. He slipped his hand from her cheek to her shoulder and then lower.

Jack knew the instant he'd pushed her too far. Willow froze in place, her lips suddenly hard and unyielding when they had been soft a moment before. Half a second later, she was on the far side of the couch and he was aware of the chilly absence of her body close to his. Not even the fireplace could take the place of her warmth.

"I—I'm sorry," he said instinctively, although he wasn't entirely sure what he'd done wrong. Reaching out to touch her had felt like the most natural thing in the world to do. But he'd been incorrect in his instincts where Willow was concerned. He had barely grazed her chest. He hadn't even gotten far enough to feel the weight of her breast in his hand before she was gone. Maybe he'd moved too fast with someone he hardly knew. Maybe she'd had second thoughts about making out with her strange visitor with an unknown past. She was right to hold back. He could be anyone, anything. He couldn't find any prison tattoos, but maybe he was afraid of needles. He didn't think he was a bad person, but how many good people wash up on a beach in his condition?

"It's not your fault." Willow tugged her robe closed with her fists, effectively closing off her body from him. "I just… I never should've kissed you. That was stupid of me. I led you on and I shouldn't have. You're in no condition for…"

"I'm feeling better every minute."

She wrinkled her nose. "That's the medication, not the curative powers of my kisses. There are other reasons. It's a bad idea all around." Willow got up from the couch and went to stoke the fire with the iron poker leaning against the stone hearth.

Jack reached out for her, but the low grumble of a growl stopped him short before he could grasp her wrist. He looked to see that her dog was no longer asleep on his pillow but had moved between the two of them and was watching Jack warily. He drew back his hand and the growling stopped.

"It's okay, Shadow bear," she said, reaching out to stroke the dog's head. "He's very protective of me."

"I can see that."

He leaned back onto the couch, letting Willow escape and soothing the concerns of her furry guardian. There was no sense in pushing her. Like it or not, he was stuck with her on this island until the storm blew through and the ferry was running again. There was no reason to make things more awkward with his host than they already were.

But what he did know, deep down, was that he'd never kissed a woman like Willow before. And he liked it. Very much.

"What are you doing?"

Sawyer looked up from his suitcase with a guilty but determined look on his face. Kat wouldn't be happy with him, but he had no choice. "I'm packing to fly to Seattle."

Kat sighed and sunk down onto the bed beside his luggage. "Just because Finn's body wasn't one of the four they recovered doesn't mean he's alive, honey. That hole that blew into the side could've sucked him out over the ocean or the woods well before the crash and we'll never find him."

Sawyer continued to pack. "That's what they told me. It's very logical, of course. But I've got to go. I've got to at least look for him. It might be a lost cause, but he's my twin brother. He'd do the same for me."

"Would he?"

Sawyer paused and looked at his wife. The beautiful redhead had been the center of his universe since she marched into his sister's wedding reception and slapped him hard across the face. Now, in her third trimester of her pregnancy, she was practically glowing with radiant beauty. But he wouldn't let her talk him out of this.

With a heavy sigh, he tossed his toiletry bag into his suitcase and flipped the lid closed. "My brother is a complicated person to love. There are times when I've resented the hell out of him. Times when I felt like he practically got away with murder, living his life without consequences while the rest of us cleaned up his messes. He's a hedonistic playboy. Absolutely. But deep down, my brother is a good person. And yes, I do think he would look for me. He might seduce my nurse while sitting by my bedside while I was in a coma, but he'd be there. So I have to go."

Kat nodded in resignation. "How long do you think you'll be gone?"

"A couple of days at the most. I really don't know what I'm going to do once I get there. Talk to the local police. The coast guard, maybe. Visit a few hospitals and see if they have any John Does I could try to identify. But I know I'm tilting at a windmill."

Kat pushed herself up from the bed, belly first, and wrapped her arms around him. Sawyer buried his face in her auburn hair and inhaled the scent of the shampoo she used. He needed to breathe in enough of her to last him until he got home.

"If you need anything while I'm gone, call Mother or the girls. I know Morgan or Jade would be here in a flash. Actually, what about staying with one of them while I'm gone?"

"I'm pregnant, not an invalid. I'll be fine alone. I lived alone a long time before the Steele family crashed into my life."

"Yes, well," he said in a begrudging tone, "don't be surprised if they drop in to check up on you."

"You told your sisters that you're leaving?"

"Yes," he admitted.

"*Before* you told me?" Kat asked with an irritated arch in her eyebrow.

He had to tread carefully here with his hormonally charged wife. "Morgan and Jade were both there this afternoon when we got the news about the dental record results. We discussed me going out there. Otherwise, of course I would've told you first. You're my wife. The mother of my future child. You're my world. That will never change."

Kat dropped her forehead against his chest as her annoyance faded away. "Hurry home to me, Sawyer Steele. My baby has probably already lost one father. I need the other one."

Willow looked at herself in the bathroom mirror and frowned. She felt stupid. It had been two days since the kiss and she'd been dancing around Jack as though he were going to jump her bones at any moment. Ridiculous. He hadn't so much as looked at her suggestively since the night of the storm. He'd been a perfect gentleman and guest.

Initially, he slept a lot. And as his pain and the associated medications decreased, he was even helpful around the house. He'd attempted to cook a few times and tidied up the best he could. He'd helped her clean up outside after the storm, too. He couldn't haul broken branches or climb up on the roof to throw a tarp over an area that had lost shingles, but he did what he could to be a help and not a hindrance while Willow did those things.

But he hadn't laid a hand on her. Jack probably thought she was scared of him, and she felt bad about that. Honestly, he hadn't done anything wrong. When Jack had kissed her, she'd panicked. It wasn't because she didn't want to kiss him. She did. So badly. It was just that she hadn't kissed a man since her treatments and surgery.

In the moment, it was all too much. Before that night, she hadn't given any thought to how she'd react in that situation because part of coming to this island was to make sure she was never put in that kind of scenario. Living alone, writing her books, isolating herself on this island…it was all by design. She wanted to put that chapter of her life, and everything that came with it, behind her.

She'd lived the past fifteen years of her life knowing that one day, she would likely develop breast cancer. Her grandmother and mother had both succumbed to it within a few years of each other. They'd had the gene that predisposed them to breast and ovarian cancer, and with her family history it was almost a certainty. And after years of screening, a questionable spot had finally shown up on her mammogram. Willow knew the instant she saw it that it would be cancer. And she was right. The doctor had been optimistic since they caught it so early. Perhaps only a lumpectomy and some chemotherapy would be required.

Willow was not so optimistic. She'd watched her mother slowly wither away as she tried all kinds of holistic remedies. Mother insisted the mainstream treatment was worse than the disease, and in a way she was right. But by the time she finally agreed to the chemotherapy, there was no real point.

Willow had firsthand experience with what this cancer could do. So when the doctors delivered the bad news, she had already decided what her path forward would be. It was drastic. Her doctors seemed surprised that she wanted to take it that far. But she couldn't be dissuaded. A full mastectomy and a full hysterectomy was the only way to be certain. If she survived the breast cancer, the BRCA gene still left her vulnerable to relapse and ovarian cancer, as well. So she had them take it all. If she didn't have any of those parts, they couldn't try to kill her later.

Rain told her she was acting out of fear not logic, but Willow didn't want to tiptoe around this. She would use a sledgehammer on the thumbtack of her cancer. And it was just as well. As she'd alluded to Jack, Willow had no interest in passing this curse on to another generation anyway.

The doctors thought she might regret her decision. Her sister certainly disagreed. She was very vocal about it. But Willow had made up her mind and it was her body. And after the painful surgeries, a long recovery and chemotherapy, she didn't ever want to see the inside of another hospital again if she could avoid it.

And she hadn't regretted it. Until now.

Turning around, Willow started the shower to let

the water warm up. Then she pulled off her shirt, padded mastectomy bra and pajama pants. Looking down at the mangled remains of her chest, she knew exactly why she had panicked that night on the couch. She had opted out of the reconstruction surgery. She couldn't bear going through more procedures and more pain just so she could fit the image of what a woman should be. Where her breasts once were, now was only flat, rippled skin with a pair of scars that were still pink and healing.

No one had touched her chest since the surgery. But Jack had come very close. When she was alone, she didn't bother with the mastectomy bra that gave her the illusion of a slight figure. After Jack's arrival, she'd put one on, but she hadn't worn it to bed that night.

What would've happened if she'd let him touch her? If he'd realized she was a shell of the woman she'd once been? There were no nipples to harden and press against his eager hands. No full globes for him to caress. She couldn't bear to see the desire in Jack's eyes die away when he realized the truth. Willow would rather run and have control over the situation than be rejected.

But as his lips had touched hers and he'd moaned with desire, it had felt so amazing. It was nice to be wanted as a woman again. Even for just a moment, until she ruined it all.

When she came into the living room after showering, Jack was propped up in the recliner. He had made himself a bowl of cereal and brewed a pot of coffee for them both.

"Good morning," she said, as she went into the kitchen and poured herself a cup.

"Good morning," he responded. "You have an amazing cereal collection."

She chuckled as she added cream and sugar to her cup. "My sister wouldn't agree. She says I don't eat real food."

"Well, these Lucky Charms are great. Oh," he said, setting aside his bowl, "your cell phone was ringing while you were in the shower."

"Thank you." Willow walked through the living room to where she'd left her phone on the charger. The missed-call banner on the screen said that Doc had called. She hit the button to call him back and he picked up a moment later.

"Good morning, Willow. How is our patient doing?"

She glanced over her shoulder at the man in her easy chair. "Jack's getting around better."

"Jack? Has his memory returned?"

"No. He still has no idea who he is. But we had to call him something."

"Ah, that's a shame. I was hoping for a miraculous recovery. Did you two fare okay with the storm? The power was out for a long while this time."

"It was fine. I had a fire going and the generator kept the food from spoiling."

"I'm glad. I'm sorry I didn't call sooner, but I had a tree land on our carport and I've been dealing with that. I figured if there was an issue, you'd call. But today I have some good news. The ferry to Seattle is up and running again. I called over to a friend of mine at Harborview Medical Center. They're expecting Jack later this afternoon. With any luck, they'll be able to track down who he really is and he'll be out of your hair before too long."

Willow didn't respond. She didn't know what to say. She hadn't been expecting this call so soon. Of course she wanted Jack to get the help he needed. But at the same time, there was a part of her that wasn't quite ready to let him go yet, either.

"Willow?"

"Thanks, Doc," she said. "I'll let him know." Willow hung up the phone and took a sip of her coffee. "Good news."

With a groan, Jack pushed up from his chair and carried his bowl into the kitchen. "What's that?"

"Our connection to the mainland is restored. We can finally get you to a real doctor in Seattle where they can take X-rays and treat you properly."

"Oh, okay," he said, although he didn't sound very excited. She tried not to think too much about why.

"Maybe they'll even be able to check the missing-person reports to see if someone is looking for you. I'm sure your family is worried."

"If I have one," Jack said.

She was certain he had one. A man in a designer suit with an expensive watch didn't go missing without anyone noticing. Even if he didn't have family, he had friends, employees or a lover who would know he was gone. Maybe that was why she was hesitant to take him to Seattle. The knowledge that he probably wouldn't come back.

"I can check the ferry schedule and drive you down there when you're ready."

Jack turned to Willow and frowned. "Wait. You're not going with me?"

She knew it probably sounded horrible, that she would just drop a man with brain damage on a boat and wave goodbye. But she couldn't go back there. Harborview was where she'd had her surgeries and treatments. She just couldn't. Just thinking about the scent of the disinfectant and the long stretches of linoleum-lined hallways made her chest tighten with anxiety.

"You'll be fine. I'll give you some cash to get a cab from the ferry terminal to the hospital."

"It's not a question of how I get to the hospital," Jack said. "I mean, what happens when I finish my exam and all the tests? What if no one is looking for me? Where do I go? I know I don't have any right to ask anything of you, but I don't want to go alone. I know I'm just some stranger that's been sleeping in your guest room for a few days, but you're basically the only person in the whole world that I know. You're my only and best friend right now. I'd really like you to go with me."

Of course, he'd managed to make her feel terrible for not going. "I don't like hospitals, Jack."

He approached her and cupped her upper arms with his warm hands. "Please, Willow," he pleaded. His large brown eyes were like a big, sad puppy dog, wearing away at her resistance. "I'll find a way to make it up to you, I promise."

She shook her head, knowing that it was a lost cause. She was going back to the hospital. At least this time they wouldn't be sticking *her* with the needles.

Five

Jack stepped through the doors from the MRI wing of Harborview Medical Center and found Willow waiting for him there. It had been a long day of tests and exams, but thankfully this was the last one. The nurse had told them he could go for the day, but to stay in town. They would reach out to him tomorrow with the results and he might need to come back for more tests.

Willow was curled in a ball in the corner of the waiting room. Her knees were drawn up to her chest with her large cardigan wrapped around her. Her head was resting against the wall with her eyes closed. She looked so small and fragile sitting there. As though she were the patient instead of him.

He felt guilty. She told him she didn't like hospitals and he'd asked her to come with him anyway. It had apparently been a stressful day for her just being here.

He supposed that after losing several members of her family to illness, a place like this probably held a lot of bad memories for her.

It made him wish he could treat her to a night out. A nice dinner and a stay at a fancy Seattle hotel. It seemed like the right thing to do. If he had a penny to his name. A lot of things about his life had felt weird since he'd woken up without his memory, but not having any funds at his disposal bothered him more than most.

"Hey," Willow muttered as she sat up and sleepily rubbed her eyes. "How did the MRI go?"

"Fine. I found out I'm not claustrophobic, so that's good to know." He grinned at her, trying to lighten the mood. "I'm all done for the day."

Willow looked down at her watch and frowned. "The last ferry to the island left an hour ago, so it looks like we're staying here tonight."

"It's for the best," he said. "The doctors said I might need to come back in the morning if the test results find something that concerns them."

She nodded. "I should've thought of that before we left and brought an overnight bag for us. As it is, we'll have to find a pharmacy where we can get some essentials for the night. Hopefully we can find something nearby."

Jack walked over to where she was sitting and held out his hand to help her up. "I'm sorry today ran long. I promise you that once I have things straightened out, I will pay you back for everything. Not just the hotel, I mean. But food, clothes, medicine, your time… I know I've been an inconvenience from the moment you found me."

Willow looked down at his hand touching hers and gently untangled her fingers from his own. "It's not a problem, Jack, really. I have plenty of money. I have the time. To be honest, your arrival is the most exciting thing to happen in my life in a long time. If it wasn't for the fact that you were hurt, I'd enjoy the change to my routine. Life will surely be boring without you."

There was a sadness in her eyes when she spoke that Jack hadn't noticed before. It did feel like their time together was coming to a close. He couldn't hide out on her island forever. Eventually he would get his memory back or someone would come looking for him. Part of him wished it weren't true. Like somehow things would be easier if he could start fresh with Willow and never look back.

"Okay. Let's go find a hotel," she said. "And then we'll get something to eat. I'm sure you're looking forward to something other than soup and breakfast cereal."

"I don't have a single complaint," Jack replied with a grin.

They headed down the hallway together to the exit of the hospital. As they were reaching the lobby, they passed a woman in a wheelchair. Jack didn't pay much attention to the patient, but a few steps later, he realized that he was walking alone. Turning around, he saw Willow frozen in her tracks. Her wide eyes were locked on the woman in the wheelchair, her lips trembling but wordless.

Jack turned to the woman in the wheelchair to see what he was missing. This woman was likely a cancer patient at the hospital. The thin remains of her hair were wrapped in a bright pink handkerchief. Her face was thin and sunken in with dark circles beneath her eyes. She was the embodiment of frail with arms that looked like a rough nurse could snap them putting in a new IV. Her eyes were shining gems, the spirit still alive despite the ravages of the illness that had brought her here.

He looked back at Willow and the pieces finally clicked into place. This woman had cancer. Being in the hospital was bad enough, but seeing her like that no doubt reminded Willow of losing her mother and grandmother to it. He didn't know how long ago they'd passed away, but judging by the look on Willow's face—large, fearful eyes, tense jaw and firmly pressed lips—it wasn't long enough. She actually looked like she was riding along the edge of panic.

As if on cue, Willow drew in a ragged breath and started frantically wheezing. The woman in the wheelchair watched in alarm as Willow clutched her chest and backed up hard against the far wall to brace herself.

"Willow?" Jack asked, unsure. "What can I do?" He knew better than to ask what was wrong when she could barely breathe and waste the words.

"Leave," she managed between gasps.

Jack didn't hesitate to wrap his arm around her and guide her to the front exit. Outside, he led her to a concrete bench and sat her down. The sun was just setting and the cool air was a refreshing shock to him after so many hours in the hospital. He hoped it was the same for her. Some nice fresh air without the scent of disinfectant and death tainting it.

Willow dropped down to the bench and buried her face in her hands. After a few moments, her shoulders were shaking with raw tears instead of the desperate breaths of her earlier hyperventilating.

The whole situation was unexpected for Jack. Since he'd woken up on the beach, Willow had been his rock. Strong. Independent. Seeing her break down like this was unsettling. Unsure of what else to do, Jack sat on the bench beside her and wrapped a comforting arm around her shoulders.

"I shouldn't have asked you to come," he said after a few minutes of silence. "You told me you didn't like hospitals, but I was being selfish, not wanting to come here alone. I'm sorry, Willow."

She shook her head, wiping the tears away with the back of her hand. "No. You couldn't have known. Even I wasn't sure how it would be. I got cocky after going all day without more than a twinge of anxiety. And then I saw her and everything hit me all at once."

"I imagine it brings back a lot of bad memories of losing your family."

Willow stiffened beneath his embrace for a moment and then nodded. "I have nothing but terrible memories from hospitals." She took a deep breath and sat up straight. "Enough of that. Let's get out of here and find a place to stay tonight. It's getting late, and I'm starving, so I know you've got to be, too."

And just like that, his strong Willow was back, taking charge of the situation and putting her emotions in check. Reaching out, he took her hand to help her up, but this time, he didn't let her pull away like she usually did and she didn't fight it. There was shared strength in their touch, a hum of awareness and energy that they both needed tonight. It might've felt like junior high to some people, but Jack liked having that connection with her.

He was suddenly desperate not to lose it. Tonight or maybe ever.

"I hope you like Thai food," Willow said as she unpacked a sack of takeout.

They'd found a nice hotel a block or so from the hospital that had availability and a room with two queen beds and a kitchenette. While Jack showered, Willow had gone in search of dinner and a pharmacy to pick up some essentials for the night. She'd returned about an hour later with toiletries and enough Thai food to feed an army. She'd followed her nose to a place down the street and if the scents were any indication, they were in for a treat. She hadn't had good Thai or even Chinese food in ages. It wasn't exactly an option on her tiny island.

Jack came out from the bathroom wearing only his sweatpants from earlier. His blond hair was still damp and curling at the edges, and the steam from the bathroom had left moist highlights along the ridges of his stomach and chest. Willow had to look away and tried to focus on setting out dinner instead.

"Thai food, huh? I don't know if I like it or if I've even had it before, but it sure smells good."

They settled down at the small table for two the room provided. The cartons and containers of various Thai delicacies took up nearly every inch of the table, leaving them barely enough room for their plates and the sodas she'd purchased at the pharmacy.

They were both exhausted from a long day and ate in relative silence for a while. Even in the quiet, however, Willow was aware of a change between them. Something had shifted today. She had always been attracted to him. And he'd kissed her, so she supposed he was into her on some level. But neither of them had really pressed the issue since that night on the couch.

But today, when he'd taken her hand outside the hospital, things changed. The attraction was still there, but there was more to it. An affection. A need to support and care for each other in a way that went far beyond an emotionless hookup. And it made things both easier and harder. It made her relax around him. She was far more comfortable with Jack than she'd been with anyone in years. Even on such a trying day. But that kind of comfort threatened the walls she'd built to protect herself. Before too long, she was certain she was going to let Jack get close to her. And when he left, it would leave a catastrophic mess in his wake.

Even so, she knew she couldn't resist him. She wanted to reach across the table and take his hand again. To feel his skin against her own. She felt not so alone with him there. It wasn't until that moment that she realized how miserable she really was on her island.

She thought she was protecting herself going out there. Convincing herself that all she needed was her books, her coffee and her dog. But it wasn't enough and she knew it. Having Jack around made it impossible to lie to herself any longer.

"Can I ask you something?" Jack finally spoke up as they finished their meal.

Willow sat back in her chair and pushed the half-eaten plate of pad Thai away before she ate more and made herself sick. "Sure." She was happy to get out of her own head and the turn her thoughts had taken.

"That first night we spent together…when the storm hit and the power went out. I kissed you and everything seemed to be going well until it wasn't. Did I do something wrong?"

Maybe her thoughts were safer. "No. Like I told you, I just realized it was a bad idea," Willow said as she got up and carried a few empty food cartons into the kitchenette.

Jack didn't let her escape the conversation so easily. He followed her with the last of their dinner and set it on the counter beside her. "Are you sure that's all it was?" he asked as he leaned against the counter. He was so near to her that her senses were flooded with the scent of his freshly washed skin and the heat of his body.

With a sigh, Willow turned to face him. The movement put her so close to him that they almost touched, but she felt childish taking a step back. "No, that wasn't all it was," she said, letting her gaze fall to his bare collarbone. "I panicked, okay? It had been a long time since I'd been attracted to someone and it felt like we were moving too fast."

Jack's hand came to rest at her waist. "Willow?" he asked softly.

She couldn't answer with him touching her like that. The hem of her shirt just barely brushed the waistband of her jeans, and his fingers had come to rest on a fraction of her bare skin. It was a simple touch, and yet it made her heart leap in her chest and her breath catch in her throat. He'd kept his distance since that first night, something that had both relieved and disappointed her. But he'd been a stranger then. And too injured to move. Now he was neither of those things. It was a question of if she could allow herself to open up to him.

"Yes?"

He slipped his finger under her chin and tilted her head up until she had no choice but to look at him. She felt her cheeks flush with embarrassment and excitement as her gaze met his. His brown eyes searched her face as his lips tipped upward in a smile of encouragement. "That's what I hoped."

Willow almost couldn't hear him for the blood rushing in her ears. Being here in Seattle seemed to be bringing their attraction to the surface, maybe because they both knew they were one step closer to losing their chance to be together. Eventually they would find out who he really was and he would return to his life. If this was their moment, they needed to take it.

"Why would you say that?" she asked.

Jack slid his hand around to her lower back, pulling her body flush against his own. "Because I've laid in bed alone each night thinking about that kiss we shared and worrying that I might not ever get to kiss you again because I screwed up somehow."

Willow gasped at his words. She'd never had a man say something like that to her before. Not even before she got sick and allowed herself the luxury of dating.

"I've fantasized about holding you in my arms again. I know that I shouldn't because I don't know anything about myself, or if I'm even good for you, but I can't help it. Now that we're off the island, it feels like I'm that much closer to leaving you and I don't like it. It makes me want to throw caution to the wind and not hold back anymore."

The longer he spoke, the more she fell under his spell. He was right. They were going to lose their chance and she would spend the rest of her life kicking herself for passing up the opportunity. Yes, she was ashamed of her body. But there had to be a way she could work around that and still get what she wanted. She had to.

"Then don't," she said, boldly meeting his eyes.

He narrowed his gaze at her for a moment. Then Jack's lips met hers without hesitation. His kiss was powerful yet not so overwhelming as to scare her off a second time. Willow stood on tiptoe to wrap her arms around his neck and draw herself closer to him. When his tongue sought hers out, she opened to him and melted into his touch.

She had thought the kiss in front of the fire was amazing, but that was nothing, nothing like this. This kiss was like a lightning bolt, shocking her dormant inner core back to life. As his hands rubbed her back and his fingers pressed greedily into her flesh, all she could think about was how badly she needed Jack.

"I want you," she whispered against his lips.

Jack broke away from her mouth and trailed kisses along her jawline to the sensitive hollow of her neck. "Whatever you want, it's yours," he said in a low growl at her ear.

His mouth returned to hers, hungrier than before. This was no longer just a simple kiss. They'd officially moved on to foreplay. Without breaking the kiss, he walked them backward through the little kitchenette until her legs met with the small dining room table where they'd just eaten. Willow eased up until she was sitting on it with Jack nestled snugly between her denim-clad thighs. She could feel his desire pressing against her, sending a shiver of need down her spine.

Jack slipped his hand beneath her shirt to stroke the

smooth skin of her back and press her even closer to him. He moved to lift the hem and remove her T-shirt, but Willow grabbed his hand and stopped him.

"I need to leave it on. Please."

He frowned, confused by her hesitation, but he didn't argue with her.

"My chest is very…sensitive," she said. "I don't like having it touched." She left out why. She also left out that she was wearing one of her padded mastectomy bras to give her some shape where she no longer had any. "I'm sorry," she murmured, feeling the need to say something.

"Don't be sorry. If you don't like something, just tell me." Jack quickly moved on from her shirt, leaving it in place. She felt his hand slide down her stomach to her jeans instead. She lifted her hips as he slid them and her panties down her legs.

As he stood, his eyes devoured her long legs splayed out in front of him. He kissed her again and let his hand wander over her bare thigh as he did. Jack dipped his fingers between her legs, brushing over her sensitive skin and sending a shiver through her whole body.

He did it again, harder, and this time Willow cried aloud when he made contact. "Jack!"

Clearly encouraged by her response, he stroked again and again until she was panting and squirming at the edge of the table. He built up the release inside her so quickly, she could hardly believe it until it was almost too late.

"Stop," she gasped, gripping his wrist with her hand. "Not yet. I want you inside me."

"Very well," Jack agreed. His gaze never left hers as he slipped out of his pants and kicked them aside.

He settled back between her legs, and Willow felt him press against her.

"Yes," she hissed as he slowly sank into her.

He gripped her hips, holding her steady as he started to move in her. Every stroke set off fire bursts beneath her eyelids as they fluttered closed. Willow arched her back and braced her hands on the table as their movements became more desperate.

How had she even gotten here? This morning, she'd reluctantly boarded a ferry to escort Jack to the hospital. And now, she was having sex with Jack and on the verge of her first orgasm in ages. She could feel it building inside her. He coaxed the response from her body so easily, as though they were longtime lovers.

"So close," she said between ragged breaths.

Jack seemed to know just what to do to push her over the edge. Rolling his hips forward, he thrust harder, striking her sensitive core with each advance. In seconds, Willow was tensing up in anticipation of her undoing.

Then it hit. It radiated through her body like a nuclear blast. She clung to Jack's shoulders as the shock waves of pleasure made every muscle tremble and quiver. They rode through it together. With her final gasp, her head dropped back and her body went limp in his arms.

"Willow," he groaned, thrusting hard into her. He surged forward and gasped against the curve of her throat as he poured into her.

Willow cradled him against her chest as he recovered, the sweat dampening the cotton and pressing it to her skin. Thoughts swirled through her mind as the sexual haze faded away and she realized what they'd just done. What she'd just done.

Before she could say anything, Jack straightened up and kissed her tenderly on the lips. "To the bedroom?" he asked.

Yes, a bed was exactly what they needed. Leaving their clothes where they lay, they made their way into the other area of the suite. They tugged the blankets down and curled up together in the plush, clean cotton. He tugged her back against him and wrapped his arms around her waist.

Willow was on the verge of falling asleep, content in his arms, when her cell phone rang. With a groan of displeasure, she rolled over and looked at the screen. It was the hospital.

"Hello?" she answered.

"Yes, can I speak with Mr. Jack Doe, please? This is Dr. Dunne with Harborview Medical."

She passed the phone over to Jack, who quietly conversed with the man for a few minutes. Willow was anxious to hear what they had to say. They'd called sooner than she expected. Hopefully it wasn't bad news. She wasn't sure she could face returning to the hospital tonight.

"What is it?" she asked as he hung up the phone.

Jack had a strange expression on his face as he looked at the phone and seemed to struggle with what he'd just heard.

"Are you okay? Did they find something serious?"

"I'm fine. Nothing more than we already expected."

Willow didn't understand. "Okay. Then what's wrong?"

He cleared his throat and passed the phone back to her. "First thing this morning, they took a photo of me with some basic information and sent it out to the

Seattle police department to see if there was a match for any of their missing-person cases."

Willow's heart skipped in her chest. No. No. No. No. No. Not so soon. Not when things were so good between them. She'd never thought she'd have anything like she'd shared with Jack after beating cancer. She wasn't prepared to give it up yet. And somehow she knew that Jack's next words were going to change everything.

"They got a match almost immediately on a case reported to them yesterday. Apparently my twin brother is here in Seattle looking for me. And my name…is Finn Steele."

Six

Jack sat nervously at a diner booth with Willow beside him. They'd arranged to meet with the man claiming to be his twin—Sawyer Steele—for breakfast the following morning. He'd barely been able to sleep the night before and had already downed two cups of black coffee since they arrived. His feet anxiously tapped on the tile floor, his mind racing with the possibilities of meeting this man.

"Maybe you should switch to decaf, Jack. I mean, Finn? Maybe? This will be an adjustment."

"You're telling me." He'd hoped that hearing his real name would be enough to unlock his mind, but no luck. "Finn Steele" meant nothing to him. He felt more like Jack Doe than anything.

The door of the diner opened and a bell chimed to announce a customer. Both Jack and Willow looked up at once to see if it was the man they were expecting.

There was no question. The man standing at the entrance looked exactly like Jack. A rich, powerful, confident version of Jack he couldn't begin to relate to. Sawyer was tall, with the same blond curls in a different style. When the man turned and made contact with the same brown eyes, he smiled and rushed over to their table.

"Finn! Thank God."

Jack stood to greet the stranger, not expecting the violent hug that met him instead. He groaned with the pain of the impact, taking a step back as soon as he could to clutch his healing rib cage.

"Oh no, I hurt you. I'm sorry. They didn't tell me anything on the phone except that you had amnesia. Are you okay? I can't believe you're alive. They told us that you were dead, but I just couldn't believe it."

It was a lot coming at Jack all at once. He wasn't quite sure what to say to the man, so he held out his hand to gesture for him to sit across from them. He settled back into the booth beside Willow and clutched her hand for support beneath the tabletop. "I've got a few broken ribs. The bump on the head has been the biggest problem. I was pretty beat up in general when Willow found me. I felt like hell for a couple days, but it's better now. Thanks to Willow's expert care, of course."

Sawyer finally turned to acknowledge the silent woman sitting beside Jack. He smiled at her and looked back at his brother. "I should've known that no matter what situation you'd gotten into, you'd find a beautiful woman to care for you."

"Excuse me?" Jack asked. He didn't like the man's tone. Or rather, he didn't like what his tone said about Jack. Perhaps he was more than just a flirt.

"Wow. You really don't remember anything. Nothing at all?"

"Nothing personal. I don't know who I am, or what I was like. I certainly don't know how I ended up on that beach."

Sawyer's brow went up in surprise. "You washed up on a beach?"

"We're not sure," Willow said, finally speaking up. "I found him unconscious on the beach not far from my house on Shaw Island. It's part of the San Juan Islands off the coast here."

Sawyer shook his head in amazement. "That's wild. That's got to be more than two hundred miles from where the plane finally went down."

Jack sat upright, his brother's words a surprise. He'd imagined a dozen ways he could've ended up on that beach and none of them had involved a plane crash. "You're saying I was on a plane?"

"Yes. You were flying back from Beijing on a corporate jet. They're still not sure what happened, but there was an explosion. I guess maybe you were sucked out of the plane over the ocean before it went down in the national forest lands. The crash investigators were insistent that you were dead even when we couldn't find your body because you could've ended up anywhere. Honestly, until I saw you just now, I was worried they were right. It's a miracle you survived."

Jack had been given so much information and yet the pieces still weren't coming together in his mind. He couldn't quite believe that he'd survived a plane crash any more than he could believe he was used to flying on private jets and traveling to China. None of this life Sawyer described seemed like it could be his.

"Can you tell me who I am?" he asked. "You're obviously my twin brother, but what else should I know?"

Sawyer nodded and gave him a soft, understanding smile that made Jack like him a little more than before. "It's a lot to absorb, I know. I shouldn't have thrown it at you all at once, but seeing you sitting here…" He shook his head and blinked away a shimmer of glassy tears in his eyes. "Your name is Finn Hamilton Steele. Hamilton is our mother's maiden name. You live in Charleston, South Carolina. Our whole family lives there. You and I are both vice presidents for the family company, Steele Tools, which was founded by our great-grandfather and is currently run by our father, Trevor Steele."

"Steele Tools, as in the company that makes the hammers and screwdrivers you can find in almost every home in the country?" Willow asked.

Sawyer nodded. "Yes. If you haven't already guessed, Finn, you're also ridiculously rich."

The waitress chose that moment to arrive at their table. They all forced themselves to order breakfast and coffee, sending her away as fast as possible.

"Ridiculously rich?" Jack said the words aloud, but he couldn't quite grasp the idea. He was wearing a five-dollar T-shirt from the Shaw Island General Store that Willow had had to buy for him. He didn't have a solitary dime in his pocket. "Are you sure?"

"Unless you've managed to blow your entire billion-dollar trust fund on women and sports cars, then yes. I don't think even you could waste money that quickly."

Jack got a sinking feeling in his gut. For anyone else, hearing that he was a billionaire likely would've been good news. But he couldn't help but home in on his brother's words: "women and sports cars." It made him sound like he was some kind of wild playboy. He'd known almost immediately that he had a great fondness for women, but Sawyer made it sound as though he had a different one on his arm every week or something.

"Am I married?" He held his breath, hoping the answer was no. It didn't sound like he was, but who knew? Perhaps he wasn't Mr. Monogamy. But he didn't want to be that guy. If he was married and didn't know it, his romance with Willow couldn't be held against him, but he still didn't like the idea of it.

"Ah, no. You're not married. Not even close. You proposed to my wife earlier this year, but she turned you down. That's the closest you've gotten to the altar."

Jack frowned. That sentence didn't even make sense. He decided to ignore it and focus in on the fact that no, he hadn't cheated on his wife with Willow. He was free to be with her if he wanted to.

He took a deep breath and finally started to relax into the booth. He wasn't a criminal. He wasn't married. It was a relief to know he hadn't drawn Willow into some messy intrigue by making love to her last night. He could deal with anything else he found out about himself just knowing that much was true.

"So, Finn, huh?" Jack gritted his teeth as he said it. The name—like the rest of his new identity—felt like wearing someone else's shoes, but he'd have to get over it.

"Our dad loved Mark Twain's stories when he was growing up, and all of us are named after different characters from his books. Our older brother is Tom. Then there's you and me and our younger sister Morgan. He got her name from *A Connecticut Yankee in King Arthur's Court.* Oh, and we also have a sister named Jade, which has nothing to do with Mark Twain, but that's a long story for another day."

He didn't doubt it. Everything about his life seemed impossibly complicated. It made him want to go back to Shaw Island and hide out with Willow forever.

"They're all going to be thrilled when I tell them the news. I didn't want to say anything until I knew for sure that I'd really found you. Mother has been a wreck. They'll want you home as soon as possible. I took one of the company jets here to look for you, but you don't have to worry about flying home. After the crash, we had a crew of technicians go over each one in the fleet. It's perfectly safe." Sawyer turned to Willow. "I'm sure you'll be glad to get this guy out of your hair. I can't imagine taking in someone who has no clue who they are or how they got there, but you're a good person. There's a reward for information about Finn. Our parents will happily pay it to compensate you for the inconvenience of it all."

"I don't need any money." Willow had been tense and mostly quiet since Sawyer had walked in. Now Jack could almost feel the waves of irritation coming off of her. She wasn't happy about any of this, and frankly, neither was he.

It would all be so much easier if his memory would return. Then his whole life wouldn't feel like he was reading someone else's biography.

"When would we leave?" Jack asked.

"As soon as you're ready."

Jack looked at the beautiful woman beside him and wasn't sure he would ever be ready.

* * *

"I want you to come with me."

Willow stopped in her tracks just inside their hotel room and turned to face Jac—*Finn*. After breakfast, Sawyer had returned to his suite at the Four Seasons to call family. This was their first chance to speak privately since the bomb of his identity had been dropped on them both.

"What do you mean come with you? Where? To the Four Seasons?" He was supposed to be meeting his brother there later to make plans to return home.

"No. To Charleston. I want you to come back with me."

Finn—*right on the first try, finally*—had to be out of his mind. "What reason do I have to go to South Carolina? You're going home to your family and your old life. You don't need me there."

He shut the hotel room door and closed the space between them. He wrapped his arms around her waist and pulled her close, his scent wearing away at her resolve. "That's where you're wrong. I do need you there. Just like yesterday at the hospital—I need your support to get through this. These people might be my family, but I don't know them. Right now, you," he said, looking into her eyes, "are my whole world. I can't remember a time when you weren't in my life." Finn smiled. "Don't make me do this without you."

Willow knew she would eventually relent—she couldn't tell him no when he looked at her like that—but she had to voice her concerns first. "I grew up dirt-poor on a commune. I don't know the first thing about how to act around rich people. I'll embarrass myself and you in the process."

"I could never be embarrassed by you," he insisted. "And I'm in the same boat. I don't remember anything about my life. I don't feel like a billionaire. Sawyer could've said I was a circus clown and I would shrug and go along with it because it all feels wrong to me anyway. But all that talk of being a vice president and having trust funds… I feel like this is all some cruel prank being played on me. The only truth, the only constant in my life right now, is you. You're my lifeline, Willow Bates."

It was nice to be needed, but Willow could feel the anxiety tickling at the back of her brain. She was going with him to help ease the transition. No more, no less. She shouldn't expect anything other than a week together. But she couldn't help but feel a bit used. "And when you're comfortable in your old life again? When you get your memories back? What then? I come home to Washington and we pretend like none of this ever happened?"

"No, of course not." Finn ran his palms reassuringly along the backs of her arms. "I'm not sure what I'm walking into here, but we'll figure things out as we go. I'm not ready to give this—you—up yet. But under the circumstances, we can't promise each other anything, either. All I can tell you is that if you get there and you don't like it, you can leave whenever you want. I won't ask you to stay. But go with me."

Finn reached up to brush a honey-gold strand of hair from her eyes. "Please."

"I'll see if Doc can keep Shadow," she said with a heavy sigh of resignation. "But I'm not staying more than a week no matter what. I have a life, a deadline. And I won't impose on Doc any longer than I have to."

"A week is perfect." Finn grinned and the single dimple in his cheek appeared, tempting her to lean in and kiss it.

She watched him for a moment before giving in to the urge and pressing her lips first to his dimple, and then to his lips. "I think Finn suits you. It's sort of a mischievous name. Like that smile of yours."

He shrugged. "It's growing on me. It could've been worse."

Willow pulled away and looked around the hotel room. "Well, we need to check out if I'm going to make the next ferry. I'll talk to Doc, pack a bag and then meet you and Sawyer at the Four Seasons. Okay?"

He nodded. "Just don't take too long. Sawyer has threatened to take me shopping this afternoon."

She looked him over, eyeing the clothes she'd bought him that first night. It certainly wasn't what you'd expect some tool magnate to wear. "You could probably use some clothes that don't say San Juan Islands on them. Speaking of which, is there anything you left at the house that I should pack for you?" He certainly hadn't left for Seattle thinking he wouldn't return.

Finn looked thoughtful for a moment and then shook his head. "The only thing I need is you."

Willow rolled her eyes dramatically and laughed. "I've already agreed to go. No need to lay it on so thick."

They gathered up what little they had in the room and left. She put Finn in a cab to the Four Seasons and caught another to the ferry pier.

Being away from Finn, alone on the boat, gave Willow time to think. Perhaps too much time. The whole way back to Shaw Island, she wondered if she were crazy to go with him.

This whole time, she'd thought he was a Seattle executive or something. Smart and well-to-do, definitely, but a billionaire? The heir of a tool empire that was a household name? That was beyond her wildest imaginings. Whatever girlish fantasies she might've entertained about the two of them together were dashed the instant she heard who he really was.

Jack and Willow made sense. Finn and Willow didn't stand a chance.

Maybe she was just fooling herself by going to Charleston. She was clinging to a dream that had died the moment Sawyer walked in the door of that diner. But she couldn't help herself. Despite believing it to be impossible, she'd allowed herself to develop feelings for Finn. All she could do now was make the most of every moment she could with him. And when it was over, it would hurt, but it would be worth it.

Willow had a week left with Finn. And a lifetime to hold on to the memories and hope that was enough.

"I'm sorry, could you repeat that?" Kat said with a near-hysterical edge to her voice.

Sawyer grinned and repeated his words loud and clear for his wife to understand over the phone. "He's alive, Kat. I knew he hadn't died in the plane crash and I was right. I found him."

He didn't have to be with her in Charleston to know that the stunned silence on the end of the line was being caused by her quiet tears. Third-trimester hormones were getting the best of her lately. She cried at television commercials. Social media posts. Surely this news would start the waterworks, as well, so he continued to talk and take the pressure to speak off of her.

"He ended up on an island, hundreds of miles away from the crash."

"Is he okay?"

"For the most part, but he did hit his head. We would've found him sooner if he had any clue who he was or how he washed up on that beach."

There was a moment of hesitation before Kat spoke. "Are you saying Finn has *amnesia*?"

"I know, it sounds crazy, but it's true. He's been staying with a woman for the last few days and going by the name Jack. He has no clue who he is, who I am or anything about his life before the plane crash."

Kat made a thoughtful sound on the line. "Are you sure… I mean, he couldn't be faking it, could he? Not the wreck, obviously, but could the amnesia be a ploy to try and take advantage of a little free time without responsibilities or your father hulking over his shoulder?"

Sawyer had considered that, but even Finn had limits on how low he would sink. "He's absolutely not faking it. And you know how I know?"

"How?"

"Because he's completely smitten with the woman that rescued him."

There was another long silence. "Finn is…smitten?"

"I can't think of a better word to use, but yeah. Smitten, infatuated, whatever you want to call it. He sat across the table from me at breakfast practically beaming at her the whole time. Holding her hand. I haven't seen him act that way with a woman in my entire life. Not even some good old teenage puppy love back in high school."

"This I've got to see."

Sawyer took a deep breath. "Well, you're going to get your chance. Because Finn insists on bringing her back to Charleston with him. At least for a week or so."

The news had nearly knocked Sawyer off his feet, but when Finn had arrived at the hotel, he announced that Willow would be meeting them tonight and traveling back with them to South Carolina. This was so unlike his brother, Sawyer almost couldn't believe it was really Finn, if he hadn't been the spitting image of his twin.

Finn liked everything in his life to be flashy and beautiful, be it women, cars, watches…everything. But he kept the cars and the watches far longer than the women. He adored them all, but was easily bored by them and certainly wasn't interested in the long-term care and maintenance that one required.

If he was honest, this woman, Willow, was pretty enough. She had a tiny frame, very slender, and was almost swallowed by the cardigan she wore over her T-shirt. She wasn't wearing a stitch of makeup. Her blond hair was cut short, which made her eyes seem even bigger than they were. Her face was interesting with high cheekbones and full lips that were in contrast to her lack of curves anywhere else. She wasn't what you could call traditionally beautiful, but she was the kind of oddly attractive woman you would see on a high-fashion magazine cover or catwalk.

That was not his brother's type. At all. He liked curves, flowing hair, lots of makeup and tight clothes. He liked them high-maintenance and fun to drive, like his cars. Willow was quiet, but smart and well-spoken. She seemed thoughtful and genuinely concerned for his brother without knowing anything about who he was and what he could offer her. It was refreshing, if not a little disconcerting.

"He really did hit his head hard, didn't he?" Kat noted.

"Absolutely. And it's not just her. There's a complete personality change in him. He's not as outspoken or extroverted. He isn't constantly making jokes or sarcastic comments. He actually seemed to be really serious about the whole situation. Which, of course, is not like him at all."

"Well, I can't wait to see how all this turns out. Where is he now?"

"He's in the bathroom taking a shower and cleaning up. I hauled him down to Neiman Marcus and bought him some clothes so he would at least look like himself when he arrived back in Charleston. Mother would faint if she saw him in the sweatpants and flip-flops he had on this morning."

Kat chuckled and followed up her laugh with an "oh" sound. "The baby kicked. She must think that's funny, too."

Sawyer smiled, picturing his wife and her large, round belly as she sat in the wingback chair. Lately it was the only chair in the house she could get up out of on her own. He hated leaving her and the baby, especially when they were getting so close to her arrival. But finding his brother was important. Finn was the baby's biological father, after all. Having him be a part of the baby's life was just as vital as having Sawyer around.

"I think she misses you," Kat said. "And so do I. When will you guys be coming back?"

"We may wait until the morning. I have to talk to the pilot and see what he recommends with the weather and flight time. We also have to wait for Willow to return to Seattle on the ferry."

The bedroom door of the suite opened and Finn walked into the room in his new suit. It wasn't as well tailored as it should be, but under the circumstances, it would do.

"I need to let you go. I'll see you soon. I love you."

"I love you, too," Kat said.

Sawyer hung up the phone and looked at his brother. He looked like Finn. Sounded like Finn. But he certainly didn't act like him.

Maybe, Sawyer thought, that wasn't all bad.

Seven

The moment Willow stepped onto the Steele corporate jet, she knew she was woefully unprepared for this trip. The small jet sat six guests in plush leather seats, three on each side of the aisle. At the top of the stairs, they were greeted by their flight attendant, an attractive, middle-aged brunette named Gloria, who offered them each a glass of champagne as they boarded.

"I'm so glad to know you're safe, Mr. Steele," Gloria said as she gave Finn a crystal flute of golden liquid. "I knew I had to break out our best bubbly to celebrate your return home."

"I was sorry to hear about the others," he responded, with a sober expression on his face.

Willow had learned the night before that two pilots, a flight attendant and another passenger had lost their lives when the jet crashed. Considering the state of the wreck Sawyer described, it really was a miracle that Finn had survived. The best they could guess was that he was wearing one of the plane's parachutes when the explosion tore the fuselage in half.

Gloria looked pleasantly surprised at Finn's thoughtful words and nodded. "It's a risk we accept and hope to not face in our line of work," she said. "But no worries about today. This jet has been fully vetted by the best mechanics and inspectors in the business."

"Thankfully, I don't remember the crash," Finn said. "Or anything else for that matter. So I'll be fine."

"Well, just in case, I do have some Xanax if anyone needs it."

At first, Willow thought Gloria was kidding, but when no one laughed, she accepted her drink and kept her mouth shut. The world really did work differently for the rich in ways she never even imagined.

She settled into a seat in the second row across the aisle from Finn. Putting her champagne into the polished wood cup holder, she nervously buckled her seat belt. Then, she picked up the glass and downed it all in one gulp. It was probably a waste of very good champagne, but she didn't care at the moment.

"Are you afraid of flying?" Finn asked. He was relaxing casually in his seat as though he hadn't nearly died in a plane like this less than a week ago.

"No. I've flown a couple times in my life. Coach, of course. But if I wasn't afraid before, meeting you would change that. I'm just a bit of an anxious traveler. I've spent too much time as a homebody, I think."

That wasn't entirely a lie. She never had traveled much. She had a passport, but only to go over to Canada from time to time. But really, her anxiety had kicked in the moment she met the brothers in the Four Seasons lobby. Both of them were standing there waiting for her, looking incredibly handsome. One was wearing a navy suit and the other a black suit. It was amazing how much they looked alike standing side by side smiling at her. At least until she noticed they each had a single dimple, but on opposite cheeks, like a mirror image of one another. Once she saw that, she knew that despite the new suit and the haircut, the one in black was Finn.

The fact that he wasn't wearing a tie should've given it away, but she knew for certain when he approached her and said hello with a firm kiss on the lips.

From there, things had been like one big wealthy whirlwind. It started with the beautiful brass-and-marble lobby of the hotel and the two-bedroom hotel suite that was bigger than her first apartment. Then Sawyer treated them to dinner at the nicest seafood place in Seattle and ordered a bottle of wine that cost more than her mortgage. She'd had her first ride in a limousine when their car took them to the executive airport this morning.

And now, she was on a private jet, sipping a refilled glass of champagne and wishing she'd had nicer clothes to pack. She had a few business pieces that she wore to author events and mystery conventions from time to time. Today, she'd chosen a black sheath dress with a cashmere sweater and ballet flats. It was a stretchy fabric and good for travel, but it didn't feel nice enough. She felt more like the secretary traveling with her CEO boss.

Willow imagined it would only get worse once they landed in Charleston.

She was halfway through her second glass of champagne when the jet started to taxi down the runway for takeoff. Minutes later, they were in the air without much trouble. It was a remarkably smooth ride. Once they leveled off, a chime sounded. The flight attendant got up and went to the back of the plane to do something in the galley.

In front of her, Sawyer pushed a button and rotated his seat around to face them. Reaching down between them, he pulled out a table that extended from the side and offered a large new space for Willow and Sawyer to set their drinks, paperwork or whatever else they might have with them.

"So, now that you're on the plane and you can't get away, I need to tell you about something."

Finn narrowed his eyes at his brother. "What could it possibly be? You've already warned me that your wife is pregnant with my baby. What could be worse than that?"

Willow sat stunned for a moment. She hadn't heard anything about a baby, much less one the brothers shared. She'd presumed, ignorantly, that when Finn didn't have a wife, that he didn't have children. Apparently that wouldn't be the case for much longer.

"It's a long story," Sawyer said to her with a comforting pat on the knee. "And it isn't necessarily worse news. Just not the kind that you would normally want to hear."

Finn sighed and sat back in his seat. "Okay, tell me."

"Well, you will soon learn, if you don't remember, that Mother likes to throw parties. We're always being summoned to the family home for big soirees. Charity events, weddings, garden parties for one thing or another. She lives for it. And once I told her you were flying back today, she started planning a welcome-home party for you Saturday night."

Finn didn't bat an eye. "What's so bad about that? It seems like a nice-enough gesture. I won't know anyone there, but maybe meeting them will jog my memory."

Sawyer shook his head. "You don't get it. This isn't going to be twenty folks gathering to shake your hand and have nibbles and cocktails. When Mother throws a party, it's always a catered event for at least a hundred people. There will be an orchestra playing. It will be black-tie, for sure. If the weather holds up, it will be in the gardens. Otherwise she'll have it in the ballroom."

Willow groaned inwardly. His parents' home had a ballroom? She definitely hadn't packed the right outfit for that. She didn't have any beaded gowns in her closet and if she did, they would have husky hair on them. She wasn't sure what she was going to do. Maybe one of his sisters was short and flat chested and could loan her a dress? She doubted it.

Finn seemed equally startled by the news. "Are you serious?"

"As a heart attack," Sawyer said flatly. "She's been wanting to show off that ballroom, so I bet she has it inside no matter what. She had the whole thing redone after it was blown up last year, but Morgan had an outdoor wedding, and Kat and I eloped in Hawaii, so she hasn't had a chance yet."

"Did you just say someone blew up the ballroom?" Willow asked. The craziest statements seemed to roll off Sawyer's tongue like they were everyday occurrences for normal people.

"Well, he wasn't very successful, but he did enough damage that Mother had an excuse to redecorate."

"Do people normally try to blow up our family?" Finn asked. "This seems like something I should know."

"No, that was new. Honestly, things were pretty normal with our family until we found out that our little sister had been switched at birth. We grew up with Morgan, but our biological sister is Jade. The guy that tried to kidnap and ransom Jade as a baby tried again last year, and when it didn't work out again, the guy posed as a caterer and tried to blow us all up."

Both Willow and Finn sat in stunned silence. The awkwardness was only broken by Gloria approaching everyone with individual plates of fresh fruit and croissants. At this point, Willow was happy to get something in her stomach to go with the champagne. Her head was starting to swim, and given the current conversation, she might say something rude. Were the lives of all rich people like a big soap opera?

"Anyway," Sawyer continued, "no one was hurt. And things worked out in the end. But I'm telling you, Mother's itching to have people over. She had to get off the phone with me last night so she could start making calls. Don't be surprised if there are two hundred people there to see the infamous Finn Steele return from the dead."

Finn looked at Willow and put a grape wordlessly into his mouth. She could tell from his expression that he was just as blown away by the conversation as she was. Only for him, this was regular life. He couldn't remember it, but there had been a time not long ago where he could speak about his family without batting an eye, too. It made Willow's family seem tragic and boring by comparison.

"Gloria?" Finn spoke up, turning to the back of the jet, where the flight attendant was working in the galley. "I think I'm going to need that Xanax."

"Don't leave me," Willow whispered between the gritted teeth of a feigned smile. "I don't care what anyone says or does, please stay with me."

"I was going to say the same thing to you," Finn admitted. "Aren't we a pair?"

Finn looked up at the huge antebellum mansion in front of them. It was massive with two-story columns and dark shutters that stood out against the stark white limestone. Coming down the long driveway lined with moss-covered live oak trees had been intimidating enough, but this? How could this possibly be his childhood home? It seemed impossible.

The doors flew open and Finn clutched Willow's hand. A few women around their age came out first—a blonde, a brunette and a redhead—the redhead visibly pregnant. Some men followed behind them. One had to be his brother Tom based on the resemblance. The others must be his sisters' husbands, because they were both big, dark, bearded and completely unlike the Steele men in every way. An older couple, presumably his parents, came out behind them, followed last by a tiny old woman who looked more like the Queen of England than old Elizabeth Windsor herself.

The crowd rushed forward at once. It was a cacophony of words and hugs and tears, most of which Finn could barely understand. He stood stiffly, accepting each embrace as everyone said their hellos, but not really reciprocating. The only one to keep their distance was the old woman still on the porch, leaning on her cane.

"You all are going to scare him to death. The boy doesn't know you from Adam. Look at his bewildered face. Don't smother him."

Everyone took a step back and Finn made note of who really ran this place. He would guess it was Grandma.

"Come in," she said, gesturing inside. "It's hot as blue blazes out here."

Still holding Willow's hand, Finn walked toward the house with the others in their wake. Inside the mansion was equally imposing. A large, grand staircase greeted guests as they entered beneath a sparkling crystal chandelier.

It was all very nice. And about as unfamiliar as the Palace of Versailles. Finn swallowed his frustration as he crossed the foyer. He'd hoped that coming back here would jog his memory. The people he'd just met were supposedly the most important people in his life. His family. He was in the home where he'd grown up. And yet he might as well have been anywhere, meeting any new group of strangers.

At least he had Willow here with him. He looked at her and tried to smile reassuringly. She seemed to be just as nervous as he was about all of this. But she was here. His rock when he needed her the most. He'd never be able to properly thank her for her support. Not even with all the money he supposedly had in his accounts. But he'd have to find a way.

They followed the old woman as she clicked across the marble floors with her cane to a large family room.

"Have a seat," she said as she lowered herself into a velvet wingback chair fit for a queen.

Finn chose a love seat, putting Willow beside him and keeping the others at a comfortable distance. Almost immediately, an older woman he hadn't met yet arrived and offered them both tall glasses of sweet iced tea. She also placed a platter of cookies and finger sandwiches onto the coffee table in front of them. When she was done, she reached out and cupped Finn's face for a moment, tears in her eyes. "Welcome home, Finn," she said, and then disappeared from the room as quickly as she'd arrived.

"Who was that?" Finn asked.

"That's Lena, the housekeeper. She took your accident especially hard. She's wonderful, been with the family since the children were young. Since *you* were young," his grandmother corrected. "I think you may be her favorite."

Once everyone was seated, they took turns introducing themselves in a slower fashion he might actually be able to keep up with. The older woman was his paternal grandmother, Ingrid Steele. His parents, Trevor and Patricia, were seated on the sofa. His brother Tom lurked in the corner nibbling on a cookie and saying very little. He looked more like their father than he or Sawyer did.

The woman with platinum-blonde hair like Patricia was his biological sister, Jade. The petite accountant was in sharp contrast to the massive man hovering around her—her husband, Harley. He was some kind of former military security specialist and he looked the part. The dark-haired woman with the dark-haired man were his sister Morgan and her husband, River, a real estate developer. She had left the family company to start her own charity for premature babies the year before. Lastly, there was the redhead sitting beside Sawyer. Kat. She was a wood-carving artist. She was also seven months pregnant with his daughter, Beatrice.

If he recognized any of them, he thought it would be her. The woman he'd seduced and accidentally impregnated while pretending to be his brother. It was such an incredibly shitty story to hear about himself. But he tried to tell himself that things had worked out. Kat had married Sawyer and they were blissfully happy. If the baby looked like Finn, that meant it would look just like Sawyer, as well.

It did worry him, though. How many other stories were there where he was an asshole? It sounded like he went through women like tissues. It didn't feel like that's who he really was. But they would know better than he would. The more Finn learned about his life before the plane crash, the less he wanted to regain his memory. Maybe it was better if he didn't and could just start his life fresh.

"And who is this young lady?" his mother asked once everyone else had been introduced.

"This is the woman that saved my life." Finn squeezed her hand and looked at her with appreciation in his eyes. "Everyone, this is Willow Bates. She's a mystery writer that just happened to live in the middle of nowhere where I turned up. I don't know what would've happened if she hadn't found me and taken such good care of me."

"Wait a minute," Jade said. "Are you S. W. Bates? The author of the Amelia Mysteries? I love those books. I have about a dozen."

"That's me. S. W. Bates is the pen name I use. If you bring one of the books by, I'll be happy to autograph it for you."

Finn seemed surprised by the whole exchange. He knew she wrote books and did well enough, but he didn't know she and her characters were recognizable names in the genre. "What does *S.W.* stand for?" Finn asked.

Willow looked at him with a touch of hesitation lining her brow. "My initials, is all."

"Willow isn't your first name?"

"No, but I've gone by Willow for many years now."

There was something about her expression that urged Finn not to press forward. She was embarrassed of her name, perhaps. He understood that, coming from a whole clan of Mark Twain characters. So, he'd let it go. For now. But eventually, he'd find out what that *S* stood for.

"Well, we can't thank you enough for what you did for our Finn. We really did think we'd lost him along with the others. We were making the final arrangements when Sawyer called and told us that he'd found you in Seattle." Patricia's eyes were blurred with tears as she spoke. "I couldn't believe it. You're his miracle."

Willow shifted uncomfortably. "Finn's surviving the fall was the miracle. I don't know how he ended up on my beach, but all I did was take him home and call a doctor."

"And get me medicine and clothes, and feed me and take care of me," Finn added.

Willow only shrugged. "It was what any decent person would do in that situation."

"Somehow I doubt that, but you've more than earned the reward we advertised for finding Finn."

"I don't need any reward."

"Posh," Patricia said dismissively. "You'll take that hundred grand and do something swell with it. Buy a boat. Pay down your mortgage. Give it to orphans. But you'll take it."

Finn glanced over at Willow, who seemed mildly irritated but not enough so to argue with his mother on the subject.

Patricia continued on, unfazed. "I'm sure Sawyer has told you about the welcome-home party I've been planning for you Saturday night," his mother said to the two of them. "It came together quickly, but I think it's really going to be a lovely affair. And considering everything you just said, I think Willow should also be a guest of honor at the party as the person who saved Finn. People will be so pleased to meet you, as well."

He could feel Willow tense beside him. Finn knew very little about himself, but he'd grown so familiar with Willow that he could read her like one of her books. Every flinch, every sigh, every gasp of pleasure… He knew exactly what was going on in her mind. So he spoke up.

"I'm not so sure it's the best idea right now. It's awfully soon after the accident. I'm still in a lot of pain and my memory hasn't returned. Maybe we could push it out a little bit. I'm not sure I'm ready to face all those people."

"Nonsense," Patricia said with a dismissive wave of her elegant fingers. "Everyone is dying to see you and we have to celebrate while Willow is still here in Charleston. A party might be just what you need to shake out the cobwebs in your brain."

"I also don't think Willow packed for that kind of

event, Mother. I had no idea about the party until after we'd left."

"We can take her shopping," Morgan offered brightly. "We'll have a girls' day out, just Willow, Jade, Kat and I."

"That's a great idea," Jade added. "We'll get to know her better and we'll help her pick out something just right for the party."

"It can be our gift to you," Kat said. "For keeping Finn safe. A beautiful dress for a beautiful lady."

"I don't know," Finn began. It sounded like it could be overwhelming for her to spend the day with the girls. Never mind him having to go it alone all afternoon while she was shopping.

"It's okay," Willow said. "That sounds nice. They can probably do a better job helping me pick out a dress than you could."

"Yes, Finn's much better at taking them off than putting them on," someone quipped. Maybe Tom.

Finn sighed as the others tittered with laughter. He was getting tired of those comments. Even if he deserved them, there had to be more to his life than his pursuit of women. Being a rich playboy couldn't have taken up all his time, could it?

"I do hope you two will consider staying here for a few days. Upstairs there's a whole wing of the house that's empty now that all the children are gone. It will be very private, and you won't have to worry about cooking or cleaning with Lena here to handle things."

"Mom, Finn owns his own place just a few miles from here," Sawyer argued. "It might be better for him to spend time in a familiar environment. Being surrounded by his own things might be what brings his memories back."

"And I don't want to be underfoot," Finn added. "I'd really like to see my place. You're right, the more of my life I'm exposed to the better. That's what the doctors said," he lied.

In truth, he would go anywhere he could have time alone with Willow. He'd barely gotten to touch her since they'd made love that night at the hotel. Once he'd gotten the call from the hospital, it had been all drama and personal revelations. They'd shared a bed in Sawyer's suite the night before, but it had felt awkward to do more than spoon with his brother so nearby.

He didn't care if it was his place, or a hotel, or the garden shed in the yard; he just wanted some privacy. And to stroke Willow's soft skin. To talk her out of wearing that shirt so he could worship every inch of her. She'd made noises about being sensitive, and in the heat of the moment, he hadn't wanted to argue. But they couldn't go on like this forever. Whatever she was hiding from him, he wished she'd share it with him. And she wouldn't with his family lurking around.

"Well, if the doctor said so," Patricia relented. "But don't be a stranger around here."

Sawyer looked over at Finn and winked conspiratorially. Finn was really beginning to like his brother.

Eight

"You're so petite," Morgan remarked. "Anything will look good on you, like Jade and her ballerina's figure."

The three sisters had gotten Willow up early the next day and taken her to King Street in Downtown Charleston where all the high-end boutiques and department stores were located. She'd been hesitant to leave Finn, but if she didn't want to make a fool of herself at this party, she needed his sisters to help her get ready.

So far things had gone well, but she was a little overwhelmed. The women gave no notice to price tags or sales. They just picked up whatever they liked, making Willow thankful that they'd offered to buy her dress as a thank-you. She wouldn't even pay these prices for a wedding gown. Not that she'd ever need one.

"But you've got curves," Jade complained and clutched her barely B-cup chest. "I would've killed for your boobs in high school. Hell, I would kill for them *now*."

"Boobs are overrated," Morgan said.

"I doubt River would agree with that statement," Jade replied with a knowing grin.

"Well, neither of you have to buy a maternity gown today, so I don't want to hear it. I was hoping to get through this pregnancy without having to dress up. Now I'm going to look like a giant disco ball or a humpback whale in a beaded dress."

"I think a killer whale would be appropriate since it's black-tie attire," Morgan quipped.

Kat gave Morgan a cutting glance. "I will hurt you."

Willow listened to Finn's sisters all bicker at each other like old girlfriends. None of them were related by blood or had even grown up together as true sisters, and yet they had an amazing friendship. Her relationship with her own sister was strained and nothing like this at all. Their banter was amusing to listen to, but it was also a lot to keep up with. Especially knowing that a changing room and partial states of undress were looming in her future. She didn't imagine these ladies had a lot of boundaries. She was wearing her padded mastectomy bra and hoped it was enough to cover the scars and divert any questions.

"Ladies, these dresses seem a little over the top for me." Willow glanced at a price tag and winced. "I know you said it was a gift, but I'm not comfortable letting you pay this much for a dress I'll only wear once."

Kat and Jade looked at each other with a knowing glance.

"You're new at this," Kat said, putting a comforting hand on her shoulder. "We used to be in the same boat, Jade and I, so take our advice. Rule number one, Steeles don't look at price tags. Rule number two, quality and style are paramount because everyone is expecting it from you. The sooner you accept it, the easier it will be. So don't give it a second thought. You have to look good."

"What about this one?" Jade asked, holding up a strapless pale pink gown and turning the subject away from the ridiculous amount of money they were looking to spend.

That dress would never work. Even if she could find a strapless mastectomy bra in time, she couldn't hide the scar from her chemo port, which had yet to fade. "I think I'd prefer something with straps or sleeves. Maybe a high neckline. Something a little more modest. I like the color, though."

"Next thing you'll want a matching beaded bolero," Kat said. "Too modest and you'll end up in the same dress as Patricia. We can't have that. Especially under the circumstances."

"What circumstances?" Willow asked.

"Finn's favorite color is red," Morgan said, pointedly ignoring her question. "She should wear red if she's out to seal the deal."

Willow's eyes widened. Those circumstances. "Oh, I'm not out to—"

"He doesn't even know what his favorite color is," Kat interrupted. "But his Ferrari is red, so you probably can't go wrong with that. It's a statement-making color, for sure."

He drove a red Ferrari? Even after their long discussion the day before, Patricia had gotten her way and they'd stayed at the family home overnight. Today, after the shopping trip, they would go to Finn's townhome for the first time. And apparently, they would see his Ferrari and the other personal aspects of Finn's past that neither of them expected.

"I don't understand how amnesia works, I guess. He remembers basic things, but nothing personal? He can count to a hundred and tie his shoes, but doesn't remember any of us?" Morgan asked no one in particular. She narrowed her gaze at Willow for a moment and took a deep breath as she clutched a black beaded dress in her hands. "Okay, I'm going to ask the hard question, Willow. You and my brother are… *together*, right?"

"Morgan!" Jade chastised.

"It's a valid question," Morgan argued. "You've seen how they are with each other. Have you ever seen him like that with a woman before? No. So there's something to it. There has to be. Or there will be soon if we get the right dress."

All three sisters were suddenly silent and turned to look at Willow expectantly.

"It's complicated," she said. That was an understatement. Getting involved with someone in Finn's condition was asking for trouble.

"But you guys have…?" Kat wiggled her eyebrows suggestively.

"Yes, we have. But I doubt much more will come of it than that." It was a hard truth to speak aloud, but she needed to hear it as much as they did. Thankfully, they hadn't asked if she had feelings for him. That would be a more painful conversation with an equally doomed ending.

"So with amnesia, then," Morgan continued, "did he

know what he was doing when you guys were together? I mean it should've been like his first time, right? Like being back in high school again or something. Or is it like riding a bike?"

"Morgan!" Jade repeated.

Morgan only shrugged and ignored her sister. "I'm just trying to figure out what he remembers and what he doesn't. Of all the things I'd think Finn would remember, it would be sex. Let's be honest here. He might forget his own name, but the location of the clitoris is another matter."

They turned back to Willow for the answer. "He… knew what he was doing," she explained delicately. She wasn't about to tell them that she wasn't experienced enough to know if his skills were unusual. All she knew was that it was the most incredible night she'd ever spent with a man. "He was a thoughtful and generous lover—" She stopped, certain she was blushing brighter than that red gown from earlier.

"Generous and thoughtful?" Kat scoffed. "That doesn't sound like the Finn I know. Certainly not the one that did this." She rubbed her belly thoughtfully.

"Honestly, I've yet to see the Finn we know," Jade added. "He looks like Finn and sounds like Finn. But it's more like an alien is wearing his skin."

Willow frowned. She'd heard several things from his family since they arrived that had given her pause about her relationship with Finn. He'd obviously been some kind of playboy. But other adjectives had been included in not so many words—selfish, irresponsible and a bit of a jerk. Things were okay between them for the moment, but what if Finn's memory came back? What if he returned to being the arrogant womanizer he once was? It would be over between them for sure. There was no way a man with Ferrari tastes in cars and women would be interested in the stripped, broken-down hatchback that was Willow. Not even a fancy paint job courtesy of his sisters could help her if the old Finn came back.

"Maybe his memory won't come back," Jade offered as though she could read Willow's mind. "Then he could just stay the polite, kind Finn we know now, and we'd get to keep you."

Willow perked up. "Keep me?"

"Yeah. We aren't sure when Tom will settle down, but we were pretty certain Finn was a confirmed bachelor. But the new Finn really seems to like you, Willow. Like Morgan said, he's never acted the way he does with you around any other women before. If the new Finn stayed around, you could get married and you'd be one of us."

Apparently she wasn't the only one inclined to flights of fantasy. "That's—um…that's not going to happen. Even if the new Finn stays around forever, I have a life on the other side of the country. I'd be crazy to give that all up for a man I've known less than a week."

"You can write your books anywhere," Jade pointed out.

"And Finn isn't just any man. He's one of the Steele heirs. Most women would do a hell of a lot more than move cross-country for them," Morgan said.

Willow sighed. She would intentionally lose this argument because she couldn't tell them the truth. The truth was that Finn didn't know all of her secrets. He didn't know that she had been sick. Or that she could never have his children. As close as they'd gotten, they'd only known each other a handful of days. "I wouldn't get too attached" was all she said. "To the new Finn or to me. We will probably both be gone by the end of the week."

Jade frowned and turned back to the display of dresses. "Well, in that case, we at least need to make sure you look so amazing, he never forgets you. What about this one? Even I look like I've got curves in this cut."

She held up a peacock blue, empire-waist gown. It had wide satin straps, cap sleeves, a square neckline and a flowing chiffon skirt. It might be just the style she needed to disguise her lanky, waifish figure and less-than-stylish mastectomy bra.

"That color would be gorgeous on you."

"I love it," Willow said. "But I don't have anything to go with that color. I'd need shoes at least. Maybe some earrings so I don't look so plain."

"That is not a problem," Jade said. "We're nowhere near finished with you. We'll hit the makeup area, the jewelry counter, the shoe department… You'll walk out of here looking like a million bucks."

Willow wouldn't be surprised if it cost that much, too. She tried not to even glance at the price on the dress Jade chose. It would just make her anxious. She had to tell herself it was an investment piece. Maybe one day she'd win a book award like the Agatha and need a gown to wear to the ceremony.

"Absolutely," Kat agreed. "Try it on and if you love it, we'll get the rest after lunch. I'm starving."

"You're seven months pregnant. You're always starving," Morgan pointed out and glanced down at the time on her phone. "It's just now eleven. We'll get you some pretzel bites a few shops down to tide you over."

"That's not true," Kat grumbled and followed the others into the dressing room. "But I want a frozen Coke, too."

Everyone was looking at him. It made Finn uncomfortable. He might've been the life of the party at one time, but at the moment he wanted nothing more than to be sitting on Willow's deck, scratching Shadow behind the ears and listening to the birds in the forest that surrounded them.

What gave him the most discomfort was the way the women were looking at him. There had been coy smiles, winks, blown kisses and overly grabby hugs from women who varied from barely legal to his mother's age.

He was desperate for Willow to come downstairs and join the party. He wanted her on his arm tonight. Not just to deflect attention from the female party guests, although that would be nice, but because he missed her. He'd gotten used to having her around all the time. It physically pained him when she was gone, like a piece of him was missing. He was certain this was a new experience for him, although he wasn't entirely sure he liked it. He was an independent guy, from all reports. But if that meant Willow wasn't in his life, then forget it. Nothing said he had to stay the same person forever.

He looked anxiously at his watch and then scanned the ballroom for the tenth time. It was filled with people dressed in their finest sipping champagne and nibbling on canapés. There was an orchestra playing on the stage and a dance floor with a few couples taking a spin. It was very nice, but difficult for him to believe tonight was all in his honor.

That's when Finn saw her.

At least he thought it was her. The woman who found him on the beach had changed from an island hermit to his fantasy come to life. She wore a dark teal dress that flowed around her legs when she walked, as if she were some kind of goddess. Gold-and-aquamarine peacock feathers dangled from her ears, and a headband of tiny golden flowers was nestled into her short blond hair. When her eyes met his from the other side of the ballroom, she smiled brightly and the look was complete. The hair, the makeup… It was perfection.

But it wasn't the fancy clothes and jewelry that made the difference. Willow was already a diamond. His sisters had just given her the confidence that allowed her to shine.

When she looked at him like that, the crowd around them faded away. He turned abruptly from the stranger making small talk and made a beeline straight to Willow. He stopped long enough to pluck two flutes of champagne from a nearby server and held one out to her when he approached.

She accepted the drink and took a large sip. "So," she said with a nervous quaver in her voice, "do I look okay? If I don't, I'll go. I know that this isn't really where I belong and I don't want to embarrass you in front of your family and friends."

"Are you serious?" he asked. "You're the most beautiful woman at this party."

Willow glanced around the room at the other guests

and then frowned at his champagne glass. “How many of those have you had tonight?”

“I am not drunk. You look amazing and I won’t hear another word on the subject.”

Finn spied his mother coming his direction with some stranger in tow—another person she wanted him to meet that he wouldn’t remember. Reaching out for Willow’s hand, he asked “Do you dance?” as he pulled her toward the dance floor.

If her answer was no, it was too late. It was his only viable escape and there were worse ways to go about it than pressing a beautiful woman’s body against his own.

He wrapped his arm around Willow’s waist and guided her with him in slow motion in time to the music. Leading her even in the simplest steps was a struggle as she fought his every move. She was stiff as a board and probably none too pleased with his abducting her onto the dance floor.

“I’m sorry,” he leaned down and whispered into her ear. “I can’t take any more of these conversations. It’s been one stranger after the other asking the same stupid questions about my amnesia and if I really don’t remember the accident. Or feeling me up.”

Willow tilted her head up to look at him with an arched eyebrow of confusion. “Feeling you up?”

Finn sighed and nodded. “I get the feeling half the women at this party have spent the night with me, or would like to. It’s incredibly disturbing.”

Willow looked around the crowd of people and back at Finn. “If that’s true, you have good taste. I’ve never seen so many beautiful women in one room before. They’re probably all asking themselves why you’re dancing with me.”

"What does that mean? Why wouldn't I dance with you?"

"Because—" she frowned and averted her gaze "—it only takes a quick glance to see you could do better."

Finn groaned. "I thought we agreed this discussion was over and you're gorgeous."

He couldn't tell if Willow rolled her eyes, but he imagined that she did. To prove his point, Finn leaned his hips against her own, pressing the heat of his arousal into the soft curve of her belly.

She looked back at him with wide eyes that eventually faded into a smirk. "Fair enough. Your sisters did an amazing job on my hair and makeup. And they helped me pick a stunning dress for tonight. I will give them full credit for the transformation. Maybe you're right and I look just as glamorous as every other woman here tonight. But even then, I'm uncomfortable. These people…they're all looking at me. They know I don't belong here."

"They're all looking at you because you're beautiful and they're jealous." He ignored Willow's scoff. "Apparently it's not every day that a woman catches and keeps the attention of Finn Steele. Or so I hear. But don't feel bad. I'm uncomfortable, too. Maybe more uncomfortable than I've ever been. I know my memories don't go back very far, but I'd take another round of broken ribs spent in your recliner over being at this party another couple of hours. It's unbearably awkward knowing they all expect something from me that I don't know if I can deliver. But you know what?"

"What?"

"This party is for me. And if I have to stay, I'm going to enjoy myself."

Finn dipped his head down and captured Willow's peach-painted lips with his own. She melted into his arms at last. Here, now, with her mouth open to him and her anxieties gone for a fleeting moment, he savored it. The party, the people, the awkwardness…they were all worth it because they brought Willow into his arms like this. While they'd come together physically, they'd never really had the opportunity for romance. He hadn't known until recently that he had the money to take her out to a secluded dinner for two or a nice supper club with dancing. They'd never dressed up and gone out on the town. But they had tonight and he wanted to make the most of it.

The song ended and with it, the spell he'd managed to cast around them. The world returned, and Finn noticed his older brother, Tom, joining the orchestra on stage.

"Ladies and gentlemen, if I could have your attention for just a moment, please."

A quiet fell across the room with everyone turning to the stage. Finn and Willow turned, as well, although he did it with more dread than interest. He wasn't aware there were going to be any speeches tonight. Hopefully they didn't expect him to make one. Just the thought of being up there with the spotlight on him made his palms start to sweat.

"For those of you that don't know me, I'm Tom, the oldest of the Steele children. We're here tonight to celebrate the miraculous survival of my younger brother Finn."

He paused long enough for the crowd to cheer. "But I wasn't surprised when I got the call that he was okay and coming home. You can always count on Finn to get out of a tough spot unscathed. I remember his freshman year in college, when he got caught literally with his pants down with the daughter of the dean of the university. You or I would've been expelled, but somehow, Finn became a campus hero and got into the most badass fraternity on campus without having to pledge."

Tom paused for more laughter. "And then there was the incident with the ambassador's wife. Dad paid dearly to keep that out of the news. And the time he seduced three Victoria's Secret angels over the course of New York Fashion Week alone." He shook his head. "You can't make this stuff up. Right now Finn doesn't remember any of it, but I'm sure a lot of us will never forget. I'm also certain every father in China breathed a sigh of relief when he left Beijing and their daughters behind. He was and is a legend. To my brother Finn!"

The crowd raised their glasses and cheered with laughter and appreciation at Tom's stories. A few people slapped him on the shoulder in congratulations for his notorious exploits. But Finn felt nothing but embarrassment. Embarrassment and a sudden, overwhelming sense of panic.

Finn gripped the stem of his champagne glass so tightly, he was surprised it didn't shatter in his hand. But it didn't matter. In that moment, the flood of memories was all he could focus on. With imperfect timing, the dam of Finn's amnesia gave way and he remembered it all in a rush. Now he knew his brother wasn't exaggerating. In fact, he'd left out quite a few of the salacious details to avoid scandalizing Grandma Ingrid and Mother.

Up until this moment, he had thought that perhaps his reputation had been embellished. Perhaps it was just the family joke to pick on him for refusing to settle down. But it wasn't a joke at all. It was fact.

So many women. It made his stomach ache thinking of how casually he had used them all. Even Kat. He disgusted himself with the memories he could no longer ignore.

"Are you okay?" Willow leaned in and spoke into his ear over the sounds of the people talking on stage.

"I need to get out of here," Finn said. Reaching for her hand, he dumped his champagne glass onto a nearby table and fled for the door.

"What's wrong?" she asked as they made it outside.

"Be right back with your car, Mr. Steele," the valet waiting out front said, and jogged into the parking lot.

Finn bent over and braced his hands on his knees, drawing in a cool breath. "I think I'm having a panic attack."

"We should go back inside. You can lie down upstairs."

"No!" he said more brusquely than he intended to. "I want to go home. I don't want to be around these people or in this house for a second longer than I have to."

"What happened?" Willow asked. "What set it off? Your brother's speech?"

Finn shook his head. He wouldn't tell her the truth. He couldn't. It was bad enough that he had to remember his past and come to terms with what he had done and who he had been. He didn't like himself. And he was afraid that Willow wouldn't like him, either. Not if she knew the truth. If he was honest with her about what he'd done and how he'd treated the people in his life, she would never want to speak to him again. And he couldn't bear the thought of that.

Willow was the only thing in his crazy life that made any sense. She was the anchor that kept him from being swept away by the currents. He wasn't about to drive her away any sooner than he had to.

The valet returned with his Ferrari. He tipped the driver and they got inside. Moments later, they were peeling out of the long driveway and onto the highway, getting far, far away from the Steele mansion and the memories it held.

But running away from his family only did so much. His past had returned and no matter what he said or did, it would follow him forever.

Nine

Everything was different now.

Last night, as they'd entered his town house for the first time, it had been like touring an old historic house. He'd expected to see placards explaining the different pieces of art and furniture. There was no connection, even as he looked at his own face smiling back at him from pictures.

Now, with Finn's memory suddenly restored, it was more like a haunted house than a museum. Everywhere he looked, he saw ghosts of the past. Female ghosts, mostly. And unlike at the party, he couldn't run away from his own history.

With a sigh of relief, Willow kicked out of her heels. "I looked good while it lasted." She made quick work removing her jewelry and massaging her abused earlobes.

"Yes, you did. I'm sure everyone will think I swept

you out of the party early to make love to you." And that was true enough. He'd done it on multiple occasions over the years when he'd been forced to attend one of the company's tedious fundraisers.

"Is that why we left?" Willow asked. She turned her back to him and presented the zipper to her gown. "Please."

Finn moved instinctively to her back. Ignoring the zipper at first, he opted instead to run his palms over her bare upper arms, warming her skin. He leaned in to press a firm kiss against her neck, appreciating the accessibility her short haircut provided. He loved a woman's neck and the reactions he could coax by caressing it. He could feel her shiver against his lips and smiled.

Running his fingers across her shoulders, he traced the line of her back down to her zipper. He tugged it down slowly, grazing the silk camisole he found beneath it as he traveled to the low curve of her spine. He bit his lip to smother his disappointment. He'd been hoping somehow that tonight of all nights, she might be bare beneath that gown. He still hadn't managed to convince her to take off her top.

"Maybe that is why we left early," he whispered into her ear. "Maybe I faked that panic attack just to get you into my bed."

Willow turned in his arms to face him, holding her dress to her chest. "Liar." With that word hanging between them, she turned and headed for the staircase.

"You don't think I want to make love to you?" he asked as he followed her upstairs and into the master suite.

"Oh, I believe you want me. I just don't think that's

why we left early." She punctuated her sentence by letting the gown slip to the floor.

If she had to be wearing something beneath her gown, Finn had to admit this wasn't so bad. The ivory silk chemise was edged with scalloped lace that fell high on her thighs and dipped low at the neckline. She was wearing a bra beneath it, as usual, but it was more skin than he'd seen on her chest so far. Admiring the view, he halted when he noticed an unusual scar beneath her collarbone. It seemed like a fairly new scar, making him wonder what else she might be hiding with her modesty.

Willow paid him no mind as he studied her, focusing instead on scooping up her gown and draping it over the nearby chaise lounge. She slipped her headband off and set it on the dresser with her earrings. Finally, she turned back to face him. "So are you just going to stare at me, or are you going to tell me why we ran out of that party like your ass was on fire?"

Finn looked at her for a moment, weighing his options. He didn't want to lie to her, but he couldn't tell her the truth. Not yet. She'd come cross-country to help him with his transition home. If she knew he had his memory back, she might not have a reason to stay. Especially knowing what Finn was really like. He knew he would have to tell her eventually, but not tonight. Things would fall apart soon enough when she figured out how unlovable he really was.

"It was my brother's speech," he said, which was true enough. He sat down on the edge of his bed and tugged at his bow tie. Lying to Willow made his throat tighten and he thought it might help to loosen his tie. It didn't. "Everyone seems to get a big laugh from my old escapades. At my expense. But I don't think any of it is very funny. It's one thing to go through what I have and lose my memory. It's another completely to not understand or even like who I used to be."

Willow's expression softened as she listened to him speak. She crossed the room and sat down on the bed beside him, putting a comforting hand on his knee. "You don't have to have amnesia to not like who you are or to feel uncomfortable in your own skin. I think a lot of people do, but are too scared to change or don't know how."

Finn shook his head. "But what if I can't change? What if my memory returns and I end up falling back into my old habits again?"

"Finn, if you want to change, you can at any time, memory or no. You're already so different from the man I've heard people describe. Being a womanizer or not is completely within your control. It's not like you have an awful medical condition or were in some disfiguring accident that can't be helped or changed."

There was something about the way she said the words that made Finn take notice. It made him wonder if she was speaking from personal experience. "Like you?" he asked, turning to look at her.

Willow opened her mouth, then closed it again. She turned away from him and focused her eyes onto the floor. "Yes," she said at last.

He put his hand over her own. "Tell me, Willow. Please."

She sat for a moment before she spoke, making Finn's stomach knot tighter with every second that ticked by in silence. "I told you about my mother. And my grandmother. We found out too late that they were both at a higher risk of developing cancer because they had the BRCA gene that increases their odds of getting both breast and ovarian cancers in their lifetimes. After they both got sick, my sister and I were tested and we had the gene, as well. Having the gene is not a guarantee, but with the family history, I knew it was only a matter of time. Two years ago, I found a lump and I knew what it meant for me.

"After watching what happened to my mother," she continued, "I decided that I wasn't going to mess around. My sister said I was being paranoid, but I didn't care. I was determined to live past forty-five and not pass on this curse to anyone else. So I had a complete mastectomy and hysterectomy. Then I underwent months of chemotherapy. I lost thirty pounds and what curves I had were long gone. So much of my long blond hair fell out that I had to shave my head. This scar—" she touched the area of her chest he'd noticed earlier "—is from where they put my chemo port."

Finn squeezed his eyes shut. He'd been blind to not see how all the puzzle pieces of her life fit together to create this terrible image. Blind or just selfish—he'd been focused too much on his own problems to see she'd obviously been through a lot. She was living basically as a hermit, hiding from the world for a reason. Her short haircut and small figure. The panic attack in the hospital when she saw the cancer patient. The fact that she refused to take off her shirt for him… Separately those things didn't mean anything, but all together, the answer was obvious.

"Why wouldn't you tell me about any of this?"

Willow sighed. "It's not easy to talk about, Finn.

I'm no spokesperson for breast self-exams. And it's not necessarily something I feel the need to tell a stranger that drops into my life out of nowhere."

"Is that how you still think of me? After everything we've gone through this week? After all the things we've shared? Even after we made love?"

"Of course not," Willow said. "But by the time I felt comfortable enough to tell you about my past, I didn't *want* to tell you."

He didn't understand. "Why?"

"Because on some level, it's embarrassing. I'm damaged goods, Finn. Who would want me if they knew the truth?" She turned to look at him with tears shimmering in her eyes. "For one thing, I can't have children. And for another, I didn't have the reconstructive surgery. I couldn't bear to face another painful procedure when it wasn't medically necessary. I was tired of needles and drainage tubes, medication and discomfort. I wanted it to be done. Under this chemise..." Her voice trailed off.

Willow shook her head. "I don't want you to see. I didn't want anyone to ever see. So I hid away from the world to protect myself."

Finn listened to her speak without interruption. He could feel the weight of her words as she confessed her truth to him. He'd arrived in her life and disturbed the peace she'd tried to build herself. He'd tempted her from solitude and forced her, without knowing it, to face her biggest worries and fears.

"And now, after seeing the life you've lived and the women you've known...how could I ever compete with them? They're a bunch of gorgeous lingerie models and

I'm…well, not. So I'm sorry if I don't seem to believe you when you tell me over and over that I'm pretty, Finn. It's because I know the truth. I've seen the ugliness that I've kept hidden from you."

Once she'd gotten all the words out into the world, Willow could only hold her breath and wait for everything to come crashing down around her. Even if he'd cared for her, even if Finn harbored unspoken feelings for Willow…it might not be enough to overcome this. She'd told him all there was to tell. Short of taking off her top and exposing him to the harsh visual realities of her illness, it was done.

Now it was his chance to bow out gracefully, thank her for her help and let her return to the Pacific Northwest without making a bigger fool of herself than she already had.

"You're amazing," he said at last.

Well, that wasn't what she expected to hear. She turned to him and frowned. "Were you listening to me at all, Finn?"

"Yes, I was listening." Finn got up from the bed and knelt in front of her with his hands on her bare knees. Looking up into her eyes, he said, "And what I heard was the heartbreaking story of a tragedy that befell one of the strongest women I've ever met. What I heard was the story of you fighting to live…of you making the hard decisions to keep from repeating the same fatal mistakes your mother made. You've lost so much and yet you still have so much left to give. I know because I've been the lucky recipient of your gifts."

Willow's mouth fell open. This was the point where he was supposed to tell her how sorry he was about her lot in life and walk away. And yet here he was, on his knees, telling her how amazing she was. She didn't know what to think or say to that, especially when she didn't believe it herself.

"I know it was difficult to share that with me. If I had lived a life like you have, I might be afraid to open up to another person. Thank you for sharing your story with me, Willow. I'm honored, and not entirely sure I deserve it, but I'm thankful you chose me."

"You're too hard on yourself," she managed to respond.

"I was about to say the same thing to you," Finn replied. "Maybe we're both right. But you rehashed your painful past tonight because you wanted to prove a point to me. You wanted to convince me that I could change and be a better man if I wanted to be. And you're right about that, too. You've gone out of your way to help me since the day we met. And now it's my turn to embrace the new, improved Finn Steele and help you."

"Help me?" Willow questioned. "What could you possibly do to help me? The damage is done."

"I want you to show me," he said.

Willow's heart sunk into her stomach. "No." Why would he ask such a thing of her? She didn't even like to look upon the scars herself. She wore a sports bra or tank top under almost everything, only showering without her scars covered up.

He took her hands in his and held them tightly. Probably so she couldn't escape the uncomfortable situation. "You've trusted me with your story, Willow. Now trust me with this. Please."

Finn was so stubborn. He wanted so badly to be different than he'd been in the past that he thought this was how he could do it. But he didn't understand that if he was repelled…if he even flinched at the sight of her chest, it might not help him at all, but it could set her back months, even back to square one on her mental recovery from her cancer.

"I want to make love to you tonight, Willow. But I want to make love to all of you. I want to touch and kiss every inch of your body. I don't want you to hide anything from me anymore. You're just one step away from being completely open and you need this. You've been so brave through the whole ordeal. Be brave now. I promise that this step may seem hard, but you've been through so much worse."

Willow looked down at him. He was so sincere in his words. And maybe, just maybe, this wouldn't be the nightmare she'd imagined it to be. In reality, there wasn't much risk in trying. With the party over and Finn settling into his old life, she would return home soon anyway. Either he accepted how she looked, or he didn't, but either way, she would be gone before long. Why not take the chance?

Deep down, Willow knew that was a lie. There was a risk. A huge risk. But it had nothing to do with her pride. It had to do with her heart. She had let herself fall in love with Finn. It was stupid, but she had done it anyway. If she wasn't in love with him, she never could've told him the truth about her past and she wouldn't even consider exposing her scars to him. Whether their relationship ended with a whimper or a bang, it would end and she would be crushed. But that ship had already sailed with her heart aboard. She might as well enjoy the cruise.

Without speaking, Willow untangled her hands from his and reached up for the silk straps of her chemise. She let them fall down her arms and slipped out of them until the cool fabric pooled around her waist. Then she reached behind her to unfasten her mastectomy bra. She closed her eyes, held her breath and let it slip to the floor. Then…a long and incredibly painful silence.

His hands were still on her knees, so she knew at least that he hadn't recoiled from her. But he hadn't said anything, either, which was unlike Finn. Finally, the curiosity got the best of her and she opened her eyes.

Finn was kneeling before her, just as he had been. He was looking her in the eyes with a soft smile curling his lips.

"Did you even look?" she asked. Was he playing the good guy by keeping eye contact and just not looking so he couldn't make a mistake?

He nodded. "Yes, I looked. I imagine that was incredibly painful to go through. But it isn't the most interesting part of you, by far, and I wanted to look back at your lovely face. I think I like looking at it the best. I can see all your emotions dancing there without you saying a word."

Willow looked down at her own chest for a moment and then back at Finn. If it didn't bother him, maybe she could work toward not letting it bother her anymore, either. Perhaps she'd built this all up in her mind to be worse than it was. Or maybe Finn was just deserving of the love she wanted to give him.

"I don't want you to ever be ashamed of your scars, Willow. Especially not around me. They're proof that you're stronger than the cancer. They're evidence that you're still alive. Be proud of them."

She didn't feel proud. She always felt like her actions were ones of fear, not strength, but she'd never wondered how it appeared from the outside looking in.

"May I?" he asked, reaching out to touch her.

She nodded, closing her eyes again. A moment later, she felt his gentle caress brush over her collarbones, her sternum and then lightly over her scars. It was a strange sensation. Some parts of her were numb, while others were very sensitive, but she didn't mind this. He seemed to intuitively know how to touch her. This felt right, where little else had in ages. It even managed to set alight the flame of desire for him deep in her belly.

Opening her eyes, she covered his hand with her own, then leaned in to kiss him. "Make love to me," she murmured against his lips.

Still on his knees, Finn slipped out of his tuxedo jacket and tugged off his bow tie. With a sly smile he sought out the hem of her chemise and pushed it up her thighs until the entire thing was a silk band encircling her waist. She watched as his fingers gently stroked her upper thighs, his hot breath searing her bare skin. She leaned back and braced her hands on the mattress when his fingertips grazed across the satin of her panties. Finn applied pressure to just the right spot and a bolt of pleasure shot through her.

"Oh, Finn," she whispered, her eyes fluttering closed. She felt his hands seek out the waist of her panties and gently start tugging at them, along with the bunched-up slip. Willow lifted her hips, and he slid both garments down the length of her legs to the floor. Now she was completely naked for the first time with Finn. For the first time with anyone since her surgeries.

Maybe that was why tonight felt different from the other times they'd come together. There was a newfound confidence in Finn's touch as he let his hands roam all over the soft skin of her bare thighs, creeping higher and higher. She worried for a moment that he was focusing below her waist and avoiding her chest, but then she felt the flutter of his touch as he brushed over her center and all thoughts faded away. An explosion of sensation took its place as one finger slipped inside and stroked her aching core. Her heart started racing in her chest as he pushed her closer and closer to her release faster than he ever had before.

Her orgasm was hard and intense, knocking her back onto her elbows with the powerful spasms. He stayed there on his knees until the last tremors shook her legs, and then he stood up.

He immediately had his hand at his collar, quickly unfastening the buttons of his shirt. He tossed aside his shirt and whipped off his belt. Willow sat up to help. Her fingers sought out his fly, undoing the button and pulling the zipper down. Her hand slipped inside, slowly stroking the firm heat of him through his briefs.

"Willow," he groaned, and then his mouth greeted hers. She met his intensity, stroking him with a sure, firm hand until he pushed forward and she fell backward onto the bed.

Before she could recover, Finn had slipped from his briefs and pants and was moving above her. The heat of his skin seared hers as he glided over her body. Willow's thighs parted, cradling him. He paused only as he met her gaze and hovered there.

He was such a beautiful man. The first day when

she'd found him on the beach, she'd thought he looked like a fallen angel. The angles and curves of his face were perfectly carved by a great master. She had seen him at his worst that day, and at his best today. But her favorite expression was the one he had now as he paused, motionless over her. His golden hair had fallen into his eyes, his desire for her evident in his dark brown depths.

Was it possible that a man like this could ever love a woman like her? He was a successful businessman. A billionaire famous in the Charleston society circles. He'd probably grown up going to private schools and taking horseback riding lessons. What was Willow? A nobody born to a pair of hippies. Sure, she'd written some books and done well enough, but it felt like she could never do enough to deserve the love of a man like Finn, even though she wanted it so badly her heart nearly burst at the thought.

Finn dipped his head down to kiss her and she closed her eyes to focus on the sensation of being with him. She could feel the tears gathering in the corners as the unwelcome emotions of the night swelled inside her. Things between them had moved so fast, but she'd comforted herself in knowing they'd likely never go this far. She'd let herself indulge in a fling with her unexpected visitor figuring there wouldn't be any harm in it. But she was wrong.

His lips parted from hers, the air heavy and warm between them. Finn shifted against her, his spine arching and his hips moving forward. He entered her so slowly, and then paused there. Willow savored the sensation. She wanted Finn in her blood, his scent in her lungs, his taste on her lips, so she could keep him there in her forever.

His dark eyes searched her face for a moment as he hovered, buried deep and still inside her. "What am I going to do without you in my life?" he asked. "Isn't there a chance you might be willing to stay longer?"

Her secret hadn't driven him away. In fact, it had brought them closer. Was it stupid of her to run back to her island when she had something that felt special here? She needed to get as much of Finn as she could before it ended. "Maybe I could stay a few more days."

"Really?" A broad smile crossed his face.

"Yes, really."

Finn kissed her and the moment that had hung suspended in time suddenly began to rush forward. Emboldened by her response, Finn eased back and thrust forward again. And then again.

Willow clung to him, riding the waves of pleasure as they surged through her body. She drew her knees up and locked her ankles together at the small of his back. She didn't want to let him go, not even for a second. This moment wouldn't last forever, but she would savor it as long as she could.

It wasn't long before Willow felt her release building up in her again. She bit her lip, trying hard to fight it off. It was too soon. "I'm not ready for this to end," she said. And she didn't just mean making love to Finn right this moment. She meant all of it. Adding a few days onto the trip was only delaying the inevitable. But he hadn't asked her to stay forever.

Finn propped himself up onto his elbows and planted kisses along her jawline to her lips. He kissed her thoroughly and smiled. "There will be more moments. Enjoy this one."

His hand slid up her outer thigh to her knee. He hooked her leg over his shoulder, tilting her pelvis up and driving harder and deeper than ever before. The sensation was incredible, causing Willow to cry out.

"Oh, Finn," she gasped, clawing at his back. There was no use in prolonging her release now. It was impossible. She could feel the tightening in her belly, the driving surge of the countdown inside her. "Yes!"

Willow sucked in a large lungful of air and her eyes closed. Like a tsunami, her orgasm crashed through her. She clung to Finn for dear life as every nerve ending in her body lit up and her insides pulsated with pleasure.

"Willow..." he whispered, driving harder and faster than before until he stiffened and groaned. He gasped her name one last time as he surged into her body, leaving him exhausted and trembling.

He dropped over to her side, sucking ragged breaths into his lungs as his muscular chest rose and fell. They both lay together quietly for a few moments before Willow pushed herself up onto her elbow to look down at him. Damp blond curls were plastered to his forehead. His brow was furrowed from exertion as he lay there with his eyes closed.

"You're a better man than you give yourself credit for being, Finn," she said. "I don't think the old you would've handled this the way you did tonight."

He opened his eyes, looked at her and nodded with a sad certainty. "You're right. The old Finn was far too focused on the things that don't really matter. A woman's outsides aren't nearly as important as what's inside. A good heart, a sensitive spirit and a loving soul make for a far more beautiful lady than a big rack and pouty lips."

Finn rolled onto his side and reached out to caress her cheek. "And you, Willow Bates, are beautiful both inside and out."

Ten

Sawyer finally escaped the man who had been trying to talk business with him for the past hour. He scanned the mostly empty ballroom, looking for the wife who had long abandoned him to the boring chat. He found her sitting at a corner table, her shoes discarded and her bare, swollen feet elevated on a nearby chair.

"I'm sorry," he said as he approached her.

"This may have been the longest night of my life. If I was further along in this pregnancy I might've feigned labor just so we could leave."

"You know I can't leave these things early. Mother would notice."

Kat picked up her sparkling-water-and-fruit-juice cocktail and took a healthy sip. "And yet the guest of honor has been missing in action for two hours now."

Sawyer had noticed that he hadn't seen his brother

or Willow in some time. A few people had even approached him, thinking he was Finn. "He usually finds an excuse to bail on these things early. Why did he leave?"

Kat shrugged. "The last time I saw Finn, the blood was draining from his face while Tom publicly humiliated him. I wouldn't be surprised if he escaped because of that."

Sawyer frowned at his wife. "Publicly humiliated? Finn? He loves telling those stories, especially because it gets my father all riled up."

"Maybe the old Finn enjoyed reliving his wild past. But the man that came home with you is different, honey. I don't think he's quite as proud of his escapades. He could barely look me in the eye since he got here. I don't know if he'll be able to handle being in the delivery room when Beatrice is born."

The orchestra finished their last song and thanked the remaining audience, signaling the end of the night. The catering team swarmed the ballroom, picking up the last of the dishware and breaking down the dessert bar.

Kat reached out her arms to Sawyer. "Take me home, darling. I'm through with all of this."

Sawyer knelt to slip her ballet flats onto her feet and lifted her out of the chair. He wrapped his arms around her as best he could. "You know, we agreed this baby would never come between us," he said as he looked down at the gap her expanding belly created.

"Very funny," Kat said and gave him a quick, firm kiss. "I can actually feel myself getting bigger if I sit still long enough. The third trimester is not for wimps."

"That is the last word I would ever use to describe

you. You hand-carved Beatrice's cradle. You're a force of nature." Sawyer wrapped his arm around her shoulder and walked her to the foyer. When their Range Rover was brought around, they settled in and headed back over the bridge to downtown.

"You know, I think I like the new Finn," Kat said after a few moments of silence.

"I do, too. And I like Willow. I feel like she's a good influence on him. I couldn't say that about any other woman I've seen him with before."

"The girls and I agree that she's a keeper. I hope Finn is on board with that plan."

Sawyer wasn't so sure about that. He'd never thought he would see the day when Finn settled down. Their father had twisted his arm into proposing to Kat when she got pregnant, but his heart wasn't in it. No one was more relieved when she turned him down than Finn was. "If Finn has changed for good, you might get your way. But..." He trailed off.

"But what?"

Sawyer frowned at the road ahead of him. "The doctors in Seattle said that Finn's memory would eventually return. They seemed to think it was a side effect of the swelling in his brain when he hit his head. It's not permanent. And when he does remember everything, I can't help but think things will change drastically. Especially between him and Willow."

"But he seems so disgusted by his old partying ways. You don't think that his experiences since the crash will affect him after his memory returns?"

He wished he could say yes for certain, but Finn always seemed to find a way to surprise him. "I don't know."

"Well, I'd like to think that even with his memories, Finn has changed for the better. He's had a near-death experience. And if you ask me, he's fallen in love with Willow."

"Finn?" Sawyer sputtered. "In love?"

"You've seen those two together. He may not want to admit it to himself or anyone else, but he loves her. If those two things combined don't make him want to seize the moment and make the most of whatever time he has with her, I don't know what would."

Sawyer turned their SUV onto Market Street. If Finn really did love Willow, maybe Kat was right and the new Finn would outlast the amnesia. But the nervous ache in his gut told him it was a long shot.

"For everyone's sake, I hope you're right."

Finn crawled out of bed at dawn for possibly the first time in his life. He knew now that he was a night owl. If he saw this hour of morning, it was because he hadn't yet made it to bed. He knew a lot of things now. And that was why he couldn't sleep.

He'd watched Willow sleep for a while, looking peaceful and beautiful on the pillowcase. Of course, she'd slept like a baby. Not only had she been well loved, but she'd finally lifted a great weight off her shoulders. She slept the sleep of a happy, free conscience.

Finn poured hot water into his French press and silently cursed himself. He'd had his memory back for less than ten hours and he was already acting like the self-absorbed shit he'd always been. The same person he said he didn't want to be anymore. But he'd lied to Willow. She'd been by his side through this whole ordeal. She'd held his hand as he struggled with his memory and his place in the world. And when those memories finally came back, he kept it to himself and instead pushed Willow to be honest with him.

That was rich.

He pinched the bridge of his nose as he sat at his kitchen island. Willow had given him everything he'd asked for last night. He'd pushed her to trust him because he knew she needed to let the hurt and shame go. But he'd never forgive himself for doing it while his own pants were aflame. He was the last person anyone should trust.

Finn needed to tell her he'd gotten his memory back. Sitting over his coffee, he considered half a dozen scenarios where he'd stage his memory returning in a dramatic fashion, and he realized he was only making the situation worse by piling on more lies. He just needed to be honest with her, no matter the cost.

And yet he knew what the cost would be. He had no doubt that he would lose Willow. Not because of the lies, necessarily, but because of the truth. If his memory had returned, Finn was no longer lost in a sea of strangers, fighting to understand a life that made no sense to him. She would go because he remembered now. He remembered everything. He knew why certain women had looked at him at the party with wicked, hungry gazes and why others seemed to scowl at him from the edges of the ballroom.

He wasn't lost. He didn't need Willow to hold his hand. At least, not like before. Now he was just confused on how to move forward with his life. If he didn't want to slip into his old bad habits, he had to make changes, as Willow had suggested. And he could. He was capable of being a better person. He could at least continue to be the person he'd become since the accident. But he got the feeling that the minute she returned to Washington State, those bad habits would resurface again.

Whether he was punishing himself for screwing things up with her, or just trying to forget Willow, he had no doubt he would party until her curious dark eyes stopped haunting him when he closed his eyes. And he knew that once he started down the path of booze and women, he wouldn't want to stop again. It was a hell of a lot more fun than being stuffy and responsible like Sawyer, or an ass-kisser like Tom.

Sure, finding out who he really was had carried the excitement of knowing he was rich and important. But there was also a peace and easiness in just being Jack, who didn't have a dime to his name but was happy with Willow in the middle of nowhere. Since Sawyer found him, it had been nothing but a roller coaster of emotions, culminating in last night's flood of unwanted memories. Being a Steele had baggage. And being Finn Steele made everything complicated.

"I woke up lonely in a cold bed."

Finn turned around to see Willow standing at the bottom of the stairs. She was wrapped up in a pink silk robe and wearing a pair of his bedroom slippers.

"I'm sorry," Finn replied, leaning in to give her a good-morning kiss. "I couldn't sleep."

Willow looked mildly surprised. "After all of last night's hard work, I would've thought you'd sleep like a baby."

"Well, you certainly slept like someone who had

been thoroughly and well loved. Would you like some coffee?"

"Actually, if you have some, I think I'd like tea."

"I do. It's in the far-left cabinet above the canisters. There should be English breakfast and Earl Grey."

Willow was heading over to the cabinet when she stopped dead in her tracks and turned to look at him. "What did you say?"

That's when he realized what he'd done. Amnesiac Finn wouldn't know the first thing about what was in his cabinets or where, and yet the details had rolled off his tongue as easy as could be. He'd managed to blow it almost immediately.

"How would you know all that?" Willow pressed.

"I..." If anyone else had put Finn on the spot, he would've had a quick lie or comeback to deflect it. He could say he'd seen it earlier looking for coffee or sugar or anything. The lie hung on the edge of his tongue. But not with Willow. He knew what he had because he knew every inch of this home. "It's just tea, Willow," he said instead.

The expression of contentment she'd woken with started to crumple. She bit at her bottom lip and glared at him. "No, this is about more than the contents of your pantry, Finn. When we first got here, you couldn't even find the powder bath on this floor. How long?" she demanded. "How long have you had your memory back?"

He could see the overhead lights reflecting as a shimmer in her moist eyes. "A day? A week?" Willow's voice cracked as she spoke. "Has this whole thing been some kind of charade for you to get a break from your life and responsibilities for a while at my expense?"

"Absolutely not!" Finn insisted. Yes, he hadn't been completely honest with her, but to accuse him of lying about everything? That was a low blow, especially considering the shape he was in when he turned up on the beach. It was as though she'd been waiting for him to betray her this whole time. "I just got my memory back, Willow. I swear it."

"So you woke up with your memories this morning and decided not to wake me up and share the news?" She glared at him from across the kitchen island and dared him to lie again.

He sighed and looked down. "No, it wasn't this morning."

"Was it last night, then, at your big party? Did seeing all those beautiful women remind you of the nights you've spent with them? They were all certainly looking at you like they knew more than a casual stranger."

"It wasn't like that, either. It had nothing to do with the women. They made me uncomfortable—I didn't lie about that. It was later, during Tom's awful toast. I don't know why that triggered my memories, of all things, but it did. That's why I wanted to leave so suddenly. It was too much for me all at once. All I wanted was to get away from all of those people who knew me before the accident and what I was like then."

Willow looked at him for a moment, studying his face carefully. Finn tried hard not to flinch under her scrutiny, or worse, to try and make himself look more honest and contrite. She would see right through that.

"I'm not sure I believe you, Finn. I'm not sure I believe anything you say now."

"No, please," he said, rushing closer to her, only

to have her take a large step back. "It was last night. I was scared to tell you."

"So you decided to just lie? All the while, prompting me to trust you with my biggest, most painful secrets?" Willow looked down at the gap in the neckline of her robe, and tugged it tightly closed to keep her chest and everything that went with it hidden from his sight.

Fate had the worst timing. Why would his memory have to return on the same night she'd finally opened up to him? "No. Willow, don't associate last night with this. What we shared was so special to me."

"Everything that happened last night was tainted by your lies. One of the only reasons I was comfortable sharing my scars with you was because I didn't think you could compare me to a hundred other women you've been with before. And the whole time, you had your memories of every single one."

"I assure you that the last thing on my mind last night was other women. Before and after my memory returned, you're the only woman I've thought about. How I feel about you. How special you are. How it would ruin everything if you knew the truth about me."

Finn shook his head. "I've been agonizing over what to do since before sunrise. The old Finn wasn't a very good guy. I thought once you knew my memories had come back and you learned what I was like before the accident, that you wouldn't want to stay. That's why I didn't want to tell you yet. I'm not ready to lose you, Willow."

She listened to everything he had to say and sadly shifted her gaze down to the hardwood floors. "I'm sorry, Finn, but you already have."

* * *

Willow had been dreading this moment since the amnesiac with the dimpled grin had captured her heart. She knew that when he regained his memories, she would lose him. At least, she would lose Jack. Jack was the man she had fallen for. Curious, kind, grateful…he had looked at her like his whole world was wrapped up with her on their tiny island. He was an outsider when he showed up on her beach and they were able to be outsiders together. Jack would never lie to her. Or manipulate her. He didn't have a devious bone in his body.

But Finn was never hers. He was the billionaire heir of Steele Tools. The playboy. He'd never been an outsider. He'd always been the cool guy. Mr. Popular. She wouldn't even begin to know how to relate to a man like that. It was hard enough to make small talk with his friends and family. There was no way she could continue on with Finn when they had nothing in common but a week spent together on her island.

She would cherish the time they'd had together. It had been an enlightening and educational experience for her. Willow had realized by being with Finn that she might live on an island, but she wasn't one. Keeping people and relationships at arm's length might have seemed like the right thing to do after her health scare, but it only made her lonely. And worse—vulnerable to the charms of the first man who dropped into her life.

Even coming out here had taught her more about herself and what she was capable of when she put her mind to it. She had fought through cancer, making hard choices to ensure that she would live, and now she needed to start actually living. Despite what she once believed, she could still be beautiful and desirable and have people in her life. There were people out there, men included, who would accept her as she was, once she was able to do the same. But that man would not be Finn. Their relationship was a stretch, and it was time for the fantasy she'd built up in her head to end.

It was not what she'd intended to wake up to this morning. She'd hoped for a kiss, some caffeine and maybe a return to bed. Instead, she'd been faced with a truth she couldn't ignore any longer. It was so disappointing to watch him scramble for words when he was caught in his lie. She'd heard stories about his escapades, even masquerading around as his twin without anyone suspecting the truth.

She had thought that the infamous Finn Steele would be a better liar. And she wished he was better. Or that she couldn't read him so well. Then they could both keep on pretending that his memory hadn't returned. But he'd screwed up and there was no going back to the way things had been.

"Please, Willow. What can I do to convince you that I mean what I say? Tell me. I know that I shouldn't have lied to you, and I'll do anything to make things right between us again."

Willow bit at her lip, fighting to stay strong. This needed to end. And the sooner the better for both of them. "You are who you are, Finn. Nothing can change the past. And it seems like your future might be on the same path you've already set a course for. And that's okay. There's nothing wrong with continuing to live your life the way you'd planned to before the accident. You've just got to do it without me."

"Willow—" he started to speak, but she held up her hand to silence him.

"Please book me a flight back to Seattle as soon as possible," she continued. She wasn't going to wait to hear his arguments. If he had a good reason for her to stay, she might be persuaded to do it. And if she'd learned anything about the old Finn, it was that he knew how to get his way. She didn't believe the glint of tears or the pained expression on his face were intended to manipulate her, but she could feel her resolve crumbling from seeing him hurt. "I think it's past time for me to go home."

His dark eyes watched her with a mix of resignation and disappointment. She could tell then that he wouldn't fight her on this. He knew this needed to end, as well. They both needed to move on with their separate—and very different—lives. Their paths were never meant to cross. It was an accident. And now it was time to fix it and put their paths to rights.

"If that's what you want, I'll take care of all the arrangements. If you'd like to start packing, I'll have a car come pick you up and take you to the airport in about an hour."

"Thank you." Willow took a deep breath, resisting the urge to run into his arms and bury her face in his chest. Instead, she turned and went upstairs to pack her clothes and get ready to leave.

Her small duffel bag held what she'd brought with her, but she quickly realized there was no way that any of her new pieces from her shopping trip with the girls would fit inside. It was just as well. She would never have another occasion to wear a dress like that, despite what she'd tried to convince herself earlier. Maybe one of his sisters would like to have it. It would be lovely on Jade. She hung up the dress and put it in the closet with the heels. She opted to keep the earrings and the headband; they were easier to pack.

Dressed and ready, she checked the time. She had a bit before the car would arrive, but she couldn't just stay up here. She went downstairs, dropping her bag by the front door. She could hear Finn in the kitchen.

"Please tell the driver when he arrives that I'm across the street at Waterfront Park."

Finn walked into the room, drying his hands with a towel. "I will," he said with a nod. "He should be here in about fifteen minutes."

"Thank you." Willow reached for the doorknob.

"No. Thank you, Willow," Finn said in a quiet voice that reminded her more of her sweet Jack. "Thank you for everything."

She couldn't look at him. Not if she wanted to stay strong. "You're welcome," she replied and marched out the front door without looking back. She rushed across the street to the park and found a place to sit near the famous pineapple fountain.

There were people all around. Some were admiring the fountain, while others were looking out into the channel for the famous sights of Charleston Harbor. The whole area oozed Southern charm and history. Willow didn't see any of it. She was lost in her thoughts, lulled there by the roar of the fountain.

It wasn't until a man in a black suit tapped her on the shoulder that she returned to the world. "Miss Bates? I'm here to take you to the airport. I already have your bag in the car, along with all your flight information."

Willow followed the man to the street where the

shiny black Lincoln Town Car was waiting for her. She was determined not to look over at Finn's town house as they pulled away. As she'd tried to tell Finn, there was no sense in looking back. Just look forward.

It was time to return to her solitary, but comfortable, life on Shaw Island.

Eleven

Monday morning, bright and early, Finn put on a suit and went to the Steele Tools corporate offices. He ignored the wary glances and whispers as he crossed the lobby to the elevators and headed to the executive floor. He supposed that surviving a plane crash made him subject to employee gossip. Among his other notable activities.

When he arrived at his office, his assistant, Melody May, shot bolt upright in her chair. "Mr. Steele?" she asked. "I wasn't expecting to see you this morning."

He admired the pretty, dark-haired woman who had worked as an assistant for the three Steele boys for at least the past two years. Finn had flirted with her, but to avoid more problems at work than he already had, he had maintained a hands-off policy with Melody. That seemed to offend her more than anything else.

But today, she appeared to have put that chip on her shoulder in the past.

"You don't expect to see me most mornings, Melody." Finn smiled and walked past her desk to his office.

Melody showed up a few minutes later with a cup of coffee and a handful of cream cups and sugar packets. "I'm not sure how you take your coffee, sir."

Finn felt the burn of shame on his cheeks. He'd barely done anything to deserve this job and the salary it earned him. He couldn't even be troubled to show up before lunch most days, so much so that his own assistant didn't know how to make coffee for him. He really had been a jerk to everyone in his life. "Black, thank you."

Her brows rose slightly in surprise as she set the cup on his desk. "You're welcome, Mr. Steele. Is there anything else I can do?"

"Could you put a ticket in with IT to get me a new laptop and a new corporate phone? Mine were both lost in the crash. I also need all new identification cards, credit cards, a checkbook, a passport...and anything else I normally carried in my wallet. If you can help me work all that out, I'd very much appreciate it."

"Yes, sir."

"Please call me Finn."

"Yes, sir."

"Could you also print out my calendar for the next week so I have it to reference until my new computer shows up?"

"Absolutely."

"Thank you, Melody." The woman hesitated for a moment, making Finn feel even worse for how he may have treated her in the past. "Have I ever told you 'thank you' before, Melody?"

She sat with a puzzled expression on her face for a moment before shaking her head. "I don't believe so."

Finn sighed and sat back in his chair. "Well then, to the thank you, I'd also like to add that I'm sorry. Things will be different now."

"You really lost your memory, Mr. Steele?"

Finn nodded. No one but Willow knew it had returned yet. "Finn, please, Melody. But don't worry. These changes are permanent. The amnesia has nothing to do with my ability to treat people well."

Melody smiled and backed out of the room. "Let me know if you need anything else, Mr. St—*Finn*."

His assistant disappeared from the room, leaving him alone in the emptiness of his office. He looked around at the unremarkable space. The furniture was a generic mahogany suite with leather guest chairs and a small conference table near the window. Both his brothers had similar setups. He'd added a small dry bar in the corner with a minifridge and a crystal decanter filled with Scotch. The bookshelves behind him were mostly empty, save for a few picture frames. He turned to look at them as though it were the first time.

Even with his memory back, it didn't seem very familiar. He'd never spent much time here and that had nothing to do with his assignment in Beijing. He was just a shitty employee who got away with murder because he was the boss's son.

One photo was of his whole family gathered for some event on the lawn of the estate. He couldn't remember which get-together it was for. Another was an autographed photo of him with an Italian runway model. The third was a photo of him from a ski trip in Switzerland. He didn't remember the name of the woman in the picture beside him. He wished he could blame that on the head injury, but he just frankly couldn't keep track of them all.

An unfamiliar beep sounded at Finn's desk phone. He pressed the blinking button beside the intercom label. "Yes?"

"Your father would like to see you in his office."

And that was why he rarely came into work.

With a groan, he picked up his coffee and pushed up from his chair. His father's office wasn't far, just in the corner of the building with the best views of downtown on both sides. It was positioned such that Tom's, Sawyer's and Finn's offices were easily visible to him down the hallway, as were their comings and goings. Or no-shows, in Finn's case.

"Good morning," Trevor Steele said as his son appeared in the doorway of his office. "Come in."

Finn sat in the guest chair, where he got most of his tongue lashings, and settled in for his next one. Perhaps he was in trouble for leaving the party early on Saturday. Or for surviving the crash and somehow inconveniencing his father and the company in the process. Who knew? It was always something, though.

"I know you've been out of touch for a few weeks. And I'm not sure if you recall, but when your plane crashed, you were coming home from our new facility in Beijing. It was a big responsibility I gave you by sending you out there to set up our first manufacturing plant overseas. And I have to tell you that things are going very well. The project has been an amazing success and you had a major hand in that, Finn. I'm proud of you."

If Finn hadn't regained his memories, this conversation would've been nice, but it wouldn't have had the same impact. He tried not to visually react to his father's words, just smiled and nodded at the praise. But it was the first time his father had ever said those words to him. And he hadn't realized how badly he'd wanted to hear them until this exact moment.

"I understand that you've been through a lot, and I don't want to rush you. But once you're fully recovered, I'd like you to take on more responsibility at the company."

At this, Finn's jaw dropped. He'd only been given the bare minimum to handle since he'd graduated from college. He got the feeling that his father only gave him the Beijing job to get him out of his hair for a few months. "Really?"

Trevor smiled at him and he almost didn't recognize that expression on his father's face. It wasn't his polite public smile, but a legitimate grin. "Really. I feel like this whole experience has changed you for the better, Finn. You've done a lot of growing up in the last few weeks and I'm hoping that this will be the start of great things for you and your involvement in the company."

"Thank you." It was all he could think to say.

"There's actually a few big projects coming up, so you can have your choice. When you're ready. Now, get out of here. Take a few more days. I don't want you rushing your recovery."

Trevor stood and came around the desk. He held out his arms and it took a moment for Finn to realize his father wanted a hug. He got up and hugged his father, accepting the paternal slap on the back.

"When I heard your plane crashed, it felt like a part

of me died," Trevor whispered in Finn's ear. "I thought I'd never see you again and I had so many regrets. It looks like we both have a second chance. Welcome home, son."

"Thanks, Dad." Finn left the office and found himself standing stunned in the hallway.

Growing up as one of four children, Finn had been neither the oldest, the baby nor the cherished girl. He was one of the twins, not even a whole person on his own. He learned early on that getting into trouble got him more attention than being good. He also learned that it was a hell of a lot more fun. So he took on the mantle of problem child and made the most of it.

But deep down, if Finn was honest with himself, all he'd really wanted was for his parents to acknowledge him. Maybe even to be proud of him. But it had seemed impossible until now. The moment he'd always secretly wanted with his father had happened. And all it had taken was for him to nearly die.

He should be thrilled.

And yet…the moment wasn't everything he'd hoped for it to be. Or at least, it wasn't as impactful as he expected. To actually earn a promotion, more responsibility and the approval of his father…it was everything he'd dreamed of and suddenly nothing he wanted. And it was all because of Willow.

She could've gone through reconstruction to look the way the world expected her to, but she'd made the choice that was right for her. She lived a life that made her happy, even if her sister or outsiders thought it was strange to live alone. If he'd learned nothing else from his time with her, it was that he needed to live his life on his own terms. Despite his wild reputation for hedonistic fun, he hadn't really been happy. Or fulfilled. Everything he'd ever done had been to suit his chosen role as the rich playboy son. Living in the moment had been fine enough in his twenties. But now he wanted to do what made him happy and that meant rebelling in a completely different way.

Finn had thought chasing women and partying at every opportunity was a great way to spend his free time. Most people were envious of the life he lived. And that had been enough for him until he met Willow. Or rather, until he lost Willow.

Watching her walk out of his town house had been more painful than waking up on that beach a broken man. It was like she had ripped out a part of him and taken it with her. And he knew now it was his heart.

He had never been in love with a woman before, but he was pretty sure that's what it was. He couldn't stop thinking about her and what she was doing. He smiled remembering things she'd said to him. All of his public escapades seemed frivolous and stupid compared to a private life lived with her. She made him a better man, which was no easy task.

Everything about her was so amazing. And special. She wasn't just some cookie-cutter debutante. Willow was one of a kind. And he loved her.

Now he just had to find a way to prove to her that it wasn't too risky to love him back.

For the first time since Willow bought her house, it felt empty. Doc would be coming by later to bring Shadow home, but until then, it was just her and the rooms that seemed larger and more cavernous than she remembered. Big and abandoned.

It didn't help that the house had been left in a state of disarray. They'd basically gone to Seattle for the day to see the doctor and unexpectedly had never come back. She'd briefly returned to the house to pack some things for Charleston, but she hadn't had time to do much else. Finn's blanket was folded up in the recliner he'd loved to sit in. His empty coffee cup was still on the end table. Breakfast dishes were in the sink from that morning. Her notes from her latest book were scattered around her desk. It made it almost seem like Finn was still around. Like he would step out of the bedroom at any moment and ask her for some shampoo.

She had been alone in the house for far longer than she had ever been with Finn, but he had blended so seamlessly into her life, it was as though he'd always been around. People had always asked how she could live out here by herself, but it hadn't seemed to bother her. Maybe she just hadn't known what she was missing. But now, with Finn on the other side of the country, she truly felt alone here for the first time in her life.

Willow lowered herself into the recliner and gathered his blanket into her arms. Taking a deep breath in, she could smell Finn's scent lingering in the soft fabric. She could imagine burying her face in his neck and drawing in that same smell as she kissed his warm skin. Without much trouble, she could once again feel the stubble along his jaw as it grazed her throat.

Sitting back, she closed her eyes and tried not to let herself get upset again. She'd managed to hold her emotions in check until she was out of Finn's sight. She even made it onto the plane. But somewhere over Tennessee, Willow had started crying and couldn't stop until they were nearly to Salt Lake City. She always thought the people in first class lived such charmed lives. She was wrong.

At least about herself and her happiness. Willow had set herself up to fail in this situation. The moment she'd laid eyes on the beautiful, unconscious Finn, she knew she shouldn't get attached to him. She had a million different reasons, but the idea was the same—she needed to keep her distance or she would get hurt. She needed to protect herself and her heart. Without knowing the first thing about him, she knew that handsome face would never be hers.

To think otherwise was to court disaster.

And here, as she looked around her living room, was the disaster area. Ground zero. This was where she'd shared details of her life with Finn and he'd kissed her for the first time. Even as she'd pulled away from him, she'd known that a line had been crossed in her mind and her heart. A point of no return. Every moment she spent with Finn after that would only get her in deeper and deeper until she drowned.

And now she was all alone and hopelessly in love with a lying playboy she would never see again.

No. That wasn't exactly right. Truth be told, Willow was in love with Jack. The problems hadn't truly started until Jack morphed back into Finn. Until then, things between them had been simple and pure, somehow. Now their relationship was tainted by Finn's lies.

Willow was about to go into the kitchen and deal with the mess they'd left behind when she heard her house phone ring. She picked it up quickly, figuring it was Doc on his way over with the dog.

"Hello?"

"Where have you been, Willow? I've called the

house almost every day for a week and no one has answered until now."

Willow frowned at her phone. It was her sister, Rain, who rarely if ever called, much less called repeatedly. "Is Joey okay?" she asked. The only reason she could think her sister might call that much was if there was an emergency with her young nephew.

"Joey is fine. We're all fine. You're the one I'm worried about."

"There's no reason to worry about me, Rain. I've been on a trip for a few days. Why didn't you call my cell phone? I had it with me the whole time."

Rain sighed into the receiver. "Willow, I don't know your cell phone number. Why should I bother when you never leave the house? I don't even know why you have one, to be honest. Do you get reception in the middle of nowhere?"

"I leave the house," Willow said, but it was a weak argument. Before Finn showed up in her life, she really only left the house to take walks with Shadow and to get food and supplies in Victoria. People rarely called on it, but the cell phone did work, despite her sister's concerns. "I've been in South Carolina for almost a week."

There was a long silence. "Why were you in South Carolina? Was there some mystery-book thing you forgot to tell me about? A book signing or something? I forget that you're a famous author sometimes."

"No, it wasn't for a book. It was a last-minute trip to Charleston. A vacation of sorts. I just got back into town last night pretty late."

"A vacation? By yourself?"

Willow's jaw tightened, holding in the words. They

weren't super close, but since she'd gotten sick, her older sister had attempted to take a motherly role. She knew that Rain wouldn't give up until she knew everything that was going on in her life. But that didn't mean she was going to spill about Finn at the first prompting. It was a long story with a painful ending and she wasn't sure she wanted to tell it yet.

"I was invited by a friend."

"Uh-huh."

"So how is Joey doing?" she asked in a weak attempt to change the subject.

"He's two. He's on the warpath destroying everything he can get his hands on. Steve wants to have another one, but I'm not sure I'm ready to start again. Now, who is this friend? Someone from the island?"

"Sort of."

"Sort of? Why are you being so difficult, Wil? What's going on that you don't want to tell me? Your cancer hasn't come back, has it? You did everything humanly possible to keep that from happening."

"No. No, my last scan was clear. I'm perfectly healthy." Just heartbroken.

She heard her sister audibly sigh in relief. "Then what is it? Something is going on, so tell me or I'll waste your whole afternoon. Or worse, I'll get on the ferry and come out there where you can't avoid me. You can't lie to my face, Willow. I can read you like a book."

"Fine, fine," Willow said, giving in. She really didn't want Rain showing up on her doorstep right now. "Did you read about the John Doe in the papers? The guy that just washed up out of nowhere with amnesia and no one knew who he was?"

Between the hospital's call to help identify Finn and Sawyer's attempts to find him, the story had made its way into the papers. She supposed it was just as well they had left Seattle before the reporters could swarm them with questions.

"I think Steve mentioned something about that. He pays more attention to the news than I do. What about him? Do you know him?"

"Well, yes and no. I didn't know him before his accident, but he actually washed up on my beach. Shadow found him when we were on a walk. Then we had that awful storm, so I was stuck taking care of him until we could get him to a hospital."

"I don't think I like the idea of some stranger at your house, Wil. Why didn't you say something?"

"What were you going to do? The ferries weren't running."

"Wait, I remember the story now. Didn't the papers say the guy had turned out to be some missing billionaire from that awful plane crash right before the storm?"

"That's the same man, yes. Once they figured out who he really was, I went with him back to his home in Charleston to make sure he got settled in okay. He didn't have his memory back and he needed some support. Then I came home. That's all there is to it."

"You went home with him. To the East Coast? That's not a quick trip. There's more to this than you're telling me."

"There is. And I'm sorry, Rain, but I just got back and I'm not really ready to talk about it yet. A lot of things have happened and I'm still working through it all."

"You love him."

How could she know? Her sister had a sixth sense about these things that had made Willow crazy growing up. "Yes, but it doesn't matter. It's over."

The slam of a car door outside caught her attention. "Listen, Rain, I've gotta go. Doc's pulling up outside with Shadow."

"Okay," her sister said with a dubious tone. "But this isn't over. We're going to talk more about this guy when you're ready."

"Whatever you say." Willow hung up the phone and got up from the recliner. Looking out the front window, she could see her enthusiastic dog leap from the cab of Doc's truck and run straight for the door with a loud *woo* of excitement.

Willow smiled and walked to the front door to greet him. She'd missed her fluffy boy these past few days. Maybe she'd let him sleep in the bed with her tonight.

She could use something to hold on to so she didn't feel so alone.

Twelve

It took two weeks for Finn to get his life in order. It was longer than he wanted, but upending his entire life would take a little time if he was going to do it properly. He started by gathering his family to make an announcement. He spoke quickly and firmly so they knew it wasn't up for debate. His memory had returned. He was resigning from Steele Tools and going to Washington State. Hopefully, to be with Willow, if she'd have him. But either way, he was done with his life as it was before the accident. No one protested. He hoped it was because they realized he'd finally found some direction in his life.

Next, he put his town house on the market and the desirable property sold in a day. Then he sold the Ferrari. He donated most of his furniture and household things and packed what was important, which was surprisingly little. He took a few boxes to Sawyer and Kat's place and they agreed to ship them to him when he was ready. With a single suitcase, he boarded a commercial flight to Seattle and hoped for the best.

It was a bold step on Finn's part. He hadn't spoken to Willow since she walked out of his town house and flew home. But he knew that it would take bold steps to prove to her that he was serious. Serious about her and serious about the life he wanted them to start together.

He made a few stops in Seattle, the last being a boatyard near the coast. The salesman was stunned to have Finn walk onto his lot, point out a small but luxurious yacht model he'd had his eyes on for quite a while and hand him a check. The next morning, Finn and his new yacht were in the water and on the way to Shaw Island and his future.

Finn had always wanted his own boat. His parents had a large yacht—*License to Drill*—they took out for holidays and trips from time to time, and some of his best memories had been from those trips. Now that he was hoping to live on an island, it was the perfect time to buy one of his own, albeit much smaller. It would be practical, fun, and if he'd read her all wrong and Willow slammed the door in his face, he would at least have a place to live.

It was about ten in the morning when he rounded the shore near Willow's home where she had found him that first day. As he pulled up to her unused dock, he heard a familiar howling in the distance. He smiled. She and Shadow were on their walk.

Finn tied up the boat and stepped off onto the dock. His heart pounded loud in his chest as he walked across the worn boards to the grassy outcropping that separated the wooded area from the beach.

A moment later, Shadow leaped from the trees and made a beeline straight for him. Finn crouched down and welcomed the dog, who thankfully was happy to see him. Hopefully his mama would be, too. He accepted a few kisses and scratched the dog behind his ears as he vocalized excitedly.

"Shadow!"

The dog immediately turned and ran back to the trees, where he greeted Willow. She, however, barely took notice of the dog. Her eyes were glued on Finn. She was instantly stiff, as though she'd encountered a bear on her walk instead of the man she loved.

"Hello, Willow," he said.

The line between her eyebrows deepened as her gaze danced between him and the beautiful boat just behind him. "What are you doing here, Finn?"

He took a step closer to her, and she didn't move away. "I came to talk to you."

"You rich people are so dramatic. You fly cross-country and charter a yacht to come out here, when you could've just picked up a phone."

Finn shook his head. "What I needed to say couldn't be said over the phone. It needed to be done in person."

She narrowed her gaze suspiciously, but waited to hear what he had to say. "Say it, then. I've got a lot of work to do today."

She hadn't run excitedly into his arms and blanketed his face in kisses, but she hadn't slapped him and walked away, either. He took that as a positive. "I love you, Willow. There are a lot of other things I could say, but that is the most important one. You are the first and only woman I've ever loved. And not just because I don't remember. I remember everything, and nothing from my past has ever measured up to you."

Her lips parted in surprise for a moment, but she held her ground. "I know you think that you mean what you say, but I'm not so certain."

"You don't think I love you?"

"I think that returning to your old life and all your old memories was hard for you. Having to face who you've been and what you've done couldn't be easy. I imagine it's easier to run off to a faraway place and avoid reality for a little while longer."

"Is that what you think I'm doing?" Finn asked. "Running from my life?"

She shrugged. "You tell me."

"No. I'm running *to* my life, Willow. I realized that the life I had in Charleston was full of excitement and fun, but it meant nothing. I'd very nearly been wiped from the face of the earth in that plane crash and in the end, it hadn't really mattered if I lived or died. Sure, my family would be sad that I was killed, but it wouldn't change much, because I hadn't contributed much. I took and took, and I never gave anything back. And until you came into my life, I hadn't cared. But you made me want something more."

She watched him warily as he spoke. "When you were here before, you didn't know anything about your life. You were happy with soup and cereal, and walks in the woods. It's a simple life on this island. How do I know you won't get tired of slumming out here in the real world? That you won't decide to run back home and be a rich playboy again when things aren't going your way?"

"I don't have anything to run home to, Willow."

She crossed her arms over her chest and scoffed. "You have that big, beautiful house overlooking the harbor. That fancy sports car—"

"It's all gone," he interrupted. "I sold or gave away almost everything I had. The art, the furniture, all of it. But even if I hadn't, it was just stuff. Once you left my house, it became glaringly obvious that it was just a big house full of things. The only memories that mattered were the ones I made with you, and it didn't mean anything without you there with me."

"You sold all your stuff, but you kept that cheap T-shirt and sweatpants I bought you?"

Finn looked down at the outfit he'd chosen to wear today. His San Juan Islands T-shirt and black sweatpants were perfect for a brisk day out on his boat. They were also a reminder of a happier time for him. "Of course I kept these. I kept everything that you bought for me."

Willow bit at her bottom lip. He could tell that her resolve was starting to wear thin. She wanted to believe him. She wanted to love him. He could see it. She was just scared to trust him. He'd hurt her and he couldn't expect the past to be wiped away as easily as it had before.

"So, you think you can just show up in that cheap T-shirt and say a lot of romantic things and I'll just forget about everything you did, right?"

"No. I don't expect you to forget. I know firsthand that forgetting just hides away the past—it doesn't deal with it. I only hope that in time, you can forgive. I'm not going to stand here and make excuses for why I lied to you. In the end, all I ended up doing was to drive you away when that was what I was trying so hard to avoid in the first place. But once you were gone, I realized it was far more serious than just wanting you there with me. I needed you with me. And not just to hold my hand through hard times. I need you because I love you, Willow. You took a part of me with you when you left that day, and no amount of money or women or alcohol would ever change that."

Willow swallowed hard and shook her head in disbelief. "You just gave up your whole life for me?"

"No," he said, pulling a small velvet box from the pocket of his sweatpants. "My life is here with you. And it always will be. All these years, I've been searching for something. I thought I would find it in the arms of a woman or in the approval of my father, but it never felt right once I got it. It turns out I had to forget about everything else to be able to see what I was looking for. I found it in you. You're my everything and I'm not going anywhere, Willow. Not without you."

Finn got down onto one knee in the grass and opened up the box to display the ring he'd chosen for her. "I love you just as you are, Willow Bates. And I hope that you can accept me as I am. I'm flawed. I'm complicated. But I love you so much, I couldn't stay away even knowing you might never want to speak to me again. I hope that you'll accept this ring and me along with it, to be my wife. There's nothing more in this life I want than to hear you say yes."

Willow had woken up this morning like she did most every morning. She anticipated a quiet day of writing and finally putting away the patio furniture since the season was long over. She was making a list for a trip to the mainland to get some new groceries. That was the highlight of her week. Or so she thought.

She had never expected to see Finn Steele again. And she certainly hadn't expected to be proposed to today. If she had, maybe she would've put on a nicer shirt or something. She looked down at the box Finn was holding out to her and couldn't believe the radical turn her day had taken. If she didn't know about his family and how much they were worth, she might think he was proposing with costume jewelry. It was that big and that shiny. Her mind was arguing with itself that there was no way the ring he was holding was real, but it had to be. The center stone was a bright yellow pear cut and easily six or seven carats. It was set in platinum with a thin split band that looked far too fragile to hold a stone that large.

"Is that—is that a yellow sapphire or something?" she asked. It was obviously not what he wanted to hear in response to his important question, but in the moment, she was so overwhelmed, she didn't know what to say.

Finn shook his head and stood up. He plucked the ring from the box and took her hand. He slipped it onto her finger, where it fit perfectly. It made her petite finger look even smaller with the giant stone. "It's referred to as a vivid canary diamond. They're very rare, especially in this size and quality. I actually had to buy the stone in an auction at Sotheby's in London, then I had someone from Harley's security agency fly over to England and escort it back to me. I had our family jeweler set it in a ring for you."

She couldn't stop staring at it. Partially because it was beautiful and partially because the significance of the moment had stolen the words from her lips. This couldn't be really happening. It looked like it should belong to Elizabeth Taylor or the Queen of England. Not on the hand of little, old, insignificant Willow Bates. "I don't know that I've ever seen a yellow diamond before."

"There aren't many, at least as many as bright in color or as internally flawless as yours. This stone is one in a million, easily. But so are you. You're my sunlight in the darkness. And I thought that there wasn't anything more ideal for you than a perfect bright yellow diamond."

"You certainly know how to apologize to a girl," Willow said as she fought the gathering of tears in her eyes. A yellow diamond was so perfect; he was right. And for reasons he didn't even know. It was like a drop of liquid sunshine on her hand. She hadn't thought Finn was that sentimental, but she was wrong. He'd obviously gone to a lot of trouble and expense to get this for her.

"I wanted you to know how sincere I was. I came out here with this ring and the boat, selling everything, so you would know I mean it when I say that I love you and I want to be with you. Whether or not you say yes, I had to come out here and try to make things right between us. I can't bear to think that you might hate me, even if you don't love me."

Willow shook her head and looked up at Finn. She couldn't let him self-flagellate any longer. "I could never hate you. I was hurt, but that was because I loved you so much. More than anything, I was angry with myself for falling for you when I knew that this relationship was destined to fail eventually. The odds were against us from the start, but I couldn't stop myself."

Finn visibly flinched at her words. "Do you still believe that? That we're destined to fail?"

"I think that the billionaire playboy and the reclusive mystery writer were never meant to be. But you and me, as we are now, I think we might have a chance."

"Does that mean you'll marry me?" he pressed.

Willow still hadn't given him an answer. She wanted to say yes. She wanted to scream it so loud that Doc could hear it from his property. But before she could, she had a question to ask Finn. "You said that you loved me just as I was, Finn. Did you really mean that?"

He clasped her hands in his and squeezed them tightly. "Of course I did."

"Even though we can never have a family of our own?"

Finn frowned at her. "Starting a family of my own is not something I've given much thought to. In fact, I've spent most of my life trying to prevent it. I never imagined that I would fall in love and want to get married. Until I met you. You're my family, Willow. And if it's just the two of us—"

Shadow nosed in between them at that moment and howled at being ignored for so long.

Finn gave him a pat on the head and a good scratch. "Pardon me, the three of us—then that's all the family I need."

"It doesn't bother you that I can't have your children? Please be honest with me because I don't want this to become something that comes between us later."

"If we wanted to add children to our lives, we could always adopt babies or foster as many of them as you'd like. Families take lots of different shapes and DNA isn't that important in the end. I love Morgan just as much now as I did when I thought she was my biological sister. And I love Jade even though she spent most of her life apart from us. That's not what's important.

"And even if it were," he continued, "I'm having my chance to have children. My daughter with Kat will be born before year's end. I don't know that I deserve to have the role of a father in her life, but I'd like to try. I'm already sharing her with my brother and Kat, and I think we'd all be happy to include you, too. Then she can have two dads and two moms that love and adore her. I think little Beatrice might be the luckiest girl in the whole world."

Willow had just been proposed to, and yet she'd never heard sweeter words than she had now. No matter what, she and Finn would be a family. And with his daughter, not only would she never have to feel like he was sacrificing his chance for children to be with her, but she would get a chance to be a mother. She'd never imagined that would happen for her. Or that any of this would happen for her. She took a big sigh of relief and looked up at him with a smile so big, it almost hurt. "I don't know about that," she said. "I think I might be the luckiest girl in the world."

Finn grinned and the elusive dimple in his cheek beckoned to her. She hoped that Beatrice would have that same dimple so she could kiss the baby's sweet cheeks just like her daddy's.

"That would make sense, because I'm the luckiest guy on the planet. Well, almost. Any other reasons why you think we shouldn't get married and be happy forever?" he asked.

Willow smiled and reached up to touch Finn's cheek with her hand, which was graced with a sparkling yellow diamond. "No. I think we've covered everything, so I'll put an end to the torture. I absolutely will marry you, Finn Steele."

With a loud whoop, Finn scooped Willow into his arms and lifted her off the ground to kiss her. She wrapped her arms around his neck and clung to him. Not just so she wouldn't fall, but because she never wanted to let him go. She'd done it once and she wasn't sure she could ever do it again.

Setting her back down on the ground, Finn looked at her with a wicked glint in his eye. "So, do you want to see our new boat?"

Willow grinned. "I absolutely do."

He took her by the hand and led her back down to the dock with Shadow jogging by their side. The closer she got, the more beautiful she realized it was. This was no boat. This was a fifty-foot Azimut yacht. The navy-and-white vessel tied to her dock was as sparkling and beautiful as the ring on her hand. She had always wanted something so she didn't have to depend on the ferry, but this was more than just a boat to get supplies. They could live on it. Travel the world on it.

He helped her on board and they climbed up to the sun terrace. "It can sleep eight, which is a little much, but it's the smallest one they make in this class. I could've custom ordered one, but I didn't want to wait any longer than I had to to cross the channel and get over here."

All she could do was shake her head. "It's beautiful. Perfect. Have you named her yet?"

"As a matter of fact, I have. They applied the name to the boat yesterday after I bought her. She's called *My Sunshine*."

Willow paused for a moment and looked at her new fiancé. Then she looked down at her ring. "What made you choose that?" He couldn't possibly know. Who would've told him?

Finn turned back to Willow and grinned. "I named my ship after my girl. That's a long-standing yachting tradition, isn't it, Sunshine?"

Willow's jaw dropped. "Who told you?"

"Well, after my sister mentioned that you wrote your books as S. W. Bates, I did a little digging."

"Oh, no," Willow said, squeezing her eyes shut.

"You knew everything about me almost as I learned about myself, but you…you were keeping secrets, love. When you said your parents were hippies, you didn't tell me everything. Rainbow Blossom and Sunshine Willow Bates," he announced with a smirk.

So he knew her full name. Her real name. "I haven't gone by Sunny since I left the commune. When we moved and I started public school, I told people to call me Willow. I just don't tell anyone because—" she looked at him and the amused expression on his face "—because of that!"

Finn scooped her into his arms and held her until she stopped squirming in irritation. "I promise it will be our little secret. And besides, your name will be changing soon anyway, Mrs. Steele."

"Willow Steele," she said, trying out the name. "I think I like it."

He tipped her chin up and captured her lips in a kiss. "I think I love it."

Epilogue

"Ho, ho, ho! Merry Christmas!" Finn shouted as he opened the front door of the Steele family mansion and stepped inside. He had a mountain of wrapped gifts in his arms and Willow by his side as they made their way into the foyer.

"We're back here, Finn dear," he heard his mother call out.

"Be prepared for the decorations to be over-the-top," he whispered to Willow as they walked through the main hall. Near the grand staircase was a small forest of trees with lights, silver-and-gold ornaments and a blanket of faux snow around their bases. Garland ran up each side of the staircase railing, and the scent of fresh pine and apple cider lingered throughout the house. "Mother loves Christmas."

"The tree-lined drive of twinkle lights and snowflake projections would've tipped me off even if the wreaths on each window and the garland wrapped around each column didn't."

Finn looked at his mother's handiwork with a new appreciation this year. He looked at everything with new eyes this year. His second chance at life had done that. As had Willow. And of course, his daughter. Christmas took on a whole new meaning with children in the house.

As they entered the family room, they were greeted by the twelve-foot-tall Christmas tree dripping in heirloom ornaments that sparkled in the light of the fireplace roaring nearby. As usual, the mantle was covered in garland and ribbons with stockings hanging there for everyone in the family. Thankfully, it was a large fireplace, as this year there were three new additions to the collection: one for Kat, one for Willow and one for tiny, three-day-old Beatrice.

Speaking of Beatrice, the Queen Bea was holding court in her grandmother's arms. Patricia was beaming as she held her granddaughter. Kat was resting in a nearby chair with her feet up and Sawyer hovering at her side in case she needed anything. The rest of the family was gathered around, looking at the new baby with grins on their faces and hot toddies in their hands. Beatrice, for her part, was unimpressed by it all and fast asleep.

Finn settled the presents with the others at the base of the tree. When he turned, Lena was waiting to offer them both a festive holiday beverage. "Merry Christmas, Lena," he said, leaning in to give her a hug. "You're looking radiant tonight, as always."

The woman's cheeks blushed bright red at his compliment. "You quit that, you old flirt. You're a father now, and soon to be a married man."

"I can still appreciate a lovely lady when I see one," he said with a wink.

He and Willow had settled into the couch together and he was just about to grab one of Lena's famous white chocolate–peppermint cookies when his father stood up.

"Now that everyone is here, I'd like to make a toast," Trevor said. Everyone quieted and held their glasses in anticipation. "This family has been through a lot the last few years. It's difficult sometimes to look back and think about those hard times, but then I always remember what amazing things have come from it. Without Jade being kidnapped, we never would've had Morgan in our lives. Or Jade's husband, Harley. We may have had our home bombed, but we came out of it with our new son-in-law, River, and the amazing charity in Dawn's memory.

"Finn brought Kat and our beautiful granddaughter, Beatrice, into our lives. And now, in nearly losing him for good, we gained his lovely fiancée, Willow. In many ways, despite him living on the other side of the country now, we also got Finn back, too. I never could've imagined how our family would grow and change so quickly, and for that I'm grateful."

"Now if we can just marry off Tom!" Sawyer interjected from the corner.

Their oldest brother squirmed uncomfortably in the corner. "I'm working on it," he said. "I've been seeing a new girl lately and I'm pretty sure she might be the one. I knew the moment she was introduced to me at a party."

"What's her name?" Morgan asked.

"Becky. I thought that was appropriate."

Trevor laughed. "We've needed a Becky to complete my Mark Twain collection," he noted. "I look forward to meeting her. But in the meantime, to all of you, I wish you all a very Merry Christmas, and a happy, exciting New Year ahead."

"Cheers!" a few folks yelled out and glasses clinked together around the room.

Finn smiled and hugged his fiancée to his side. He knew that no matter what the future held for him, he would face it happily with Willow. He placed a kiss on the top of her head and raised his glass again.

"To Beatrice's first Christmas!"

* * * * *